The Timeless Enemy

Book Three

K.A. Griffin

ISBN: 979-8-9890883-4-8

Editor: Kathryn Hall – www.cjhall.co.uk
Typesetter: Catherine Arthur – www.catherinearthur.com
Cover art by: Eugene Ivanov
Printed in the United States of America

For Dad, who made up stories to entertain his grandson.
If there is any good in me, I learned it from you.

CONTENTS

PROLOGUE

The suns were fixed just above the horizon as Muriel finished the final step to the top of the mesa. Surrounding her on three sides, they created a circle of colors and light that never changed. A cool breeze floated across the flat surface and teased her hair, blowing it across her face and forcing her to regret that she hadn't tied it back before leaving.

Her hair was wavy, coal black, and flowed down to the middle of her back. To the left of her part was a silver cluster of hair, giving her head a disproportionate appearance. Her blouse was white and cut to a V shape. A turquoise dress mirrored the shape of the "V" and fell about her ankles. Sandals covered her feet, and blue and silver jewelry adorned her wrists, neck, and ears.

Ahead of her, in the center of the mesa top, sat Brindle, the leader of her people. On Brindle's left stood Tye, and on her right was David. The blind man, Tye, and the deaf man, David, were Brindle's advisors and the only security she ever needed, for they were Sumatee', and they were the Blessed.

Brindle smiled as Muriel approached and watched her struggle with her hair. "You forgot how breezy it is up here."

"Well," Muriel growled, "it's not like you gave me much notice. I was summoned, and I came as requested." She removed a leather band from her wrist and then pulled her hair back, tying it with a

1

loose knot. "This is always the awkward part. What do I do next? Do I bow before my sister, do I curtsy, or do I tell you to get up and give me a hug?" With the last word, Muriel opened her arms and waited.

Brindle stood from her chair and embraced her sister. "Thank you for coming."

"Yes, yes. You called and I answered. Now, do you want to tell me why you interrupted the exceptional meal that awaits unfinished in my home?"

"Walk with me, please," Brindle said, as she held out her arm. Muriel linked arms with her sister and walked toward one of the suns.

"This must be bad," Muriel said softly. "You don't call for me unless it's bad."

Brindle paused, took a deep breath, and looked out over the land before her. "Two days ago, we lost contact with every world that we monitor. The watchers were doing a standard forward look, when one by one, we lost contact with all of them, with every world we are connected to."

"That's impossible. We are connected with tens of thousands of worlds. They don't just cease to exist all at one time. There has never been an event so cataclysmic that worlds across every known galaxy would simply disappear."

Brindle shook her head and continued to look toward the sun that hovered on the horizon. "It wasn't them. It was us. Our world, as we know it, ceased to exist...or function. I don't know which."

"But when?" Muriel argued. "When does it happen, because it hasn't happened yet?"

"You know that's impossible to calculate. Time doesn't move here. The suns never rise, nor do they set," she said, with a wave of her hand. "We can't calculate time in a precise manner. We have to look at the worlds, find the disruption point, and then try to calculate time based upon a particular world and how time moves there."

"It always gives me a headache when you talk like that," Muriel groused. "Can you just tell me what you need me to do?"

"We found the point where things started to shift. A boy dies, and because of his death, something happens that wasn't supposed to happen. And that event destroys his world, and shortly after, it destroys ours."

"What doesn't happen?" Muriel demanded. "Or what does happen? Just tell me."

"They finally find us."

That one word caused Muriel to catch her breath, and she grabbed at the necklace around her neck. "How do you know it's them?"

"You won't like the explanation," Brindle said. "It will make your headache worse. But don't doubt me when I say it's them."

"And what do you want me to do? It can't be any worse than you giving me little bits at a time."

"I need you to break our laws, and I need you to try and save the boy."

"Don't we have people already there? Don't we have travelers already in place?"

"We do," Brindle replied, "but they don't have the skill or knowledge to help, or the boy would never have died."

"Died. You are talking past tense," Muriel said. She put her hands on the sides of her head as she realized what Brindle wanted. "No, no, no, no. You can't ask me to do that. NO!"

"Muriel, sister, there is no other way, and there is no other person. You must go back, and you will have to go through the White Zone. There is no other option. You've done it before, and we need you to do it again."

Muriel walked away from her sister and started to pace around in a circle. "One mistake," she seethed, holding up her forefinger. "One little mistake, and I die a death that you wouldn't even wish on them."

"Then there can't be any mistakes. Not even a little one."

Muriel shook her head and clenched her jaw as tears started running down her cheeks. She held back the frustrated scream she wanted to let out to her sister. "I have a half-cooked dinner at home. When does this have to happen?"

"Now. Your dinner can wait. There is a bag waiting for you at the base of the mesa. All your equipment is in the bag. Tye and David will accompany you on the journey. They will make sure there are no mistakes and will get you safely there and back."

"What are my limits? What am I allowed to do? I can't show them things they don't know about. Am I supposed to break that law as well?"

For the first time in her life, Muriel wished the suns would set, and that time would move. Then, she wouldn't be able to see the agony on her sister's face; she could just rush down the stairs and escape into the darkness of night. The wind picked up on the top of the mesa, causing her dress to press up against the backs of her legs.

"Do whatever you need to do. Whatever you can do," Brindle replied." There isn't another option."

While Brindle's voice was determined, Muriel saw something else in her sister's eyes: fear. "But where am I going and how am I supposed to find this boy I've never met?"

"Fortunately," Brindle said with a nod of her head, "we have a traveler nearby, and we know exactly where to find the boy."

CHAPTER 1

The Small Space

"No, I don't understand," the chancellor seethed. "I specifically told you to put down the gun, and you didn't do it. Give me a reason why I shouldn't have you executed right here, right now." His eyes were crazed with anger, and the veins in his neck bulged. He leaned toward her, and as he screamed, spittle escaped from his lips and splattered on her face.

"I will tell you what I know," Santa Udi said, trying to control her own anger, "but will you let me start and finish?"

"You can talk as much as you want," Chancellor Brighton said with a dismissive hand gesture, turning his back on her and walking two steps away. "But know clearly that when you are done, if I'm not happy with your explanation, the guard behind you will kill you."

"The first thing I need you to understand is that Scott and Chastain are not in the room. They are not in the building. I don't have any idea where they went. But I knew they were going somewhere. Several years ago, before I joined the Ministry of Intelligence, I was in a building. I saw a man walk into a room across the hall. Within minutes, I heard the same hum that we all heard, and I saw a brilliant light come from underneath the door. When I went into the room, the man wasn't there. There were no windows in the room, and only one door was present. Where did the man go? I have no idea. However, there is a technology here, in **NHHMM**, that we know nothing about.

"The Scott boy was holding onto a clock before he disappeared. That makes no sense unless it was somehow related to what happened. I shot at the clock to keep them from leaving, to interrupt whatever was going on. If I'm guilty of any wrongdoing, it was that I didn't shoot fast enough. We need to find out what is happening, what this technology is, and who has it. If you don't think I'm the right person to do that, then tell your man to shoot me now, because I won't apologize for doing what I thought I needed to do to protect you, and to protect NHHMM."

Chancellor Brighton didn't know if Udi was telling the truth or not, but what he did know was that Ethan Scott and Star Chastain were in the room one moment, and gone the next. He heard the deafening hum and saw the brilliant light. Somebody knew something that he didn't know, and that infuriated him. He suspected Vanderschmidt, but what if it wasn't the Resistance? What if it were someone else?

"Those two kids are the best chance we have of getting the vault open. What if you killed one of them, or both of them?"

"I didn't. I wasn't aiming to kill them."

"But they could be dead, whether you meant it or not?"

"Yes, it is a possibility that one or both of them could be dead," she begrudgingly agreed. "But you still have the Craven boy."

"Then I've got nothing. Craven would have died if I put him in the cage, and you know I was never going to do that anyway."

"Yes," Udi said, trying to divert the conversation away from Ethan and Star. "Putting him in the cage would have made his father a powerful enemy. He's not going to be happy when he learns that we threatened his son."

"Stop!" Chancellor Brighton said, holding up his hand. "Don't try to change the subject. I briefed his father before we took the children to see the cage. He knew exactly what was going to happen."

Santa Udi pursed her lips together and tried not to show her surprise at the chancellor's last statement. She knew nothing about his meeting with Daniel Craven's father. He was keeping her out of the loop on strategic information, and that caused her concern.

"Here is what's going to happen next," the chancellor said. "You are going to focus your efforts on finding Ethan Scott and the Chastain girl, and you are going to bring them to me alive and unharmed. Do you know what those two words mean? Alive? Unharmed?"

"Yes, sir," Minister Udi said, her head bowed.

"Then know that when they are delivered to me, you will leave that reunion in the same condition they arrived. And one more thing," Brighton said, looking at her. "If you ever disobey any order that I give you, no matter what you think or believe, I will have you shot immediately. Do you understand?"

"Yes, I understand."

Santa Udi left the chancellor and began her way through the maze of hallways and stairs until she arrived back at her office. Closing the door, she walked over to her desk, took a glass ornament, and hurled it against the wall.

The rubble from the explosion filled up half of the ravine. Lang and the team knew where Jack Flynn was when the explosives went off, but they didn't know where he ended up. The rock tapered down from the mountain until it reached the bottom of the ravine. The problem was that almost half of the ravine was covered in rock. The part nearest the tunnel entrance was covered with massive sections of the mountain that seemed to just drop down in one piece. The part nearest the tunnel entrance was littered with mountain debris that appeared to have fallen in one piece, while smaller rocks cluttered the floor in a disorganized heap.

They had seen him fall, but the dust and the fragments of rock shooting in their direction obscured the vision of the team, and they didn't see what happened next. Everyone, including Shy, rushed to the rock in an attempt to find Jack.

"STOP!" Lang called out. "The rocks are not stable. If he's not dead, we could well crush him by going about this the wrong way. Where did we see him last? Give me a position, or a landmark."

"He was with that tree," Clapton replied.

"He was a few feet beyond the switch," Benoit commented.

Augustine agreed with Benoit, and to Lang, the markers aligned. "Then we saw him fall just over there," she pointed. "And he was to the left of the track, as I recall."

"Yes," Lang agreed. "He was to the left."

"Then we need to start ten feet in front of that spot. We take off one layer of rock at a time, so if he's still alive and in a gap between the rock, we don't disturb what is above him." As the engineer in the group, no one was going to argue with her. She had the best plan, and she was the most qualified.

It took ninety minutes of moving one rock at a time before they were able to make progress. It was brutal work, and their hands were cut, mashed, and bleeding. "I'm not much help," Shy pointed out, realizing her injuries were holding her back. "I'm going to get us some water."

An hour later, they had reached the original ground of the ravine, and Lang estimated they would find him, or what was left of him, within the next ten feet. The water retrieved by Shy helped to hydrate the team, allowing them to continue working. However, she now needed to find food, so she went back into town to see what she could find.

"Now," Lang directed, "take the top of the rock off and work your way down. We will take it one foot at a time if we have to."

There was a large rock, almost two feet in diameter, that needed to come down. It was too heavy for one person to lift, so they decided to grab it from two sides and roll it off the top, then let it fall to the ground. John Augustine got on one side of the rock, and Guy Clapton got on the other.

"On three," Augustine said. "One, two..."

"Hey. Can you get off my fingers?" a voice called out.

Clapton looked down, moved his foot, and saw the tips of two fingers sticking out from the rock.

"Jack!" Lang called out. "Are you hurt?"

"Probably so," Flynn replied with a droll tone. "It feels like half the mountain is on top of me, so, yeah, I guess I'm hurt."

"What can you tell me about where you are?" she asked.

"I can see the side of the ravine. There's a large rock above me, lying at an angle."

"What about your feet and legs? Can you tell if they are pinned by the rock?"

"Don't know that for sure. I don't have any room to move. There's something wrong with my right leg, though. It feels wet, so I'm assuming there's something broken or cut."

"Ok. Hang on," Lang said. "We're going to get you out." Then she turned to the others. "Listen carefully, before you move a rock, test it to see if it's wedged by the one above it. We start at the top, and we work down, very carefully."

Forty-five minutes later, they were able to clear the rock around Jack's arm and get a good view of his predicament. A large stone slab was wedged at a 30° angle between the ground and the ravine wall, and that small space was what had kept Jack alive. Another thirty minutes of work passed, and they were able to clear out all the rock in front of the opening.

"Hey," Jack said when he could see them, "any chance you can get me out by dinner? I'm getting a little hungry. It doesn't need to be anything special Maybe a sandwich? And I could use some water if you have some."

"Can you move your feet?" Lang demanded, ignoring his humor.

"I don't have the space to move anything, but I can tell you that my feet are not hurting me."

"Jack," Lang said, "we have two options. We can try to go over the rock above you and see if we can open a space behind it to make sure that your feet are clear."

"Or?" Jack said.

"Or, we grab your arms and try to pull you out."

"What's wrong with the last option? It sounds faster."

"If your feet are wedged in the rock, and we can't get you out, then we could disturb the integrity of the opening, and the rock above you could shift."

Above them, near the former opening to the tunnel, small rocks began to fall. CRACK! The rock face began to split, and a section of rock twenty feet wide and over fifty feet tall, fractured from the mountain and began to fall toward the ravine.

"Pull, now. PULL!" Lang screamed.

Clapton and Augustine grabbed one arm while Benoit and Lang grabbed the other. At first, Flynn didn't budge, and he felt as if his arms were about to be ripped from his shoulders. They pulled again, and his body moved. As the giant fracture landed in the ravine and on top of the rock, they pulled a third time, and Jack Flynn was free.

Like a hand slapping still water, the rock slab sent small pieces of rock further into the ravine, pelting the team with stone bullets.

They lay on the ground, choking on dust and waiting for the rock storm to stop. Stiletto Lang rolled over and look ed at the space where Jack had been only seconds earlier. The small space was gone. The rock slab rested on the ground where Jack had been and was now covered with even more rock.

"Well?"

"The bleeding hasn't stopped."

"And?"

"And I don't know what to do. I'm not a doctor. I'm doing the best I can. I've tried to close the wound, and it's now clean. Physically, I don't know what else to do."

"Let me go down to Grayhawk and get a doctor," another voice said.

"No, we can't do that. We can't risk someone hearing or seeing us. He can't travel, and we're not ready for a fight, so we would be unable to stop them."

"Victor, I don't care what you have to do, but I need you to stop the bleeding. There has to be something in that workshop of yours you can use?"

Victor shook his head. "There is a leaf that helps blood to clot, but it is also poisonous. The right amount will help the wound to close, but too much will poison the blood. I can't make tea out of it; it's too risky in his condition. I could make a poultice, which might work. It might, but then again..."

"Where are they?" Star demanded.

"What?" Victor replied, deep in thought.

"Where are the leaves?"

"Oh, the leaves. On the wall to the right. Third shelf. The second jar from the left. The label says 'WH'. But make sure you get the right jar. There is another labeled 'BB', but don't take that one. It will thin his blood. WH. Make sure the label says 'WH'."

Star burst from the room in a sprint and left the house, running as fast as her legs would carry her. Moving past the barn, she took a narrow trail that led deeper into the trees, where a green canopy provided shade over the worn path. She finally reached a small building with dirty windows and moss growing on the slate shingles. Turning the knob, she pushed open the door and rushed over to wall and her eyes raced to the third shelf. She counted out the jars as she looked at each label, then she saw it: WH.

With the jar tucked under her arm, Star ran from the building back the way she came. Out of breath, she stepped into the room and held out the jar. "WH. I've got it. WH."

"Good. Good," Victor said, taking the jar and examining the label. "Now, all I've got to do is..." He trailed off as he wandered from the room.

Ethan's skin was a ghostly shade of white. His bare chest was covered in dried blood, and the clean, white bandage around his neck was quickly turning red on the right side. His body twitched, and his breathing began to slow.

"Victor!" Roland bellowed. "How much longer?"

"Coming. I'm coming," Victor said, as he entered the room carrying a small bowl of leaf pulp. "Remove the bandage, I'll put this over the wound, and then we will bandage it up again."

Carefully, Roland lifted Ethan's head while a woman began to unwrap the bandage from around his neck. When it was removed, Victor leaned over and spread the poultice there instead. "Ok. That's it. Wrap him back up."

While Roland elevated Ethan's head, the woman wrapped a clean bandage around his neck, and outside, lightning flashed nearby, but there was no thunder.

"What now?" Roland asked as he slowly laid Ethan's head back down on the waiting pillow.

Before Victor could answer, there was a knock on the door to the home. For a moment, everyone in the room stopped what they were doing and looked at each other with an expression of dread. Picking up a crystal pistol from a table by the bedroom door, Roland left the room. "I'll see who it is," he said, in a voice that very much sounded like he expected he would have to kill someone. He opened the front door slightly, holding the pistol behind his back. Before him was a small woman with black hair and an odd silver streak down one side. Her eyes were brilliant blue, and she carried a bag on her shoulder.

"Where is he?" the woman asked.

"Where is who?" Roland replied.

"Don't waste my time," the woman said in a soft voice. "None of us has time to waste, especially him. Now take me to him."

"And why would I let you in to see anyone?"

"Because he needs blood, or he is going to die. He may well die anyway, but if you don't let me in to see him, he will die before the night is over."

Roland wanted to argue with her. The protective part of him wanted to ask her more questions, to find out how she knew Ethan needed blood and how she had come to be there. After all, that was his job. He was the protector, the person who stood between everything that could or would cause harm. It was what he had been all his life. And now, a stranger had arrived, knowing too much and wanting access to the boy Roland had raised as his own son.

"Ro," Ashlyn's voice softly called out as her hand touched his shoulder. "Let her in. If she can help, then we must let her, but if she means to cause harm, then I can assure you that we will be ready to stand in her way."

"The only thing you have to fear from me is wasting precious time when I can help him," she said, pushing on the door and forcing her way inside. She followed the voices in the other room until she could see Ethan Scott lying ashen on a bed.

"We just changed his dressing," Victor announced. "I put a poultice of Witch Hazel on the neck wound to stop the bleeding."

The woman looked at Victor with a knowing glance and then walked over to Ethan's side. "Good decision," she commented, as she looked Ethan over. "He needs blood. What is his type?"

"Type?" Roland asked.

"Sorry," the woman said. "Sometimes I forget where I am. So, here is the problem. If we give him blood that is the wrong type, it can kill him."

"Is there any way to know what kind of blood will work for him?" Roland asked cautiously.

"Parents are the safest bet, but there is no guarantee. Immediate family might work, but again, there is no way to be sure."

"We need to talk for a moment," Roland said, as he motioned for everyone in the room to join him.

The woman shrugged. "Don't take too long, he doesn't have much time."

Victor, his wife, and another man and woman joined Roland and Ashlyn outside the room, and he closed the door behind them.

"What are they doing?" the woman groused.

"It's complicated," Star replied. "They're trying to decide if they trust you and who should give the blood."

"They are wasting time."

"Yes, especially because I know that it's me. I need to give the blood."

"And how do you know that?"

"I really don't know," Star said, with a serene look upon her face. "But I know that it has to be me."

"Then lie down next to him and let's get started."

The woman opened her bag and removed a long flexible tube, each of its ends wrapped in a clean linen cloth. She then removed a thin coil of smooth rope and tied it around Star's arm just above the elbow. "This is going to hurt. It's a large needle. I'm going to put it into this vein here..." she said, thumping on Star's skin. "The clamp on the other end will keep the blood from escaping until I can get the other needle in his arm."

Star winced as, without warning, the needle was forced into her vein. She watched as her blood snaked through the tube until it reached the other end. The woman clamped the tube shut and then began working on Ethan's arm. Loosening the clamp, she allowed Star's blood to push out the air inside the tube and needle. And then, with a smooth motion, the woman pushed the needle into Ethan's vein.

"Now, just relax. Just breathe deeply and relax." She studied the tube that passed Star's blood to Ethan, and then her eyes grew wide. The tube began to glow, a brilliant blue, like liquid sapphires were flowing between them. The woman smiled in disbelief, and then she laughed just as the door opened and the man who had been talking to Roland stepped into the room.

"It's me," he said. "I'll be the one to..." And then he saw Ethan connected to Star by the glowing blue tube. "Is she a match? Will he be ok?"

"Oh," the woman said, "they are much more than a match. I don't see this very often, and it is so amazing when it happens." She watched as the glow of the tube seemed to pulse, glowing brighter and brighter.

"Then he will be alright? He will recover?" the man asked.

"I didn't say that. All I said was that the blood will not kill him. It looks as if the poultice is working." She pointed to the fresh bandage around Ethan's neck. "She will be able to replace some of the blood he has lost, but there is no guarantee. He has lost much blood, and his brain has shut down. It may be a few days, or he may never come back. Now, please, leave the room and let me be about my work." The man nodded, and the couple stepped out of the room, closing the door behind them.

"My name is Muriel," the woman said in a quiet voice, looking at Star. "What is your name?" When she got her answer, she added, "Well, of course it is. On a night like tonight, with everything else the way it is, of course, your name would be Star. There are so many things I want to tell you. So many things that you need to know."

"I'm listening," Star offered.

"I can't. I'm not allowed to say. It's not that I don't want to, but I just can't. Do you understand?"

Star shook her head. "No."

Muriel paused as she played the last conversation she had with her sister. "Arrrgh," she said, clenching her fists. "If he survives, if he makes it, I want you to tell him something. The message is for both of you, but I won't be here, so you must be the one to tell him."

"Then tell me what we need to know."

Muriel paused and then spoke with a voice just above a whisper. "No matter where or when you are, the choice is always the same. You either become what they want you to be, or you become what you were born to be."

"I don't understand," Star replied, with a confused look on her face.

"Yes, yes, I probably should have just kept my mouth shut. There's no way you could understand what you haven't yet experienced in this life. That's why there are rules and laws. Because what I could tell you could change everything, and... I may have already done that just by being here. But you have people out there in the other room that are going to try to push him where they think he should go. He must follow his heart and go where it tells him."

"I'll tell him," Star replied, "even though I don't understand what you mean. I have a question, though."

"Yes?"

"Why is my blood blue? It's never been blue before."

Muriel squinted and shook her head, then leaned in closer to her. "It's Kail-lain, Star. Kail-lain."

"Kail-lain," Star repeated, her eyes starting to flutter.

Placing her hand on Star's forehead, she watched as her eyes closed, and her breathing grew deeper. "Rest, girl. Rest. This will all make sense to you one day."

Two hours later, the woman disconnected the needles from their arms and packed up her bag. She left Ethan and Star lying side by side and walked out into the room where all the adults were seated and waiting. "Thank you for allowing me into your home," she said in a calm voice. "I must be leaving now."

No sooner than the words left her mouth, she was assaulted with questions from the curious.

"How did you come to be here?" Ashlyn asked. "We haven't left the property since Ethan arrived. How did you know he was here?"

"I'm sorry," the woman answered. "I mean no disrespect to any of you, but you wouldn't understand my answer if I gave it to you. Just know that I knew the boy was in danger, and it was critical that I made an attempt to help."

"So, we are just supposed to trust that you somehow knew we were here, that the boy needed your help, and so you came?" Ashlyn retorted, feeling insulted at the woman's reply.

"Exactly."

"Can we pay you?" Roland offered.

"No, I didn't come here for gold."

"Then can we at least feed you?" Vallow interjected. "You must be hungry?"

"No, but thank you. I have dinner waiting for me at home."

"During the transfer of blood, why did it glow with a blue light?" Roland asked.

"Again, I mean no disrespect or insult, but you wouldn't understand. It would take days to explain and even then...well, it would be difficult for any of you to grasp."

There was an awkward silence with no one really knowing how to respond.

"Is there anything else we need to do?" the man who volunteered to give blood asked.

"No, just do what you've been doing. Apart from infection, my biggest concern is that the boy may not awake from his coma." Then, looking directly at Victor, she made an odd statement: "If that is the case, then someone will have to go find him and bring him back."

Victor started to ask a question, but the woman opened the front door, stepped outside, and quickly closed the door behind her. A few seconds later, lightning flashed a second time, but again, there was no thunder. Roland opened the door to follow her out, but she wasn't there, and the night sky was clear.

Ginger Coltrane sat in the rain under a hooded cloak and shivered as she watched the building. The rain had started in the middle of the afternoon, and the current downpour showed no sign of letting up any time soon. Breathers weren't really designed for the rain, as blowing drops of water that ran down her face could get inside the filter and play havoc with her lungs. From time to time, Ginger would shake her head in an effort to keep the rain from getting inside the breather. Thunder roared, and lightning came down with a sizzling crack, lighting up the night sky. She would rather be in a pub, somewhere next to a roaring fire, drinking a beer and having a laugh with friends. But no, it was her shift, and she drew the tedious job of watching the abandoned building in the worst storm of the year. Since The Lying Fisherman closed, her new job was working for Drake Gordon, Captain of The Darkest Night. What frustrated Ginger was that she was working for a pirate, and she wasn't doing anything remotely fun or marginally dangerous. She wondered if she'd done something wrong to get this kind of pointless assignment.

Her hands were shaking, and her teeth began to chatter uncontrollably. She had at least another two hours before her replacement came. Blowing hot breath on her hands, she tried to warm them up.

It started quietly, and then it grew louder. Gordon told her to listen for a hum, and there it was. Next came the light. As the hum grew louder, the light grew brighter. It lasted for under ten seconds, and then the world near Ginger was once again quiet and dark. She watched with careful eyes to see what happened next. No one had entered the building since she'd arrived on site, yet there was now someone leaving.

Climbing down from the wall she was perched upon, Ginger moved closer to the alley where the person emerged from the building. She now had a challenging problem. There was no way she could walk silently behind the person without splashing water or creating noise. But if she stayed far enough back so the person couldn't hear her, she risked the chance of losing them in the darkness. Stay too close, and they would know they were being followed.

At the corner of the alley and the street, the person paused as if looking at a map, before turning left in the direction of the heart of New Marchant. Jumping over as many puddles as she could, Ginger tried to stay close. She waited at the corner and checked to make sure they weren't watching before she stepped onto the sidewalk and followed, trying to stay in the shadows. Two blocks down, the figure stopped at the street corner and consulted the map again.

Ginger followed for another ten minutes, stopping when the person stopped and quickly stepping into the shadows, before following once again. She was now in the city center of New Marchant. Around her were government buildings and expensive apartment buildings that housed both government employees and those who provided influence. Rechecking the map, the person turned at a large apartment building, climbed the steps, and entered through an oversized brass door.

Once the cloaked person was out of sight, she tried to close the gap quickly. In the process, two other people entered the building, and she cursed her bad luck. Then she had to wait until the doorman turned away so that she could enter without being seen. When she was finally able to slip into the lobby, she immediately looked at the floor. There were several sets of wet footprints, all of which led to the staircase. Ginger followed them up the stairs, stopping at each level to see if any of the footprints continued. On the third level were steps that went off in either direction of the main hallway.

She followed the ones to the left and noted the apartment number where the tracks stopped. Then, she went to the other end of the hallway and did the same thing. Retracing her steps back to the stairs, Ginger went up to the next level, but there were no recent tracks, so she went one level further up. There she found the third set of footprints and followed them down the left hallway until she reached the apartment where they stopped. Committing the apartment number to memory, she went down the stairs and exited the building.

Ginger had one more assignment. Her instructions were clear. She was to return to the building to see if there was any change on the inside. The rain came down heavier, and the puddles collecting water were deeper. Her feet were soaked, as was the hem of her dress that hung below the well-worn cape. Finally, she reached the abandoned building and turned into the alley. As she reached for the side door of the building, the humming sound started again. When the sound and the light stopped, she moved back into the alley and hid in the shadows, unsure of what would happen next.

The water she was standing in came up to her ankles. Her whole body shook, and for the next fifteen minutes, no one either went into the building or left. Taking a deep breath, she stepped toward the door and opened it. Standing in the doorway, between dry and wet, she removed both a candle and a matchbook from her cloak. Her cold fingers fumbled with the matches until she managed to remove one and strike it against the side of the box. When the candle was lit, she again looked at the floor, squatted down, and examined it carefully. There were tracks, muddy tracks, all around the floor of the building. Stepping inside, she followed them across the room and to a metal stairway that led up to the next level. Ginger stopped and listened again. Her heart was pounding as she realized she had no idea who, or what, could be waiting up ahead.

Her foot landed on the first step, and the wood groaned. The second step wasn't much better. Pausing, Ginger went up three more steps until the third, too, betrayed her presence. At the top of the stairs, she trusted her ears more than the light of the candle, as the glow only gave her a few feet of vision. The only thing she could hear was her own breathing.

Bending down, she could see boot prints on the floor coming from across the room. Every step she took was careful and made with a sense of dread for what might be lurking in the shadows. The steps stopped at a black mass on the floor. As she grew closer, she could tell that it was an anvil, a tool owned by the previous occupant that was too heavy to move, no doubt. Leaning next to the anvil was an envelope.

She reached her hand into the folds of the cloak and wiped her wet hand on her dress. Her hand now dry, she leaned down and picked up the envelope. The front had writing in a language she didn't understand, and on the back was a seal embellished with a strange insignia. Careful not to damage the envelope in any way, Ginger placed the item in her blouse and walked back to the stairs. She couldn't wait for the next person on watch to take her place. She needed to deliver this immediately. So once again, she stepped out into the rain and the dark of night.

Ten minutes later, she walked through the door of a pub and waited for her eyes to adjust to the light in the room. She inhaled and smelled the aroma of beer, whiskey, and sailors who hadn't bathed in days. It wasn't The Lying Fisherman, but it smelled like home. Navigating around the tables and the staggering patrons trying to stand after one too many drinks, she made her way to the darkest corner of the room. Seated at the table were Drake Gordon and Thrasher York. Gordon's long black hair was plaited, and it hung about his shoulders. While he dressed more like a gentleman than York, he was at heart a pirate both in action and in his business interests. The captain of The Darkest Night, Gordon, his crew, and his ship dominated the oceans of NHHMM, and very few people actually knew that the ship existed.

Thrasher York looked like he belonged at any pub residing in the shadiest parts of NHHMM. His hair was badly cut, and he had a scar on his face that ran from his mouth to his ear.

Wet and shivering, Ginger approached the table. She then reached into her cloak, removed the sealed envelope, and with a shaking hand, held it out for Gordon.

Looking around the room to see if anyone had noticed her arrival, Gordon looked over to York. "Can you get her something to warm her up?" he asked.

"Of course," York replied, as he stepped away from the table and walked to the bar.

"Have a seat," Gordon said in a quiet voice, "and tell me what's on your mind."

Ginger sat next to him and set the envelope on the table. "I was at the warehouse, the one you told me to watch."

Gordon nodded, still leaving the envelope where it lay. When Julian Vanderschmidt told him of the other energy surges in New Marchant, Gordon had stationed five of his people around the areas Vanderschmidt identified on a map. "Then you have something to report?"

Ginger told him about the warehouse, the hum, and the brilliant light. She told him about the man she followed and the apartment she tracked him to.

"Can you tell me anything about him?"

"No. I couldn't get close enough."

"And what is this?" he asked, pointing to the envelope.

"I don't know. I went back to finish my shift when the noise and the light started again. I waited to see if someone else would leave, but when they didn't, I went inside to explore. I found this resting next to an old anvil."

Thrasher arrived with a hot drink that smelled of whiskey and set it on the table. With Thrasher's body blocking the view of anyone who could be watching them, Gordon picked up the envelope and began to examine it. "Hmm. The letters don't make sense, and I don't recognize the seal on the back." Putting the envelope into his inner coat pocket, he motioned for Ginger to drink.

Ginger held the hot mug between her hands and let the warmth flow inside her while she waited for the liquid to cool. "What is it?"

"A little invention of mine," Thrasher said, smiling and displaying his crooked teeth. "There is some chocolate, a little milk, and a special mixture we keep behind the counter."

Sipping the drink, Ginger smiled as warmth began to chase the chill away. "Tastes like cake."

"Told ya," York said, pointing to Captain Gordon. "Pay up."

Gordon reached into his vest pocket and placed a coin in York's awaiting hand. "I don't get it. That doesn't taste anything like cake."

"Really, it does," Ginger said after another sip. "Like chocolate cake, but with a warm bite to it."

Shaking his head, Gordon looked back over to her. "Good work. Go back home, change, and get warm. I'm going to be away for a few days, so if anything else happens, come back here and tell Thrasher. He will track me down."

Thrasher raised an eyebrow, unaware that the captain had any plans to travel. "I need to get this," he said, tapping the outside of his jacket, "to my friends. They need to know what has happened."

CHAPTER 2

The Secret of Cell 2

Resting on a metal crutch retrieved from the medical building, Jack Flynn watched as John Augustine, Guy Clapton, and Shane Benoit stacked piles of wood on the four corners of the park in Arcborne. To his left, Shy Shepherd sat on a bench and watched the others work, not yet able to lift anything. Her face was still bruised and battered, and the color of her skin around her eyes was now a purply-yellow color. To his right, Otis Walton stood in the shade of a tree, trying to protect his nearly bald head from the burn of the sun.

"Are you sure they will be here tonight?" Walton asked, watching the men work.

"That was the plan," Flynn answered. A fist-sized rock had caught him just below the left shoulder blade when the explosion went off, and the entrance to Arcborne was sealed. Another smaller piece with a razor-sharp edge tore through his mid-thigh, resulting in his newfound dependency on the crutch. Using the supplies in the medical building, Stiletto Lang was able to clean the wound and sew up the tissue. He dreaded the ride on the airship back home, mainly because there wasn't much room in the cabin and he wasn't sure how well his leg would deal with the cramped quarters. The good part was that he was alive, and it would take a very long time for the chancellor to be able to get back into Arcborne. He didn't know if the tunnel itself was damaged and, if so, how much. But it would be hard work getting back there.

"And if they don't show up?" Clapton asked.

"They will. The man who dropped us off would never leave us here. He's a good friend. The kind you don't find very often. If he doesn't show up, he's dead."

Clapton nodded. "Ahhh. It's good to know those still exist."

"It is. You know," Flynn said, looking over to Walton, "you don't have to stay here. I'm sure that my friends will find you helpful if you wish to go back with us."

Walton laughed. "I'm not a rebel; I'm simply an old man. I had my moment of importance and fame, but I wasn't up to the task. My dream was to make Arcborne a different and wonderful place. I simply wasn't prepared to fight to keep that dream from being corrupted."

"I mean no insult," Flynn said, "but you are being disrespectful to those who are old and still have courage. The man responsible for our departure tonight is older than you and considerably more frail. Maintaining freedom isn't the job of the young; it is everyone's responsibility. My friend, Jonathan Vanderschmidt, is a great inventor. He designs wonderful machines, but he could never have designed a place like this. If you want to stay here, then let it be because you're a coward, not because you are old and have nothing more to offer."

"I know Jonathan," Walton said with a slight smile. "He is a genius, that one. We collaborated on a few projects back when I was at San Simeon. And he's still at work?"

"Oh yes. He won't ever retire and sit in a comfortable chair waiting to die. There's too much in his head that he wants to bring to reality. He will probably die with a screwdriver in his hand, sitting at a workbench."

"I want you to know," Walton stated, "I'm not the coward you believe me to be. The medical staff here at Arcborne gave me six months, maybe a year to live. There isn't much more time for me to accomplish anything."

"Well, then, you are probably better off sitting here in an empty town waiting to die. That's your choice. If that's what you want to use as an excuse, go ahead." Holding his fingers up to his lips, Flynn whistled. "That's good," he called out. "Make sure the green flares are loaded, and the ropes are securely tethered to the trees. The buggies look good where they are. Just make sure the knots are tight."

From the direction of the market, Stiletto Lang approached, carrying a stack of folders that went from her hands to the bottom of her nose. "Engineering and metallurgy," she called out. "Some of this stuff is really good. I couldn't leave it behind. The boss would kill me."

"The boss?" Walton asked.

"She's an engineer for Mr. Vanderschmidt," Flynn replied.

"Oh."

"You might want to put those in a building until we get it docked and the propellers are off. They could scatter the papers all over the valley."

"Good idea," Lang acknowledged. Turning on her toes, she walked to the building nearest the park and set the stack next to the door, glad to be done with the weight. Little by little, she then carried the papers in parts into the building where they would be safe from the approaching craft.

"Will you excuse me for a moment?" Walton asked.

"Sure," Flynn replied.

Walton walked away toward City Hall with his hands in his pockets and his head hanging down. He thought he had his death figured out. He would wander the valley, admiring what he created, until he could do it no longer, and then he would simply pass away. Only now, he was faced with a different ending, and he had a choice to make. He could do what he had initially planned, admiring an effort that hadn't turned out how he wanted, or he could do something worthwhile with the time he had left. Neither choice changed the ending, but the choices impacted how he got to the place where he breathed his last breath.

Apart from the masks and the crystal guns, Jack decided to abandon the remaining supplies they brought in. That space would be much better used for the files Lang had procured from the school. In theory, his plan should work. The ropes wrapped around the trees would be attached to the tethering lines hanging from the airship; the other end of the ropes was tied to the buggies. If Thrasher could get the craft in place and low enough to the ground, then the buggies could be driven to help take up the slack and keep the airship low enough to the ground for boarding. When he was convinced that everything was in order, he and the team went to a nearby café to find some dinner. Before they got within thirty feet of the building, they could smell the aroma of cooked food, and they looked at each other with curious eyes.

"Smells good," Clapton said.

"Really good," Augustine agreed.

"Walton?" Shy asked.

"Well, if it's not Walton doing the cooking, then we have a different problem," Flynn replied.

A bell attached to the doorframe rang when the café door opened. "Help yourself," Walton called out from the kitchen. They found an assortment of cooked meats and vegetables already on a serving counter, along with glasses of water for each person.

A moment later, Walton emerged from the kitchen wearing an apron. "I raided the cooler and picked out the freshest items," he said. "No use letting the best things go to waste. I also found a bottle you might enjoy."

Jack saw a bottle of whiskey sitting on one of the tables. "That will do nicely," he said. They then all enjoyed a good dinner and slowly worked their way through the bottle of whiskey until, at 11.45, Jack announced it was time to get to the park and light the fires.

Thrasher York didn't know what to expect. He circled the valley for fifteen minutes, waiting for a flare to show him where he should go. And then he saw the fires marking the four corners of a square. They hadn't discussed this. They hadn't talked about landing in the valley. It would make his job much easier, but what had happened? Why was it now acceptable for him to land in the middle of a valley surrounded by thousands of people?

It could be a trap, a ruse to lure him in. Their agreement was that flares would be launched. They'd said nothing about markers of fire. As he continued to circle, he let out a sigh of relief when he saw the first flare. It was green, and it was followed by three more coming from each corner of the square.

Adjusting the controls, Thrasher steered for the fires. The nose of the airship tilted down, and the propellers rotated on the frame, offsetting the lift from the hydrogen. Great. I'm steering a balloon full of explosive gas between four fires. Who came up with this plan?

He eased the airship down, lower and lower, until he could see the images of people around him. With the night filter of the mask, he saw two people in front of him grab the rope tether from the frame of the airship and attach it to other tethers on the ground. The ropes wrapped around tree trunks and were then tied to the end of a buggy. Thrasher took the airship down even further to give the people on the ground more slack in the ropes. When he could feel the ground resisting the downward thrust, he waited until the ropes were tied off and someone on the ground signaled him with a wave of their arms. Thrasher then cut the power and hoped the airship would stay in place. It did.

Opening the door, he saw Jack Flynn hobble up to the carriage. "You're getting better at this," Flynn called out.

"Maybe, but I would rather be back on land or water. What happened?" Thrasher pointed to Flynn's leg.

"Long story. I'll fill you in on the way back."

"Where are all the people?"

"Longer story," Flynn replied.

"Well, as long as there's no one shooting at us, I'm good. Let's get your people on board and get out of here."

Lang and Clapton carried the folders from the building, putting their cargo in the back of the passenger compartment. They helped Shy into the airship cabin and then assisted Flynn. Lang and Augustine climbed on board next, while Shane Benoit and Guy Clapton stayed on the ground to cut the tethers when they were finally loaded and ready to leave.

"Ready to go?" Thrasher called out.

"Hang on," Flynn said. From the corner of the square, Flynn saw a figure emerge. It was Otis Walton, and he was carrying his own stack of folders. He walked to the edge of the passenger compartment. He looked up inside as he took in the technological marvel that was floating before him.

"Do you have room for me?" he asked with a humble expression.

"Why?" Flynn retorted. "I thought you were too old to be of any value. I thought you just wanted to die a peaceful death."

"Because I thought about what you said. I'm not ready to die, and I think I might have something that you will find useful," Walton stated flatly.

Flynn looked at his eyes. Earlier, they were filled with the acceptance of his own fate. Now, they offered the promise of something different. "Shane," Flynn called, "take the papers from the man and help him climb up."

"Are you sure?" Thrasher whispered. "The Council hasn't approved this."

"Yeah, I'm sure," Flynn replied, secretly glad that Walton had changed his mind. "I'll handle the Council."

Walton got on board with the awe and excitement of a child in his eyes. This device, the airship, was something they had conceptualized at Arcborne, but had never been built, and Otis Walton was about to fly in it. As a young boy, he had dreamed of one day being able to soar through the sky, and now he was about to fulfill that dream. Thrasher turned on the motors and pushed down on the levers to force the passenger compartment onto the grassy surface below. The tethers were cut, Benoit and Clapton climbed into the compartment, and the airship climbed upward and into the night.

As the craft gained altitude and Thrasher circled Arcborne in an upward trajectory, Walton peered down into the valley below, gazing at the city's lights as they twinkled. I forgot to shut off the lights, he thought, and then he laughed.

Since Roland's escape, Miles Doggert oversaw eight other residents at Hardscrabble, the small prison below the Chancellery. Some were in for a few months, and others lasted under two weeks. Doggert was never told why they were in the horrid place, or what happened to them when they were finally removed. Not officially, at least. He would, of course, pick up bits and pieces of the residents' former lives as they tried to negotiate with the jailer for better food and an extra blanket, or propose riches to Doggert if he would aid in an escape. Sometimes, the residents told him everything, hoping their argument was sound, and that anyone listening would act as judge and pardon their offense. "I didn't know she was the chancellor's wife," cried one. Followed by, "It was only a kiss." It was clear that Hardscrabble wasn't just a place to put those whose existence threatened the state, but more often angered Chancellor Brighton.

All of the residents, however, had two things in common. Each guest was in the worst place in NHHMM, and none of them ever occupied Cell 2. Of the six cells in Hardscrabble, every cell was occupied at one point or another. The only exception was Cell 2. The last resident of that cell was Bartholomew Quick, who was pretending to be Thomas Tolliver. Doggert didn't pick which guest stayed in which cell; that was determined by someone else further up in the Ministry of Punishment and Rehabilitation, but no one was ever assigned to Cell 2.

With no guests to watch over, Miles Doggert decided to go against his usual cautious nature and chose to explore the unused cell. Pulling open the heavy door, the hinges made an unnerving screeching sound. He lit a match by scraping it against the stone wall, and then lit the wick of the oil lamp he carried. Cell 2 appeared to be like the other cells in the hall, with a thick layer of dust covering everything. There was a cot, a blanket folded on the end of the bed, and an empty bucket. He pushed the cot with his foot, and it moved a couple of inches. And when it did, its legs left a mark in the dust. The walls were stone, the door was solid, and at first glance, everything seemed to be in its proper place. The only structural difference he could see was a two-foot-wide steel column on the back wall opposite the door. The column wasn't unusual; it provided the underlying support for the massive structure, and Doggert pushed on it to ensure it was secure. Seeing nothing of interest, he turned slowly to his right, scanning the walls, when his eyes caught a brief shadow. He stopped, looked again, but saw nothing. Doggert repeated the same movement, and when he did, he saw the shadow again. Reaching down with his free hand, he felt where he thought the shadow should be. Sliding over the joints where the stones met, he felt a smaller stone that seemed to protrude further out than the others. His heart began to beat faster as the small stone seemed to be loose at his touch, and grabbing it with his fingers, it came off in his hand. Squatting down and holding up the lamp, he noticed a metal knob recessed in the hole where the stone was placed.

Doggert studied the knob for a moment, as well as the stone that had covered it. The stone was hollowed out in the center so it would cover the metal knob, and if it were pushed all the way in, it would have been seamless with the other stones. Taking a deep breath, he pulled on the knob. It moved, and from inside the wall, he heard a mechanical CLUNK. Standing up, he pushed on the wall with his shoulder, and it moved inward. Built into the wall was a small doorway about five feet tall. Were it not for the protruding stone, he would never have known the door was even there. How many times had he been in the cell and never noticed the outline of a door? He couldn't remember the number.

He held up the lamp and stuck his head into the opening. There were stairs leading down and a stone on every side. Summoning up every bit of the bravery he had, he cautiously moved down one step after another, ready to retreat at a moment's notice. He guessed there must have been twenty steps before he reached the bottom. A door to somewhere was his expectation, but there was nothing but a long, dark hallway. The air smelled old and musty, and after five minutes, he began to feel like he was walking uphill. The air changed as he moved further in, and the floor started to level out. He could smell food, and up ahead, he could see what looked like a flat wall. No matter how much he searched, he couldn't find another knob like the one in the prison cell. Perhaps I missed it. He was about to turn back and see if he had passed something further back in the tunnel, when he decided to see what would happen if he pushed on the wall. POP!

The wall moved forward just an inch, and light flooded the tunnel. Doggert quickly extinguished his lamp and listened carefully before he pushed on the wall again. He could hear voices, the clanging of metal, and someone giving loud orders. Leaving the lamp in the tunnel, he pushed on the wall. It moved, but only slightly, and so he pushed harder.

The wall was really a disguised metal door, and slowly it began to move. Fixed to the outside of the door was a layer of brick that, when closed, filled out a brick wall at the end of an alley. To his right was a stone wall, and to the left, the alley opened up to a busy New Marchant street. Traffic bustled down it, and people walked along the sidewalk, paying no mind to the mixture of smells coming from the alley.

Doggert finally realized where he was. On the outside edge of the massive Chancellery was a kitchen that prepared the food for all the staff in the building. The alley was for food deliveries, and he knew it was a busy place, as every day he walked past the location on his way to and from work. He knew he had to get the door closed quickly, but he first needed to find out how it could be opened from the outside. The bricks around the door looked perfect, and he couldn't find any that were loose. There was a large metal bin for trash, and from the lack of odor of decaying food, Doggert guessed the bin had been collected earlier that day. The only oddity he could find was a sign on a metal pole at the end of the alley just away from the door: DELIVERIES BY APPOINTMENT ONLY. Grabbing the pole, he tried to move it. It wouldn't budge, not to the right, to the left, or when he pushed it. But when he pulled it toward the street, it did move, and from inside the brick wall, he heard a mechanical noise.

Releasing his grip on the pole, he pushed hard on the brick door. CLICK. Pulling a handkerchief from his coat pocket, he held it over his nose as he'd left his breather back in the jailer's office. No sooner had he made it to the street than he came face to face with a delivery buggy that nearly ran him over.

"Move it!" the driver yelled. "We need to make a delivery." Keeping his head down, Doggert waved at the driver and hurried back down the sidewalk toward the staff entrance to the Chancellery that he used every day. This had got to be worth something to Jack Flynn. However, with The Lying Fisherman currently closed, he had no idea how to reach him.

CHAPTER 3

The Stranger in the Rainbow

The world was a rolling meadow, arrayed in colors that defied his imagination. Focus seemed to be just beyond his grasp. It was better that way. The blend of colors was far more desirable than the ones with crisp lines, where every hue and shade was distinct. The fuzzy, blurred edges felt better. They let him float aimlessly, and they required nothing of him. No focus, no attention. He felt numb. Occasionally, he would focus, but only for a moment, and then it was peaceful again. He liked peaceful. Peaceful required nothing of him.

In the corner of his eye, something moved, and he tried to focus. It was a shape. A person, perhaps? But this shape was different. It commanded him to concentrate, and while everything else was the fuzzy, sleepy collage of colors, he couldn't blur this shape, no matter how much he wanted to.

He moved to the shape. It was bright, yet soft. Not a brilliant, blinding light, but a soft glow that provided its own sense of peace and calm. The voice was saying something. He could hear it, but he couldn't make out the words. Even as he grew nearer to it, the voice never changed in volume. He listened to the shape and watched it until the blur of colors called him back. He liked the colors. He liked the way they were fuzzy. They made him feel...

The shape reached out to him; it took his hand. It felt warm against the cold of this place. And as if it could feel him start to

30

waiver, the colors seemed to grow more vivid. He liked the colors.

"ETHAN!" the shape called out in a voice he finally recognized. "ETHAN. NO. ETHAN! COME BACK!" It was Star.

He sat up with a gasp and then immediately groaned in pain. There was movement around him, and a familiar voice that was in the room for a moment, and then gone.

"It's ok," Ashlyn said. "You're ok. Just lie back down. Easy now. You need your rest."

"How did you get here? Where – am – I?" He tried to take in the room, noticing the walls were a pale yellow, and beside the bed was a window that let in light, but not direct sunshine. This wasn't the Chancellery, it wasn't Arcborne, and it wasn't the metal room he remembered last. This was different. There were pictures on the wall, drawings, and beside him, sitting in a wooden chair, was Ashlyn. A blue dresser, with drawers of alternating color, was positioned on the wall at the end of the bed, and on the top of the dresser was a vase of flowers with delicate, violet petals.

"You're safe, and Pops is here."

"Pops..." he said with a slight smile. "Where is Star? Is Star ok?" He tried to sit up again, but his mind was sloppy, and his usual precise mental focus was missing.

"Star is fine. She just stepped away for a bit. She'll be back soon."

"Where is Pops?"

"He went to let everyone know you're awake."

"I've been asleep?" he asked, his eyes foggy.

"Yes, for days."

"I must have been really tired," he mumbled. "Where is Star?" he asked again.

Pops stepped through the door, followed by a man and two women Ethan didn't recognize. "Ah, you are back with us," Pops said, walking over to the side of the bed next to Ashlyn. "I'm so glad to see you with your eyes open."

One of the women went to the other side of the bed and kissed him on the forehead. "Thank you," she said. She was thin, her brown hair pulled back, and she looked at him with an appreciative gaze.

"For – what? What did I do? And who are you?"

"I'm Star's mother, Vallow. You saved her. You brought her back. Thank you."

31

"Hello, Star's mother," Ethan said, his eyelids getting droopy. "Where's Star?"

"She'll be back soon," Ashlyn answered.

"And who are those people?" he asked, looking at the man and the woman in the doorway.

"They are our neighbors," Vallow answered, hesitantly. "They've helped care for you over the last few days."

"Thank you," Ethan replied with a crooked smile. "Why does my back hurt? And why is this thing around my neck?" He pulled at the bandage. "I'm thirsty. Can I have some water?"

"Certainly," Ashlyn said. The woman in the doorway rushed out of the room and quickly came back carrying a glass of water. Ashlyn stood up from the chair, allowing the woman to take her place.

"Let me help you," she said, gently placing her hand behind Ethan's shoulder and helping him up to the water she held in front of his lips. "Slowly. Go slowly," she said, as tears streamed down her cheeks. "Take your time. It's going to hurt a little as you try to sit up, but you're going to be just fine."

Victor Chastain sat under a tree with green leaves and white blossoms. He wore brown trousers, a bright green waistcoat, and a white shirt with rolled-up sleeves. His salt-and-pepper gray hair was long, about his shoulders, and was pulled back behind each ear. His brown shoes were badly worn both at the soles and on the toes, and the laces on his left foot were fastened together with knots.

He smoked a pipe with a long, narrow stem and a short, round bowl. Looking over his toes at the tree opposite him, he watched his daughter, Star. Dressed in blue pants with the cuffs rolled up, and a pale red shirt and white stripes, she leaned up against the tree with her shoulders and head resting on the trunk. Her eyes were closed, and she looked restful...at peace.

Victor would never have asked her to do this, but she had begged to help. And it was only after he failed twice himself that he reluctantly agreed to let her try. He watched over her, not quite sure when she would wake, but with the absolute confidence that she would, indeed, awake back up from her current state.

While everything they told him was factually new, none of it was a surprise to him. But if worlds could be punctured, and people traveled through the holes to other places, why wasn't it possible that there were other planes of thought where people could move and exist? That was the part that frustrated Victor. He could accept the reality of what he had learned, but why couldn't others accept what he knew to be true? It was, perhaps, an irony, but it was also his reality.

Star twitched. Her body shifted, and her breathing became shallow.

He drew deeper on his pipe and leaned forward expectantly.

Her eyes flew open wide, and a smile as big as she could muster lit up her face. In a flash, she stood up, looked at her father, and said, "I FOUND HIM! I FOUND HIM!" And without another word, Star ran through the open field, into the trees, and down the hill to the house below.

Smiling, Victor exhaled and stood up, brushing the grass from his trousers. With a slow, meandering walk, he followed Star, completely unwilling to rush after her.

Ethan had just finished his drink of water when Star ran into the room. Completely unaware of the adults nearby, she rushed over to the side of the bed where her mother had been and kissed Ethan's forehead on almost the exact same spot.

"Star!" Ethan mumbled. "When did you get here?"

"We arrived together, from the Chancellery," she replied.

With her reply, a part of Ethan's brain began to push through the fog and the pain. He remembered the Chancellery, the machine he was supposed to defeat, and the gun that Santa Udi was about to fire. "We've got to get you out. Hold on, Star, and don't let go." With his left hand, he reached wildly for her until he caught her arm.

"Ethan," Star said in a calm and quiet voice. "We're safe. You got us both out safely. I am in no danger: We're in no danger. We're safe."

At the sound of her words, his face relaxed, yet his hand remained affixed to her arm.

Victor Chastain entered the room, carrying a saucer and a cup containing a brownish, greenish tea with an aroma of both ginger and thyme. He walked over to the woman holding the glass and exchanged the cup and saucer for it. "Now that he is back with us, he is going to feel the effects of what he went through. This will help him with the pain."

The woman helped Ethan sip some of the tea, and at the taste, he jerked his head away. "Now, drink all of this," she said. "I know it tastes a little off, but you must drink all of it. Every drop."

Ethan cut his eyes over to her, smiled, and then leaned forward to finish the tea. The impact was almost immediate. He loosened his grip on Star's arm, but let his fingers slide down it until they rested on her hand. The anxiety on his face diminished, and he drank the tea until the cup was empty.

"Do I know you?" Ethan asked Victor in a protective voice.

"No," Victor said, smiling. "But when you are feeling better, we can talk."

"That's my father," Star said.

"It's nice to meet you, sir," Ethan murmured, trying to hold out his hand. But searing pain caused him to grimace and pull it back.

"It's nice to meet you, too." Victor smiled. "And, thank you."

"Why does everyone keep thanking me?" Ethan asked the neighbor sitting beside him. The woman started to reply, but Ethan's brain had jumped to a different topic. "I had a strange dream," Ethan said to Star, as the mixture in the tea began to surge through his body. "I was in a place where there were colors everywhere. Fuzzy colors. They were all around me. They were beneath my feet, and above me, and all around me." He gestured with his weak hand. "You were there. I saw you. At first, you were saying something to me, but I couldn't understand what you were saying. And then you yelled at me."

"I know," Star replied, sweetly. "I was there." She had barely finished her sentence when Ethan's eyes closed and he fell into a deep sleep, induced by Mr. Chastain's tea.

Ethan slept for the remainder of the afternoon, although he woke up once and was able to drink half a cup of broth before returning to sleep. The neighbor woman helped him with the broth. She was good at this, and he wondered if she might be a nurse. And when he was finished with the broth, she helped him with the tea.

"Why does my back hurt?" he asked, as his body rushed back to slumber.

"You were shot, four times," the woman replied.

"Four times?" he said, holding up four fingers.

"Actually, five. Four in the back, and one in the neck. That's why you have a bandage there," she said gently.

"Whoa. That's a lot. Why am I not dead?"

"Do you want the easy answer or the hard answer?"

"I don't think I can do the hard answer today," Ethan said, shaking his head from side to side. "Ouch. That hurts. I shouldn't do that anymore."

"Yes, it's best that you remain still. But the short answer is that your waistcoat is made in a very special way with a very special sort of fabric. The bullets didn't penetrate the fabric. You're bruised and have some rib fractures, but the bullets didn't enter your body."

"But this one must have," Ethan said, pointing to the bandage on his neck, "because the waistcoat only comes up to here." He moved his hand to his shoulder. "It doesn't go any higher, and my neck is above that."

"That's right," she said. "And that was the one that caused us the most trouble. Between the time you were shot and when we were able to get to you, you had lost a lot of blood."

"But you saved me!"

"No, we saved you. We all worked very hard to save you. But it was Star that found you."

"Was I lost?"

"In a way. She and Victor, her father, can probably explain that better than I."

Ethan's eyes started to flutter. "I like you. You're nice."

"Thank you," the neighbor said, as her lip began to tremble. "That makes me happy."

He slept for the remainder of the night, and in the morning, he was both hungry and alert. The woman was gone, and strangely, he remembered most of what they had talked about the night before. In her place was her husband, sitting in the chair, watching every move Ethan made.

"Did you sleep well?" the man asked after a moment.

"Yes, I think so. I don't remember dreaming, but I don't remember anything else, so I guess that means I slept well."

"Good," he replied. "You need your rest. The body heals faster when it gets the rest it needs." He was a big man, tall and wide across the shoulders. His dark brown hair was pulled back behind his head, and his eyes were strong, but at the same time, kind.

"I remember you from yesterday, but I didn't get your name," Ethan said.

"We, my wife and I, live next door to the Chastains, on the other side of the barn. We teach school here in the area. Three of the towns nearby all send us their children, and we teach them. Star has told us a lot about you."

"Yeah? What did she say?"

"She said that you were smart, brave, kind, noble, and that you were the best Conquest player she had ever seen."

"She is amazing herself, don't let her fool you."

"I know," the man said, and laughed. "After her grandfather passed, I became her teacher, and it didn't take long before she won more times than I would like to admit."

"You were able to beat Star?" Ethan asked, somewhat amazed.

"We have a tally sheet somewhere. She probably knows where it is. I think I may be a few matches up on her, but overall, our total of wins is very close."

"That's impressive. Star rarely loses."

"Maybe when you are better, we can play a match or two."

"I would like that."

"Are you hungry?" the man asked.

"Starved."

"I think that Vallow has been cooking all morning, hoping she would have something that you like. If you will excuse me, I think I can find her in the kitchen."

"Where is your wife today?" Ethan asked as the man stood up.

"Sleeping," he replied. "She and Star took turns by your side during the worst part of this. I don't think either of them has slept much for the past few days. They have a lot to catch up on."

"That was nice of her," Ethan said. "I like her. She's very nice."

"I'll tell her you said so. That will make her happy. Now, let me see what Vallow has cooked for you." He left the room, leaving the door open. From inside the house, he heard a voice cry out.

"He's awake! Oh, I bet he's hungry." Rushing into the room, Mrs. Chastain looked like she had been working in the kitchen for hours. Her apron was spotted with flour, some kind of fruit filling, and several types of batter. "Are you hungry?" she asked.

"Famished," Ethan replied, smiling. It was impossible to look at

36

Vallow Chastain and not like her, as she always seemed to have a beaming smile on her face. Her eyes sparkled, and each sentence that she spoke seemed to end on an upward inflection point that just seemed to make her words sound happy.

"Ok, just tell me what you want. I have eggs, some skillet ham, blueberry pancakes, and some strawberry tarts. If none of that sounds like what you want, just tell me and I'll try to make it."

Ethan laughed. "It all sounds delicious," he said. "May I try a little bit of everything? Would that be alright?"

"A little bit of everything coming up," she said. And a few minutes later, Vallow Chastain came back into the room with a plate full of everything. She had taken the time to cut it all up into small bites so that Ethan wouldn't have to manage a knife and fork.

Star's teacher came into the room also, with a plate of his own, as Vallow went back into the kitchen to continue cooking. "It's good, isn't it?" he said.

"Really, really good," Ethan mumbled through a mouth full of food. "I'm glad there was some left for you," he added.

"Oh, you have no idea how much food is out there. You could probably feed half the town of Tearmann from what's in the kitchen, and she's making more."

"That's really kind of her, but I still don't understand why? I figured out how to get us out of where we were, but I don't see how I saved her."

"As Star tells it," the man began, "she held on to you, you held on to her, and the clock while the clock was chiming."

"Yes."

"And then the door opened, and the lady with the gun was standing there."

"Yes, I saw her aim the gun, and then..." It started coming back to him. Santa Udi pointed the gun at Star, and he lifted her up and turned so that his back was facing Udi.

The man watched him with pride as Ethan pieced it all together. "Let me show you something," he said, placing his plate on top of the dresser and reaching down to retrieve something from the floor. As he held it up, Ethan could see his waistcoat. The right side was covered with a dark brown stain: his blood. Turning it around, he saw four indentations, where it looked as if the fabric was nearly poked through, but still held in place. Two indentations were to the left of his spine mid-back, one near his shoulder blade, and the last was a quarter inch away from the third.

"She was a good shot. The two near your spine would probably have killed Star, and the fifth shot, the one that hit your neck, would have hit Star in the head if you hadn't moved her. That's why her parents are so appreciative. You saved her life because you turned your back on the woman, moving Star out of the way."

When it happened, Ethan didn't really have time to think about it. He simply wanted to protect Star, and he did the only thing he could. He turned her away from the gun. For him, it wasn't a heroic act, or even a noble act; it was simply the only choice there was to make, so he made it. "Ok, thanks. I understand now."

The man put down the vest and took his plate from the dresser. "Have you tried the ham?"

Ethan nodded. "It's great. I got some syrup from the pancake on one piece, and it tasted even better with a little bit of sweetness."

Inside the kitchen, a few feet away, Vallow listened to them talk about her food and her daughter, and she smiled, a pleased and satisfied smile.

A little later in the morning, Star peeked around the corner into the bedroom to see if Ethan was awake. "Come in," he said. "I can't sleep anymore, and I'm getting tired of sitting here."

"Ah, aren't you the grumpus this morning," Star said playfully.

"I'm sorry. I'm just a little cranky."

"It's ok," Star replied. "My mom told me you ate a lot for breakfast."

"I did. She is an excellent cook. Everything was amazing."

"Good. She enjoys cooking for someone new. She gets to try out things that she knows the rest of the family might complain about."

"There was nothing to complain about. It was delicious."

Star moved the chair over to his bed and sat down, pulling her knees up to her chin and wrapping her arms around them. "Where do you hurt the most?" she asked.

"My back," he said, without hesitation. "The neck stings and throbs when I move, but my back hurts every time I breathe."

"My father said it's because the bullets cracked the ribs in your back. It will take a while to heal, so don't expect to be pain-free in a few days."

"I'm just glad to be alive and out of Arcborne."

"It's my turn, you know."

"Your turn for what?" Ethan asked.

"My turn to say thank you. You kept your promise and got me home. You saved my life, and you didn't even hesitate. Thank you."

"You're right." He reached gingerly for her hand. "I didn't have to think about it."

"You weren't doing well for a while. It was like you'd decided that you just weren't going to come back. That's when I went looking for you."

"I don't understand what you mean. Where was I?"

"I don't want to tell you," she said.

"Why? Why would you not want to tell me?"

"My family, especially my father, is viewed as an oddity in the area. They like to call him crazy, but he isn't. And I'm afraid that if I tell you, you may feel the same way. Roland and Ashlyn were skeptical at first. I just don't want you to not like us."

"Star, in the past year, I've seen enough things to make me believe that I'm crazy. You don't have to worry about that. Nothing will ever make me think that you are odd, crazy, or anything other than wonderful. So, tell me what happened."

"Do you know how you told me that your inventor friend figured out how to open holes between worlds and places?"

"Yeah."

"And we both believe that's real. You've experienced it twice, and I've experienced it once, but we both know that it's real."

"Yes, we both know that it's real."

She took a deep breath. "My father is a bit of a philosopher. He's really quite smart. He believes there are different layers of consciousness. And he believes that just as we can poke holes between worlds and locations, we can also poke holes in the consciousness of our minds."

"Ok. I don't know where this is going, but I believe what you're saying is true."

"My father says there are several layers of our mind, probably more than we will ever know. There is the layer that we live in, the part that we are experiencing right now, the dialogue, the facial expressions that we both notice, the touch of our hands; this is the first layer. The next layer is kind of an in-between state when we are sleeping. Our dreams can be crazy things, or frightening things, or things that make us laugh, but they don't last for long, and they are easy to wake up from."

Ethan smiled and nodded slightly. "I'm still with you."

"The next layer is where you were. The way my father describes it, it's a place where you are more than asleep, and you are very close to death. The fuzzy colors you saw, the ones you described, make you feel calm, peaceful, and reluctant to return to the place we are in now. If you come back, then you are mentally alive again. But if you decide to stay, you die.

My father has figured out how to poke holes in the levels of our minds, just as your inventor friend figured out how to do the same with locations. Twice, my father went to that place of color to find you, and both times he did. Both times he spoke to you, both times he told you to come back, but you didn't know him. He meant nothing to you. He was simply a shape with a voice you didn't recognize. And so, both times, you turned back to the colors and away from him."

"And then you came?" Ethan asked.

"And then I came. My father didn't want me to try, and we argued and argued for hours while you hung on the edge of death. Finally, he agreed to help me. We went up to his favorite place, a meadow up on a hill beyond the trees. He walked me through the steps I needed to take. He helped me poke through from where I was to where you might be. And I began to search for you. There were other people in this space of color, but I couldn't help them. They didn't know me. It seemed like days upon days that I searched. In reality, it was less than two hours. And then I found you."

"That's what I dreamed," Ethan said.

"But it wasn't a dream. I was there. I kept talking to you, and you would look at me as if you could hear me, but you didn't understand what I was saying. Then you would turn away and gaze at the colors. I would call you back, and you still couldn't understand me, and you would turn away again."

"And then you took my hand, and you screamed at me," Ethan said, and laughed.

"Yes. Yes, I did that," she said, blushing. "But you weren't listening, and I had to make you hear me, so I screamed at you."

"And you did. I did hear you, and I came back."

"Then you believe me? You don't think I'm crazy?"

"Of course, I believe you," Ethan said. "I just finished the story for you. I remember it. You couldn't be making up something that only I know about, unless you were really there."

Star's face beamed.

"But I have a question," Ethan said.

"Please. If I don't know the answer, you can ask my father."

"If you can poke a hole in that part of my mind, to the place of the colors, then is it possible that you could make a hole in this level of my mind, and reach me the same way?"

Star shook her head. "I can't do that, but my father says it is possible."

"Is this something I can learn?"

"That's a question for my father." She thought for a moment and then scrunched up her shoulders. "And I need to apologize to you for something."

"What?" Ethan said, raising an eyebrow.

"I almost killed your grandfather."

"And how did you almost kill one of the toughest men that I know?"

"With a pitchfork," she replied, squinting. "But it wasn't my fault. Really. I didn't know it was him."

It was midday when Roland came back to visit Ethan. He was awake and looking out the window. "Feeling better?" he asked.

"Pops!" Ethan said, leaning up to hug him. "It's so good to see you."

"It's good to see you too," he said, hugging him gently. "Tired of being in bed?"

"Yeah, I'm tired of just lying here. I need to move around some."

"Ok," Roland said. "Let me help you up. We'll get you outside for some fresh air. How does that sound?"

"Great. Let's go."

Roland helped Ethan put on some pants and shoes. They had wrapped a cloth around his chest to help add some stability to his torso, but his insides still ached as he tried to move.

At first, Ethan was unsteady on his feet. The muscles in his body fought over which part needed the most protection from the pain, so he shifted and repositioned his stance until he found the most comfortable posture. Roland took him by the arm and helped him across the floor until he was able to stand on his own. The house was modest in every way; clean and warm, but there was nothing in it that was excessive or elaborate. They stepped out into the warm sun, taking small steps and trying to keep steady.

To the left and back was the barn, and directly to the left was the home of the couple that taught the local school children, or at least that's what Ethan surmised. "It's quiet," he commented. "Where is everyone?"

"They're off doing other things," Roland said. "They're giving us some time to talk."

"That doesn't sound good," Ethan said, looking over at him.

"It's all good, but it's a lot to take in, and everyone believes that it's best you hear it from me." They began to walk down the path to the house and across the road. "There's a path that leads over to a field, just that way. It's an easy flat walk. Let's go."

Following the path for several minutes, they eventually came to a wide-open field of lavender, the aroma strong, but pleasant. "This all belongs to a farmer named Mr. Cleo. They say he grows the best lavender in all of NHHMM."

"Star told me about a dessert that her mother makes for her every year on her birthday. It's called a lavender-blueberry crumble. She missed her birthday in Arcborne, so I had a baker make one for her."

"You know she almost killed me," Pops said, over-exaggerating.

"Yeah, she mentioned that. Can you tell me your side of the story?"

"I heard the hum. I saw the light and rushed to the barn. We knew you had the clock with you in Arcborne, because Jack placed it with your belongings. We put the other clock in the barn in case you figured out how to get back to us. Anyway, Star heard me coming and grabbed a pitchfork. I saw you bleeding on the barn floor, and this wide-eyed blond girl was standing between us with a pitchfork. You know firsthand how the trip can impact you. Star wasn't any different, but she was barely able to hold herself up, yet she had the tines pointed at me, and she wouldn't let me pass. I would go this way," he added, laughing and moving his body to the side, "and the pitchfork followed. No matter how I moved, she wouldn't let me pass."

"But she didn't actually stab you?"

"No, but it makes for a better story." Pops laughed. "She is a special one, that girl. She was willing to fight a grown man when she could barely stand up, just to protect you."

"She is special," Ethan said, nodding his head.

It was clear that Pops was avoiding the conversation. Whatever it was they were going to talk about, he didn't appear to be in any rush.

"What is it?" Ethan asked. "What is it that you want to talk about?"

"First, I want to thank you. I would still be in jail or dead if it weren't for you. You took a big risk for me, made a big sacrifice, and Ashlyn, Jack, and I will be forever grateful."

"Pops," Ethan said, "you are my family. You are the only family I have, and I would do anything for you. It wasn't a sacrifice. It was no different than what you did for me."

"I know, but still, it's important that I thank you." They stood on the edge of the lavender fields, and as the wind shifted, the aroma came back to them, teasing them for a moment before it disappeared again.

"After you won, I'm sure you figured out that we escaped by the metal ship beneath the fishing boat."

"Yeah," Ethan said. "Once I got the watch, I knew that's how it had to happen."

"When we were safely on The Darkest Night, I asked Captain Gordon to do two things. First, I asked him to lie to Professor Wimberly and you, and say that he had seen us die on the boat. I did that to protect both of you, should the chancellor's people decide to interrogate the professor. Secondly, I asked Jack if he would retrieve the clock in the harbor house and have Mr. Vanderschmidt connect it to another beacon, another clock. The day they took you away, Jack followed after you as soon as it was dark, and was able to put the harbor house clock in the buggy with your possessions."

Ethan smiled, knowingly. "I recognized the clock when I was in the Chancellery, but I had never noticed it before then. And I had it in my possession all the time?"

"Yes. We couldn't leave you a note explaining it all in case one of the chancellor's people found it. We hoped you would check your watch and find it."

"I didn't think to do that," Ethan murmured. "I used it to check who was around me, but not for what was around me."

"Doesn't matter," Roland said. "It all worked out. Shortly after that, Ashlyn and I had to leave to go on a journey. I needed to track down something for both of us. Because I'd spent so many years watching over your father, he and I had special codes and secrets. We had a special code that only he and I knew. I needed to see if he'd left anything for me after you and I went away. Ashlyn and I started by going to your grandfather's coastal home. Now it's owned by the chancellor, but it still has its secrets. I found a clue there that could only have been left by your father. That clue took us to another place, and when we got there, a further clue took us to somewhere else, and that one to still another. Ultimately, we came here, to Tearmann, and I placed the beacon that drew you here in the barn you just saw. That's how you arrived here."

"But why here? Why did you come here?" Ethan asked impatiently.

"Because I believed that if your parents were still alive, they might be here in Tearmann."

"And?"

Pops hesitated for a moment before answering. "We found them, Ethan. Your parents are still alive."

His mind raced as if he were playing a game of Conquest. The dots were connected, and in seconds, everything became very clear. "It's the neighbors, isn't it? The teachers."

"Yes," Pops answered.

It made sense. She'd looked at him with tenderness, and spoken to him as he always imagined a mother would talk to her child: Drink it all. Every drop. And her husband looked at him with a sense of pride when they talked about how he saved Star. "I want to see them," Ethan said. "I want to see my parents."

"Let's go, then," Pops said.

"What do I call them?" Ethan asked on their way back.

"The town knows them as Nicholas and Natalie Polowski. I suppose you could call them by those names, or by Ryan and Anne. Probably Mom and Dad would be better." Pops laughed, then added, "But that's up to you."

He stood outside the door of his parents' house, unsure of what was going to happen when he knocked. His stomach turned, and he was afraid he might say something wrong. Ethan had always believed them to be dead. Even when he heard the story of them upon his arrival at NHHMM, he never really thought they had survived. He took a deep breath and knocked on the door.

The floors creaked as footsteps crossed the room, and then the door opened, and Anne O'Connor stood before him. "Mom?"

She carefully hugged him and began to cry. "I am so, so, sorry. It was never supposed to happen this way. When you left, you could barely walk, and now...you are almost grown."

"It's ok, Mom. I understand. You did what you had to do to keep me safe. I understand that now."

From behind him, footsteps approached. Ethan's head turned, and he saw his father. His big arms wrapped around them both, and he held them so tight that Ethan grimaced.

There was a celebration that night that neither the Flynns, the Chastains, nor the O'Connors had ever experienced before. There were stories to tell, and the telling began. Tears of joy fell down every cheek. Years of life that needed to be learned, and it all started on this night.

In the midst of the stories and laughter, singing began in the kitchen, and it carried into the living area, where Ethan, Star, Breeze, and Victor Junior were seated. The adults sang as Ethan's mother brought in a chocolate cake with fifteen candles on top.

"Happy birthday, son," Anne O'Connor said. "I didn't forget. I could never forget."

Ethan smiled, and a tear ran down his face. It was a very, very good day.

CHAPTER 4

The Meeting of Minds

Jonathan Vanderschmidt shuffled into the laboratory, nodding his head at those already in attendance. With the exception of Ashlyn and Roland, all the members of the Council were present and seated, including the two newest members, Charlotte Mayberry and Captain Drake Gordon. Vanderschmidt removed two folders from his desk and then gently lowered himself into an overstuffed chair with rollers on the base.

"Good morning, and thank you for coming at such short notice. We have so much to talk about. So, so much." He tapped the top folder. "We have both good news and some concerning news. And mixed in between, we have some decisions to make."

"How good is the good news?" Captain Gordon asked.

"I should say, on the whole, very good," Vanderschmidt replied.

"Then give us the good news first, because I already know the bad news."

"Agreed?" Vanderschmidt asked, as he looked at the others in the room, who facially indicated for him to continue. "Very well, we shall start with the good news." He paused for a few moments, then said, "Roland and Ashlyn have located Ryan and Anne O'Connor. They are both alive and well, hiding in a remote town, and waiting to assist in any way they can."

The news came as no surprise to Jack. He had long suspected that the O'Connors were somewhere in hiding, because if they'd been located by the chancellor, he would have wasted no time presenting them to the public as traitors. "But what about the boy?" Jack pressed.

"Another piece of good news," Vanderschmidt said with a smile. "He was able to escape from the clutches of the chancellor along with the Chastain girl and is now recuperating with our associates."

"Recuperating?" Jack asked.

"It seems Ethan was shot five times in the process of escaping, and we owe Mr. Chamberlain much credit, as four of the bullets did not penetrate the vest his shop created. The fifth hit his neck, causing him to lose a significant amount of blood, but they were able to nurse him back to health. He will be just fine."

"Can we get the rest of our team equipped with the same kind of clothing?" Merten Ashwillow asked.

"Already working on it," Chamberlain said with a satisfied smile.

"When do we move the O'Connors back here with us?" Charlotte asked.

"I would suggest," Vanderschmidt replied, "that we leave them exactly where they are. The chancellor already believes the Flynns to be dead, and he knows nothing about the O'Connors. Ethan and the Chastain girl are two of the most recognizable faces in NHHMM. The closer they get to a highly populated area, the more likely they will be recognized."

Most of the Council members were nodding their heads in agreement, and those who didn't, Vanderschmidt merely ignored. The last coded telegram from Roland had indicated that those in Tearmann insisted they remain where they were and give Ethan more time to recuperate, so it really wasn't something that would be brought up for a vote.

"So, I hope you've enjoyed the good news, because I feel it will soon be overshadowed by what is in the next folder. But before we get to that, Jack, please update the group on what happened in Arcborne."

Jack recounted the story of his journey, telling them of the school, the factory underneath, Shy's capture, the evacuation of the city, and his efforts to seal the entrance to the valley. He spoke for almost an hour before pausing and beginning to take questions.

"Why did you feel it was necessary to seal up the valley?" Merten Ashwillow asked.

"What they were creating were ways to further enslave the people of NHHMM," Flynn began, feeling a little defensive and unappreciated. "It was a research facility, much like this, but infinitely larger, with a focus on things that we are not involved with. They were working on chemicals to subdue large parts of the population, branches of medicine to influence the thoughts and opinions of people on a large scale, and weapons, which could obliterate anyone who would stand against them. By sealing the valley, we will set them back months, if not years."

Ashwillow nodded. "I understand," he said. "The information I've received from my sources is that the tunnel experienced a partial collapse. They estimate that it will take several months to clear the debris and restore structural integrity before it is safe to use again. As a result, they have tightened security on the western tunnel and have increased the number of trains passing through each day. They will now be moving freight and people through the western tunnel twenty-four hours a day, every day of the week."

"Did everyone get out of the tunnel unharmed? The students and people of Arcborne?" Jack asked.

"According to my sources, the only people unaccounted for were some of the guards, the head administrator, Otis Walton, and one other member of the staff."

"And, speaking of Mr. Walton," Vanderschmidt said, leading the conversation in a different place. "Why did you bring him to us, Jack?"

"That man was responsible for the creation of Arcborne. He knows its secrets. The chancellor and Dean Maria Vasquez effectively stole it from him and turned what was to be a grand educational and social experiment into a weapons factory. He didn't want to leave, but I kind of humiliated him into leaving along with us. Not only did he provide us with an overview of every citizen and student, but he brought us a detailed design and layout of the other city by the western tunnel."

"Do you think he is genuine?" Pine Carstairs asked.

"He is dying," Flynn replied. "He has six months, maybe a year left to live. He has nowhere to go and nothing to lose. Walton will be an ally for us if we want him."

"I've had a chance to look over the folder of the other city," Vanderschmidt added. "It aligns with the reports that Mr. York and my grandson brought back from their trip in the airship."

"But what do we do about Walton?" Professor Wimberly asked.

"My opinion...is that we let him work with our engineers. He could probably shave months off what you are currently working on. I'm not trying to be crass, but let's learn everything we can from him while he's still alive," Jack offered.

They debated the topic for another ten minutes before finally voting to grant him access to information relevant to projects already in development at Arcborne, while keeping the information unique to the Resistance out of his reach. It was a decision that everyone could agree upon.

"Now, to the more troubling items," Vanderschmidt said with a furrowed brow. "As some of you know, I've been getting some odd readings on my instrumentation. Power surges similar to the kind that we saw when we opened the hole from NHHMM to the world where Roland was living. I recalibrated my instrumentation and found beacon signals on a different frequency than we are using. Oddly enough, one of the beacons came from the ocean. I sent my grandson, Julian, out with Captain Gordon to see what they could find. At the same time, I discovered a beacon we traced to an abandoned building in New Marchant. The captain assigned a team of people to watch the building around the clock, and he has news relating to both beacons, and none of it is good. Captain?"

Gordon stood from his chair and walked over to a large map. "The ocean beacon that Mr. Vanderschmidt mentioned was located here," he said, pointing at the map. "We were able to trace it using some stronger equipment that Julian brought aboard The Darkest Night."

In great detail, he recounted the story about the first appearance, the second appearance, the battle, and then the deactivation of the beacon and the interruption of the three other ships from appearing in the water.

"And you are sure it wasn't a NHHMM warship?" Flynn asked.

"Positive," Gordon replied. "We don't have a ship that big. The design was different; the tactics they used were different. And, there is this..."

Walking over to a table, he picked up a large black flag and held it up with both arms, extended so the Council could get a clear view. In the center of the black fabric was a diamond with a green dot at its center. Above and below the diamond were strange letters that none of them had seen before.

The Council was in a state of shock. A warship had entered NHHMM using technology that only the Resistance had. "What kind of weapons did they have?" Jack asked.

"Black powder cannon," Gordon answered. "No different in range or size than what the Navy ships have. It really wasn't a battle. As long as we stayed outside of their range, we could easily destroy them."

"And there were three more coming?" Jack followed up.

"Yes. Julian ripped out the guts of the beacon before they arrived."

"So, it was an invasion," Chamberlain said aloud. The Council members began to talk amongst themselves, and Vanderschmidt had to raise his voice and tap on the floor with his cane to shut them up.

"But there is more," Vanderschmidt said. "Yesterday, one of Captain Gordon's people delivered this note found at the site of the other beacon."

Gordon gave them a step-by-step description of the arrival of the first person and the appearance of the note. It was a somber description that no one enjoyed hearing.

"And the note," Vanderschmidt said, "is written in the same characters as the flag."

"Then we have spies among us," Charlotte said in a grim tone.

The Council debated for over an hour about what to do next. Professor Wimberly, Ashwillow, and Carstairs wanted to continue observing and gathering information. Vanderschmidt and Chamberlain wished to take defensive steps, while Captain Gordon and Jack Flynn believed the best course of action was to continue developing and deploying the advanced weaponry they already possessed.

Charlotte Mayberry was the only one who didn't argue for a position. She was already plotting out in her mind what she wanted to do. She was a newcomer to the Council, and she doubted that her opinion carried much weight. Hence, she had already reached the conclusion that she would do whatever was assigned to her, while doing what she believed was necessary.

Ultimately, they divided the Council's focus into three distinct areas of effort. Gordon and Jack Flynn would focus on applying the knowledge gathered from Arcborne and deploying their current technology to protect strategic assets. Chamberlain and Vanderschmidt were tasked with developing technology to better locate and potentially block the signals of the beacons. Since Professor Merten Ashwillow and Charlotte Pine Carstairs were still in New Marchant and had not yet been compromised, they would remain in their positions and gather any available intelligence.

Charlotte listened with satisfaction as the assignments were given. It was what she was going to do anyway, so there wouldn't have to be any deception on her part.

When the meeting was over, she approached Captain Gordon and then pulled him aside from the others. "I need a favor."

"Why am I worried?" Gordon said, squinting his eyes.

She smiled. "No need to be worried. I simply need an asset from you."

"An asset? The ship is off limits. That's the only asset I have."

"Technically," Charlotte began, "The Darkest Night actually belongs to Jack. And if I were to ask him the right way, he might give me what I want. But I'm not interested in his ship. Who was the person doing the surveillance on the building? The one that found the note?"

"Ginger Coltrane."

"I want her. I'll take over her pay."

"I don't own her," Gordon said, chuckling. "Tell her what you want, and if she wants to work for you, that's fine with me."

"I know," Charlotte quipped, "but I was being polite. She's involved with your team, and I wanted you to know what I was up to."

"What exactly are you up to?" Gordon asked. "It kinda sounds like you're up to no good."

"Captain, I'm always up to no good."

With his breather firmly on his face, Miles Doggert left through the side entrance of the Chancellery and started a quick walk to his destination. As he passed the alley that led to the secret door in the brick wall, he decided to go through with it. A year ago, he would never have dreamt of going down into the streets and pubs around the harbor at night. It wouldn't be safe for a man like him, but a year ago, he hadn't met Jack Flynn, Thrasher York, or any of the others. A year ago, he would never have thought of breaking the rules, but now he was an accomplice to those who had broken a man out of Hardscrabble. And now, he was walking into one of the roughest, most dangerous parts of New Marchant, out of his own free will.

He was looking for someone, anyone, that he could recognize from The Lying Fisherman pub, in the hope that he could get word to Jack Flynn and tell him about his discovery in Cell 2. The first two stops yielded nothing. He encountered drunken men and women that he would rather forget, but no one who looked familiar. His third stop was a pub called The Black Mule. He stood by the bar for several minutes, studying every face he could see. He was just about to leave when he spotted Thrasher York sitting at a table in the corner of the pub. Motioning for the bartender to come over, Doggert asked, "The man in the corner, what's he drinking?"

"It depends on who's buying. Him or you?"

"I'm buying."

"Chandler's Park."

Doggert winced when he heard the words. Chandler's Park was generally accepted to be the finest whiskey in all of NHHMM. And it didn't come cheap. "I'll have two."

The bartender wiped out two glasses with a rag, and Doggert wondered if drinking from a clean glass made the costly drink taste like it was worth the money. He settled up with the bartender and walked over to the corner table carrying the drinks. "Can I join you?" he asked.

York looked up, recognized Doggert's face, and motioned for him to sit. "And how have you been doing in the most foul place in this land?"

"Still alive. Still working. Not a guest in that place, and I'm not dead yet. So, it could be worse for me."

Thrasher took the glass, brought it to his nose, and inhaled. "I see Casey talked you into the good stuff."

"He said that's what you were drinking."

"Thank you but know this: Anytime you want to drink with me, you are always safe with rum."

Doggert nodded. "That's good to know," he said. "Is it safe to talk here?"

Thrasher's eyes quickly scanned the room. "For the moment, yes. There are a couple of strangers near the door. If they move our way, I'll let you know. Salute!" Thrasher took a long drink of the whiskey and placed it back down on the table.

"I've got some information that might be of value to our mutual friend."

"Our mutual friend is moving around quite a bit right now, and I don't know when I'll see him again."

"It's not urgent," Doggert said after taking a sip of the whiskey. It really was exceptional, and clean glass or not, he could see why it cost more. "It's just something that may be useful one day."

"Go on," Thrasher prodded.

"There are six rooms where I work. Your friend, our recent guest, was in room 5. The room across from him is room 2. Since the escape, no guest has been placed in room 2. Not one. I got curious and examined the room closely today since we currently have no guests. There is a hidden door in the room that opens into a passage, which ultimately leads to a secret door in an alley on the far side of the Chancellery. There are no guards posted by the passage entrance in the alley, and there are no guards anywhere along the way."

"So, that's how he did it!" Thrasher exclaimed. "We've always wondered how that man, whom we knew as Bartholomew Quick, could be in two places at once. He could come and go from Hardscrabble without being seen or heard."

"He said his name was Tolliver, but if you say it was a man named Quick, I believe you."

"Yeah," Thrasher said, throwing back the rest of the whiskey. "Quick worked for the Ministry of Intelligence. He was posing as a member of the Resistance to get the identity of the man in the other cell." Thrasher was careful not to use Roland's name, as he didn't know what Jack had confided in Miles Doggert. Waving at the bartender, he ordered another round, and a look of horror came across Doggert's face. "Don't worry," Thrasher laughed. "This round is on me."

Doggert finished his drink and waited for the replacement to arrive. As he looked at Thrasher, he realized something. These people, the outcasts that the chancellor branded as traitors, were the only ones who actually seemed genuine to him. They were real. Once he got past their rough and threatening exterior, they were quite likable.

"So, does this passage have a lock? Is it hard to get into?"

"Well..." Doggert began.

"Yeah, yeah. You want to be paid before you tell me."

"No," Doggert said, almost offended. "I don't want anything for this. I was just going to say that while the door is hidden, the lock and key are in plain sight." The bartender delivered the second round, and Doggert told York about the sign and how easy it was to get inside.

"But someone, if they were inclined, would still have to get out of a locked cell to get back into the Chancellery."

"That's just it," Doggert replied. "Cell 2 is never locked because there isn't anyone in it."

"So, we, I mean the person, could get past all of the security and make it up to the Chancellery without ever being seen?"

"Exactly," Doggert beamed.

"I don't know when I will see him next, but I'm sure our mutual friend will be pleased to get this information. And you want nothing for this?"

"Nothing."

"Then drink up, my friend, and welcome to the oft-short-lived life of pirates, no goods, outlaws, and rebels."

The thought of being someone who willingly broke the rules appealed to Doggert. Throughout his whole life, he had followed the rules, stayed in the shadows, and rarely taken any kind of risk. If the words of Thrasher made him feel uncommonly free, the feeling didn't last for long. It was the phrase "oft' short-lived life" that kept bringing him back to the reality of his wife and children.

"Oh, my," he said, looking at his well-worn pocket watch, "I'm late for dinner." He thanked Thrasher for the drink and hurriedly left the bar. Thrasher motioned to a man whose nose bent to the left thanks to more fights than he could remember.

"Bull, please see that our friend gets home safely."

"Sure thing," the giant of a man said.

Thrasher watched the men leave and then started to think about all the interesting things they could accomplish with a secret door into the very heart of the government.

Ginger looked at the paper in her hand and grew more uncomfortable with every step she took. Her clothing didn't fit in, her hair was a tangled mess, and she had none of the training to survive in such a place. Standing at the front of the steps that led up to the large, four-level, brownstone home, she swallowed hard. There must be some mistake. Gordon must have written down the address wrong. *No one in a place like this could ever want to talk to someone like me.*

As she looked at the front door, trying to decide what to do next, it opened. A stunning brunette stood on the other side, wearing a white blouse and a form-fitted black skirt that fell just below her knees. "You're punctual," she said with a radiant smile. "That's a good thing. Please, join me."

Ginger Coltrane didn't know exactly how to respond. She climbed the steps, entered the building, and promptly felt more out of place than she did before. The rooms around her were neither extravagant nor pretentious, but they were clean, bright, and spacious. There was no unnecessary clutter or furniture. No accessories were placed to either intimidate or impress. The home was actually much like the woman that greeted her: sleek, well-kept, but not overly ostentatious.

Closing the door, the woman led her into a sitting room, where she turned and introduced herself. "My name is Charlotte Mayberry."

"Ginger C - C - Coltrane," she stammered uncomfortably.

"It's nice to meet you, Ginger. Please, have a seat," Charlotte said, motioning to a sofa beside them.

"It's probably better that I stand," Ginger said, looking down at her soiled dress. "I wouldn't want to ruin your furniture."

"Nonsense," Charlotte argued. "That's why we have furniture, to sit upon. If you aren't going to sit, then I have to stand, and these shoes are not exactly comfortable, so you are doing me a favor by sitting."

Staying as close to the edge of the cushion as possible, Ginger sat down and tried to recall a ladylike pose she had once seen. "Mr. Gordon said that you wanted to see me."

"I did," Charlotte said, nodding. "And did he also tell you that you can discuss anything with me?"

"Yes, ma'am. He said I could trust you as I trust him." Noticing a hole in her dress, Ginger folded the fabric over in the hope that Charlotte wouldn't see it.

"You were the one stationed to watch the abandoned building the other night? The night when the note was found?"

"Yes."

"Our mutual friend told me about how you followed the new arrival through the rain and into an apartment complex. He also told me that you followed the wet tracks through the building to identify the apartments that could be associated with the person."

"I did."

"I'm impressed," Charlotte said, "and I don't impress easily. That was both crafty and smart, and those two characteristics have great value to me. I want to offer you a job."

"But I have a job at The Lying Fisherman."

"You had a job. The pub is closed, and when it opens back up, you can go back to that job if you wish. But, if you want to work for me, I'm offering you a job now."

"Doing what?"

"Do you want the detailed specifics, or the big picture view?"

"The big picture," Ginger said. "I've found the specifics tend to take care of themselves."

"Exactly. The person you saw the other night is a spy. I suspect there are more. We're going to find them, discover how they're connected, and determine why they're here. Is that a big enough picture for you?"

"Yes," Ginger said with a sly grin. "What do you want me to do?"

"First things first. You and I are going shopping. To do what we need to do, you and I need to be able to go anywhere without looking out of place."

"Good," Ginger said. "Because right now I feel very much out of place."

Ethan was healing faster than anyone expected. The bandage was off his neck, and even though he would forever have a nasty scar on the left side, he could live with that. It would serve as a daily reminder of the chancellor and the kind of people he employed. The ribs were still a problem in more ways than one, however. Not only did it hurt when he lifted anything, but his inability to contribute to a rural life was wearing him down. He was frustrated and felt useless. Everyone had work to do. His parents taught school, Ashlyn worked on the property, as did Pops, when he wasn't off in the nearest town, sending and receiving telegrams from the members of the Council.

They had devised an elaborate system of coded words and destinations, ensuring that there was no clear way to track any message consistently coming to or going from any one person. Using the name of Archibald Bingham, Pops was almost invisible to anyone who might be monitoring telegrams for specific names.

While Star's brother and sister were at school during the day, Star, her mother, and even Victor Chastain had things to keep them busy on the property or in town. There wasn't much he could do but sit in the green bench-swing in front of the Chastain's house, and go back and forth.

He didn't know how long Pops and Ashlyn planned on staying in Tearmann. For all he knew, it could be a long-term thing, but he didn't think so. Neither of them seemed the type to want to play the role of farmer or rancher. Sooner or later, it would all come to an end. He knew it. He just didn't know when. Santa Udi would eventually send someone back up to Star's home when they didn't turn up anywhere else. As he thought it over, Ethan knew that if it were his job, this would be one of the first places he would search.

There was an uncomfortable ache in his heart as he thought about it. He didn't know if he could be happy here, knowing there was a war coming. His father and mother seemed to be the people to lead the rebellion, but would they? And if they did, Ethan knew he would have to be at their side. Then what would happen to Star? Would he have to leave her here? Would she want to come with him? How could he even think about that? He was fifteen years old. Was it even right for him to have that thought?

Getting up from the bench-swing, he called out, "QUINN!"

Within seconds, a black flash came around the corner, and the dog immediately went in search of a stick. Finding the stick for Ethan to throw wasn't a problem. The challenge was getting the stick from Quinn's mouth so he could throw it. She wanted him to tug on it with her, but his torso wouldn't allow that. The trick was to get her to drip the stick, which she was trained to do, and then pick it up before she retook it. On the third attempt, he succeeded.

With his left arm, he tried to throw the stick with an overhand motion, and was promptly rewarded with a stabbing pain. To make matters worse, the stick barely went fifteen feet. Walking up the hill through the trees, he would occasionally retake it from Quinn and toss it further up the incline with an underhanded motion that didn't seem to hurt him as badly. He made his way up to the meadow and found Star's father sitting up against a tree, smoking his pipe.

"Hello, Mr. Chastain. Are we interrupting you?"

"Not at all," he replied, shaking his pipe hand back and forth. "Find a tree and make yourself comfortable."

Ethan carefully sat down, but still the effort made him grimace. Quinn dropped beside him, panting and rolling over on her back in the grass. "It's nice up here," Ethan commented as he looked around the meadow and rubbed Quinn's belly.

"It is, without question, my favorite place around these parts. I'm just enjoying it while I can."

"What do you mean?"

"That's what's bothering you, isn't it?"

"I don't understand."

"What's going to happen to us all when they show up looking for you and Star? That is what's bothering you... Isn't it?"

Ethan was dumbfounded. "How did you know that?"

"Think of this as your first lesson," Victor said. "Star told me you asked several questions about what I think and believe. She said you asked if it was possible to penetrate a mind in its current state. She also said you wanted to know if I could teach you. You have your answer."

"You mean yes, you can penetrate a mind?"

"Exactly. You now have proof. And yes, to the other, as well."

"But what did you mean about enjoying it while you can?"

"I'm not a political man; I'm not a fighting man; I'm just a man who thinks. The chancellor wants both you and Star, probably you more than her, but nonetheless, they will come looking for what they want. I'm not a fool. I know that I can't stop them. I know that Star wants three things: She doesn't want to be a prisoner to the chancellor, no matter how nice the surroundings; she doesn't want to be isolated from her family, and probably, most importantly, she does not want to be separated from you. As her father, I could counsel her against keeping close to such dangerous company, but it would do no good. She has argued, and quite well, I must confess, that we would be in this situation even if she had never met you. If true, and I believe it is, I would be in even a worse position to protect her all by myself."

"So, you will leave this place?"

"Young man, it would not be my first choice, but it is the right choice."

Ethan thought for several minutes before speaking. He needed to be careful. Victor Chastain had just given him his personal thoughts, and while it made Ethan feel better, it would come at the sacrifice of something Victor held dear. "Are you in my mind now?" he asked.

Victor smiled and shook his head. "No. I will never do that again without your permission. I did it this once so that it would prompt this conversation. But I won't do it again. There could come a time when it would be more than...awkward."

"Ok," Ethan replied, completely missing Victor's reply. "May I ask you some questions?"

"Of course. Ask away."

"What does it sound like? When you are in a person's mind?"

"That's hard to describe. It's like a thought, more than it is a conversation. And it's hard to filter. Walking up the hill, your brain was telling your body what to do. Step here, avoid that. The hardest part is filtering out the parts of your thoughts that you aren't even aware of, and finding the non-automatic thoughts that are most important to you at the moment."

"Could you puncture the mind of an animal?"

"Yes. It can be done, and it's surprisingly understandable. It's not like you have to learn a dog language," he said, pointing to Quinn. "You can just hear the thoughts. I don't know how else to describe it."

"And what is Quinn thinking now?"

Victor laughed. "I don't have any idea. Maybe she wants you to throw a stick."

"How long did it take you to learn to do this?"

"Most of my life. First, I had to learn what I believed, and then I had to determine if it was real, or just a dream." Lighting a match, he held it up to the pipe bowl and took a puff. "Have you ever heard the term leadership?"

"Of course."

"This is a lot like leadership. There are some leadership traits that anyone can learn, but the best leaders often possess instinctive qualities. They can improve what they do, but they are born with a gift in leadership that is stronger than other traits they may possess. There is no guarantee that anyone can ever accomplish these things.

No special words that can create this skill, and no charms that can enable it."

"But Star has that trait?"

"Yes, but how much of it she has...only time will tell."

"I'm sure you are very, very proud of her."

Victor drew deep on his pipe and then slowly exhaled. "Very proud. But I'm more proud of who she is, and who she is becoming, more than I am proud of what she can do."

They sat in silence under the trees on the edge of the meadow. Victor smoked his pipe, Quinn chewed on a stick that was every bit as long as she was, and Ethan shifted around on the grass, unable to get comfortable. "Sitting doesn't seem to agree with you," Victor said after he exhaled. "Are you up for a short walk?"

"Sure," Ethan quickly replied, glad to be able to get up from the ground.

"Need help?" Victor said, offering his hand.

"No, but thanks." Ethan forced himself up. He felt a need inside to impress the man, so despite the searing pain in his back, he got to his feet. It was stupid, and he knew it. If taking a few bullets for Star didn't impress him, then it was unlikely that trying to stand up on his own two feet would have any additional influence. "Where are we going?"

"My workshop. It's behind the barn. I want to show you my little part of the world."

Following the path between the trees, they made their way down the hill and to the back of the barn. On the other side of the dirt walkway in the back of the barn was a shed about the size of a bedroom. The shed had a window on either side of the door, vines growing up the walls, and sweet-smelling purple flowers hanging in an arch above the door. "Please, come in," Victor said.

The first thing Ethan noticed was the pungent odor. It was as if every available plant and animal scent had been crammed into one small room, and to Ethan, most of it smelled like death. The shelves, running from floor to ceiling, were stacked with bottles and jars, seemingly filled with every type of plant. In the middle of the room was a worktable holding scales, measuring instruments, and an assortment of small knives and scissors. On the back wall were the cages housing birds, toads, and what appeared to be rainbow-colored salamanders. Taking a match from his vest pocket, Victor struck it on the table and then moved the small flame to a lamp hanging over the worktable.

"Wow!" Ethan exclaimed when he could better see the room. "What is all of this?"

"Inside this room is the science that I know."

"Science?"

"Yes, my boy. Science. Do you see that container on the middle shelf?" He gestured towards it. "Third from the left? Chew on the bark of that tree, and it will help you with pain. Add that bark with the roots of the jar just above, and it will aid with poor digestion. But if you add the bark with the petals from that jar with the pale-yellow flowers, there is a good chance that you will be dead by morning."

"So, you are a chemist of sorts?"

"Of sorts."

"And this is the stuff you have been researching?"

"Oh no. The things I just told you are fairly common in the medical arena."

"Basic herbal remedies," Ethan said, finishing Victor's thought.

"Yes, but they're not taken seriously. When things are free and readily available, it's hard to charge and make a profit, isn't it?"

"Yes, but..."

"But the tonics prescribed for us represent verifiable science, isn't that what you're thinking? They've been verified and proven both safe and effective."

"Are you in my mind?" Ethan asked.

"No, but that's the common argument I often receive. Give me what is safe and approved, even if it's not what's best for the patient."

"What's in this jar?" Ethan said, pointing to a small jar in front of him.

"That is the dried glandular excretions of a particular toad."

"Sounds disgusting," Ethan said, shrugging and wincing at the pain.

"But if you combine that with some dried tree pulp in just the right way, you can travel to another place, here..." He tapped the side of his head. "Just as easily as you can step through time and worlds, with the right crystals, of course."

"Is that sarcasm?" Ethan asked, raising an eyebrow.

"Oh my goodness, no. I don't think that men like Mr. Vanderschmidt take me seriously, as he and those like him tend to only believe that things they model, test, and replicate prove real science, but I wasn't being sarcastic. I'm completely serious."

"Mr. Vanderschmidt says there is no magic, only science. Is he right?"

"Magic is just undiscovered science, and science is simply the elimination of yet another mystery."

"That really doesn't answer my question."

"It isn't my place to define the world for you. What do you think?"

"I think I agree with you, but if it is science, it's very fuzzy science. It doesn't feel exact."

"I think the primary difference between you and me is that the fuzziness feels normal to me. I'm comfortable with fuzzy science and mystery. I get the feeling that it makes you uncomfortable."

"Not as much as you think. Grasping the reality that the right assortment of crystals brought me from one world to the next was as fuzzy to me as anything could ever be. The place where you and Star found me, the place with the colors, what was that? Was that a dream, a mystery, or science?"

"You're a smart young man. You tell me."

"Star and I both remembered the same thing, so it wasn't a dream. It can't be a mystery because you've been able to go there several times, but...but it doesn't exactly feel like science, either."

Victor laughed. "Welcome to my world," he said. "One day, one day when all the mysteries are gone...we will call what I've learned 'science', but until then, I will be just an oddity who dabbles in mysteries that others call magic."

Ethan took in his words and tried to make sense of them all. "What's that?" he asked then, pointing to a blue-green mound on the edge of the worktable.

"Ah, that. That is a bit of a sandwich Vallow made for me several weeks ago... Perhaps I need to clean in here more often than I do."

CHAPTER 5

The Insulting Friends

It was a casual lunch, devoid of elegance or pretense. The food was simple, and the location was nothing more than one of Vanderschmidt's workrooms. What was most notable about the meal was that it was the first time in over fifteen years that Jonathan Bledel Vanderschmidt and Otis Walton had spoken to one another. The first few minutes of the conversation were especially awkward.

Walton knocked on the door, and Vanderschmidt invited him in. "Welcome, Otis. Please, come in."

"Thank you," replied the stooped-shouldered Walton. "You have an impressive place here," he added. "Must have taken you years to build all of this."

"It took a few," Vanderschmidt replied, "but it wasn't as bad as it could have been. "This was originally a massive quarry that the cities used for stone. It was abandoned during the excavation of the tunnels because the rock being removed from them was much cheaper than carving it out of the ground. I bought the land, and the hardest part of the work was already done. All we had to do was build; we didn't have to move the rock."

"Makes sense. An excellent move on your part."

"Did you have to excavate Arcborne, or did you just build over the valley floor?"

"A little of both," Walton answered. "We really had to scrape out the edges of the bowl and make it flat, but then we had to construct the layers up to what would become the new valley floor."

"I bet the natural springs and the water run off were a nightmare to fix."

"That was the worst part, but we came up with a solution. The water needs for a city of 4,000 are significant. The snowmelt and rain were channeled into grates that led to the lower levels and a large reservoir. The natural springs were channeled there as well. We never ran out of water, and we never reached capacity."

As Walton was speaking, Vanderschmidt opened a bottle of wine and poured two glasses. Offering one to Walton, he raised his glass in a toast. "To solving the biggest problems in life."

"Cheers," Walton replied. "So, why don't we solve the biggest problem in this room? The one we aren't talking about."

"We parted ways over philosophical differences," Vanderschmidt said, choosing his words carefully. "That was a long time ago."

"And you accused me of selling out my dreams for power and influence," Walton quipped.

"True," Vanderschmidt replied. "But, as I remember it, you accused me of being a capitalist, who cared more about money than people."

"Fair enough," Walton agreed. "I guess we were both guilty of being too quick to speak."

"Yes. We were young and rash."

"Really?" Walton laughed. "Can you be young and rash at sixty-five years old?"

"Obviously, we can!"

They ate dinner at a laboratory bench and caught up on old times, discussing the mistakes they had made and where NHHMM had gone terribly wrong. And when the food was finished, Vanderschmidt put his napkin on the makeshift table and spoke. "Otis, come with me. I want to show you something. I want your opinion."

They left the room and strolled down the hall until they came to an open door.

There were two tables in the room. Spread out on one of them was the black flag from the strange ship. On the other table was the buoy. "A little over two weeks ago, a ship appeared on our waters. It

64

just materialized right in front of our ship The ship was flying this flag. Do you recognize the symbols?"

"No. I've never seen anything like this."

"One of our people observed the destruction of the ship," Vanderschmidt said, without offering more detail about how or who. "He estimated that there were at least 250 people on board. This," he said, pointing at the buoy, "was sending out a signal. After the ship was destroyed, we looked for survivors. We found one, but the man deliberately slipped into the water as the rescue boats approached. Evidently, he didn't want to be captured."

"Oh my!"

"During the rescue effort, the buoy started to hum and glow, and three more ships started to appear. We were able to disable the buoy before they completed their arrival."

"This wasn't a naval ship?"

"From NHHMM? No." Vanderschmidt touched the man's arm. "Otis, I need to make something clear. We now have two enemies: the chancellor and these invaders. Fighting two enemies at a time is never a good place to be. We need all the help we can get."

"What do you want me to do?" Walton asked. "How can I help?"

"We need an advantage. You know what was being developed in Arcborne. You know what was reality, and what was simply theory. We need you to give us solutions. Give us that amazing brain of yours, and help us win."

"You know by now, of course, that I don't have very long. Maybe six months?"

"Otis, that doesn't matter. You can do more in one month than most people can do in a lifetime."

Vanderschmidt's words were genuine...real, and for the first time in a very long time, Otis Walton felt as if he were actually needed for something. And in that moment, he remembered what it felt like to have a warrior's mindset. A mindset that wouldn't accept defeat and work until he persevered. Chancellor Brighton had a formidable enemy that wasn't afraid of death, because he was already dying.

By the end of the afternoon, Ginger Coltrane looked nothing like the woman who arrived at Charlotte's front door. She went from looking like she was fit for little more than serving beer and having fights, to someone who would turn heads as she walked down the street. Underneath the dirt, the tangled hair, and the dress that bore the dirt and smell of New Marchant, was a beautiful woman. Not only did Charlotte equip her with bags upon bags of clothing, but she also set her up with an apartment in the same building as the person she had followed almost a week before. Once the new purchases were safely put away at her new apartment, they returned to Charlotte's place.

While they were shopping, they devised a story that would satisfy anyone curious enough to ask. Ginger had recently moved from Oppolsby after the death of her mother and was seeking employment as a clerk in a retail establishment. Should someone ask how she could afford such an apartment on a clerk's wages, she would simply say that her mother left her a modest sum when she died.

Over dinner, Charlotte spelled out her expectations. "I want you to find out who the person was who came to the apartment that night. You have three apartments to consider, and at least that many people. Ask questions, but ask them cautiously. When you identify who it is, let me know. Find out everything you can about the person, and if they have friends, find out who they are. We need to know names, where they work, where they go for fun, and most importantly...why they are here?"

"How quickly do you need this?" Ginger asked.

"Don't rush it," Charlotte replied. "Don't take chances. We aren't after one of them; we are after all of them. If you need help, I'll get it for you. And you need to remember that the words that come out of your mouth must match the image you want people to accept. You will need to go slow and give the inside of you time to catch up with the new person on the outside. If your speech and manners sound like you're from the street, that will override how you look. This is all new for you, so don't get into a rush."

"Ok."

"I know it was raining when you followed the person, but what were your initial thoughts? Male or female?"

"Male."

"Based on what?"

"The height could have been a man or a woman. He was wearing a cloak, so I really couldn't see the build."

"Then why a man?"

"The walk. The stride was longer than what I would expect a woman to have."

"Anything else?"

"He wasn't from New Marchant. He kept looking at a map. He wasn't familiar with where he was going."

"Then that is where you start. Your first option is a man, or a tall woman, who isn't from the area."

"Do I need to help you clean up the dishes?" Ginger asked.

"No, why?"

"Because I have work to do, and over the next few hours, when the locals are drinking, they will be the most talkative."

"Good idea," Charlotte said, and smiled. "Wait, just a moment before you leave, I have something for you." Leaving the room, she came back a few minutes later with a small leather pouch in her hand. "Assorted coins for food, drink, and bribes if you need them."

"Thank you." They walked toward the front door, and Ginger stepped outside.

"Stay safe," Charlotte said.

"I'll be in touch," Ginger announced as she went down the stairs and disappeared into the night.

Her first stop was the pub directly across from the apartment. It was more upscale than she was used to, but a pub was a pub. She knew how to navigate that environment. Ginger took a quick peek in the window and concluded that her current clothing would be suitable for this crowd. But before she entered, she needed to do something else. Three doors down from the pub was an apothecary. Walking up to the counter, she smiled at the young man working there.

"I'm in need of a map," she said. "Do you sell them here?"

He smiled and pointed at a metal rack on the counter two feet away. "Yes."

"I'm so sorry. I wasn't paying attention." Taking the map, she paid the man at the counter and went back outside. She walked to the pub, went inside, and picked out a table near the corner.

A few minutes later, a woman approached the table and gave her a smile. "What are you drinking?"

"Wine, please," Ginger replied. The woman went back to the bar, and Ginger unfolded the map, spreading it out on the table.

The waitress brought over a glass of red wine and handed it to Ginger. "I'll let you put it on the map if you want."

"Oh, sorry," she said, taking the glass. "I didn't think about that."

"New in town?"

"Yes," Ginger replied. "I guess a big map makes it obvious."

"A little. Can I give you directions anywhere?"

"I've moved in just across the street, and I'm just trying to get my bearings, but thank you."

"Let me know if I can help. We get a lot of regulars from across the street."

"I do have one question."

"What do you need?"

"I was in the lobby earlier today, and I found a cufflink," she said, making up a story as she spoke. "I thought it might belong to a man I saw, who also looked like he was new to the area. He was also carrying a map. Does that ring a bell for you? I'd like to return it, but I don't know anyone yet."

The waitress thought for a moment and then shook her head. "No one comes to mind, but I will keep my eyes open."

"Oh, thank you." Ginger smiled.

She sat at the table for another hour before paying her bill and walking down the street to another place. The night was just getting started, and there were still stops to make.

Ethan was nervous. He had been told about his father's skill at Conquest, and he saw firsthand how well Star, his latest pupil, had played the game. His mind rushed to the possible outcomes. What if he beat his father quickly? What could that do to their relationship? Would he be humiliated?

Should he deliberately lose? Maybe that was the best solution. Play the game, play hard for most of the way, and then make a mistake, or at least make a move that wasn't a bad move, but not a great move. However, if he couldn't make it believable, would it appear as condescending and insulting to his father?

And it wasn't like it was going to be a private match. They were going to play after dinner in the Chastains' living room. It was the biggest of all the rooms in either home, and Ethan believed there would be a crowd watching. That was the last thing he wanted, though, an audience.

Anne and Ashlyn made the bulk of the dinner, leaving Vallow to make dessert. Mrs. Chastain was persnickety about the lavender she used, knowing full well that some of the strains were great for the aroma, but not at all as good for cooking. She wanted the culinary strain for the lavender-blueberry crumble cake she was making. So she made the walk down to Mr. Cleo's farm to pick out exactly what she needed.

The table wasn't large enough for all of them to sit at, so the adults ate at it while the four children sat in the living room. "What's wrong?" Star asked, seeing the tension on Ethan's face.

"I'm not looking forward to this match," he replied quietly.

"Why not?"

"I'm afraid that if I beat my father in front of an audience, he might be upset with me. I'm thinking that I need to make some mistakes."

Star laughed and moved her hand over her mouth. Her eyes had a mischievous sparkle about them. "I think," she said, when she swallowed her food, "that you should focus on playing your best game. I heard him talking to Roland earlier. Eventually, someone will have to open the vault. Your father wants to know which of you had the better chance. He's not going to show you any mercy just because you're his son."

"He's that good?" Ethan asked, with concern showing on his face. She nodded. "Mm-hm."

"So, you think I should treat him like any other opponent?"

"That's your decision, but if you don't, you may find it's you that loses in front of an audience."

When dinner was finished, the table was cleared, the dishes were cleaned, and the kitchen was once again back in order. With six adults and two teenagers helping, the clean-up didn't take long at all. Vallow timed the dessert perfectly. While the crumble cake was baking, she mixed up the lavender and blueberry with the syrup drizzle. She checked the cake, removed it from the oven, and set it on the counter to cool before she sliced it. Just before it was cut into squares, she added the drizzle to the top by letting it ooze over the crumble from a small bowl that she moved back and forth over the cake.

The pieces were put on clean plates, and the families moved into the living room to finish up the meal.

Ethan couldn't believe that Star thought the one in Arcborne was better than this. It was exceptional, warm and sweet, and it seemed like the perfect way to end a meal. "Mrs. Chastain," Ethan said, pointing to the cake with his fork, "this is amazing."

"I agree," Anne added. "Why does the lavender taste so much better than the other ones I've tasted before?"

As Vallow started to tell her about Farmer Cleo's different strains of lavender, Ryan picked up a long tube from beside the fireplace and carried it into the kitchen, then sat at the table. Opening the end of the tube, he removed a rolled-up piece of leather and spread it out on the table. It was a traveling Conquest board. A leather pouch, wrapped with string, held the dice, the pieces, and a narrow rectangular metal timer.

"Son?" Ryan called out and motioned for Ethan to come over. Carrying his plate, Ethan sat at the table opposite him. "Let's finish our dessert before we play."

"Ok."

"Nervous?" his father asked.

Ethan smiled. "A little."

"Don't be nervous. I want you to play your best game. When we take back the country from the chancellor, it will fall on me to determine who will play the machine to open the vault. I need to know if that is to be you, me, or someone else. So, if you can defeat me, that's not going to bother me. But we need to find out. Does that make sense?"

Ethan felt relieved. His father had just asked him to play his best. "Yes, sir. I understand."

They set the board up and set their dessert plates aside. Ethan had the high roll, so he had the first move. Even though it had been almost two months since he'd played, he immediately picked up the form he had before. The first twenty seconds of the match were a surprise, as his father's moves were every bit as fast as his own. Ethan would reset the timer with a ding, and his father's response was almost immediate. The steady sound of "ding, ding, ding" brought everyone from the living room to the area where the dining table was located.

When it was his turn, Ethan looked up to his father. "I think we can put the timer aside."

"Yes," Ryan said, with a big smile. "We don't need it."

Ten minutes passed, and the game was deadlocked. Then it happened. In the middle of the game, Ethan's brain went to that place where his moves seemed to slow down. He not only knew his father's best options, but also the move he was most likely to make. Ethan would roll the blocking die with one hand while moving his game piece with the other at the same time. As soon as the die turned over, he would make any necessary adjustments to the board that the die and his plan required.

Roland had never seen him play like this. His eyes grew big, and he felt like he was watching a machine. Star watched the match with an odd smile on her face, wanting both to win, but seemingly dazzled by the contest.

Ryan didn't flinch. Unintimidated by Ethan's speed, he kept making one perfect move after another. And then he didn't. The second he removed his hand from the board, he saw it. He had given Ethan a little window of opportunity. Not a big one, but one that didn't exist a move earlier.

Ethan saw, took advantage of it, and then was lucky enough to get a good result from the blocking tile roll. The match lasted another ten minutes before Ethan was able to move his piece into the center of the board.

Ryan offered his hand across the table to his son. "Congratulations, Ethan. Well done. I am so proud of you."

Shaking his father's hand, his heart soared, not because of the victory, but because of his father's words.

Star's little brother, Victor Jr., asked Ethan if he would teach him how to play the game. At seven years old, it was time for him to start learning. Looking over to Star, she nodded her head. "We would kill each other if I tried to teach him," she said.

He worked with Victor for thirty minutes before the boy got bored and wanted to do something else. Putting the pieces, the timer, and the dice back into the bag, Ethan rolled up the board and placed it in the metal tube. He slid the leather pouch into the open space in the middle of the tube and then sealed it up.

Looking around the room, he couldn't see Pops, his father, or Victor Chastain, and he got up from the table and walked outside in search of them. He found all three standing around a tree in the moonlight. Pops and Mr. Chastain were smoking on their pipes, while

Ryan O'Connor joined them in conversation. To Ethan's surprise, the men didn't stop their conversation or change the subject as he approached.

"I agree," Victor Chastain said. "They will come. It's only a matter of time. If you will allow it, my family and I would like to join you when you leave."

"Of course, you are welcome to come," Ryan said. "I would be terribly hurt if you didn't. You and your family have shown Anne and me kindness beyond our wildest expectations. And you are right. They will take Star and Ethan, and I doubt any of the rest of us will survive. We have to be ready to leave, and I insist that you and your family join us."

"What can I do to help?" Ethan asked.

"We were talking about that before you arrived," Roland said. "We, as a group, need to develop a plan for when that time comes, and we welcome your input. But your father has asked me to help him with another project as well."

"What's that?" Ethan asked.

"You've been developing your mind, but it's time that we helped develop the rest of you. The day they arrive, your life will become much, much harder. You need to be stronger, you need to be faster, and you need to be able to take care of any one of us. Our families are here, and you need to take your place in being able to protect those around you."

"Ethan," Ryan said, "Roland...Pops played that role for me. He taught me how to be strong, how to fight, and how to kill if necessary. He has agreed to help me do the same thing for you. You've recovered enough that it's time we start."

"When?" Ethan asked.

"Tomorrow morning," Ryan replied. "Early tomorrow morning. Please note that I stressed the word early."

"Great! That sounds wonderful. How early?"

"Early," his Pops replied. "I'll wake you up when it's time to start."

Ethan looked over to Victor to see if he had anything he wanted to add.

Putting his hands up, Star's father shook his head as he looked at Ethan. "No, no. I'm not the one to help you with any of that. I have no skills in those areas. I am a pacifist by nature, but I'm wise enough to know that evil people can't be reasoned with. I'm happy to teach you the things that I know about, but these guys are the resident experts on the other stuff."

Ethan laughed. "Ok, but I would like to learn more about the things you know, too."

Changing subjects, Ryan asked his son a question: "What happened back there in the match? We were playing at a fast pace, and then it was like your brain just shifted into a different speed."

"I don't know. I first noticed it at the school in New Marchant. I don't know what happens, or why, but to me, time seems to slow down. Maybe my mind is moving faster for some reason, but what slows me down isn't not knowing what to do, it's actually waiting on my body to do what I tell it."

"Anne," Roland said, winking at Ryan. "He had to get that from his mother. You were certainly never that quick."

"What are you talking about?" Ryan retorted. "How do you know I wasn't just going easy on you all those years when we were playing?"

The two traded barbs back and forth for the next few minutes. Victor smoked his pipe and smiled, while Ethan seemed to be the happiest, he had ever been. So, this is what family is like.

Victor Chastain looked on in silence as the others spoke. He, too, had noticed that moment in the game when Ethan's mind seemed to move like lightning. But unlike the others, Victor already had a theory about why and how.

When Star's brother and sister were in bed, the adults began discussions about the reality of government discovery and the plan they would implement. Vallow Chastain wasn't enthused about the idea. She understood, but she didn't like thinking that the world they knew might change forever. Keeping a close ear to the conversation, she worked in the kitchen, baking something that smelled good. At the same time, she would occasionally step into the doorway to make sure she could hear what was being said.

"There is really only one access point to get here quickly, and even that isn't quick. Traveling through the other villages from the other side will add at least another day and a half to the journey. They will come, en masse, right up through town and into your front doors," Roland said.

"Then what do we do?" Victor asked.

"The barn is the key," Roland answered. "We move the bell from your front porch into the barn. The first hint we get that something is wrong, we ring the bell to alert everyone that we are in danger. Everyone comes to the barn. We can hold off almost everyone so that you can get out."

"But what about everyone else?" Vallow asked from the kitchen.

"We will get everyone out," Ryan assured her. "We've requested some additional supplies, which will probably arrive sometime in the next few weeks. That will give us the advantage we need. Roland and I have been working on the tunnel from my house to the barn for over a month now. It's complete. The one to your home should be done within a week. If the entrances to the barn are covered and unapproachable, then crawl your way to the barn through the tunnel."

Vallow's lip began to quiver. Victor walked over to her and put his arm around her. "Maybe this will never happen, but we have to be ready."

"That's right," Ashlyn said. "We get ready, we live life, and if we grow old here...great. If it doesn't work out that way, then we have a plan."

"But there is another option," Ethan said, without looking up at the others. He knew his idea would be dismissed before he even offered it. It was a good plan, but his primary motivation was to gauge Star's perspective.

"What's the other option?" Ryan asked.

"They don't know that you and Mom are alive. Apart from Star, I doubt the Chastains are on anyone's list of troublemakers. No one knows that Pops and Ashlyn are here. They're looking for Star and me, no one else."

Star quickly figured out where Ethan was going, and she interrupted him. "We can leave. Ethan and I can leave and take the trouble with us."

"There isn't a need for anyone's life to be upturned," Ethan added, glad to have Star's support. "We leave and stay away until you are ready to stand against the chancellor. Then it doesn't matter. They will be looking for all of us."

"Absolutely not," Anne stated. "No. You will both be safer here with us."

"She's right," Vallow interjected, her eyes beginning to well up with tears. "We have a plan, a good plan, and we need to stick to it."

"Pops?" Ethan asked.

Roland rubbed his jaw, looked over at Ashlyn, and then at Ethan. "I vote yes."

"THIS ISN'T A VOTE!" Anne interrupted.

"I know it isn't a vote. Ethan asked me for my view, and I replied. His logic is sound."

Anne glared at Roland and then at her husband expectantly. "Ryan?"

"The Council is in agreement that we should stay here," Ryan stated flatly. "I believe it is best that we stay here in Tearmann until we can stay no longer. This isn't a vote; there isn't anything else to discuss."

Ethan started to argue, but he felt Star's hand on his arm. Inside, his blood was boiling. He wanted to debate with them all, but he kept it to himself. "I understand. There is a plan, and everyone wants to stay. I understand, but I don't agree."

"If you will excuse us," Star said softly. "We're going to take a walk for a bit. Ethan?" She gently pulled on his arm.

They walked to the edge of Farmer Cleo's property without saying a word. When they were well away from the others, Ethan finally spoke.

"Why are they doing this? There isn't any doubt that you and I leaving is the best for everyone else."

"Because you're thinking strategically and logically. They're thinking like parents. Your parents just got you back. To them, you are still a baby who needs their protection. They don't want to lose you again. I'm not sure, but I don't think it ever changes. A parent will always want to protect their child. Even when they can't, and even when it makes no sense."

"I suppose," Ethan mused, pondering her words.

"Would it have made a difference if Pops said no?"

"I don't know. Probably. Maybe. But he didn't."

Star still held onto Ethan's arm. "You know, Ethan Scott, if we were going to leave anyway, it would probably make sense to wait until the supplies are delivered. There are probably things coming from

Mr. Vanderschmidt that might be of value to two rebellious children who wanted to keep their families safe."

Ethan smiled and placed his hand over hers. "I like the way you think, Miss Chastain. I really like the way you think."

CHAPTER 6

The Training Begins

It was a pleasant enough dream, as dreams go. The sky was a deep blue, and fluffy white clouds drifted slowly overhead, pushed by a gentle breeze. He lay back in the high grass of a meadow and chewed on a small tree branch. On the ground next to him was the outer bark of the branch. He didn't seem to have a knife, so he must have peeled the bark away with his fingernails. The blue sky began to fade away into black. The white clouds started to transform into oblong, crimson shapes that pulsed with no apparent pattern, and with each pulse, the red clouds seemed to glow. The one at the top of his vision stood out from the rest. Not only was it larger than the others, but the glow was brighter, too. It looked familiar to Ethan, but he couldn't place it. As he studied the cloud, the black space beneath it started to take on shades of gray. And then he understood. Beneath the large red cloud was a cluster of smaller red objects, and next to that was a nose.

He gasped and sat up when he recognized what he was looking at. The woman from Arcborne, Noola Klaar. The blind woman whose eyes were replaced with crystals and whose face was deformed by crystals embedded all over it. And then he remembered.

Was Noola able to get out of Arcborne? Was she still alive? He was angry with himself. He'd completely forgotten about her after arriving in Tearmann, as he'd also forgotten about his last conversation with the chancellor. He needed to tell Pops. He wanted the Resistance to know what he knew. But he also needed sleep, and the sunrise was still several hours away. Lying back down, Ethan rolled over on his side and tried to go back to the meadow with blue skies and white clouds.

He found his dream meadow, and somehow the same stick seemed to be in his left hand just as he remembered it. From the corner of his vision, he saw a lumbering figure approach from his right. It was a bear. Strangely, the bear walked with a familiar stride. It looked friendly enough, so Ethan continued to chew on his stick and watch the clouds. Coming alongside him, the bear let out a loud snort, but Ethan ignored it.

Lifting its right paw, it pushed Ethan's shoulder, rolling him over on his side. "Hey," Ethan called out. "Mind your own business. Move along now, and let me be."

The bear looked at him, opened its large mouth, and began to growl. "GRRRRETHAN. GRRRRWAKE. GRRRRUP. EEEETHAN. WAAAAKE. UUUUP." The bear pushed him again, and Ethan opened up his eyes and looked into Pops' face.

"Ethan. Time to wake up. Time to start training."

"What time is it?" Ethan asked, glad to see that Pops' teeth weren't nearly as long as the bear in his dream.

"The sun is just coming up. Get dressed and meet us outside."

Since his recovery, Ethan had moved out into the barn. His parents only had two bedrooms in their small home, and he couldn't take the room from Pops and Ashlyn. Star needed her room back as sleeping with her sister in the small bed wasn't practical, so the best available place was the barn loft. The only thing up in the loft to bother him was mice, but that wasn't much of a problem. The Chastains kept a mouser in the barn, a yellow cat with a white face and white stockings on its feet, called Maze. She never bothered Ethan. The closest she came to an annoyance was when he could see her green eyes staring at him as if he were an intruder in her domain.

Evidently, Maze was a skilled huntress, as Ethan hadn't seen a live mouse since he took residence in the barn. He heard them from time to time, scurrying underneath the hay and across the wooden floor, but he trusted Maze to take care of the problem, and she did.

He was dressed and outside the barn within five minutes, where he heard Ryan and Pops talking. "So, about thirty minutes?" Ryan asked.

"Yeah," Pops replied. "Give or take."

"Ok, see you back here in around thirty-ish. And, Ethan, try to keep up," Ryan said, messing Ethan's hair about.

"Let's go," Pops said, beginning to jog off into the tree line.

"Where are we going?" Ethan asked as he followed.

"Up the hill, to the meadow. Three times around the meadow and then back down. Next week," Pops added, "it becomes four times around the meadow. And then five, and then we change it up a bit."

"No problem," Ethan replied.

"You think?" Pops smiled as he increased his speed. They made it to the top of the hill, and Pops started the first loop around the large meadow, staying just on the edge where it met the trees. For the first half of the loop, Ethan was able to keep up with Roland's pace, but then he started to fall back. He kept running, hoping Pops would see him struggling and then slow down so that Ethan could keep up. But he didn't.

As Ethan was halfway into his second lap, his lungs were burning, and his feet felt like lead. He could hear Pops' footsteps coming up from behind. "Every day, you will get better. Every day will be a struggle until one day you realize that your body is ready, and you will then make me work to stay up with you. Keep that thought in mind. I promise you it will happen. See you at the bottom," Pops added as he passed Ethan.

"Wait!" Ethan called out. "Wait. I need to talk with you." He watched as Pops stopped and then began to walk toward him.

"Can it wait until we are finished?"

"No, I need to tell you some things that are best said in private. You can decide who else to tell about part of it, but for the other part, I need you to give me your word that you won't tell anyone."

"I don't know that I can do the last part. Since I don't know what you're telling me, I can't really promise not to share it with anyone. I'll try to respect your wishes, but I can't give you my word that I won't repeat it."

Having lived with Pops most of his life, Ethan knew he wasn't going to budge on his request. "I just need you to know that I gave my word I would protect a secret."

"Then why are you telling me now?" Pops asked.

"Because I don't really have a choice. A life could depend on me not telling you."

"Do you realize that you just asked me to do something you are unable to do?"

"Yes, yes, but just hear me out. I think you'll understand why I asked you to keep a secret."

"Fair enough," Pops said as he walked over to a tree and leaned up against it. "I'm listening."

Ethan told him about Noola Klaar. He told him about the accident and her new abilities. "Does any of this sound familiar to you?"

"Yes. I remember the explosion. I remember there was a lab assistant who went missing, and I remember that Mr. Vanderschmidt's wife was also killed in the explosion."

"But that's the important part. She didn't die. The vice chancellor's men found her, and her face was so marred that no one recognized her. At first, they kept her on an island, and then they moved her to Arcborne. She didn't think it was safe to give them her real name, so she said she was Noola Klaar."

"But they never found the body of the lab assistant," Roland mused. "So, if the woman in Arcborne is Vanderschmidt's wife, Angeline, where is the lab assistant?"

"No idea," Ethan answered, "but my concern is Mrs. Vanderschmidt. Did she get out of Arcborne? Is she there by herself? Is she able to find food? Is she even still alive?"

"I'll send a telegram asking for the names of everyone who got out of Arcborne. That's easy to find out. If she is still there, then we use Mr. Vanderschmidt's airship to get back in and find her."

"No, that's where my promise comes in. I promised I would keep her secret. She doesn't want to be found. She doesn't want her husband, her sons, or her grandchildren to see her like she is today."

"Let me think about this," Pops said, a frown appearing on his face. "First, I need to find out who didn't get out of Arcborne, and then I've got to figure out how I get back in."

"We," Ethan corrected.

"We?"

"We. I'm going with you. I know where to find her."

"And you aren't going to tell me so that you can go."

"Yes, sir. I've got to go with you."

Pops rolled his eyes. "And I'm guessing that Star is going to want to come with you as well. Do you have any idea the amount of trouble that is going to cause me?"

"I do."

"Well, if we get Ryan to come, that will probably pacify your mother, but I don't know how we're going to get the Chastains to go along with this."

"It gets worse."

"How does this get any worse?"

"That's the second part." Ethan paused, fully aware of what was going to happen next. What Pops was about to hear would simply be something he already knew, or it could very well create a rift between Ryan, Ethan's father, and Pops, whom he knew as his grandfather. Ethan had just experienced a new family, and he was now concerned that it could be shattered.

"The night we escaped, Chancellor Brighton told me some things. He wanted me to be a part of his team. I negotiated for some time with Star and the answer to some of the questions. The time I bargained for allowed Star and me to escape, but the answers to the questions were disturbing."

"What did you learn?"

"The chancellor said the leadership of NHHMM rotates between the three oldest families. He said that Declan O'Connor was an accident. He was not a part of the three families and should never have been elected. He also said that NHHMM is actually a country, not a world, that there were actually three countries, and that the military of NHHMM exists, in large part, to keep the other countries hidden. If there are other countries on this planet, are they friendly? Could they be allies? Could they be yet another enemy we have to fight?"

Pops shook his head. "I don't know anything about this."

"But does Dad...Ryan, know anything? And if he does, why don't you know?"

Ethan watched as Pops furrowed his eyebrows and seemed to start a channel of thought that would explain it, only to realize that the answer he wanted really wasn't an answer at all. And just for a moment, it seemed as if Pops' face showed betrayal.

"I'll use the clock we have positioned in the barn and travel to Vanderschmidt's place. I'll learn what I can there, and then come pick you up in the airship they used to get Jack and his team into Arcborne."

"When are you leaving and when will you be back?"

"Look for me around midnight, here at this meadow. I'll leave this afternoon when we're finished with the training I've got planned."

"And what about Dad? Are you going to talk to him?"

"I haven't figured that out yet. I want to hear what Vanderschmidt knows, and perhaps I'll speak with Ryan. Right now, I'm going to do what I think is best, and that may not align with what your father wants."

"They aren't going to give me permission to go with you."

Pops put his hand on Ethan's shoulder. "Ethan, you are fifteen years old. You are old enough to serve in our military, and you are one of the smartest people in our world. You're going to have to make your own decision on this one."

"But if I tell them what I'm going to do, they will try to stop me."

"Then don't tell them," Pops said as he started to turn away. "We've still got things to do. Remember, three laps around and I'll see you down at the barn."

Before Ethan could respond, Pops was already fifteen feet away from him and running with a smooth stride, leaving him standing in the shade of a tree.

Ethan paused as he finished his second lap. Putting his hands on his hips and struggling to breathe, he slowed to a walk. He was a little angry and humiliated that he had been left behind, but that didn't bother him nearly as much as knowing he was about to make his parents, and more importantly, Star's parents, angry. He hadn't experienced anything from them since their arrival other than praise and support. Now, their daughter's hero was leading her off in the middle of the night. He couldn't imagine how that would turn out well for either of them.

Catching his breath, he started running again. Twenty feet from the edge of the meadow where Pops went down into the trees, Ethan picked up his pace. He thought going downhill would be easier than going up, but he was surprised. It wasn't possible to actually run downhill, as he had to use a more controlled fall with his body. His knees would absorb the impact, and he had to keep his weight back over his heels. Once, he overcompensated and fell hard on his bottom. Another time, he clipped a tree with his shoulder and scraped his arm, but he was learning. Upon reaching the bottom, he was gasping for air.

There, his father and Pops were standing before a metal bowl filled with water. A metal ladle rested in the bowl, and that was Ethan's new objective. Ryan took the ladle, filled it with water, and offered it to his son.

"Take it slow," he said. "A little at a time, or you will get cramps, and you won't be able to finish."

Finish? What is there to finish?

When he was done drinking the water, the men led him into the barn, leaving the barn doors open, and he noticed some changes in there since he'd left. Two ropes were thrown over one of the rafters, and small loops had been tied at the ends. Inside the loops were pieces of steel that flattened out the bottom of the loops. On two of the support columns, ropes were attached to pulleys.

His father took off his shirt and jumped up slightly, grabbing the metal on the bottom of the loops. "You start off with ten, with your palms turned toward you," he said, lifting his body up and then lowering it back down. Try to get your chin level to the tops of your hands." Ryan finished out the other eight of the ten and then dropped to the ground. "This will strengthen your shoulders and arms."

One of the ropes, anchored to a high pulley, had a loop on one end, a bag of rocks on the other. "Here, you put one hand on the loop and your other hand on top of the first. Keeping your arms straight, move them down across your body to the opposite knee twenty times, and then switch sides. This will strengthen your torso."

They showed him other exercises to strengthen his arms and then ensured that he could perform each exercise correctly.

"Your goal," Pops said, "is to increase the weight you lift by ten percent each week. You will also increase the number of repetitions by the same amount, and if you can do more, that's great. But don't overdo it, or you could spend weeks recovering."

"The loops," Ryan said, pointing over to the ones hanging from the rafter, "will be the hardest thing for you. They are the hardest for everyone, but you're still recovering from fractured ribs. If the pain is too great, stop. Do only as much as you can."

When Ethan had completed the things they had outlined, he was tired and his muscles were quivering. "Now, go get cleaned up," Ryan said. "You did great today. You'll start hurting by tomorrow, but that's normal. I've got to get to the school. I'll see you this evening."

"Meet me back here in the barn around one o'clock," Pops said.

"What happens then?" Ethan asked.

Pops winked. "I start teaching you the other stuff."

He didn't have any time to waste. His parents could give him a place to stay, but with Arcborne closed, Renny Patel needed a job. After another morning of searching for work, he sat down on a park bench, pulled an apple from his shoulder bag, and took a bite. There was work if he were a sailor, and there was work if he wanted to be in a kitchen or a shop selling goods, but he wanted to utilize his education and skills. Arcborne was turning out to be both a blessing and a curse for him. No one in Mason Point had ever heard of the place, so even though the education he received was beyond what he could get in the university system, it meant little to those who would consider hiring him. To them, his education looked incomplete.

Finishing his apple, Renny walked across the street to a building that sold metal components and raw panels that could be pressed, cut, or welded into any desired shape. A customer stood next to the counter, reviewing an invoice. At the same time, several empty buggies waited in line in front of the building.

"Just sign here," the clerk said, "and we can load the items into your buggies."

"Are they good where they are?" the man asked between coughs. "Or do I need to move them in back?"

"In back would be better," the clerk said.

The man signed the invoice and motioned to a driver standing near the doorway. "Around in back," he said, gesturing with his arm.

"Thanks, Mr. Cashman," the clerk said. "We will start loading as soon as the trucks pull up. Here is your copy of the invoice and the materials list." The clerk slid the papers toward the man. Placing them in an empty folder, Mr. Cashman placed three other folders on top, then rushed outside and gave directions to his drivers.

"Good morning, sir," Renny said when the clerk was free. "My name is Renny Patel, and I'm looking for work. I'm good with numbers and would make a good addition to your office staff."

"Not hiring," the clerk said. "No openings." Without another word, the clerk left the counter and walked into the back room.

Feeling dejected, Renny walked away toward the front door. On the floor, near the door, he spied a folder with several papers exposed. Taking the folder, he examined the documents inside. The folder contained the materials list and invoice given to Mr. Cashman, and Renny guessed it must have slipped out of his hand as the man left the building. But the numbers didn't add up. The totals for each grouping listed were consistently more than the number of items requested. If the buyer wanted four sheets of copper, he was charged for six. If he needed forty-eight bolts, he was charged for fifty-eight.

Renny left through the front entrance and ran around the building as fast as he could, while Mr. Cashman was supervising the loading of the material in the buggies. His drivers and the crew of the supply company carefully loaded the items into three long buggies. "Sir," Renny said, approaching Cashman, "may I have a word?"

"Of course. How can I help you?"

"My name is Renny Patel. I was just in the building when you left, and I believe you may have dropped this." Renny handed Cashman the folder. The man opened it and nodded.

"Yes. This is mine. Thank you."

"Sir, I don't mean to cause problems, but I think you need to look carefully at the numbers. They don't add up. According to the math, he is charging you 18.6 percent more than he should. The quantity of items is correct, but the totals don't match the unit costs."

Cashman studied the number for a minute and then looked up at Renny. "How did you do this so quickly?"

"I'm good with numbers, sir. It's easy for me."

"Just a moment," Cashman said. "I'll be right back."

Five minutes later, Cyrus Cashman returned from the building with a smile on his face. "The scoundrel," he said. "I bet if I check my other invoices, I'll find he's done the same thing. I'm on to him now."

"Glad I could help," Renny replied.

"Here," Cashman said, offering him some coins. "Take it as a reward for helping me catch a thief."

"No, thank you." Renny shook his head. "But if you have an opening, I would like to work for you."

"Do you know what I do?" Cashman said, raising an eyebrow.

"No, sir, I do not. But it looks as if you're manufacturing something, and I've had some advanced education on building financial models, together with the utilization of debt for business growth."

"Have you now?" Cashman laughed, a hacking sound emitting deep in his lungs. "Climb in," he said, motioning to the first buggy, "and I can tell you about my business on the way to work."

"Does that mean...?"

"Yes," Cashman said. "You are now an employee of CMR."

"Very good," Renny beamed. "And what does CMR stand for?"

"Cashman Mechanical Riders," Cyrus Cashman replied, with a confident grin.

Pops met Ethan in the barn at one o'clock. Summer was beginning to give the afternoons a warmth that bordered on hot. There was still a crisp breeze in the low mountains, but in the barn, where there wasn't as much breeze, Ethan was already sweating.

"Before we get started, there are some things that you need to know," Pops began. "What I'm about to tell you is every bit as important as what I'm going to teach you. For most of my adult life, I was either in the military or with the protective team that kept the chancellor and his family safe. I'm going to teach you the same thing that I taught all the new members of the security detail. I'm telling you this because there will be times when you doubt me. And that's ok. It happens with everyone. But the more you doubt, the longer this will take, and I don't think we have a lot of time." He paused for a moment, then continued: "First things first. Have you ever been in a fight at school?"

"Not really. I've had times when I was nose-to-nose with some guys, but it was always more talk than anything else."

"That's not a problem, but it does open up the door for the first lesson. You're tall, and you're going to be as big as your father. The men and women of the world are not going to look at you as a child, but as a threat. They're going to treat you like an adult who can do them harm.

"The first thing you need to get into your head is that fighting never ends up well for anyone. Always avoid it if you can, but if you can't, don't try to talk your way out of a problem. Talk is for children.

It's what a bully says to intimidate you, and it's what you say in return, hoping that he goes away. In both cases, the goal is to make the other guy back down. It doesn't work that way with adults. If someone is intent on doing you or someone you care about harm, they aren't going to talk about it. They won't give you a warning; instead, they will simply take action. So, the first rule is don't waste your time talking. They already know what they are going to do, so talking to them only wastes your time and gives them an advantage."

"So, what do I do?" Ethan asked.

"You attack. We'll get into the specifics of how as we go forward. The second thing you need to wrap your head around is that there is no such thing as a fair fight. There is no gallantry in a fight. Your goal is to protect the ones that you love, the ones you are tasked with protecting, and that includes yourself. Your opponent is going to hit, kick, scratch, or hurt you in any way that they can. Do you understand?"

"Yes."

"The next thing you need to understand is that you will get hit, kicked, scratched, and hurt. If you don't think it will happen, then you're fooling yourself; the first time you're hit, it will shock you. And when it shocks you, your opponent will have the edge. If your opponent has a knife, you need to understand that he will probably cut you. You must be ready for that. My job is to help make you ready. Now, tell me what is most important."

"Always avoid a fight if possible."

"Good. What else?"

"Don't try to talk my way out of a problem, and there is no such thing as a fair fight."

"Very good."

"And I need to understand that if I fight, I will get hurt."

As soon as Ethan finished the sentence, Pops pushed out with his palm, shoving Ethan backwards.

Ethan fell to the floor and looked up at him, stunned. It didn't hurt, but it stung, and he stared at Pops, unsure of what was happening.

"That's what I'm talking about. Right here. For no reason, I shoved you, and you are shocked. You're looking at me in astonishment. If I really meant to harm you, it would already be over. In that moment of shock, I would attack you all the more. Do you understand?"

"Yeah. I get it."

"Now," Pops said, "stand beside me." Ethan got up from the barn floor and moved to Pops' left. "Everything has to do with your feet. You always want to keep your feet in the right position so that it's harder for you to lose your balance. Try to keep one foot forward, with the back foot at about a 45° angle. If your feet are side by side, it doesn't take much to put you out of balance. So, let's work on that. I'm going to stand opposite you, and as I move, I want you to mirror what I do, keeping your feet opposite mine."

They worked in the barn for two hours, and by the time they were finished, Ethan was drenched with sweat. But knowing that Pops had trained his father the same way made it easier for him. He didn't feel stupid or inadequate. He simply knew that he needed to listen, and he did his best to learn from a man who was probably more dangerous than anyone he had yet to encounter.

"Hello," a voice said. Otis Walton looked up from his desk in Vanderschmidt's research center and saw Jack Flynn standing in the doorway.

"You certainly look better than the last time I saw you. Leg all healed?"

"For the most part," Flynn said as he entered the office and looked over the walls covered in notes and drawings. "I hear Vanderschmidt has put you to work."

"He has," Walton replied. "I'm just doing my part, looking for something in the Arcborne data that might give us an advantage."

"Hmm." Flynn nodded with something else clearly on his mind.

"How can I help you?" the old man asked. "I get the impression that you aren't here for a social visit."

"I need you to tell me everything you know about Arcborne's twin."

"You mean the city off the western tunnel? They call it Retribution."

"What kind of name is Retribution?"

Walton shrugged. "It's a military installation. What kind of name did you expect it to have? Peaceful Valley?"

"What do you know about it?"

"Everything. Nothing. I am familiar with the structural layout of the place because I oversaw the design. I know how many people it will hold. I am aware of the number of buildings in the original design. I am familiar with the structural elements that make it work. But I haven't been there in almost two years. So, while I know a lot about what it was supposed to be, I know nothing about what it is now."

"Fair enough. Was the entry point similar to Arcborne?"

"Originally, yes, but I don't know what modifications, if any, they've made recently. Are you planning on blowing it up also?"

Jack Flynn ignored the question. "Can you give me any idea about what they might be using or developing there?"

"No idea. We must assume that since Arcborne was a research facility run by the same people, they're trying to bring some or all of the Arcborne research into a weaponized reality. Other than that, I have no idea."

Flynn thought about Walton's words as he paced back and forth with his hands behind his back. "I need you to do something for me, and I need it to be your top priority."

"Is this a Council-approved request?" Walton asked with a sly smile.

"No," Flynn replied, smiling back, "but I can make it one if need be. It's a slight variation on what you're already doing. With just a little bit of a twist."

"What do you need?"

"I need you to look at the Arcborne data and tell me which of the projects are the easiest to create and mass produce. I need to know what to look for."

"Look for?"

"Yeah. I'm going into Retribution, just like I did Arcborne. I'll need maps or drawings of the buildings as you remember them. We need to know how big a threat Retribution poses."

"And if it is a big threat?"

"I'm going to do my best to cripple their operation before I blow the western tunnel and seal everyone inside."

"That's a little cavalier, don't you think? You're just going to blow up a tunnel and seal in thousands of troops and civilians? Just like that?"

"Spare me the moral black and white. We have the chancellor essentially declaring war on his own world, along with an unknown enemy that could arrive at any moment. We can't allow the chancellor or the invader to use what's in Retribution against the people of NHHMM. So, I'm sorry if that sounds insensitive, but I'll do whatever I have to. Even if that means sealing up the western tunnel."

"Is it hard?" Walton asked after a moment.

"Is what hard?"

"Is it hard stepping back and forth into this pale light of moral ambiguity?"

"It gets easier every time," Flynn replied, without hesitation.

"What if there is another option?"

"Please...please give me another option where my team and I have a better chance of survival. What is this other option? Tell me."

"We can talk to the chancellor. We can tell him about the invaders. He needs us as much as we need him."

Flynn laughed out loud and shook his head. "That's your other option? To talk reason to a man that's already tried to kill everyone I know? Feel free to take that idea up with the Council. Really. Be the grand negotiator. But, Mr. Walton, evil doesn't change its nature out of necessity. It adapts, but it still remains what it is at its core. Evil will always be evil, no matter how you dress it up and hope it will be something else."

Walton smiled at him and nodded. "I'll get you what you need. I'm assuming you're in a rush?"

"I need it by the end of the week."

"And you shall have it by then. But I want you to understand that I will take my idea up with the rest of the Council."

"That's great, Otis. I wish you luck, I really do. You are dying. I get that. You have nothing to lose. Just try to make sure you don't sacrifice anyone else in your pursuit of madness."

CHAPTER 7

The Unexpected Reunion

Every evening, when her day was over, Ginger Coltrane would fill out a report and send it back to Charlotte Mayberry. After three days, she didn't feel any closer to understanding what was going on. The strangers, all men, didn't follow any discernible pattern. There were always five that left the building every evening, and they didn't return until two or three o'clock in the morning. And when they returned, there was always a newcomer to the group. Shortly after they left the building by the side door, they would split up and go into different parts of the city. She couldn't follow all of them, and they never went to the same place twice. The ones she could follow would stop at every street intersection, make notes on a small pad of paper, and then continue their walk until they stopped and returned the way they came, checking or adding to the notes already made.

Before they returned to the apartment, they would stop at the warehouse, and she would hear the usual hum. Ginger guessed they had found an effective way to stop the light from coming through the windows, since she could no longer see it. And every night, when the men left, she would see a new face. Until now, she had only been an observer, but based on the instructions she just received by courier, that needed to change. Charlotte wanted one of the notebooks to study, and there was no way to get one without moving from the shadows and interacting with one of the strangers face-to-face.

She had already picked out the stranger. He arrived the night before and walked with an uncertain step back to the apartment. He was smaller, both in height and frame. The others moved with cautious confidence, but this one seemed either unprepared or uncertain about what he was doing. He would be Ginger's best chance. She named him Mouse.

Dressed in ordinary street clothes rather than those of a lady, Ginger waited across the street from the alley exit for the men to appear. At nine o'clock, they exited the building and then began to split up into smaller groups. Two continued on straight. The Mouse was in a group of three that turned to the left and proceeded to the city center of New Marchant. She followed them, staying in the shadows and out of reach of the gas lamps.

At the next intersection, the group split again, and Mouse continued down the street, while the other two turned left and continued on their way. Based on what she already knew, he would walk and take notes for another two to three hours before he retraced his steps. If she moved too soon, she would lose valuable information. Moving too late, however, would be dangerous. The closer the man got to the others, the greater the chance they could intervene. And so Ginger stayed in the shadows and watched every move that Mouse made.

Ashlyn listened quietly as Roland recounted his conversation with Ethan. When he finished, she asked him a simple question: "When are we leaving?"

"We aren't. I'm leaving. You need to stay here and help keep an eye on everyone."

Ashlyn laughed. "If you are going, then I am going. Or, said another way... If I don't go, you don't go."

"But..."

"No. I don't want to hear it. I thought I made it clear that I'm not going to be separated from you again. I gave you up for two years, I'm done with that."

"It makes no sense for..."

"Love, it doesn't have to make sense. It's just the way it's going to be."

"Love, I really don't think you can stop me."

Without warning, Ashlyn jumped on Roland, wrapped her arms around his neck, and her legs around his waist. She moved her lips to his ear and whispered, "I could stay on you like this for hours. You remember, don't you?"

Roland flinched as she nibbled on his earlobe and smiled. "Yes, I remember."

"So, love," Ashlyn asked again, "when are we leaving?"

On the edge of Farmer Cleo's lavender field, Star and Ethan were having a similar conversation. "Of course I'm going," Star snapped.

"Just think for a moment about the position this puts me in. Your parents are going to hate me if you come with me. Perhaps not your father, but your mother will not be happy. You saw her face when we offered to leave."

"Was it the right thing to do back then?" Star asked.

"Yes."

"Then it's the right thing to do now. And what about your parents? What are you going to tell them?"

"I'm going to write them a note and leave it on the kitchen table."

"So rather than asking for permission, you're just going to ask for forgiveness after you've already gone?"

"Yeah, that was my plan," Ethan said, with a nod of his head

"And Pops will pick us up at midnight?"

"Great, then we'll have plenty of time to write notes to our parents. I'll be right back," Star said, standing up and walking towards her home.

"Where are you going?" Ethan asked.

"Paper, pencil..." She turned back and smiled. "I could carve it into the table with a knife, but a pencil and paper would probably work better."

It was the doorman who finally gave her something meaningful. Ginger's time in the nearby restaurants and bars had been unproductive. She learned about all kinds of interesting and questionable people, but she could find nothing on the man from the rain. The doorman was elderly, having spent his career in the army, and his semi-retirement consisted of opening doors and offering security to the residents

In reality, Yochem Pardue had a bad back, a gimpy knee, and couldn't run more than half a block if his life depended on it. He split his time with three other doormen, rotating shifts as needed. Currently, Pardue had the night shift. He had another sixty days left in his three-month rotation, after which he would return to days.

Ginger, who was always one of the last residents to make it back at night, made a point to bring Pardue something from wherever she'd been for the evening. The man was as thin as a rail, and no matter what decadent dessert Ginger brought him, he never seemed to gain any weight.

"Quiet night?" Ginger asked as Pardue opened the door before her.

"Yes, ma'am," he nodded. "It's the middle of the week. Not a lot is happening. It will pick up on the weekend, it always does."

"Brought you something," she said with a mischievous grin, as her hands held it behind her back. "Guess what it is?"

"Tell me where you went. You have to give me something to work with."

"Hanover's," she replied, teasing him for a moment.

"Chocolate cake?"

"Close. It's a raspberry chocolate cake." She produced the brown paper bag from behind her back.

"Thank you," Pardue said as his eyes grew big at the description. "You are too kind to me."

"There's a fork in the bag. Why don't you try it while I'm here? I'll watch the door with you while you eat."

Pardue shuffled over to a table, opened the bag, and removed the fork and cake, which were resting on a piece of brown cardboard. He went back to Ginger and sat down on the wooden stool carefully positioned by the building entrance. Taking a bite of the cake, he smiled, a big chocolate-icing toothy smile. "This is wonderful!"

"Good. I'm glad you like it. I'll have to try it myself the next time I'm there."

He took another bite of the cake, savoring the sweet gift, and nodding his head at the taste. "Mmm."

"Can I ask you a question?"

"Mm-hm." Pardue nodded, still chewing.

"Do you ever encounter residents or their guests that don't quite seem to belong?"

Pardue raised an eyebrow. "What do you mean by 'belong'?" he said, after swallowing his mouthful.

"Maybe their clothing doesn't look just right. Maybe their communication is different. I don't know. They just don't seem like they're locals."

"Yep," Pardue answered. "All the time. We get people in from all over NHHMM. Some come here on business. Some have work at the Chancellery. Some stay here for just a few months, and some for an entire year or longer."

His answer was absolutely no help. She had to try another approach. "Do you know every resident of the building?"

Pardue shook his head. "No. I don't sign the leasing documents. Residents are not supposed to sublease their apartments, but I believe it does happen. Especially on the fifth floor."

"What happens on the fifth floor?"

"There is one apartment - 506 - that seems to have a lot of people coming and going. We've had a couple of complaints from some of the other residents about excessive noise and odd singing coming from inside it. When that happens, the doorman must go investigate and tell the resident to quieten down."

"Same people every time?" Ginger asked.

"Oh no," Pardue said, as he cut another piece of cake. "Same apartment, but never the same people. I knock, and a man answers, always a different man. I tell them to hold it down, and he gives me a blank stare and says nothing. I leave, he closes the door, and that's all that happens until I get another complaint."

"But it's not the same person?"

"No. It's always someone different."

"That's so strange," Ginger mused.

"Either the tenant is sub-leasing the apartment, or it's a very, very large family."

Ginger thought it over for a moment. This was the place. It had to be apartment 506. She'd already tracked wet footprints up to the fifth floor, which stopped at that door. "Can you break a rule for me?" she said with a girlish smile.

"Maybe," Pardue replied, already deciding that if it was remotely legal, he would do it. "What do you need?"

"Can you tell me who has the lease in apartment 506?"

"Honestly, I don't know."

"Oh," Ginger said, despondently letting her emotions show.

"But I can find out," Pardue said with a wink.

They chatted for another five minutes while Yochem Pardue finished the piece of cake. Ginger then wished him goodnight and took the stairs up to the fifth floor, then cautiously walked down the hallway toward the apartment. The building was relatively new and well-constructed, so there was no creaking of the floor as she walked. The apartment was located at the end of the corridor. While there was another apartment directly opposite the door to 506, there was nothing beyond except an emergency stairway down to the lower level.

Walking to the exit, she slowly pushed open the door and looked into the stairwell. There was a dim gas lamp above the metal stairway that snaked its way down to the street level. Placing her ear against the wall that adjoined 506, she listened. She could hear voices. Three or four. Maybe more. She couldn't make out any words, only the sounds of men's voices.

They had to be using the emergency stairway to go in and out of the building. Pardue and the other doormen would recognize regular faces coming and going through the main entrance, and Pardue had said there was a new face every time he had to knock on the door.

Ginger stepped back into the hallway and placed her ear against the wall. Again, she could hear voices but couldn't make out any words. She checked the door to the stairway. It didn't lock, but when she checked the other side she found that the knob wouldn't turn and there wasn't a keyhole. It had to be a turn lock. Leaving the door ajar, she went down the stairs until she reached the first level. At the bottom of the stairs was a metal door, and when she turned the knob, the door opened onto an alley on the side of the building. Reaching out, she tried to turn the alley-side knob. It was locked.

As she tried to remember the combination, she heard voices approaching from above. Her first thought was to move out into the alley and further into the night. She decided, however, to crawl under the stairs and hide in the shadows. The voices grew closer, and the steps on the metal stairs grew louder. Several men were coming down the stairs, and her heart began to race when Ginger realized that she couldn't understand any of them.

They were obviously trying hard not to draw attention to themselves. Several of the men spoke in whispers, and she could hear their steps directly over her head. She could also smell them, a mix of body odor and food that filled the stairwell. Staying in the shadows, Ginger watched as the front man turned the doorknob and waited until the last man was out of the building and the door to the alley had closed. It was only then that she stood up, slowly opened the door, and stepped into the alley.

After fifteen minutes, she was confident of their destination, and then they surprised her. One minute they were all in a group, all five walking together, and then they split up. One continued forward, two turned to the right, one turned to the left, and the last man quickly stepped away from the streetlights, pausing at the corner of the building. Ginger crossed to the other side of the street from the waiting man and then continued forward and into the night. Checking over her shoulder, she looked to see if the man was following her, but there was no sign of him.

She quickened her steps and turned down an alley, then pushed her way through a gap in the wooden fence at the end. Stepping around piles of debris, she followed the fence until it joined a brick wall. Hiking up her skirt, Ginger climbed the fence and carefully walked along the top until she felt the brick underneath her feet. There, she sat down on the brick and waited. Before her was the building where she saw the first man arrive. The door had been repaired, and many of the windows as well. From the mouth of the alley, a dark shape appeared and walked toward her. It was too dark to make out the figure, but she definitely recognized the smell. The man walked to the side door of the building, unlocked it, and stepped inside. Over the next five minutes, the remaining four men from the apartment arrived and entered the building. As the last man was in, Ginger could make out another approaching figure from the street. This one was smaller and walked with a quicker stride.

The door was opened, closed, and then Ginger heard the locking mechanism click into place. At least it isn't raining this time. She shifted on the wall and prepared for a long wait. And then, no sooner than she thought it, the first raindrop fell and splattered on her cheek.

Twenty minutes later, her whole body shuddered as the rain kept falling. She feared that those inside were waiting for a break from it before they left the building. Ginger wanted to go. She desperately wanted to leave. Still in the dress she wore to dinner, she hid in the corner of the alley beneath the wall she had perched on before, every stitch of clothing clinging to her body. The door lock turned from the inside, and she willed her body to be still. She held her breath as the door opened. Out stepped the last person to arrive, the smaller person, who quickly left the alley, evidently not wanting to be caught out in the weather any more than was necessary.

Ginger started to follow, but she stumbled. Her cold, wet body wasn't functioning correctly. This was her only chance. The others would probably leave shortly after the first, but she didn't want to wait for them. She wanted the person who had just left. Where was she going? She caught her fall by grabbing onto a piece of brass pipe that was acting as a rain gutter. Staggering to the corner, she saw the figure approaching the intersection of a nearly deserted street. She was making too much noise this time, as her feet splashed in the water, but fortunately for her, the person ahead didn't seem to be paying any attention. After a few blocks, Ginger thought she had a rough idea of where she was going. Ahead lay the housing district for government officials who needed to live close to work. These were the ones who really didn't have any freedom in their life. They started work early, ended late, and then continued working after dinner and until bedtime.

The person walked at a quicker pace, occasionally crossing the street suddenly, and proceeded to a large, exclusive apartment complex. By the time Ginger could catch up, they were through the lobby, up the stairs, and out of sight. She followed and tried the same trick as before, but the results were not the same.

"I'm sorry, miss," an armed soldier said as he stepped out of the shadows and blocked her movement. "No matter how bad the weather outside, you are not allowed to wait out the storm in the building."

"Yes, yes, I'm sure," Ginger agreed. "But this is different. The person who just crossed the street and came inside dropped their keys on the sidewalk. I just wanted to try to deliver them. I know how frustrated I would be if I lost my keys to everything."

The guard smiled. "That's kind of you," he said. "If you give them to me, I will hold them for the resident. I'm sure she will be glad to get them back."

98

"Can you give me her name?" Ginger gambled. "I'd like to write her a personal note. You never know, there might be a reward in it for me."

"I'm not allowed to give out the names of our residents for any reason. But if you give me your name, I will be sure and tell her when I deliver her keys."

It is a woman! Reaching into her bag, she produced the keys to her mailbox and apartment. There was nothing to identify the building or apartment location on the keys, so she didn't think it could be traced back to her. "Yvette Dupuee," she replied, giving the guard her keys.

"Thank you," he replied. "Now leave."

Moments after Ginger left the building to again face the cold night rain, the guard looked up as he heard the quick steps of heels on the tiled floor. "A woman was just here," he said. "She said you dropped these." He offered the keys to a dark-haired woman who bore a cruel smile.

"They are not my keys," Santa Udi said. "And what was the name she gave you?" The guard looked confused, as if she would know. "She followed me all the way here. I was waiting in the hallway to see what I could learn."

"Yvette Dupuee." The guard nodded that he understood.

"Obviously a lie, but it doesn't matter," she said, looking closely at the mailbox key. "We will find her soon enough."

The rain lasted another two hours, and when it was over, Mouse finished his walk around the city and began his return to apartment 506. He turned quickly, and when he did, he thought he saw something in the shadows further down the street. He paused and looked intently at the space with a cautious eye. After several minutes of seeing no movement, he continued his walk, checking his notes at every intersection. At Ferris Street, he stopped at the corner and reviewed his notes again. The sound of footsteps came from his right, and before he could lift his head to look, he was sent sprawling into the street, the notebook and pencil flying from his hands.

"Hey, watch where you're going," a young woman in dirty clothes yelled. "You don't go standing on the sidewalk for no reason in the dead of night." A slight pause, then, "And I think I've hurt my shoulder because of you."

Mouse started to yell back at her but stopped after just a few intelligible words. Rolling over to his knees, he began to stand up when he felt the point of a knife pressing into his back. "Now, give me everything in your pockets and I won't cut you, but be quick about it."

To her surprise, the man understood. He reached into his trouser pocket and removed some coins. "And I'll have the breather, too." He went to remove the breather and watched the woman scoop up the notebook with her free hand. The breather detached, Mouse slowly turned around, and offered it to Ginger Coltrane as he studied her face.

"My orders are to cause no trouble." He said, thinking about every word. "But soon, very soon, those orders will change. I will remember you, and I will find you. You beg for your life. You have my word."

"I will look forward to that day," she replied, trying to maintain her composure. Grabbing the breather from Mouse, she began to back away down the sidewalk, never taking her eyes from him until she could see the darkness of the alley where she had been hiding. Then, stepping into the alley, she ran as fast as she could toward Charlotte Mayberry's home.

"I will look forward to that day," she replied, trying to maintain her composure. Grabbing the breather from Mouse, she began to back away down the sidewalk, never taking her eyes from him, until she could see the darkness of the alley she had been hiding in. Then, stepping into the alley, she ran as fast as she could toward Charlotte Mayberry's home.

Neither one of them knew what to expect, so when the moon was blotted from the sky and the wind swirled around them like a tornado, they were awestruck. The tall grass in the meadow whipped their legs, and then they heard the quiet whine of the electric motors. Dirt and debris bit into their faces, and they covered their eyes until they recognized a familiar voice.

"Climb up," Pops called out. Ethan looked up through squinted eyes and saw a metal ladder roll down. "We'll keep it as steady as we can."

Star went up the ladder first. Watching her struggle, he realized it would be easier if he provided some kind of anchor to keep her from swaying back and forth. Dropping to the ground, he grabbed the ladder with both hands. When Star disappeared into the metal compartment, Ethan started up. As he climbed, the airship would jerk as the natural wind flowed all around it. He was climbing blind, his eyes stinging from the flying dirt. Finally, he felt a hand on his shoulder and heard Pops' voice.

"Got you," Pops said. "Two more steps."

Ashlyn closed the sliding door and slid the handle into place to lock it.

"Welcome aboard," Clyde Vanderschmidt said, looking back over his shoulder. "I'm Clyde."

"This is Mr. Vanderschmidt's grandson," Ashlyn said.

"He was the only available pilot," Roland pointed out, trying to cut off any questions that Ethan might ask.

"Any problems leaving?" Ashlyn asked.

"No," Star said, shaking her head. "The problems will come when we get back."

Ethan looked over the compartment at the marvel that allowed them to sail through the sky. "They were working on something like this at Arcborne. But it was smaller, built for one person."

"Already done that one," Clyde commented. "Not for the faint of heart, but it's an amazing ride if you have the stomach for it."

"Are they all like this?" Ethan asked as he listened to Clyde.

"All of them," Roland answered. "Genius kind of runs in their family."

Ethan knew not to mention Noola Klaar in front of Clyde, so he tried to speak in code. "And how did you convince the Council to let you use this thing?"

"It's purely strategic," Roland said, shrugging. "We'll place a beacon in Arcborne. I convinced the Council that we needed a safe place in case Mr. Vanderschmidt's research was compromised and we had to leave. What better place than Arcborne?"

"Makes sense," Ethan said with a grin, happy that Noola's secret hadn't been betrayed.

"How long will we be up here...flying?" Star asked.

"About three or four hours," Clyde replied. "Depends on what kind of wind we are flying into."

"Anything else that we need to know?"

"Not really. Some things in life are still a mystery," Roland answered.

"We did get a list of names for you that might be helpful," Ashlyn commented. "The evacuation of Arcborne created an unexpected problem for the chancellor. There are now thousands of people talking about a place that doesn't exist. Our information says that Brighton is rounding up the former employees and some of the students. Either he's trying to recapture their knowledge, or he wants the voices to vanish. This," she said, handing a folder to Star, "has the home addresses of all the students. We may be able to use some of them if they are inclined."

"Is there a light in here?" Star asked, wanting to look over the names.

"Yes, but we can't use it," Clyde said.

"Why?"

"Most people aren't ready for the reality that we can fly. And we especially don't want the chancellor to know that we can."

Charlotte Mayberry wasn't accustomed to people knocking on her front door in the middle of the night, and there certainly wasn't any precedent for someone pounding on it. Sliding into a robe, she walked downstairs, peeked out the window, and saw Ginger Coltrane looking much like she did the first day she'd met her: Unkept, dirty, and disheveled. Pulling back the bolts on the door, she opened it.

"Come in. Quickly." Ginger stepped through the door, and Charlotte closed it behind her and slid the bolts back into place.

Ginger started off fast, barely pausing between words, as if she were in a race to tell what she knew. "I did what you asked, I followed them, and I got a notebook with their writing. I can't read it. And the man threatened me. His eyes were black, and it felt like they were daggers. He said he was ordered to do no violence, but that would soon change, and when it did, he would find me and make me suffer."

"Ok," Charlotte said slowly. "Breathe and let me get you something." Walking over to the bar, she poured a clear liquid into a small glass and then offered it to Ginger.

"No thanks." Ginger shook her head. "I don't need water right now."

Charlotte laughed. "This isn't water. And you don't want to sip it. Just drink it down all at once."

Ginger's whole body shuddered as she followed Charlotte's instructions. "Clear whiskey?"

"Of a sort. Now, tell me, is there any chance he, or the others, could have followed you here?"

"No, I was careful. I stayed in the shadows, changed directions several times, and kept an eye over my shoulder."

"And he saw you...this way?" Charlotte motioned to her appearance.

"Yes."

"Not to worry then. I almost didn't recognize you. When you're cleaned up, a man will be looking at your curves rather than trying to remember if you were some street girl who bumped into him one night."

"Yes, I understand. Sometimes I look in the mirror and I don't even recognize myself."

"May I see the notebook?" Charlotte asked.

After handing it over, Ginger stood and walked to the bar. "May I?" she asked, holding up her glass.

"Of course, but go slow. It's pretty strong stuff."

The notebook was like any other that you could buy on twenty street corners around the city. She started at the first page and studied everyone until there was no more writing. Every corner was identified in NHHMMian, just as the street signs would have them listed. And underneath was a word she didn't recognize. At least Charlotte guessed it was a word. They were symbols or letters, she wasn't sure which, because it wasn't the NHHMMian alphabet. Every important building was labeled the same way. The banks, the police buildings, and the telegraph locations were all identified. Each page, even the ones without words, was made of two rows of rectangular boxes. And the top and the bottom were the names of the cross streets. The top of any page would lead to and continue to the bottom of the next page. It was a crude but effective map that anyone could follow.

"You did very well," Charlotte said aloud, as she looked over the last pages.

"They are a scary lot," Ginger replied.

"What else can you tell me about them?"

"Nothing. They all look different. Some have black hair, while others have brown. Some are taller and some are heavier. Some of them speak our language, but it isn't easy for them. Others in the group sound just like you and me."

"So, there is nothing about them that would stand out if I passed them on the street?"

"No, they look like anyone else. Some are light-skinned. Others dark. Some have beards, others don't. Their eyes and their hair are different colors."

"Interesting," Charlotte mused aloud. "I'm going to give this to a person that I know. She's very good with puzzles, and I hope she can help me come up with a letter conversion process of sorts. My hope is that we will be able to ultimately read what is being written. Now," she said, changing the subject. "I want you to go take a bath and clean up. I'll give you some of my clothes. They won't fit well, but I don't want you going back there dressed like you are. Should the man be out in the lobby of the building, he might notice you."

"Good idea. And what is this?" Ginger motioned to the glass. "It tastes like peaches."

"That is called Glow. It's made up in the mountains from some kind of corn distillation process. Everyone who makes it puts a name in front of the word Glow. They flavor it in different ways and bottle it differently. This one is called Reaper's Glow."

"The maker's name is Reaper?"

"Probably not, considering this is illegal and the maker doesn't want to end up in jail."

"Why is it illegal?"

"Taxes, my dear. Taxes. It's illegal because the maker doesn't want to pay tax on his profits."

"I'm surprised this isn't something that we sold at The Lying Fisherman. Sounds like the kind of thing Mr. Jack would be involved with."

"You never know. He probably is."

Thanks to Otis Walton's forgetfulness, there were still lights on in Arcborne as Clyde Vanderschmidt navigated the airship below the mountains into the bowl they created. As the ground was smooth in the open area outside of the town center, Ethan directed him to land the craft about two hundred yards south of the last visible light. When it was still a few feet above the ground, Roland jumped out of the cabin and rolled out. Immediately, Ashlyn threw several large canvas bags out into the night.

From the darkness came a groan. "Are you trying to hit me with those bags?" Roland asked.

"Sorry, dear. Didn't see you."

Clyde rotated the motors so that they pushed the airship down, allowing him to rest the bottom of the cabin on the ground. Ashlyn, Ethan, and Star stepped out and then quickly moved away from the airship.

Once the engines were off, Clyde jumped out of the cabin with a long hammer and two long rods. He drove the rods into the ground and tied a rope that hung from the nose of the airship to one of them. When it was secure, he moved to the back of the craft and repeated the process. With the propellers off, the rest of the crew started picking up the canvas bags.

"Which way?" Ashlyn asked.

"We will head toward the lights," Ethan answered. "When we have our bearings and find the main street, it's not far to the school."

"Where do we start looking first?" Roland said as they began their walk.

"I suggest that you and Ashlyn look for a location to place the clock, and Star and I will go to her office and start there. She will recognize the two of us, but you and Ashlyn will catch her by surprise."

"But how will she recognize you if she can't see?" Ashlyn questioned. It was clear that neither Roland nor Ashlyn really understood what had happened to Noola Klaar.

"The best way I know how to describe it is that she sees frequencies. I have a frequency. Star has a frequency, and both of you have frequencies. Our watches and the clock you brought have frequencies."

"We've met her before," Ashlyn added. "Wouldn't she recognize our frequencies as well?"

"Maybe, but I doubt it. She hasn't interacted with either of you since the explosion that destroyed her vision. I suspect she knows you're friendly because of your watch. She knows that Mr. Vanderschmidt made them, and you wouldn't have it if you weren't trustworthy."

"She knows... But it's dark outside?" Roland said with surprise.

"Yeah, she's probably watching us right now if she moved above ground. Remember, she doesn't see light or dark. She sees frequencies."

When they reached the center of the city, Star provided them with a verbal description of the area. As she pointed directions, they could all smell the odor of rotting meat and produce. Before Ethan and Star could begin their search for Noola Klaar, Roland reached into a bag and gave him a flare gun.

"Any problems, anything concerning, fire this off and we will come to you."

"Got it," Ethan replied. "We'll check back within two hours."

"We'll be here."

The moon was three-quarters full, and once they knew where they were, it was easy for Ethan and Star to head to where they were going. They found the path leading up to the school and then made their way over to the strategy building. The quiet made them both feel uncomfortable, however. The place was designed to house thousands of people, and yet the only sound they heard was the whisper of a night breeze and the crickets talking back and forth to each other.

From the basement, they gained access to the buildings below ground. No sooner had they stepped into the hallway that led to Noola's office when they heard a voice call out:

"Ethan! It's good to have you back. Please, bring your friend and come join me."

CHAPTER 8

The Dagger to the Heart

"You look better," Jack said after Shy sat down opposite him at The Listing Ship. It was mid-afternoon, and the lunch traffic had cleared, leaving them as the only ones in the restaurant. The bruises and swelling were gone from her face, but it didn't look like how he remembered it. He thought it looked a little crooked.

"Thanks," she said with a half-smile. "There are a few small scars that are permanent, but so far, it hasn't kept the men away. How's the leg?" She hadn't seen him since he was walking with a crutch.

"I've got a large scar that will be permanent, and I'm hoping it doesn't keep the women away!"

Shy laughed out loud. "I'm sure it won't."

"Have you been keeping busy?"

"Oh yes," Shy grinned. "There will always be people who have too many things in their lives. You know...clutter. Sometimes that clutter sparkles, sometimes it has numbers on it. I simply help them realize that they can live quite nicely with less."

"Mmm. When I do that, I'm called a pirate. What does that make you?"

"It makes me the one who frees their souls from their dependence upon material things. Doesn't that sound more noble than being called a thief or a pirate?"

"Perhaps, but I'm not sure the judge would agree should you be arrested."

"We'll find out if they catch me. So, Jack," Shy asked, changing the subject, "what's on your mind? I know you didn't call me here just to catch up. Prior to Arcborne, we had never met, so I know this isn't a social visit."

"You're right. I need your help."

"Does it involve me being shot at, chased, and beaten mercilessly?"

"Like last time? Er...maybe, but I'm hoping we can both avoid injury and scars," he answered.

"Then please, please tell me about it, because I'm so incredibly bored."

Jack told her about the strange ships in the ocean and the real probability that there could be an invasion of some kind. And then he told her about Retribution. "It's the functional, military twin sister of Arcborne. What they came up with in theory in Arcborne is being made into weapons in Retribution. We've got to get in there, find out what they have, assess the threat, and then...well...it depends on what we find."

"You are going to blow up the tunnel and seal everyone in," she said after a moment. "With no tunnel, they can't move out troops and weapons."

"Maybe. It depends on what we find there. We can't have the chancellor using those weapons against us, and we can't take the risk that everything, the people, the technology, and the weapons could be used against us by an invader."

"I'm in," Shy stated, without reservation in her voice.

"Shy, there are families there. Maybe even children. It's not just soldiers. We were lucky the last time. We may not have the option of being kindhearted this time around. If you want to change your answer, right now is the time to do it."

"No. I've seen how Arcborne was laid out. There was food, water, and the ability to last an entire town for months, maybe years. If Retribution is as important as you say, someone will eventually try to dig them out. It may only buy us a few months, but I can sleep at night knowing that what we might do could be the difference between freedom and slavery."

"Are you absolutely sure?" Jacke asked after a moment.

"When do we leave?"

"I'm working on that. We need a better cover story than we had the last time. I've got a connection on the inside that is supposed to provide me with the names and descriptions of the people being moved into Retribution. She says that sometimes it's workers, and sometimes new soldiers. Sometimes both. Once we have a list and a date, we can go from there."

"Any idea how long this will take?"

A slender brunette with short hair pulled behind her ear walked past the glass window of the restaurant. She stopped at the entrance, looked at the sign on the door, and then came inside. "Any minute now," Jack said, as he looked at the woman. "Shy, I'm sure you understand, but this meeting needs to be over. I'll be in touch."

As Shy stood up to leave, the woman approached the table. "Booking your dates, one after the other now?" she asked.

"This is business, dear," Shy replied, and then she grinned as she added, "I'm not into scars. See you around, Jack."

Jack winced at the comment. "Sinead, it's good to see you. Thanks for coming."

"Scar? How does she know about the scar?" Sinead asked.

"Because she was with me when I got it, but I'm guessing you probably aren't going to believe that."

"Of course, I believe you," she said, with a dismissive gesture. "She didn't really look like your type." Looking around the room, she made a disapproving face. "Is this place safe to eat in?" she asked, sitting down in the chair vacated by Shy. I'm not going to get sick from the food, am I?"

"Not unless the cook heard you say that. What do you have for me?" Jack tried to change the subject.

"Fourteen new arrivals are coming to the location you asked about. These papers," Sinead said, sliding an envelope across the table, "have everything you want to know."

"Perfect." Jack smiled. "Thank you."

"You aren't going to do anything bad with this information, are you? There are perhaps one hundred people in the government who are cleared to discuss this. You aren't going to get me in any trouble, are you?"

"Look, Sinead, you know that some of my business ventures are a bit on the gray side of the law. All I want to do is make sure I know who my customers are so that I can bring in what they want. I've got another shipment going in over the next two weeks, and I can tell by looking at their profiles what they are most likely to drink. The military only provides residents with a limited choice of what they have access to. This list will help me bring in the right things. If there are fourteen wine drinkers, for example, I'd best make sure that my shipment isn't only whiskey and rum."

"And you can tell that by a piece of paper?"

Jack nodded. "For the most part. An officer or a business person isn't going to want the standard spirits the military provides. They will want something more expensive. A soldier below a certain rank can't afford the good stuff, but they'd like to have something a little better than military provisions. As a general rule, not always, women will prefer wine, as will the non-military personnel. That's why I need to know this information." Jack was making it all up as he was talking, but he felt that his story sounded credible. "No one will ever see me with the list, and there's no way that it will get back to you. I will just amaze my new customers with my ability to have what they want."

"That makes sense, and...I guess that doesn't sound too bad."

"The colonels and majors all know what I'm doing, and they look the other way because I bring them the things they can't get there."

"I understand. And you're sure it's safe to eat here?" Sinead whispered as she used the table napkin to wipe off the utensils.

"Sinead, you know I wouldn't lie to you."

When the sun lost its battle with the moon and darkness settled in over New Marchant, Ginger left her apartment dressed in the oldest, most tattered clothes she could find. Leaving the building by the side stairway, she pushed open the door and began her walk to the old warehouse. She knew it was a risk, but she needed to know if there were more new arrivals. Stepping out onto the sidewalk, she kept her head down and did her best not to make eye contact with anyone. Had her head been up, she might have noticed the shadow from across the street that moved and began to follow her movements.

This far, there hadn't been any activity until ten o'clock, so she knew she had time to get into position and watch the side door from the alley. Thankfully, there was no rain, and the weather was pleasant. After weeks of looking, asking questions, and buying drinks for strangers, she was finally making real progress, and it felt good.

At first, Mouse made her uncomfortable, and while she would admit that to no other...he frightened her. And when she had time to really think about it, her emotions changed from fear to anger. Who were these people who thought they could come into her world and make it their own? She wasn't afraid to fight for what she believed in, but then she thought of her little sister, who was her complete opposite. Her sister was meek, always worried about offending others, and not one to ever fight back over anything. For almost all of her life, Ginger was little more than a deception, pretending to be someone else, living a life that wasn't normal for her, and telling lie after lie. But now, she had a feeling of nobility about her work. She could make a difference, and she wanted to help protect those who couldn't defend themselves.

Two hours passed, and there was no movement in the warehouse that she could see. There was no hum, no brilliant light. It was as if they knew she was there and decided not to show up. Maybe they changed their plans when Mouse told them what happened? Maybe they have moved on to somewhere else?

At eleven o'clock, Ginger moved from the nearby rooftop onto the fence and then dropped down into the alley below. She stepped up to the warehouse door, turned the knob, and felt it give way to her push. The hinges creaked slightly, and she froze in place. There was no sound on the first or second floor, and she felt a sigh of relief. Stepping inside, she closed the door behind her and began a stealthy climb up the stairs. She would only be inside for a few minutes. There, she would check the anvil, ensuring there were no messages or anything else of value, and then return to the apartment to get a good night's rest. Reaching the top of the stairs, Ginger turned toward the anvil when a voice called out.

"You are late. We have waited a long time." Ginger felt arms wrap around her and throw her across the room. Landing on the floor in a heap, gas lamps began to illuminate the room. Three Yehudis blocked the stairs, and six more began to surround her. One man held back and kept his distance. Crawling backwards, she found herself in a corner. Placing her right hand behind her back, she grabbed the handle of a thin blade tucked in the back of her skirt. When she was in the corner, the other men joined the ring around her.

"This is the one?" a large man with blond hair and blue eyes asked.

"Yes," Mouse said. "She is the one. Please give me the honor of killing her."

"No," the man replied, dismissing him with a wave of his hands. "Our orders are clear. We cause no physical harm yet..."

"That's probably a good idea, because I would really hate to hurt any of you," Ginger chided.

"You do not speak to Yehudi man unless we give you permission, and I have not given you permission."

"This is NHHMM. I don't need your permission to speak. So, if we aren't going to fight, then I will take my leave of you and find something more interesting to do with my time." Ginger stood up and adjusted her skirt.

"I didn't say we didn't have a use for you," the large man said, "I only said we weren't going to harm you. There is much you can tell us."

"Torture me for information? I don't know much, but if you are trying to get me to talk, threats are probably not the best way."

"Take her," the heavy-set man said, and two men rushed forward, grabbed her arms, pushed her to the floor, and held her down.

"We don't need to do this," the man in the back of the room said.

"SILENCE," the man replied.

"What is your name, Sir?" Ginger asked.

"Niven, and these men are in my charge."

"Well, Niven, I'm not really sure what kind of torture you have in mind, but you and your men are not going to be able to entice me to talk. That's not going to happen," Ginger said with disgust in her voice. "But do you have a cute sister? Could she join us? I might be more talkative if she joined us."

The large man looked confused, and then her words sank in

His hands began to shake, and the veins in his neck began to bulge as his face twisted with rage.

"You insult every man here with your words, and I personally will cut out your tongue."

112

"No," the man in the back argued. "Our orders are clear. We are not allowed to do harm to anyone until the appointed time. You just said it."

Without a word, the Niven turned, drew a pistol, and shot the man in the back of the room.

"Well, that wasn't very nice," a woman's voice said from the top of the stairs.

The men turned, and shock was on their faces when they saw a woman wearing odd clothes and a metal attachment on her face. In each hand was a strange pistol, and without taking her eyes off the men, she asked, "Are you okay, kid?" Charlotte asked.

The man holding Ginger's right hand reached for a knife stuck into his waistband and moved it toward her throat. Without hesitation, Charlotte shot the man on the right, and then the one on the left. And then, the room exploded with shouts, gunshots, and screams. When it was over, the men of the Yehud lay dead and wounded on the floor. Ginger's thin blade was covered in blood, and Charlotte Maybury holstered a pistol, removed her mask, and pointed to the second pistol at a man squirming on the floor.

"Can I have him?" Ginger asked.

"Absolutely," Charlotte replied.

The man writhing on the floor was Mouse, and Ginger stepped over to him and knelt down beside him. "How do we activate it?" she asked, pointing to the anvil.

Mouse spat in her face.

"This is what is going to happen next. If you tell me how to activate the anvil, I will send you home alive."

"You would do that?" the man said.

"I will send you home alive, because I want you to deliver a message."

"And...And if I don't tell you?"

"Then we will figure it out the hard way, and you will surely bleed out before we can send you back."

"Our leader. In his jacket is a metal box with buttons on it. He pushes the top button to go home. Press the button. I'm near the metal bender, and it will take me home," he said, pointing at the anvil. As he spoke, Charlotte went through the leader's pockets and found the box.

"Top button?" Charlotte asked, pointing to the top button.

Mouse nodded. "What's the message?"

"Tell your leaders that the women here are slaves to no man, and if you bite us, we bite back. And one more thing: Tell them that if they use this anvil, this metal bender again, they had better be able to swim, because we are going to drop it into the bottom of the ocean."

"Nice touch," Charlotte said with a smile. "Now, you," she continued, looking at the man, "lean up against the anvil, and kid," motioning to Ginger, "move over to the stairs."

Charlotte took a step closer to the man and the anvil. "How many seconds after you press the button until it is activated?"

"Seconds?"

"How many counts. One, two, three... How far can you count before you go home?"

"Five. Five counts."

"Thank you," and she immediately pushed the top button on the box. Sliding the box into her jacket pocket, she stepped away from the anvil as the room filled with light and a deep resonating hum.

"Can you help me?" a voice from the back of the room called out when Mouse was gone.

"What is your name?" Charlotte demanded when the man came to and started to look around the small room. He lay on a bed that was slightly propped up next to a window, allowing the early morning sunlight to brighten the room. His shirt was off, and a clean linen cloth was wrapped around his waist. Three inches above his right hip bone, a pinkish-red color stained the wound dressing.

"I am not going to die?"

"Not yet. What is your name?"

"Dueral. My name is Dueral Fabarge."

"How is it that you speak our language?"

"We are trained. We are all trained before we go into any new place to speak the home language."

"So NHHMM isn't the first world you have entered?"

"No. It is three for me. This one makes three," he said, holding up three fingers.

"Mr. Fabarge, I am going to ask you some questions about your world, your reason for being here, and your plans. You will answer my questions, or I have no use for you. And if I have no use for you, then it makes no sense for me to keep you alive. Do you understand?"

"I understand, and if you will do two things for me, I will answer any questions you have."

"What do you want?" Charlotte asked.

"You must swear that you will not send me back. Let me stay here, even if as a prisoner, but you cannot send me back."

"Agreed. And what is the second thing?"

"May I have something to drink? Water?"

"Ginger, can you find this man a glass of water?"

Without a reply, Ginger stepped from the dark corner of the room, put the thin blade back into the waistband of her skirt, and left.

Dueral Fabarge woke to brilliant sunlight coming in a window beside him. He raised his hand to shield his eyes, and then his brain began to process the data, past and present, and his heart began to race. His fingers began to slide over his body searching for injury or restraints. When he reached his abdomen, he grimaced with pain. He could feel a bandage, and as he tightened his stomach muscles in his effort to sit up, searing pain overwhelmed him.

Footsteps. He heard footsteps coming in his direction, and he panicked. His eyes darted around the room looking for a way out, but there was only one window and one door.

"Back to the land of the living?" Charlotte said from the doorway.

Fabarge looked at her with confusion. "Who are you?"

"I'm just the one who saved your life last night."

Memories flooded back to him. The shooting, the battle, and the request for sanctuary, but this woman looked different.

"Confused? Don't worry, I'm the same person. "Last night, you saw me in my uniform, accompanied by my tools of battle. I'm not fighting right now, and this is the normal me."

"And the other woman?"

"She's here, getting some sleep. Are you hungry?"

Fabarge thought for a moment and then nodded. "Yes. Very."

"Good, you will function better when your stomach is full. Let me help you up." Charlotte slid his legs from the bed he was lying on, onto the floor. Fabarge groaned throughout the motion and, after a moment, tried to stand up. Charlotte took his arm until he could catch his balance. "The kitchen is just through the doorway. I apologize for the condition of your bedroom. We didn't think you would be able to navigate the stairs, so we brought a bed down from upstairs and set it up down here in the laundry room. It's not much, but it will do until you can move around."

She led him into a large, well-equipped kitchen with a large wooden table positioned near the far wall. On the table were scrambled eggs, ham, fruit, and pastries. "Please, sit down," Charlotte offered.

Fabarge slowly worked his way down into a corner chair and wrestled with it until he could scoot it closer to the table.

"Do you take coffee or tea?" she asked.

"Coffee," he replied.

Bringing him a cup of coffee, Charlotte sat down next to him in a chair at the head of the table. "Make yourself comfortable and eat anything you want. As much as you want. We'll probably be here for a while, possibly through lunch, so relax and let's get to know each other. To start with, tell me about yourself and why you are invading our world."

"May I eat first?" Fabarge asked.

"No, we don't have time for that. Consider this a working breakfast. Eat and talk."

"I told you my name last night. Do I need to repeat it?"

"No. Dueral Fabarge. Did I pronounce it correctly?"

"Close enough," Fabarge answered.

"Is Yehud your home?"

He peeled an orange and shook his head. "All captured men serve in our Army. When they conquered my home, I became a soldier for them." He bit into a section of orange and smiled. "I haven't had one of these in over two years. Thank you."

"What is your role here on our planet?"

"I am gifted with words. I believe you say 'language'. My job is to understand the nuances of the languages we enter so that we better fit in. I'm also good with drawing pictures, so I assist with mapmaking."

"Did you do those things in your old world?"

With the orange finished, he added some ham and eggs to his plate. "Yes and no. I was a teacher of young adults. I taught them other languages we have in our world."

"You have more than one language in your world?

Fabarge finished a bite of ham and eggs before answering. We have many nations, and many languages."

"We only have one nation here," Charlotte commented.

"No, you have three nations. They all have the same language, but there are three."

"No. One," he said, holding up one finger. "I have seen them. There are three."

Fabarge was calm, confident, and Charlotte couldn't believe he was lying to her. Three nations? How can that be? "I want to know more about these other nations, but we can talk about that later. Why are the Yehud here and what do they want?"

"The Yehud are traders...world traders. We use our technology, our ability to move from one world to the next, and take the local resources that we want so they can be traded to other worlds."

"So, what do the Yehud want from our world?"

"Your world is different. They are running out of crystals, and they've discovered you have them in abundance. That's the first thing. The second...They want your young people...Your children. People are what they trade the most. By taking the young, they get two things. They deplete future generations, making it impossible for a rebellion to take place, and they make gold by selling the young for pleasure."

Charlotte's jaw dropped. Despite her knowledge of the darker side of NHHMM, even she could not fathom that there was a market for the young. "And there is a market for that?"

"Oh yes," Fabarge said, finishing the ham. "Some worlds value dark hair. Others prefer females, others males, and some both. It's the same way with skin color and height. The emperor has a detailed ledger that shows what worlds want what kind of people and for what task."

"Yes. Task. Regardless of age, if the youth is physically fetching, they will be sold for intimate acts to the wealthy and powerful. If the youth is homely, they will be sold for pleasure to the military troops. The young men or those with special skills will be sold for manual labor, conscripted, or sold into brothels. The latter applies to the women as well."

Putting aside the horrors of selling people as commodities, the business side of Charlotte's brain found the business approach to genius. Their ships appear. The transaction is completed, and the ships disappear, moving to home or the next world on the docket. There would be no interaction with law enforcement or the military. It was a profit while making sure no world ever had young soldiers to use in a revolt.

"Do you have family?" Charlotte asked.

Fabarge's face dropped, and his demeanor changed. "No. My wife died during our invasion. We never had children."

"I'm so sorry to hear about your wife. Do you wish to return home?"

"There is nothing for me there beyond a death sentence. I can't go to any world owned by the Yehud. They will conscript me again, or if they learn I deserted, they will kill me. Are you going to keep me here as a prisoner?"

Charlotte thought for a moment as she bit the end off a strawberry. "I have no interest in making you a prisoner. I could turn you over to our government, but that wouldn't do either of us any good."

She took another strawberry and looked up at him. "Do you want a job?"

"Doing what?"

"Doing what you do now. You are a spy. You are average enough that you wouldn't be noticed, but you could navigate just about any social setting I can think of. I would need you to shave your beard. If you agree, I'll equip you with clothing and a place to stay. I will pay you well, and you will never have to do the bidding of the Yehud again."

"What exactly do you think a spy does?"

"Anything I want...of course."

CHAPTER 9

The Sight of the Blind

Ethan and Star entered the room, and he reached for the switch that controlled the light. Noola Klaar stood before them, clutching a chair for support. She was frail, and the bones beneath her skin were pronounced. She was also starving. There were cuts on her arms and hands, and the left side of her face was bruised, her lips swollen.

"I'm going to get some food and water," Star stated when she saw Noola's condition. "I'll be back as soon as I can." And without waiting for a response, she hurried back into the hallway.

"Do I really look that bad?" Noola asked.

Ethan wasn't sure how to reply. While he didn't want to be disrespectful or rude, he also didn't want to minimize her condition. "When was the last time you had something to eat?" he asked.

"A few days ago, maybe. I don't really remember."

Taking her free arm, he spoke in a soft voice. "Why don't you sit down. I've got the back of your chair. Just slowly ease down to the seat, and then we can talk. Ok?"

When she was seated, he pulled another chair over next to her and sat down.

"What happened to your hands and face?" he asked.

"I tried to venture out on my own to find food, but it didn't go very well," she said, turning her palms over to show him her cuts and scrapes. Remember, all I see are frequencies and patterns. Food

119

doesn't really translate well through my new eyes. I remember that I used to be able to see mold on old bread, or the color of meat when it was unspoiled, or the color of vegetables when they were fresh. Now, I have to rely on my sense of smell for those things.

"I made it once to the market where produce was sold, but I can't really see depth either. I must feel my way up or down stairs, and a small drop or depression in the height of the ground can prove dangerous. That's what this is from." She gestured to her face with her hand.

"How long have you been without food?"

"I had some things here in my office that lasted for a day or so. Then I expanded my search, one room and one level of the building at a time, finding what I could."

Tears filled Ethan's eyes, and he took her hand in his. "I am so very sorry. I was taken from Arcborne before it was evacuated. I only heard about what happened a few days ago, and when I learned that you were on the missing list, I came here as quickly as possible. If I had only known everything sooner, I could have been here faster. You wouldn't have suffered."

"It's alright," she said, patting his hand. "You are here now, and it sounds like your friend has gone to get some food."

"We have food. We brought food and water."

"We? You and your friend?" she asked, with a questioning voice. "So, you and Star climbed the mountains and carried food and water here to me?"

The look on Noola's face showed concern, and she sat up a little straighter in the chair.

"Yes, ma'am. Star and others, but we didn't climb the mountains. We came from a craft that floats through the air."

Noola nodded her head. "Thank you for being honest with me. Remember, I see frequencies. I saw your watch as it descended from the sky. I saw another frequency, similar to your watch, but I also knew it wasn't present when Star was in the room. I knew there were others, and I'm sorry if I pretended ignorance, but I'm not quite sure who I can trust. After all, it appears that you didn't keep my secret."

"I'm sorry, but I didn't know any other way. In my heart, I felt that you must be starving, and I needed help to get here."

"Did you tell my family?" Noola asked.

"No, but I did tell the man who raised me. You've met him. His name is Roland Flynn. He and his wife know about you."

"Anyone else?"

"No. There is another person here with us, but he doesn't know anything about your presence here in Arcborne."

"And who is that person?"

Ethan paused, not wanting to answer her question. "Your grandson, Clyde Vanderschmidt."

Noola gasped and covered her mouth with her hands. "You can't tell him about me. Please. You can't."

"You aren't going to be here alone much longer. Important members of the Resistance will be coming. Things are happening that I've just learned about. Our planet is being invaded by people from another world. Arcborne is the ideal location for us to establish a center. Without access to the tunnel, there is no way for an army to get here. During this visit, we will establish a portal here. That way, members of the Resistance can come and leave without any kind of transportation. You will have company, and you will never run out of food or water."

"And I will have my greatest nightmare become a reality."

Looking down at the floor, Ethan took a deep breath and started to speak. "It's selfish, you know."

"What's selfish?"

"Depriving your family of who you are, because of vanity."

"How easy it is for you to judge me when you haven't lived a single hour as I have," Noola retorted. "How could anyone love me? My face is scarred from the blast. Crystals are buried in my face and eyes. Where is the beauty in that?"

"So, then you believe that beauty only resides on the outside. What would you want for Clyde? Would you want him to love someone who was appealing on the outside, but dead on the inside?"

"Of course not, but that isn't the same thing," Noola argued.

"It is exactly the same thing. I would think that I could never want anything more than for someone to just love me for who I am. Clearly, I've been looking at love and family the wrong way."

Noola pursed her lips together and stared toward the corner of the room. "How old are you?"

"Fifteen."

"You are an old soul," she said after a moment. "Wisdom does not usually find a home in someone so young."

"What does that mean, 'old soul'?"

"It means that this is probably not your first life. Somewhere in your past, you lived to be an old man who grew wiser with each passing year, because what you are speaking now comes from someone who has lived far more than fifteen years."

Ethan wasn't sure how to respond. It wasn't something he had thought about before. He'd never had the time to think about another life when he was too busy trying to survive the life he was living.

"And what if they turn from me in disgust?" she added. "What if they never want to see me again? What if they see me as a monster?"

"Then stay here in your office. I can ensure that you will never go hungry, and you will always have access to clean water to drink. There are no doors that are locked for you. The only barriers you face are the ones that you create yourself."

Nina Mineaux flipped the pages back and forth, peering at every character, symbol, and mark they contained. Pushing her glasses down to the tip of her nose, she studied one page more carefully than the others.

"What do you think?" Charlotte asked.

"Huh?" Nina said, looking up from the paper and over her glasses.

"What do you think?"

"At first blush, I'd say we are fortunate."

"This is just a transliteration of our NHHMMian letters, punctuation, and numbers."

"A what?" Charlotte asked.

"Transliteration. It means that every aspect of this language is identical to ours. Identical. The only difference is that the marks or symbols are different. Because they labeled their writing of the word directly beneath the building or street, as it's written here in NHHMM, it's not at all hard to translate."

Charlotte looked confused.

"Here, let me show you." Nina walked over to the chalkboard in her classroom. She taught three courses at South Central: NHHMMian grammar, Cryptology, and Literature. "I know this street intersection. This is Magda's Bakery. Next to it is the Capitol

Bank. Notice," she said, quickly writing on the board, "that each word has the same number of letters. There is a mark here showing that the bakery belongs to Magda. The symbols are different, but they are still marks. The spacing between characters is the same."

"This is easy to figure out?"

"Simple, but that's what's so odd. If what you say is true, and I'm not sure I believe it —that there are people here visiting from another world —the odds against two different places mirroring each other's language and words are just... I don't even know how to calculate it all."

"I'm not sure I understand," Charlotte replied.

"What is this?" Nina said, pointing to a small frame on her desk.

"It's a picture of your daughter, Gabrielle."

"Ok," she said, breaking the chalk in half and giving one piece to Charlotte. "Go over to that side of the board and make up a word for 'daughter'. It can be as long or as short as you want. The letter placement doesn't have to follow any of our grammar rules. I'll make up my word on the other side of the board. When you are ready, let me know and we will compare them."

Charlotte followed Nina's directions, made up a word, and wrote it on the board. "I'm finished," she said.

"So am I," Nina replied. "Now, let's step back and see what we have."

Charlotte had written the word MISTUUBNIK. Nina's word was I-bin.

Charlotte laughed. "They are nothing alike," she said. "Nothing."

"And we are spelling the word with characters that are common to us."

"I see your point, but what does this mean?"

"My best guess is that these worlds are somehow connected. Either they, whoever they are, based their language on NHHMMian, or we based our language upon theirs."

Star, Roland, and Ashlyn were walking up the hill toward the school, carrying water and an assortment of fresh food, when they saw Ethan walking in their direction. Holding on to his arm, Noola took cautious steps, looking so frail that she might break with one wrong movement.

Roland dropped his things and rushed over to them. "Can I help you?"

Noola shook her head. "Ethan says you raised him?"

"Yes, ma'am," Roland replied. "For the most part."

"You did well. Are you Roland? Roland Flynn?" she said, holding out her hand.

"Yes. I'm Roland," he replied, accepting her hand.

"I remember you. You were the one keeping Ryan O'Connor in line." Without giving Roland a chance to reply, she added, "I'm Angeline Vanderschmidt."

"It's good to see you alive," Roland replied. "We were afraid we might not get to you in time."

"Thank you," Angeline replied. "Can I get something to eat and drink, and then can you take me to see my grandson. Well, I won't exactly see him, but I'm confident I will know his voice."

The Council met at the well-protected Vanderschmidt research facility in a room that was fifty feet below ground. Except for Roland, Ashlyn, and Ryan, everyone was in attendance. Mr. Vanderschmidt tapped his cane on the floor to get everyone's attention when it was time to start.

"I only have two things that we need to discuss today. If there are other items, we will have plenty of time to discuss them. Since both items are somewhat related, I've asked Charlotte Mayberry to begin with her new information, as it may well be relevant to the second topic. Charlotte..."

Charlotte Mayberry stood and walked over to a large table at the front of the room. "In our last meeting, we learned about the attempted invasion of NHHMM, and of this black flag that was attached to the ship we destroyed," she said, lifting up the corner of the flag. "I can now tell you exactly what the writing means. The letters spell out a phrase which is translated as 'Yehud Subdues All.'"

"And you know this how?" Campbell questioned.

"Since our last meeting, I retained someone to follow and identify those who are spying on our world. At my direction, this person acquired one of their notebooks. I took the notebook to a friend of mine who is knowledgeable in grammar, literature, and cryptography.

She has not only decoded the notebook...that we acquired, but also the letter left in the warehouse."

"And...?" Jack asked impatiently.

"The front of the notebook has a series of prayers written, which identifies the deity they worship as Yehud. However, the letters refer to their leader as the emperor of Yehud. I have the translations here on the desk for you to review. It appears that the invaders are a conquering world, based upon the flag and the prayers. The flag says 'Yehud Subdues All,' and the notes and salutation on the letter appear to solicit Yehud to aid them in their current conquest... NHHMM."

"And how do we know that the translations are correct?" Professor Wimberly asked.

"Nina Mineaux, one of your teachers, did the translations."

"Oh," Professor Wimberly replied. She knew Nina Mineaux to be brilliant, thoughtful, and anything but rash. If Nina Mineaux said this was the translation, then Wimberly knew it had to be correct.

The people in the room broke out into a series of smaller conversations, each discussing what this could mean and the impact on their world. Charlotte passed around the notebook, letters, and translations to Campbell, who reviewed them and then passed them around the circle.

Vanderschmidt took control of the room by tapping his cane again. "Thank you, Charlotte. I don't recall the Council authorizing this course of action, but it is clear you have given us something very valuable. Now," Vanderschmidt said in an effort to move the group to the second item, "before we discuss this in greater detail, I think that the next item will be valuable to our effort as well."

"But I'm not finished," Charlotte interrupted. "There is more that you need to hear."

"Very well," Vanderschmidt conceded. "Please continue.

"Probably the most important thing that Ms. Mineaux told me is that the two languages are directly related. The only difference between the two languages is that the letters are different characters. The grammar, the number of characters in each word, and the punctuation are exactly the same."

"What does that mean?" Merten Ashwillow asked.

"She says that the two languages are built upon each other. That either our language is based on the language of the Yehud, or it is the other way round," said Charlotte.

The room burst out into both conversation and questions, with only one person sitting quietly in his chair. Jonathan Vanderschmidt didn't say a word, but his face was contorted with emotion. He gripped the knob of the cane until his knuckles turned white. His brilliant mind was sorting through the memories and facts that resided there. He bit on his bottom lip as he contemplated Charlotte's words.

"Jonathan," Professor Wimberly whispered, leaning over from her chair toward Vanderschmidt, "you need to get control of this."

"ATTENTION!" he called out. "Let me have your attention. We can debate and theorize after we have the facts. We must have the facts. Charlotte, please continue."

She began by explaining the special assignment she had given to Ginger Coltrane. Jack Flynn gave Drake Gordon a disapproving look. In Jack's mind, Ginger was never a part of The Darkest Night's crew, but more one of his own personal associates from the staff of The Lying Fisherman.

Step by step, Charlotte explained what Ginger accomplished leading up to the night of the conflict with the Yehud, and the survivor named Fabarge.

"And how did you happen to be in the warehouse that night?" Jack's voice had a mix of frustration and skepticism. "And why didn't you take steps to make sure Ginger was never in any danger?"

Charlotte raised an eyebrow and cocked her head a bit to the side. "My Dear Jackie, I sensed she would soon be discovered, so I made sure to keep a personal eye on her to ensure that no harm came to her. What is it that's bothering you? Are you upset that I didn't ask anyone's permission to do what I thought was right, or because I didn't kill everyone in the room, or because of something else completely different? Please understand I'm not here to seek the Council's blessing for what I've already done. I'm not seeking anything. I'm simply trying to give this council some insight into the adversary's intent on taking over our world."

An uncomfortable silence filled the room, and the tension between Charlotte and Jack could be felt by everyone.

"If there are no other interruptions, I will continue with what I've learned. The Yehud are a political group that uses religion to promote their political and military agendas.

"Can you explain what you mean by a religious group?" Pricilla Wimberly asked.

"They believe in an all-powerful god, a deity, a creature that commands all people to behave in a specific way. They believe that the emperor is the voice of their deity, and he interprets the deity's words to the people. Their beliefs are delivered to the people by the emperor as laws or decrees. The decrees are called The Laws of Yehud, their god, and as a result, the followers of these laws are called the Yehudi. I don't have a complete understanding of the Yehud. I only have bits and pieces. To the Yehud, women exist to serve men and to bear them children. The penalties for breaking the laws of their god are harsh, severe, and have no foundation in what we would call justice."

"Did the prisoner give you any idea of what they do when they take over a world?" Vanderschmidt asked.

"The men are enslaved, conscripted into their military or into their factories, and the women are traded like commodities."

"But why are they here?" Jack demanded. "What do they want with NHHMM?"

"May I finish, please?" Charlotte said, showing frustration. Not waiting for an answer, she continued. "But that is not the worst part of what they do. They take the children. That's why their ships are so big. The first thing they do when they take over is to remove the children. They literally ship them out to their home world and then sell them to wealthy buyers in every world they come into contact with. Girls. Boys. It doesn't matter. According to Mr. Fabarge, there is a book that their emperor keeps. It is a book of buyers and orders. Orders are placed from the worlds they've conquered or made contact with. Gender, age, skin color, hair color, eye color, and the list goes on and on."

There was silence in the room. No one said a word, but a look of shock and disgust was on every face.

"So, Jack, to your question. Why NHHMM? Somehow, they know about our crystals...and they want them. They want to enslave our world, mine our crystals, and use them to continue their expansion to the next world. As disgusting as we may find it, taking the children is its own type of brilliance. Depending on how you define a generation, every world they take over loses one to two generations nearly immediately. Then they farm the remaining population as they age. There can be no resistance because the Yehud continually controls the population."

"But their technology is inferior to ours?" Chamberlain asked.

"Yes. Based upon what I was told, the Yehud only use the crystals to move from one place to the next. Either they see no need to develop other uses for the crystals, as we have, or they lack the scientific knowledge to create new applications."

"How are any of them already here?" Jack asked, without looking at Charlotte.

"There is no way to know. Our prisoner says they have at least fifty access points set up across NHHMM, and several people have already been placed in our government. As for how many people of the Yehud are already here, I have no idea."

"And where is this man, Fabarge?" Captain Gordon asked. "We need to learn more from him. We need to understand where they are weak. Where we have an opportunity to defeat them."

"Recuperating," Charlotte replied. "He was shot by one of his own people."

"Where is he, then?" Gordon asked.

"He's asked me to give him time to heal before he has to fall under the scrutiny of questions. He will be able to speak with any of you when he is better."

It was clear to everyone in the room that Charlotte had no intention of giving them access to Fabarge, and that realization felt like a betrayal. With her refusal, the Council meeting ended on an awkward note. Vanderschmidt declared the meeting over, and they quickly dispersed, leaving the room and breaking into groups of two and three. Jack caught Charlotte as she headed for the door.

"Can we talk?" he asked.

"Not tonight," Charlotte answered. "There are too many things to think about at present, and I'm not exactly in the mood to talk with you right now.

Clyde Vanderschmidt was tinkering with the left motor of the airship when Roland approached. "Clyde, do you have a moment? I need to speak to you."

"Can you give me a few minutes? I...need...to...finish this adjustment," he managed to say, as he tugged on a wrench inside the motor.

"This is important."

"Yeah? And so is making sure this motor is secure. We don't want to be airborne and have the propeller start to swing. It could cut right through the cabin. I'm almost done...just be patient."

"James Clyde Vanderschmidt," a voice behind him called out, "stop what you are doing and come give your grandmother a hug."

Clyde froze in place, tilted his head to one side, and then slowly turned around. His eyes grew big as he looked upon the woman he believed to be dead, and then they narrowed as his brow furrowed and confusion took over his expression. "Gram, where have you been? What happened to you?"

Angeline released her grip on Roland and took a cautious step forward. She raised her arms and held them open, then motioned with her hands for Clyde to come to her. When he was a toddler, she would have scooped him up in her arms, but that hadn't been possible in years. Clyde was five the last time she saw him, and she was content to simply hold him. He wrapped his arms around her and lifted her frail body off the ground. The emotion of the moment washed over her, and she cried unshed tears.

Roland backed away from Angeline and her grandson, walking toward the others in town.

"How did it go?" Ethan asked as Roland approached.

Roland nodded. "Pretty well, I'd guess. I don't know if Clyde is going to leave Angeline here or if he is determined to take her back. I think it's probably best if they come to her, but that's not my decision to make. You, however," he said, putting his hand on Ethan's shoulder, "made the right decision. I don't think she would have lasted another week."

Ethan didn't reply. He just looked at Angeline and nodded his head.

For the next few hours, Ethan and Roland worked to move Angeline's things from her office to an abandoned residence near the center of town. The move would put her closer to fresh water and allow her to access the sunshine if she decided to stay. Her filing cabinets were the biggest challenge, as the two had to move them down the stairs to the electric underground train. Once they figured out how to work the train, all they had to do was navigate the last set of stairs up to ground level.

Star and Ashlyn spent their time looking for the right place to set up a portal. Enclosed in a hinged metal box to protect it from the elements, the clock inside would allow members of the Resistance to move from their current location to Arcborne in seconds rather than hours or days. They decided to place the box far out in the field on the far side of the city, close enough to allow supplies to move into the town, but far enough away that nothing could impede the actual movement of people and things.

The stench of rotting food and meat made their stomachs wretch, so their final task of the trip was to clean it out as much as they could. They debated about burning it all, but Roland argued that the wild animals posed a bigger threat than the smoke would ever create. After all, no one noticed the smoke from fireplaces when Arcborne was open. When the last of the trash was moved to a heap, away from town at the base of the mountain, Roland set the rotting food ablaze. They walked back to the center of the city, where they found Angeline and Clyde sitting at a table in the bakery, where Ethan had given Star her birthday gift.

"Hungry?" Clyde asked. "I've got some food cooking in the kitchen."

"Very," Ethan answered. "What are we eating?"

"Couldn't make much with the supplies we brought, but I've got some beef stew in the pot. Carrots, potatoes, and onions. Got some bread warming, no..." He sniffed. "Burning. Excuse me." He stood up quickly and rushed into the kitchen.

"How are you feeling?" Star asked as she sat down next to Angeline.

"Overwhelmed," she said. "Emotionally. Physically. Overwhelmed."

"Can I get you anything?"

"No. I'm just trying to absorb everything that's happened."

"I'm sure it's a lot to take in," Ashlyn said.

"Can you tell us what happened?" Roland asked, and Ashlyn cut him a look that clearly said he was being pushy.

"About this?" Angeline replied, pointing to her face.

"Yes," Roland replied, as Ashlyn rolled her eyes and shook her head.

"It's alright, dear," she said back to Ashlyn. "He isn't being rude."

"But I thought you couldn't see?" Ashlyn queried, embarrassed that she had noticed her reaction.

"Every living thing has a frequency. Crystals have a frequency. I can see your frequency. Your frequency is in your arms, hands, and fingers. It's all throughout your body. If you move your arm, I can see the frequency move. And I've even been able to learn how that translates to a disapproving shake of your head. I can't see your eyes, mouth, or nose, and if your fingers aren't spread very far apart, I can't identify each one, but I can tell if you're waving at me. Don't ask me how it all works. I've not figured that out yet. My best guess is that some...several of the crystals ended up on or near my optic nerves. I could be completely wrong about that, but that's my suspicion."

"But what happened that caused the explosion? Do you remember?" Roland asked.

"My team and I were working late in the warehouse facility. We were measuring and logging the frequencies of different crystals. Because the crystals react to each other in powerful ways, we kept them separated by color. Each color was in its own secure part of the building. While we've discovered red, white, green, and blue crystals on our planet, none of them, in any combination, deliver the kind of cataclysmic explosion that happened that night. I think someone outside of our team introduced a different element into our environment."

"What do you mean?" Roland knew how carefully the research was monitored, and the thought of someone else entering the secure workplace concerned him.

"From the windows in the laboratory, we saw lights moving in the warehouse. It was common for the security team to make regular rounds in the building, but it didn't move like them."

"Move?"

"Yes. The guards were very systematic in their movements. They would go down one aisle, and then another. These movements were random, like someone was looking for something, but wasn't sure where to look."

"Then what happened?"

"There was an alarm button in the lab, and I pushed it. If it were an intruder, the security guards would handle it. If it was nothing, then the guards would check it out and make sure. We were scientists. We weren't prepared to confront a stranger in the dark." Angeline cleared her throat and then reached for a glass of water that sat before her on the table. Her hand felt its way across the wood until she touched the glass. She took a long drink and then continued:

"Once the alarm started, we heard movement and voices. The last thing I remember was a crash, like someone had run into something. I could hear crystals falling from the shelves onto the ground, and then there was a horrific groaning. It sounded like our very world was being ripped apart. There was a blinding yellow light and then an explosion, unlike anything I've ever experienced or learned about. The glass in the windows shattered and flew toward me. And then...then it seemed like it was sucked back in the other direction. Right after that, a wave of crystals came through the window, battered my body, and took my eyes."

"Who's hungry?" Clyde said as he exited the kitchen, carrying a bowl in each hand.

He was greeted with stunned silence from everyone in the room, except Angeline. "I'm hungry," she said.

As everyone else ate, and Clyde updated Angeline on the rest of her family, Star got up and slipped outside. Walking to Angeline's new home, she went inside. She took the folder she brought from the airship, containing the home addresses of every student and faculty member at Arcborne. She carried it back to the bakery, took her seat at the table, and began to scan over the names on the list. Some of the names brought a smile to her face, and others, like Daniel Craven, caused her to frown.

"What are you doing?" Ethan asked, noticing the folder.

"Just looking over the list of home addresses of the other students. I've got Dorn, Tristin, Meghan...and here is Renny."

At the mention of Renny's name, Clyde stopped his current conversation and looked over to Star. "Renny Patel?" he asked.

"Yes," Star answered. "Renny was one of our few friends. Ethan more so than me, but yes, we know him."

"I love Renny," Clyde exclaimed. "He has an amazing mind, and he has been so much help to us in a short time."

"But how do you know Renny?" Ethan asked.

"He works for a company that my grandfather put money into. Outside of helping manage the company's finances, he's been helping the company adapt the electric motor we have to a rider."

"What's a rider?"

"It's a two-wheeled motorized machine that you ride like a horse. It features fat tires that allow you to drive it almost anywhere, and it is remarkably fast. As I understand it, Jack Flynn rode one when you went to Arcborne to deliver the clock, so you could get back to us when you noticed it."

"Yes, but the problem was I didn't notice it. Not until a short time before we used it to escape."

"Clyde, is there a portal there at the company?" Star asked, pulling her hair behind her ear.

"Of course. There is a storage room that they keep empty. We go there from our research facility, and they come to us."

"But does he know what we are all mixed up in?" Ethan asked cautiously.

"I don't know. I don't say much about anything that's going on with my family or the Resistance. That was drilled into me from the time there was a Resistance."

"What is the clock setting you use?" Star asked.

"One."

"Ethan," Star offered, "maybe we can go visit him sometime."

"I like that idea. Maybe..." Ethan started, before Roland cut him off.

"There will be time to reconnect, but we have other problems to sort out before that day may come."

CHAPTER 10

The Angry Goodbye

The White House on Founder's Square would never make it on Jack Flynn's top ten favorite restaurants in New Marchant. It was everything that he wasn't. The guests, both well-groomed and well-behaved, exuded smiles and were quick to offer the perfect compliment for every occasion. "Oh, that's a stunning dress," or "I just adore what you've done with your hair." On the few occasions that Jack felt obligated to dine at The White House, he always felt the smiles he was greeted with would soon be followed by some kind of knife slipped silently between his shoulder blades. As much as he hated the place, it was Charlotte Mayberry's favorite place to dine, so when her invitation to dine with her at eight p.m. was delivered, he knew he would attend regardless of his dislike of both the restaurant and the patrons. He was going away, going away to Retribution, and he didn't know if or when he would return. Charlotte needed to know that, especially in light of their last interaction.

His preparations for the trip were complete, all the papers for him and Shy were finished, and in a week, he would depart New Marchant on what he hoped would be an uneventful journey into the heart of the chancellor's war machine. With polished black boots, a black suit, and a gray waistcoat, Jack looked deserving to be at The White House. Still, the usual sly grin he carried and his tendency to stare at the beautiful women for a few seconds too long would tell all the regulars that he didn't really belong. Opening the door to the restaurant, he quickly scanned the room. He saw Charlotte sitting at a corner table, radiating beauty and elegance.

Jack waved off the white-gloved maître d'hôtel who attempted to stop him at the door and walked directly toward Charlotte. She stood as he approached and gave him a playful smile. Her dress was made from a shimmering gold fabric that hugged her figure and accentuated her curves. Her brown hair was pulled up loosely behind her head with wavy tendrils falling just in front of her ears. Standing, she took Jack's hand and kissed him gently on the lips.

"You clean up so well," she said, smiling. "Have you figured out yet that I like the place, not for the food, but because it forces you to play the part of a gentleman, for at least one night?"

"And you, dear Charlotte, are a vision. How could anyone in this place even notice me when you are nearby?"

"See what I mean?" she said, sitting back down. "This place brings out the best in you."

"I was going to say it was the company of a beautiful woman, but I think you're right...it must be the sophistication of this pompous lot." He gestured with a sweep of his arm.

Her nose wrinkled when she frowned. "You were doing so well, and then you just had to add in that last part."

"We both know that I would never be in this place if it were not for the woman who sits before me."

"That's kind of you to say. Thank you. What are we drinking tonight?"

"I'm curious. I wonder if they would have my drink of choice..."

"Rum?"

"Glow."

"I'd have to agree with you on that. The White House isn't the kind of place that would serve bootleg spirits."

"Then you understand my predicament."

"Yes, Jackie, and that's why I took the liberty of ordering wine. And don't worry, I picked one even you would enjoy." As she spoke, the sommelier delivered the wine, poured a glass for Charlotte, and then moved to fill Jack's glass. Jack motioned for him to stop and then spoke in a voice so low that the employee had to lean in to catch his words.

"I've got a special request," Jack said. "How difficult would it be to get a serving of Glow?"

"We are a reputable establishment," the sommelier bristled. "We don't have non-licensed spirits on the menu."

"And what is your name?" Jack asked.

"Hennessee."

"Well, Hennessee, let's pretend for a moment that I was...the chancellor. Would you be able to serve me an item not on the menu then?"

"But, sir, you are not the chancellor."

"Clearly," Jack replied. "Let's try this another way." Reaching into his jacket pocket, he removed a small bag. Opening it, he took one coin out and placed it on the table. Charlotte raised an eyebrow, and a sly smile adorned her lips. "Let me know when you can find my drink."

Jack then placed another coin beside the first. "You see, the trick to this game is knowing what my limit is. Take too long because greed got the best of you, and I take them off the table. Act too quickly and you get less than what I would have paid."

Hennessee looked at the two coins and then back over his shoulder. With a look of somber resolution, he looked back at Jack and didn't flinch. Jack waited a moment and then reached into the bag and placed a third coin next to the other two. "Does the chancellor have a preference?" Hennessee asked.

"Do I have options?"

"No, sir, I was just being polite," he answered, reaching for the coins.

Jack placed his hand over the coins. "When the drink is on the table," he said, then added, "And make it a healthy pour."

"Of course." And with a nod of his head, Hennessee left the table and disappeared around the corner.

"Such drama over a drink," Charlotte noted, with a roll of her eyes.

"I was making a point," Jack said.

"What point? That you can overpay for bootleg spirits?"

"No, that they do sell it, and I've learned that I need to charge them more."

Charlotte laughed. "You sell them the Glow?"

"Of course." Jack smiled as Hennessee returned and placed the glass in front of him. Scooping up the coins from the table, Jack put the gold in the sommelier's hand. "That's not entirely accurate," Jack continued after Hennessee left the table.

"What's not accurate?"

"I don't technically sell it to this place; someone else does it for me, but now that I know what they think the price should be, it's clear I need to charge more."

"Can we order food now, or is that going to be a long process as well?"

Their dinner orders were taken, and the food was finally served. Their conversation was unnatural, with long pauses between each topic, and Jack couldn't help but feel that they were both avoiding something, putting something off. Following this awkward silence, there was no other option but to ask her directly: "What are you not telling me?"

"What do you mean?"

"This, this evening doesn't feel right. Something's off."

Charlotte sighed and nodded her head. "There is something, but I don't feel like you are yourself, either. Why don't you tell me what's on your mind, and I'll tell you what's on mine."

Jack nodded and looked into her eyes. "I'm leaving tomorrow. I don't know when I'll come back, or even if I'll come back."

"Where are you going?" she replied, with a scowl on her face.

"I can't tell you that."

"So, that means you are up to something and the Council hasn't given you its approval."

Without giving her a reply, he just smiled at her.

"That's a shame. You see, the reason I invited you to dinner was to propose that we become business partners. I'm about to start a new business, and I won't have time for the Council any longer. And to answer your next question...I can't tell you that."

"Have you told the Council?"

"No," she answered, with a slight shrug. "You are the only one who knows I'm stepping away, and I'm the only one who knows why."

Jack let out a slight laugh. "So, you aren't going to give me even a hint?"

"Will you?"

"Ah, now we are negotiating."

"Not really. Jackie, you would lose if this were a real negotiation. I would call this more like...pre-departure foreplay."

"Go ahead," Jack replied as he raised his glass to his lips. "You go first."

Charlotte went to speak, stopping before a single word came out, and then thought for a moment. "When are you going to start thinking about yourself? The Council doesn't listen to either of us. They're behaving like a scared child, afraid of what will happen if they make the wrong decision. I don't need a hint to know what you're about to do. It is Resistance-related; it has to be. Ever since your father got back to NHHMM, you don't seem to have any other focus."

"My father has nothing to do with the decisions I make."

"Really? Then put your plan aside and join me. I'm about to embark on the greatest business venture NHHMM has ever known and will ever know. Put aside the battles you see on the horizon and join me. Let's build something spectacular." She put her hand across the table and waited for him to take it in his. He didn't. "But I really didn't think you could do that." She sighed, pulling her hand back. "Jack, you aren't your father. He has this fatalistic nobility about him that says he must always do the right thing, even if it isn't good for him. That isn't you. I really don't know why Ashlyn puts up with him. He goes away for years, leaves her alone, and then he takes her off on another high moral quest that will probably end in disaster. Don't waste your life trying to be like him. Put the Council aside and join me."

Swilling the clear liquid around in his glass, Jack gritted his teeth and then took a deep breath. His eyes flashed like fire, and he put both hands on the glass so she couldn't see him shaking with anger. He brought the glass to his lips, opened his mouth, and tossed the remaining Glow to the back of his throat. It burned as it slid down, and he winced a bit. He resisted the urge to tell her not to speak about his father like that, because he knew it would only prove her point. Reaching into his jacket pocket, he removed the small bag and placed several coins on the table. "Foreplay's over, my dear. I wish you the best of luck in your business venture. And while you're off becoming even more wealthy, I'll do my best to make sure that NHHMM is still a place worth living in." Standing up from the table, he gave her a slight bow and left the restaurant. For the first time in his life, he felt a little like his father, and he wasn't sure at all that he liked the feeling.

"Oh, Jackie," she said aloud, as she watched him leave. "You have no idea how much you will regret this decision."

No matter how hard he tried, Clyde could not motivate his grandmother to return home with him. Angeline was resolute in her decision. She wanted to meet with her husband, Jonathan, first, and she wanted him to come to Arcborne. After they had a chance to meet with each other, she would expand her reintroduction to the rest of the family.

When the sun finally fell below the mountains and drifted below the horizon, Clyde gave his grandmother a hug, kissed her on the forehead, climbed into the metal airship cabin, and sat behind the controls. Ethan and Roland untied the tethers and pushed the metal poles back and forth until they were able to remove them from the ground. Then they placed them into the cabin and slid the door closed.

"Clear?" Clyde asked through an open window.

"Clear," Roland called out. "Travel safe."

Clyde turned on the engines, and a minute later, the propeller rotated down and the airship rose slowly into the night sky. Ethan watched until it disappeared over the mountains and out of sight.

Ashlyn took her husband's hand, and they started walking out into the field toward the portal.

"Coming?" she called out, looking over her shoulder towards Ethan and Star.

"In a bit," Star replied. "We're going back to search some of the buildings we didn't get to when we were here last."

Unconcerned because of the security that Arcborne created, Roland waved at them. "It's probably better this way," he said to Ashlyn. "It's probably best if we take the wrath of their parents before they get home."

The bowl that was Arcborne's base reverberated with the loud hum coming from the field. After the brilliant light was gone, Star slid her arm around Ethan's and turned him toward the school.

"What are you up to?" Ethan asked with a curious look.

"Would you agree that we're going to be in trouble with our parents when we get back?"

"Most likely."

"So, if we are already in trouble, why don't we do something that will be both fun and strategic?"

"Then the plan is to get into more trouble than we are already in," Ethan said, shaking his head.

"Exactly, but it's all very logical and smart. We enter the school, as I mentioned to Ashlyn, so I didn't lie. We look around for a few minutes, and then we use the portal to visit Renny. It's still early enough that he might be there. We've got the folder containing the addresses of all the other students. Renny may know something about some of them, and we need to make contacts outside of the Council. If we do have to leave everyone, it will be nice to have a contact point with someone else." She looked up at him with a sly grin. "What do you think?"

"I love it. Our parents can't be that much more upset with us than they already are. But now we'll have the ire of Roland and Ashlyn to contend with."

"I don't think so," she said, as they started up the hill to the school. "I think they would probably approve."

"Maybe. But I'm more worried about our mothers. What word do you think we will hear more than once?"

"Irresponsible. Reckless, maybe."

"Irresponsible is my guess."

"Then let's find something that will be worthwhile, but let's change our destination."

"Where are we going?" Star asked.

"Dean Vasquez's office. We might find something useful there. She doesn't seem the type to keep important information far away from her control."

The massive great room of the student residence hall was deathly quiet, and each word they spoke seemed to echo around them. As soon as they made the turn to the hallway leading to the dining area, they were hit with a smell far worse than the center of town. At least in town, there was the natural air circulation that pushed the odors of rotting food away, but here, in the residence hall, the stench coming from the kitchen was overwhelming. Ethan gagged from the smell and pulled his shirt up over his nose. Star took a clean, white napkin from a dining table and held it up to her face to filter the air.

The last and only time he was in Dean Vasquez's office was when she was yelling at him, but he still remembered. Taking a right at a connecting hallway, he continued on toward the closed door at the end of the wooden floor. "Do you think it will be locked?" Star asked with a muffled voice.

"Probably," Ethan replied, as he turned the doorknob and pushed on the door with his shoulder. It didn't move. Unsure if it was a turn lock, he used the combination he remembered from the doors in the basement of the department buildings. It didn't work. He went through the sequence options involved in a four-turn lock, and still the door would not open. "Be right back," he said, running back down the hallway. Two minutes later, he was back, carrying a meat cleaver.

"How was the kitchen?"

"Disgusting. Really disgusting." Sliding the blade of the meat cleaver between the door and the frame, he pulled on the handle, and the door popped open. They stepped inside, and Ethan closed the door behind them. Pulling his shirt away from his nose, he cautiously inhaled. While the room smelled musty, the aroma of rancid meat fortunately hadn't invaded its space.

Star found a switch for the electric lights and turned them on, revealing the room's vast size. Along the entire wall behind Dean Vasquez's massive wooden desk was a bookcase filled to capacity on every shelf. In the right corner, opposite the bookcase, sat a round metal table, and on it were pictures of what Ethan assumed to be Vasquez's family. In the left corner was a model of Arcborne, complete with the school, the city, and the surrounding mountains on every side.

Ethan immediately moved to the desk and began opening the drawers. Two were locked, and he used the meat cleaver to pry them open, just as he had done with the door. There was nothing of any great importance that he could find, and so he turned to the bookcase instead.

"Come look at this," Star beckoned.

Ethan stood behind her and looked over her shoulder as she spoke. "There are four peaks on the mountain ring, like the four points on a compass. But the stone pedestal it's resting on is square, and the mountain peaks don't align with the corners."

Ethan looked it over and nodded. "Yeah, it doesn't look right to my eyes either, but..."

As he spoke, Star put her hands on two of the opposite mountain peaks and tried to rotate the model. It moved, and when it did, a popping sound was emitted behind them. They turned to look at the bookcase and saw that the far-left section was no longer aligned with the others.

Ethan walked over to the section and examined it with a careful eye. On the middle shelf, underneath the wood, was a small metal plate that extended an inch below the book support. Putting his hand under the shelf and his fingers behind the plate, he jerked it back. Star smiled as the model shifted back to its unaligned position before it was rotated.

"Again?" she asked.

"Yes." The model rotated, the mechanism behind the wall popped, and the bookcase shifted slightly. This time, Ethan put his hands on the section and pushed. The bookcase slid back, and he stepped into the darkness beyond. After finding a light switch, he stared in awe at what was before him. Star came through the new doorway and stood beside him.

Opposite them was a blackboard that filled the entire wall. On the board were chalk-drawn boxes, each titled with notes that appeared to be priorities. The side walls and the rest of the doorway wall were lined with metal filing cabinets, each with three drawers. A metal table, about four feet in diameter, was positioned in the center of the room along with a leather chair that boasted overstuffed arms. On the table were three wooden trays, each four inches tall, filled with papers.

"Where do we begin?" Star said as she took it all in.

"We don't have time to go through all of this right now. Not if we still want to try and see Renny. Let's take the three trays on the table back into town and then see if we can find Renny. Before we leave for Tearmann, we can pick up the trays and take them home. Make sense?"

"Yes," Star said with a nod. "We can always come back for more when we have time, but this should at least give us something to support our delay in getting back to Tearmann."

Finding a match for Jack was easier for him than it was for Shy. Eight of the fourteen people headed to Retribution were men, and of those, Jack could reasonably be a match for five of them. It would require a new identification paper, but that wasn't a problem for someone with his connections. Shy, however, was a different situation. Only six women were making the trip. Three were married to men also going, and one was an engineer with advanced degrees. As good as Shy was, Jack knew she couldn't pretend for long to know technical information that she'd never learned. Either of the other options would work based upon her preference, and Jack had his own point of view, but it would be Shy's choice.

When his dinner date with Charlotte was over, Jack meandered over to the place where Shy rented a room, still angry about how the date went. He was ready to resolve the next part of his plan. Shy opened the door and gave him a look of exaggerated surprise.

"This is an unexpected surprise," she said, looking him over. "You obviously dressed up for someone. I've heard your dates go well into the early morning. Losing your touch with Sinead?"

"I wasn't with Sinead tonight, but nothing is going on with her. She complains about everything," Jack answered. He entered the apartment without Shy's invitation and promptly sat down on a red-print cushioned chair and crossed his legs. "After you left, all I heard was that the plate hadn't been washed properly. The meat was slightly undercooked. The vegetables were overcooked. The waitress wasn't quick enough, and the overall seasoning of the meal was off."

"And can you imagine what it'll be like when you're married, and she isn't on her best behavior?"

"That's not going to happen." Jack shuddered. "Never. No. Not if you gave me a choice between her and a life in Hardscrabble."

"All I can say is that as a girl, watching another girl, she has a different idea. Every girl likes the bad boys like you, and they all think they can rehabilitate you. And then when they do, if they do, they don't like you as much."

"I'm beyond rehabilitation, and it really doesn't matter; we will be on our way a week from now. Can you leave that quickly?"

"That was fast. Of course, I can leave by then. I don't have anything holding me back here. Who are we going to be?"

"My job will be easy. I'll be Wilhelm Klein, the new manager of The Black Valley Tavern, and you have two choices. You can be Shilo McKenna, who will work as a civilian with the military kitchen staff, or Lois Pebblesmith, who is some kind of mechanic."

"A dishwasher or a mechanic? That's what you've got for me?"

"I never said dishwasher. The paper said kitchen staff, and I said kitchen staff."

"Well, I don't know much about machines, and the kitchen job may give me a more flexible schedule."

"I agree," Jack said quickly, "and there's less chance you will make a mistake with your name. Shy could always be a nickname for Shilo."

"But what is going to happen to the real Klein and McKenna?"

"That's the easiest part. Wilhelm Klein resides in Oppolsby, and McKenna lives here in New Marchant. In the next few days, they will receive job offers that pay them twice what they will make in Retribution. They'll take the legitimate jobs offered by one of our members, and we will take their places."

"What happens if one or both of them notifies the government that they're taking a different job?"

"I've thought about that. Their new employer will ask them if there is a current employer that needs notification of their job change. If they say yes, then our people will take responsibility for doing that, and any paperwork will get lost in transit."

"Clever," Shy said, nodding her head. "We'll need identification papers."

"Now that I know who you are going to be, I can have them created and ready by tomorrow evening."

"Is there anything else I need to bring?"

Jack shrugged. "Honestly, I have no idea. I don't know how thoroughly they'll search us or our things. I've got a way to bring in a mask for each of us, but we can't risk bringing in weapons. They can receive telegraphs, of course, but we may have trouble accessing the equipment. And, we don't know how heavily it's monitored. I've already arranged with Thrasher a set of code words for what we may need, and he's developed a way to accurately drop supplies to us if we need them. All of the new arrivals will be on the same train. I don't know if we will be in the same train car, but it would make sense to me if we were. You can expect that you will be drugged going in, just as they do everything else."

"But I don't have to be...drugged?"

"Not if you can avoid it. I just don't know their process. Will they try to deliver it in food, or in drink, or have they developed something else? The only thing I'm confident about is that they won't allow anyone to see how to get into the place, or where it actually is. That's a secret they'll try hard to protect."

"Do we know each other...inside?"

"If we're all on the same train, then it would make sense that we could have already met. If they have an orientation of some kind for the new people, we could meet there. If not...then we'll have to wait for a natural introduction. Until then, we are strangers in a new place doing a new job."

"And our job is to get as much information as we can?"

"Yes, until we have what we need or the situation changes, that is the plan."

"If we don't know each other," Shy argued, "how are we supposed to communicate?"

"Thanks for reminding me," Jack said, feeling stupid. He reached into his jacket and removed several pieces of folded paper. "I almost forgot. In this paper is a code, known and used by fewer than twenty people in our world. It takes our NHHMMian alphabet and substitutes a series of symbols in place of what we know. But it's more than that. It also changes the basic grammar rules. The papers hold the key, and no one can decipher what you write without that key. Do what you can to memorize the basics before you get there, but above all, don't lose these papers. It'll be hard at first, but I've given you examples of what a sentence would look like normally, and how it would be encrypted."

"How did you learn this?" Shy asked.

"All you need to know is that I grew up with it, and it works. You could paint a message on the wall with red paint across from the Chancellery, and the message would still be safe."

"Thank you. I will keep it safe."

"I'm leaving you with the paper Sinead gave me about Shilo McKenna. It has your departure date and time. I'll have your new identity papers sent over to you as soon as they're ready."

"Be sure and give Sinead my best if you see her before we leave," Shy taunted.

Jack just glared at her and shook his head as he left her apartment.

CHAPTER 11

The Kindness Repaid

Renny Patel held the mask up to the right side of his face, and it quickly adhered to his skin. This mask was connected to a three-foot wire, with two prongs on the end. Turning off the lights to the testing arena, he straddled the rider and sat down. He then inserted the end of the wire into a plug on the steering column and then started up the rider. The only sound the machine made was a slight whirring noise as the crystal-powered generator began to spin. Next to the right-hand grip were two buttons, red and black, and he pressed the black button once. The dark arena immediately sprang to life in shades of green and gray.

Turning the right grip slightly, the rider began to move, and Renny was able to steer around the arena with confidence. Pushing the black button a second time, he put his left hand up to the mask. His hand looked red and fuzzy. There was minimal temperature variation in the arena, so he pushed the black button two more times until the green and gray view returned, allowing him to safely continue his ride.

Next, he pressed the red button several times in a row and watched as the items on the other side of the arena seemed closer and larger. He needed to push the button three more times before his view was back to a standard magnification. The design would work for now, but it wasn't ideal. Renny decided that he needed to split the red button to allow the driver to adjust the magnification up and down with a single touch. Driving the rider over to the arena wall with the light switch, he stopped the machine and turned on the lights. Releasing the mask, he removed it from his face and then unplugged the wire.

It was at that exact moment that he heard the hum coming from a room on the other side of the arena. He dismounted and placed the mask on the saddle before rushing out of the arena and bursting into his office, where he checked a large calendar that hung on the wall. A quick glance told him what he needed to know. There were no scheduled arrivals at the warehouse. He sprinted down the hallway and saw that the door was opening. Throwing a shoulder against it, he pushed the bolt lock closed and then backed away.

"No one is scheduled to be here tonight. Announce yourself, or I will shoot. I have a gun, and I know how to use it," he said, with no gun in his hands.

"Renny," a familiar voice said. "I don't think you have a gun, and do you really want to shoot me with a gun you don't have?"

"Ethan?"

"It's me and Star. Can you let us out?"

"Of course!" Renny slid back the bolt and opened the door. "What are you doing here?"

"We came to see you," Star said, and gave Renny a hug.

"But how did you know I was here?"

"The short answer is Clyde Vanderschmidt. And the long answer is going to take a lot more time," Ethan added. "But what are you actually doing here? What is this place?"

"I work here. I handle the accounting needs of the business, and then I get to work on the fun things."

"What fun things?"

"Oh, Ethan. You have no idea! We make the most amazing things here," Renny said proudly, as he walked them back to his office. "I can't wait to tell you all about it." They went inside, and Renny closed the door behind them. There were shelves all along the walls filled with notebooks, as well as several filing cabinets. Renny's desk was immaculate, not a paper out of place. "Sit down." He gestured to the chairs in front of his desk. "Where have you two been? I kept searching the newspaper for news of the two of you, but I found nothing."

"Ever since Arcborne was shut down, Star and I have been in hiding up in the mountains with some people who were able to help us," Ethan started. He avoided mentioning the exact location and the family and friends who were helping them. It wasn't that he didn't trust Renny. After all, the Vanderschmidts trusted Renny, but he still didn't know who Ethan really was, or anything about Ryan and Anne.

"We heard they were looking for you. It seems like every week, someone is coming into town asking about you, but we never learn anything from them."

"That's why we need to be very careful about what we say to you, Renny. Sooner or later, they're going to find us, and it will be bad for anyone who has any link to Star and me."

Renny laughed. "But, my friend, it will go badly for all of us here if the chancellor learns what is going on. I'm sure you have secrets, but we have secrets here as well. So, please, be honest with me."

Ethan knew he was right. If Renny and his employer were working with Mr. Vanderschmidt, he probably knew about things that were beyond their understanding. Taking a deep breath, Ethan quickly told him about the purpose of Arcborne, the Strategy Department, and the Conquest National Championship. He told him about their escape and the actions of Jack Flynn to seal up the tunnel. The only thing he held back was his real name and the time differential between NHHMM and the other world he called home.

Renny's face showed surprise, but something about him had changed. To Ethan, Renny seemed to have grown up in a matter of weeks. He was self-confident and appeared unfazed by the things he'd just learned. It was as if he was thriving in his new job and environment.

"Promise something for me," Renny said.

"Of course," Ethan replied.

"Promise me that the two of you will come back, so that we'll have more time to talk."

"We promise," Star replied.

"I think," Renny said, "my employer and his family are still here. I want to introduce you to them before they leave."

"Their whole family is still here?" Star asked with a curious look.

"Oh yes. Mr. Cashman. His wife. Their children. This is like a second home to them. They have a special room for their children, located in the building, allowing them to spend more time here. Come with me. Let's see if we can find them."

Star and Ethan followed Renny as he left the office and walked down the hallway. As they turned the corner to a connecting hallway, a short woman in a navy-blue dress approached from the other direction. "Mrs. Cashman," Renny said excitedly. "Please allow me to introduce two very dear friends of mine. We went to school together. This is Ethan and Star."

"It's a pleasure to meet you, ma'am," Ethan said.

"Have we met before?" Mrs. Cashman asked as she studied his face.

"No, ma'am. Not to my knowledge."

"It's funny. I never forget a face, and yours looks very familiar. And I'm sorry, I didn't catch your last name."

"O'Connor. Ethan O'Connor."

Renny shot him a sideways glance, but Mrs. Cashman just stared at Ethan as if she were searching through her mind, trying to find the connection between them.

"Well, Ethan O'Connor, it is a pleasure to meet you...again. If you went to school with Renny and you are half as smart as he, I'm sure you will do well in life."

"Thank you, ma'am. Being half as smart as Renny would be an amazing accomplishment."

"We're going to see Mr. Cashman," Renny said. "Ethan knows Mr. Vanderschmidt, and I wanted to ask him if it was ok for me to show Ethan and Star what we're working on."

Mrs. Cashman kept staring at Ethan, seemingly oblivious to Renny's comments.

Warning bells were going off in Ethan's brain. Does she recognize me from the Conquest Tournament? His photograph was on the front page of every newspaper in NHHMM. Does she recognize me from a poster that the Ministry of Intelligence passed out?

And it was at that point that Mrs. Cashman found the connection she was looking for. Looking at Ethan's face again, she began to smile. "Please, wait right here. Don't move," she said in an excited voice, and then she rushed down the hall and disappeared into a doorway.

"What did I do?" Ethan whispered to Renny.

"Honestly, I don't know."

A few moments later, the boys could hear excited voices coming from the room that Mrs. Cashman entered. And then moments after that, a man's voice called out, "RENNY!"

"That's Mr. Cashman. Let's go. He doesn't sound angry, but he rarely raises his voice. He has a cough, and the yelling makes it worse." Renny and Ethan walked down the hall to the office. Renny stepped inside, and Ethan waited in the doorway. Mr. Cashman sat behind his desk, and his wife stood beside him.

"Come in, young man, come in. And you also, miss," Cashman said, with a rattle in his chest. Ethan stepped into the room, not wanting to get too far from the doorway in case they had to make a fast exit.

"Step a little closer to the light," Cashman requested, and Ethan took two cautious steps toward the desk. "Cassie, you are right. It is him. It is him!" A broad smile came across Cyrus Cashman's face, and he started to laugh. But only for a moment, as the laughter triggered a cough deep in his lungs. "Sit. Sit," he said between coughs, and he motioned to two chairs opposite his desk. Cassie Cashman poured a glass of water from a pitcher on a small table next to the desk and offered it to her husband. Taking in the water with small sips, Cashman got his coughing under control.

"Do you recognize us?" Mrs. Cashman asked.

Ethan frowned. "You look familiar. Your husband more than you, but I can't place either of you."

"Everything that you see here is because of you," Cassie said softly. "Everything. The fact that my husband is still alive is because of you. The fact that my children are healthy is because of you...because of your kindness and generosity. Does that help you remember who we are?"

Ethan's mind was racing, and he sorted through every encounter he'd had since being in NHHMM. "The family in the alley in New Marchant," Ethan said out loud.

"Exactly," Cyrus Cashman stated, with a nod of his head. "I was unemployed, and my family was living on the street. I had no breather, and we had no food. You gave a stranger 2,000 in gold, and the very coat from your back to keep us warm. We are alive today and thriving because of you. Thank you."

Ethan smiled and nodded his head. "But you give me too much credit. I didn't even know how much money I had. I just wanted to help."

"And this," Cashman said, spreading out his arms, "is what your gift did. We were able to get off the street. The gold allowed me to finish a prototype machine I was building. When that was done, it enabled me to find a business partner who invested in my idea, and from that investment came this factory."

Ethan smiled. "I'm glad to see that you and your family are doing well. I don't even know what you do here, but Renny says that you're doing amazing things."

"Well," Cashman said with pride, "we were doing some amazing things before I found my business partner, and now...now what we are working on is beyond anything even my imagination could come up with."

"Can I show them, Mr. Cashman?" Renny asked. "Can I show them what we're doing?"

"The test arena?" Cashman asked. Renny nodded. "Absolutely. We would already be dead if it were not for him. Take him anywhere he wants to go."

"Before we leave," Ethan cautioned, "I need you to understand that people are looking for us. Powerful people. And if they find us with you, I'm afraid they will not treat you well. Because while Ethan O'Connor is my name, most people know me as Ethan Scott."

"Conquest savant? Then you must be Star Chastain," Cashman said, looking at her.

Star nodded. "It's nice to meet you, sir."

"And you also. Yes, they're looking for you, but you're safe while you're with us. Do you recognize those letters on my wall?" He pointed to three metal letters, painted red, each two feet tall. The letters were CMR. The middle part of the 'M' was inlaid with silver.

"No, sir."

"The letters stand for Cashman Mechanical Riders. What does the top of the M look like?"

"It's...a V."

"Yes, it's a V, because my partner in this business venture is named Vanderschmidt. Jonathan Bledel Vandershmidt. And it's the marriage between my invention and his that makes our project more than amazing."

Ethan laughed out loud. "I like the design, and I like the way you hid Mr. Vanderschmidt in plain sight."

"Yes, so we know all about you, Ethan Scott-O'Connor. In fact, when you traveled to Arcborne, your friend Jack followed you on my prototype machine. But until today, we had no idea that you were the one who showed us such kindness."

Roland had reached his breaking point. For the last hour, he had been lectured and berated by parents who blamed him for being irresponsible. Three times earlier, he tried to speak, and three times he was cut off mid-sentence. The attack was coming from Anne, Vallow, and Ryan. Victor Chastain sat quietly in his chair and took it all in. Ashlyn could see the explosion coming, and she tried to calm him with a gentle touch on his arm or shoulder, but even she could see it was getting to the point of no return.

"THAT'S ENOUGH!" he roared, and stood from his chair. "I love and respect each of you, and you..." Roland said, pointing a finger at Ryan, "I've served you for all of your life. I've cared for your son and protected him at the expense of my own life. So, here's what's going to happen next. You will all sit in your seats, without uttering a single word, and I will speak. If you interrupt me, we are finished, and Ashlyn and I will leave tonight. And when I am finished speaking, if you don't want us here, we will leave when you tell us. But let me make it very clear. We will not be chastised for another moment for doing what we believe is right. Is that understood? Just nod your heads, because I don't want to hear any of you speak."

Anne, Vallow, and Ryan sat in stunned silence. Victor reached into his vest pocket, retrieved a match, and lit his pipe as he crossed his legs and settled into his seat.

Roland began to pace. "Ethan is brilliant, and Star is at least Ethan's equal. They are strategic in their thought, logical in their methods, and have already gone through more things in their life than people twice their age." He then pointed at Ryan and Anne. "And before you start trying to blame Star for being a bad influence on your son's actions," he added, before pointing at Vallow. "Or you... If you try to blame him for the same thing, remember this: Star saved your son's life with her blood transfusion, and Ethan saved your daughter's life by taking five bullets for her."

The only time Roland stopped pacing was when he was talking directly to one of the parents. "I don't understand what their relationship is, and I don't know how two people so young can be so well connected. However, understand this: if you want to continue a relationship with your children, you must accept that they are more than you think they are. I've known Ethan longer than any of you, and I know there is something special between the two of them. Don't ruin your relationships by trying to blame someone for your fear.

"Now, let's get to the facts, because if you want to blame us, you will be doing that long after we've gone. Yesterday, Ethan asked me if everyone in Arcborne had gotten out safely, because there was someone important who might have been left behind. I was able to confirm that the person Ethan was concerned about was reported as one of the few people still missing. He convinced me that we needed to look for someone named Noola Klaar, who was still possibly in Arcborne. And this person was scarred by an explosion. SHE HAS NO EYES! How is any man or woman supposed to survive with no help, no food, and no water when they can't see?

"I made the decision to use the portal and go to Vanderschmidt's research facility. I also decided to bring the airship back to Tearmann. Ashlyn decided to accompany me to Arcborne. Ethan insisted on going because Arcborne is an actual city, and he had the best chance of finding Noola Klaar. Star decided to go with Ethan. She chose that. We, Ashlyn, Ethan, Star, and I, all made the decisions to go do what we thought was right. I gave Star and Ethan the responsibility of telling you they were going because it isn't my responsibility to act as an intermediary between your families.

"And guess what? We found Noola Klaar. She was starving, dehydrated, and we brought her the food that saved her life. And, she got to hug her grandson, whom she hadn't touched in years." The look on Ryan's face showed complete confusion, as he knew the airship was a Vanderschmidt invention.

"And the blind woman, Noola Klaar?" Roland continued. "Her real name is Angeline Vanderschmidt. She is Jonathan Vanderschmidt's wife. Now, think for a moment about what you are going to say to Jonathan when you tell him why Ashlyn and I left. You tell him that his wife wasn't worth the anxiety that you, as parents, experienced in one...single...day."

Roland finally paused and deliberately looked at each parent, one at a time. He made eye contact with everyone except for Anne, who would not look at him. "Your children are coming back. I'm not sure if it will be tonight or tomorrow, but they're coming back. They are responsible and trustworthy. They have already offered to leave to keep everyone safe. Don't give them another reason to leave. Don't be that stubborn and narrow-minded.

"I'm finished. We are going to sleep now. We will pack our things, and we can leave in the morning, if that's what you want." Roland then held out his hand to his wife. "Let's go." Ashlyn stood up, took Roland's hand, and they left the Chastain's' home.

"I'm going to my workshop," Victor said, standing up. "He is absolutely right about everything, and we were absolutely wrong with how we treated them." From a small pouch, he stuffed some more tobacco into his pipe, then lit the bowl and walked outside. By the time he closed the door behind him, the Flynns were out of sight.

Star sat on the saddle of the rider, completely transfixed by Renny's directions.

"Ok," she said, putting her hand on the right grip. "I rotate it forward if I want to go fast, and toward me if I want to slow down."

"Yes. Squeeze the metal bars in front of the hand grips to stop. The one on the left controls the breaking mechanism on the back wheel, and the one on the right controls the front wheel. Always use the left one first."

"Why?" Star asked.

"If you use the right one first, you will fly over the front. It's not fun. I know from experience. Are you comfortable with how to operate the mask?"

"I think so."

"Then hold the mask up to the right side of your face." Star's head pulled back as the mask attached to her skin.

"Well, that feels strange."

"You'll get used to it. Now, plug in the wire and start when you're ready. Call out if you want the lights off. Remember, start slow and..."

Star turned the right grip and sped away from Ethan and Renny. "We should probably get behind this wall," Renny offered.

"Is she supposed to go that fast?" Ethan asked as he stood beside a short wall outside the dirt arena.

"No. She's either going to be naturally good at this, or she'll never make the turn at the corner."

It was a feeling Star had never experienced. Her heart was pounding as if she were feeding on the power of the motor. The wall seemed to race toward her, and without panic, she turned the handle to the left. She felt heavy, like the top of her wasn't in balance with the rider, so she leaned into the turn. Pulling back on the grip, the motor began to whine, and her speed decreased. Once she was out of the turn, she rolled the grip forward, and the rider shot off into the next segment.

After two trips around the arena, Ethan heard her call out: "LIGHTS!"

Renny chuckled, leaned over the wall, and turned off the switch that controlled the lights.

Quickly toggling the switch, Star could now see in the darkness. Her heart raced faster, and to her, her face felt like nothing but a smile. As she approached the short wall where Ethan and Renny were standing, she pressed the button that would reveal her heat, and she saw their red glows. "Lights!" she called out a second time, and then she slowed the rider down and brought the vehicle to a stop.

Renny switched on the lights as Star pressed the button to release the mask. "This thing is...AMAZING!"

"Isn't it?" Renny answered.

"Ethan, you have got to try this."

"I will, but not tonight. Now that we have established the connection to the portal, we can access it at any time. We need to get back. Do you have the papers?"

"Yes, in my pocket." She dismounted the rider and walked over to Renny. "Here are the home addresses of all the students in Arcborne," she said, giving him the papers. "Since we can't be seen around NHHMM, it might be good if we can locate some of our friends. We've heard that the chancellor may be picking them up and making them disappear. If you can check in with any of them around here, it might be beneficial, because they have skills and knowledge we might all need one day."

"I can do that," Renny said, nodding.

"Please give the Cashmans our thanks."

"Of course." He gave them both a hug and started walking toward the door. "Let me get you the portal, and then you can be on your way."

They used the portal to get back to Arcborne. There, they said goodbye to Angeline, took the trays, and then walked out into the field to the portal. "How bad do you think it's going to be?" Star asked.

"Bad," he replied, as he set the clock to 9.58, wound it, and closed the metal door. Ethan held out the trays with his arms extended. "Hold on tight."

Star slipped between Ethan's arms and put her arms around his neck, and he dropped his arms around her waist with the stacked trays in his hands.

"Any second now..." Ethan said.

And before the hum started and the light ripped open the night, Star kissed him until they arrived in the barn. The kiss finally stopped when Anne spoke, and the first and only word out of her mouth was, "Irresponsible." She promptly turned around and left the barn.

Vallow held out her arm, and Star came to give her a hug. "I'm glad you're ok," Vallow said, "but please don't do that to us again."

Star didn't reply, but hugged her mother tightly. She wasn't going to make a promise she couldn't keep. "I'm hungry," she said, "Do we have anything to eat?"

"Of course," Vallow replied. "Do you want anything, Ethan?"

"No, thank you," Ethan answered. He watched as Star and Vallow left the barn, and then he looked at Victor and Ryan. "Ok. I'm waiting. Let's get it over with."

"Did you really think there would be no reaction to the two of you leaving?" Ryan asked.

Ethan shook his head. "No, I figured this would not go well."

"Roland told us why you left. I...we understand the motive, but you leave a note on the kitchen table, and think that everyone will be ok with that?"

"Neither of us wanted an argument. Neither of us wanted to fight with our families. Would either of you actually have been supportive if we told you what we were going to do?"

"No," Victor answered. "None of us would have been supportive, and that would have been our mistake."

"Then what would have been worse? Doing what we did, or telling you, then having you tell us 'No,' and then having us disobey you?"

Ryan, realizing that he didn't have a valid argument, shook his head and smiled. "What's in the trays?"

"We went back to Dean Vasquez's office and found a secret room. It seems the room was to house the things that she didn't want anyone else to know about. We took these three folders from a table, but we haven't had the chance to go through them yet."

"No?" Ryan questioned.

"We made another stop along the way that Roland and Ashlyn knew nothing about." Ethan knew they would find out sooner or later, so he thought it was better to just get it over with.

"Where did you go?" Victor asked.

"To see our friend, Renny Patel, from Arcborne. His employer is a business partner with Mr. Vanderschmidt, and they set up a portal in their factory. Star and I took the list of addresses of the Arcborne students that Pops gave us to give to our friend. And no, Pops didn't ask us to give the names to Renny. We can't track any of them down from here, and we hoped that Renny might be able to help. Every student at the school is smart, and they have skills that could be useful to the Resistance. We thought it could be helpful if we could make contact with talented people who might be able to help us."

"Sounds reasonable to me," Victor commented. "Now, if you will both excuse me, I'm going to go back to sleep. Let me know when you want to start your training with me."

"Tomorrow...this morning?" Ethan quickly replied, realizing the sun would be up in a few hours.

"This afternoon," Ryan interjected. "This morning, you are going back to your physical training."

"Ok. I'll see you and Pops in the morning."

"Maybe," Ryan muttered to himself, walking out of the barn.

"Good night, Ethan," Victor said. "It's all going to work out. Don't worry."

"Thank you." When he was alone in the barn, Ethan opened the door to a small feed room and put the trays from Arcborne inside. As he climbed the ladder up to the hay loft, one thought occupied his mind: That could have been much, much worse.

CHAPTER 12

The Yellow Crystal

Roland and Ashlyn slept under the stars as they were both too angry to have any further interaction with the group. Roland wasn't sure how the situation would play out or what the others would decide, but he no longer cared. In his heart, he knew that Anne had little to no experience raising a child and that she was acting out of a purely emotional response. Still, she spoke to him as if he were a servant who had failed in his duties. He would not put up with that again.

"What are we going to do if they want us out?" Ashlyn asked, struggling to fall asleep.

"I think we should go to Arcborne. There is plenty to plan and do before it becomes the new base for the Resistance. Now that we have a portal there, we can come and go as we please."

"What do you think Ethan will do?"

"I don't know," Roland answered, staring up at the sky. Far away from the city, the stars were brilliant and beyond his ability to count. "He could go to Arcborne, Vanderschmidt's facility, or maybe even to Mason Point to stay with his friend. Star could convince him to stay here, if that's what she wanted, but I doubt that would happen. They seem to be aligned on everything. It will be an interesting night. If Ryan and especially Anne can't recover and control their anger, Ethan and Star will leave.

"I've got to tell you, Ro," Ashlyn said as she rolled over onto Roland's shoulder. "Watching you go military on them was impressive. I enjoyed it..."

"Well, when we figure out where we are going to live, we can discuss how much you enjoyed it.

When the sun first peeked over the trees, he slid out from under the blanket and tucked it around Ashlyn. Pulling on his boots and buttoning up his shirt, he looked over to Quinn and whispered, "Stay." The dog sat down at Ashlyn's feet and then curled up into a ball.

He walked down from the meadow and headed toward the barn, thinking Ethan and Star had arrived back in the early morning, but wanting to make sure. As he passed the corner of Ryan and Anne's small home, a voice called out to him.

"Can we talk?" It was Ryan. He was sitting in a chair outside the front door.

Roland nodded. "Come and join me."

"Where are we going?" Ryan asked, standing up and joining Roland.

"The lavender fields seem like a good place to talk."

They walked for several minutes in silence, and as they neared the fields, Ryan finally spoke. "I'm sorry for the way that played out last night."

"Thank you," Roland replied.

"Can we fix this?"

"You apologized. It's already fixed."

"What about Ashlyn?"

"She's more forgiving than I am."

"Then we are good?"

"For the most part. I do, however, need to give you some advice regarding last night, and then I have a different topic to discuss."

"Ok," Ryan said, uncertainty in his voice.

"If you think you are ultimately going to lead our world and this Resistance, if you want that role, you are going to manage Anne's interaction in your political affairs. You can't have a spouse undermine a leader's action with irrational behavior. I would say the same thing to her if the roles were reversed. A leader who yells and pouts and broods, while wanting to punish others for perceived failure, is a tyrant."

"I know," Ryan agreed. "We spoke about it until a little over an hour ago. She and I are both aware of the impact this could have on our team and our efforts. She's going to apologize to you both later, and to the children as well."

"Apologize to the children for what?"

"When Ethan and Star finally showed up, she only spoke one word to them, and it was not kind."

"Then there is nothing else I need to say about it."

"And the other topic you wanted to discuss?"

Roland paused, thought for a moment, and then looked at Ryan. "What do you know about the other nations in our world, and the impact they have on our military strategies?"

The look on Ryan's face told Roland the most important thing he wanted to know. Ryan had heard about the other nations. He looked down, trying to buy time as he came up with an answer.

"What's the context?"

"What do you mean, 'what's the context?' It's a simple question."

"I'm trying to understand why you would ask me that question, and why you would ask me now?"

"And you still haven't answered my question."

"I know a little, and I know nothing."

"Yesterday, when Ethan told me about Noola Klaar, he also told me about what he learned from the chancellor before he escaped. Brighton told him there were three other nations in our world and that our military, specifically the navy, was actively engaged in keeping our ships away from the other nations and keeping them away from us."

"That's what I've heard," Ryan commented.

"And that leads us to my next question. Where did you get your information, and when?"

"You are making this personal, aren't you?"

"Not at all," Roland said, stone-faced. "I'm a part of the Resistance Leadership Council. Making strategic plans with incomplete data is a foolish act. This information is new to me. It may be new to the Council. But every plan that we have made can change based on your answer."

"A year after my father was elected, an odd visitor came to the Chancellery. His clothes were ill-fitting, and he carried a package. He asked to see my father and said he was an ambassador, an emissary. When my father finally saw him, the man offered congratulations from his people and then handed over the package to him.

Dad asked who his people were, and the man shrugged and said, 'We are the sons and daughters of your father's fathers.' The man left without telling my father anything else."

"What was in the package?" Roland asked.

"A yellow crystal."

"But I've never seen a yellow crystal before."

"Neither have I, and I never personally saw this one. I'm only telling you what he told me."

"So, is it just one nation, or are there more?"

"Honestly," Ryan said, with an exasperated tone, "I don't know. If Brighton says there are two others, then he would probably know better than I. My father and I had one conversation about this, six months before the Oppolsby Rebellion. We never spoke about it again."

"Do you have any idea where the yellow crystal could be now?"

"I have no idea. Most likely, Brighton has it. I'm sure that everything my father had ended up in the hands of Chancellor Brighton."

Roland listened, and his mind tried to piece together the options. The invaders could be from a different world or one of the nations in NHHMM. And if they weren't from NHHMM, could they be potential allies...or potential enemies? He tried to think of the best-case scenario, but couldn't come up with one. The Resistance wasn't in a position to recruit new allies when they had no intelligence about where or who those allies might be. And why would an ambassador give a crystal to Declan O'Connor, and did every new chancellor get a crystal after their election?

"Ok," Roland said after a moment.

"That's it?" Ryan asked, looking relieved.

"That's it. We will need to brief the Council at a later time, but this will require a face-to-face conversation. No telegrams."

"I agree. Are we training today?" Ryan asked.

"Absolutely," Roland answered, as he started his way back to the barn. "He needs to know that the work doesn't wait just because he had a late night."

When Ethan's physical training was over for the day, Roland walked into Tearmann, ordered a beer at the local bar, and sat at a small table. Before he left, he took a piece of paper, an envelope, and a pencil from the kitchen in Ryan's home. The paper and envelope he removed from his back pocket, and the pencil he retrieved from the resting place on his top right ear.

He thought for a moment, and then he began to write a lengthy message composed in the symbols he used in the secret code, which was only understood by a small group of people. It took almost an hour to complete the letter, and when he was finished, he placed the letter in an envelope and then wrote "Jack Flynn" on the outside.

Roland finished his beer and then walked back to the barn, where he set the time on the clock and activated the portal. Five minutes later, the barn lit up for a second time, and Roland was back.

"So, what do I do first?" Ethan asked as he sat down in the meadow and leaned his back against a large tree.

Victor Chastain sat opposite Ethan and methodically spread a clean cloth on the ground. Then, from his leather bag, Victor began to remove items and place them on the fabric. "Just a moment," he replied, not looking up from his work. The last things he removed were a small jar of water and a drinking glass.

Ethan watched with curiosity, and Victor positioned everything on a cloth just as a doctor might before a surgical procedure. There were two vials: one contained a substance that resembled a tincture of some kind in a brown bottle, and the other was a tiny jar with yellow flakes. The latter he handled gingerly as if it were of great value.

"Before we get started, I want to ask you about something."

"Sure..." Ethan replied cautiously. "What do you want to know?"

"When you played Conquest with your father, during the game, you...you seemed to speed up your game. Something about you changed. What happened?"

"I really don't know, sir. When I'm angry, or really, really focused, my mind seems to go to a different place. Everything around me seems to slow down, but my mind speeds up. I'm not sure how else to explain it. I don't really have to think, or I'm not aware that I am."

"Has it been that way all of your life?"

"No, not that I remember. I've always been faster than anyone that I've played, but not like this."

"When did you become aware of this increase in speed?"

Ethan thought for a moment, staring at a honeybee buzzing around some wildflowers. "During the tryout for the Conquest team at school, I guess."

"But never before, not that you can recall?" Victor asked, stroking his beard.

"Not that I can recall." Ethan nodded, not sure where the conversation was going.

"Am I correct that in your old world, where you came from, time moves faster there?"

"So I'm told. It's a six-to-one ratio, they say. For every year that you age here, it's like six years there."

"Interesting. One more question before we get started. Are you ever able to shut your mind off? Just exist in the moment you are in, and not think about what you need to do or what problem you need to solve?"

"Sometimes," Ethan said, feeling like that was the answer he needed to give. "But not often."

"Hmm."

Ethan wondered if the "Hmm" was a good "Hmm" or a bad "Hmm."

"If this is going to work for you, you need to try very hard to get to that place. I want you to let your mind be free and not shackled, to do the things you need to do or the things you worry about."

"I don't know that I can do that."

"That's what all of this is for. I'm going to mix a few things into a glass of water, and I want you to drink all of it. It will taste like burned spices at the back of your throat after you swallow. It's not a good taste, but there are definitely some worse things."

"Ok."

Victor immediately began mixing everything together. The jar containing the water was emptied into the glass along with a few drops from the vials. The water was still clear and colorless. Carefully, he took the small container with the yellow flakes and put two into the glass. As he stirred it all together with a small spoon, the liquid turned a bright blue color. "Drink this, all of it. Then close your eyes and

164

relax. You will feel different for maybe fifteen minutes. Colors will be more vivid. Light will be brighter. Look for me, because I will be there. And when you see me, try to talk to me, and I will talk to you. When you open your eyes, I want you to tell me what we talked about."

"And this is how Star learned?"

"For the most part. She already can quieten her mind, but if she didn't...she would have done this as well."

Not understanding much of what Victor was talking about, Ethan took the glass and drank it all. It did taste like burned spices, something he'd never even thought about, assuming there wasn't such a thing as a taste of 'burned spices'. But he now knew what that tasted like. Closing his eyes, he began to relax.

Darkness surrounded him on all sides. Before him, above him, below him, and behind him on either side, he felt like he was standing in a cloud of darkness. A breeze began to move around him, and it shifted the dark clouds, allowing him to see color and light beyond them. He reached out to push the clouds away with his hand, but they didn't budge. And then, from his left, the breeze grew stronger, and an array of color and light began to overwhelm him. He recognized the place. He had been here before. The colors were like shapes, distinct and different from each other. Then, suddenly, they were no longer shapes, but a beautiful palette of overlapping colors. And as he watched, the colors began to take on geometric shapes once again.

Ethan was aware of people around him. Most were wandering all about him, but one person caught his eye. This person was moving with intent, their path of movement a direct line to where Ethan was standing. The person, a man, stopped as he drew near Ethan, and he began to speak. As he did, a bright light seemed to consume the space around them. It was Victor. But as Victor's mouth moved, Ethan's ears could hear nothing.

"Louder," Ethan said. "Can't hear you."

Victor smiled and spoke again. Ethan shook his head. He could hear a garbled sound, but no clear words.

"Again," Ethan shouted. "Louder."

"My mind cannot shout," Victor replied in a soft voice just above a whisper. "Listen more closely."

"That's better," Ethan nodded. "Thank you."

"In the barn, on the second shelf to the left of the entrance, is a bucket. Over the mouth is a soiled cloth. Underneath the cloth and inside the bucket is a folded paper with writing on the inside. It's important that you tell me what the writing says. Can you do that?"

"Yes," Ethan replied. "I can do that."

Victor seemed to move back away from him, and as they ceased their dialogue, the bright light disappeared, and the dark clouds rolled in from every direction.

Ethan's eyes fluttered, and he calmly stared into the eyes of the man across from him. "Thank you," Ethan said, with genuine sincerity in his voice.

"You are quite welcome. Did you find me?"

"You know that I did."

Victor smiled and drew deeply on his pipe. "Did we talk?"

"You know that we did."

"And what did we talk about?"

"Just a moment," Ethan said as he stood up and then proceeded to run across the meadow and down to Victor's workshop. He entered and quickly located the bucket and the paper. As he picked up the paper, his eyes glimpsed a dusty book leaning on the shelf above. Taking the book, Ethan inhaled deeply and blew the dust from the cover. It was a leather-bound book with the title tooled intricately into the leather. The Handbook of Time, Worlds and the Hazards Therin. The author's name was Trosh Reitan. Taking the book in his other hand, Ethan sprinted back up to Victor. Five minutes later, Ethan appeared beyond the tree line, and he ran across the meadow to Victor. In his hand was paper, crushed under his grip. Catching his breath, he held up the paper and showed it to Victor.

"Science is merely a mystery solved. A mystery is an answer science has yet to discover."

"Very good," Victor laughed. "Very, very good."

"I love...this... Who...said...this?" Ethan asked, still trying to catch his breath.

Victor raised his hand and, with a sheepish grin, replied, "Me."

The excitement of his first lesson with Victor Chastain kept them in the meadow talking for several hours. Ethan peppered him with questions about what he'd experienced.

"How long did it last? Will I need the drink every time I do this? What was in the drink? What were the colors? Did I really say what I thought I was saying? Why couldn't I hear you well at first?"

Victor laughed. "Slow down, and I will answer what I can. As I mentioned, it will last approximately fifteen minutes. That's the normal time. That's how long it lasted for you. What's in the drink? It's my secret recipe. All you need to know is that everything is natural. It comes from the world around us. As for how long you will need it, well, that depends on whether you can learn to relax and live in the moment you are in. Now, the colors, I haven't figured out yet. I don't understand the geometric shapes, either. Did you speak out loud so that someone else could hear if they were nearby? No. You didn't make a sound. The reason that you couldn't hear me at first is that you didn't really believe that you could. You saw my mouth move, so you assumed you should be able to hear it, but you didn't. So, you listened more closely, and you heard something. Then it became clear. You went from doubt to belief, to practice."

Ethan absorbed everything he was saying like a sponge, and he remembered the earlier part of the conversation. "You were asking about how I play Conquest and when my rapid play started to happen. What are you thinking?"

"I was afraid you were going to ask me that."

"Why?"

"Because," Victor said, "I don't know how you will take my answer."

"I trust you," Ethan replied. "Just tell me what you are thinking."

"I don't doubt your ability to play Conquest. You are a prodigy. There is no doubt about that. But I think something else is happening. Even though you were born here, in NHHMM, you've spent the bulk of your life in the other world. Time moves much faster there. I think that because you are now here, where time evidently moves much more slowly, your mind can function, calculate, and respond faster than the people here in NHHMM. If I'm right, there is more to moving back and forth through time than just the movement of the hands on a clock or the pages of a calendar. I don't know for sure, it just seems like a plausible theory."

"Then I didn't win because I played better. I won because I cheated."

"No, no. I wouldn't say that at all, and I certainly don't believe that. I think you function in this world very well on your own. However, I also believe it is possible that when you are under stress or must apply extreme mental focus, your brain operates at a faster rate than anyone in our world. And I think it's because you spent so much of your life in a place where time moves six times faster than in NHHMM."

"If what you are saying is true, then the longer I stay in NHHMM, the more my mind will re-adjust to moving at the same speed as everyone else?"

"Not necessarily. There are too many unknown factors. If this change is real, when did it start? Was it an incremental change that happened year over year? Did it have to do with the hormonal changes that occurred as you got older? Was it triggered by our local environment? or is this just how you would have been if you had never left in the first place? There isn't any way of knowing right now. Just be aware that there may be other things that show up in your life. Some may be good. Others not so good."

"Hmm," Ethan grunted. He didn't like the idea that he might be only a fluke of science. Something more than him was born to be, and that didn't feel natural or right. But it bothered him more to think that the overwhelming speed that he possessed might fade over the years. And then he had a different thought: What if I keep getting faster rather than slower?

Sensing Victor wanted to finish up, Ethan decided to ask him about the book he found. "Can you tell me what this book is about?" Ethan asked, holding it up for Victor to see.

Victor frowned and held his hand out. Sensing his displeasure, Ethan put the book in his hand. "This book," Victor said, "Is something you were never meant to see, and I must ask you to forget you ever saw it."

"I'm sorry if I offended you by bringing it up, I was just curious after seeing the title. And to be honest, I don't think I can actually forget that I saw it."

"Nor do I," Victor mused. "I really should have done a better job of hiding it. Regardless, you did not see this book, and I cannot discuss its contents. Do you understand?"

"Yes, Sir," Ethan replied with a nod.

Then, pretending the book didn't exist, Victor patted him on the shoulder and said, "You did well today for your first attempt. "Then he walked back down to his workshop without speaking another word.

CHAPTER 13

The Reluctant Leader

Star insisted that Ethan join her in town, and no matter how much he questioned her, she wouldn't say why. "Does it involve food?" Ethan asked.

"Not saying," Star replied, with a sparkle in her eyes.

"Come on. Give me a hint."

"Nope."

"How much farther do we have to go?" Ethan asked as they neared the edge of town.

"Not much," Star said, not offering him any information.

On the far side of Tearmann was a community park ringed with trees. It was a wide-open green space, with soft, lush grass. A favorite place for picnics and local celebrations, the only people in the park today were mostly familiar faces. Roland, Ryan, and Victor were adjusting small barrels around the park. At the same time, Anne, Vallow, and Ashlyn sat on the grass talking to one another. The Chastain children, Victor Junior and Breeze, were sitting off to one side, and there was a young man and a girl who looked to be a little older than Star, carrying on a conversation.

"What is this?" Ethan asked.

"You'll see," Star replied.

It was Ryan's idea. He'd heard Ethan talk about it when he was at Arcborne. Everyone was tired and on edge, and it was clear that

Ethan was growing increasingly frustrated with the constant waiting. It was also hard on Roland and Ashlyn. Neither enjoyed the waiting. Victor helped Ryan with the setup, and they recruited Wart Pinsley and a local girl named Rose Talbot to join them. Rose was two years older than Star and had a crush on Wart, so she was happy to accept the invitation to play.

"What's going on?" Ethan called out as they neared the group.

"We're going to have some fun," Ryan said. "We're going to play a game."

"Yeah? What kind of game?"

"Borkin," Ryan said. "We've got a ball." He motioned to one sitting in front of Victor Junior. "We have goals, we have a way to keep time, and we have ten players. We just need you to tell us the rules."

Ethan's eyes lit up. He knew about the game from Renny Patel, but he had never played. He'd only watched. "I like this!" He walked toward the couple standing over to the side. "I'm Ethan," he said, offering his hand.

Wart took his hand and shook it. "I'm Wart Pinsley, and this is Rose."

"Good to meet both of you. Have you ever played Borkin?"

"Never even heard of it," Rose replied.

"Ok. The rules are pretty simple, and it moves fast." Ethan called everyone over and began to explain the rules. "There are five goals," he started. "We need to make them a little smaller, but the layout is perfect. The field is shaped like a pentagon, with the five goals positioned in the middle of the flat sides. There are five people on each team, but only nine players are allowed to play at a time. When the first team has possession of the ball, they are in offense, and the opposing team, the defense, only plays with four team members. The two sides switch after five minutes. The team that was on offense then plays defense with only four players, and the other team plays offense, with their fifth player coming on the field. Make sense so far?"

"What's the object of the game?" Wart asked.

"To score as many goals as you can when you are on offense. A goal is scored by throwing, rolling, or kicking the ball through a goal. The goals are the small open spaces between the barrels. The team with the most goals after three sets of play is the winner."

"Doesn't sound too hard," Rose commented.

"Yes, but there are a few tricks," Ethan said. "First, you can't run with the ball. You can pass it to another person on your team, or you can move it through the goal, but you can't carry it. Second, the clock never stops, so if you kick it hard through the goal, and you have to chase it, the clock keeps ticking. And...the team on offense has to chase it down. So, even though the team on defense is at a disadvantage, having only four players, you always have to play smart."

"What if a player on defense intercepts the ball on a pass?" Ashlyn asked.

"They leave the ball where it is, and the offense has to start over on that spot," Ethan answered.

"And after a goal is scored," Roland asked, "how does play start again?"

"You start again next to the goal you just scored at, but you can't score again on that goal until another of your teammates touches the ball."

"Ok," Ryan said. "Anything else?"

"Only one thing," Ethan answered. "If a defensive player knocks the ball out of the playing field, the offense gets a free attempt to score from the middle of the field. And if the player intentionally kicks or throws the ball out of bounds, then the opposing side gets five points. That keeps the defense from deliberately wasting time by making the offense chase it."

"So, all we have to do now is divide into teams," Roland commented. "What's the best way to do that?"

"I have a suggestion," Ashlyn said, grinning. "The girls will play the boys. That seems fair, doesn't it?" She looked at Anne.

"Hardly," Anne laughed. "I think we should give them some kind of advantage. You know, something to give them a better chance."

"Done," Ryan said, with a gleam in his eyes. "Boys against the girls. And you girls can go first."

"Can you give us a minute?" Vallow asked. "We should probably meet as a group for a minute or two so that we have a plan."

The two teams stepped away from the others and devised different strategies for how they would play the game. After a few minutes, the teams walked onto the field. Victor Chastain sat by his children as Roland, Ryan, Wart, and Ethan scattered out around the area, with Wart and Ethan each taking a position so they could reach the

172

open goal. At the same time, Roland and Ryan centered themselves between the open goals.

Ashlyn started with the ball in the middle of the field and passed it over to Rose with a roll. Star faded back to the open goal, and Vallow followed her about ten feet over to the left. Rose passed to Star, and Star deflected the ball with her foot to her mother, who immediately rolled it back to her. With a winding arm motion, Star rolled the ball at the open goal and was able to get it beyond the barrel before Wart or Ethan could pick it up.

Ashlyn let out a yell, and Rose ran after the ball. Ethan groaned when the ball went past, and Star gave him a smile followed by a curtsy, while holding out the edges of her pretend skirt.

The girls scored three more goals before Breeze called out, "TIME'S UP!"

Vallow offered to sit out their defensive round, and the boys controlled the ball, determined to make up the score. They scored three quick goals, and then things went awry. Victor found himself all alone in front of one of the goals and started waving his hands to get Ryan's attention. Seeing him out of the corner of his eye, Ryan rolled the ball towards Victor. All he had to do was tap the ball with his foot, and they would have scored a goal with plenty of time to score more. Instead, he pulled back his right leg and kicked the ball hard. It went through the small barrels, but it also sailed thirty yards away.

Throwing up his arms, proud of his accomplishment, Victor yelled, "YES!" By the time Ethan could chase down the ball and get it back into play, their time was up. The two teams finished the first round tied at 4-4.

By the second round, the teams were beginning to figure out how to play. The defensive effort was getting better, and the scores were lower. The game was getting more physical. Ashlyn positioned herself beside Roland on one play. When Wart tossed the ball toward Roland, Ashlyn threw her hip into Roland and pushed him out of the way. The ball flew past him and right into Rose's arms.

Roland hit the ground and immediately looked up at his wife. "Oh! Sorry, dear," Ashlyn cooed. "Are you alright?"

"Just fine," Roland replied, quickly getting to his feet. And taking the ball from the spot where Rose dropped it, he made a high looping toss over to Ethan, who immediately rolled it to the goal. Ashlyn had a chance to kick the ball away, but when she turned to run, she saw Roland. He crouched down and lifted his wife up on his shoulder as the boys scored another goal.

"Oh, I'm sorry, love. Did I get in your way?" Roland smirked.

"Isn't that a foul or a penalty or something?" Ashlyn yelled at Ethan.

Ethan grinned. "Maybe...probably. But since we don't have a referee or an official rule book, it looks like fair play to me."

At the end of the second round, the boys were up 7-6. Not only was everyone having fun, but the residents of Tearmann had also stopped their daily work to watch the game. They didn't understand the rules, but it was still entertaining to watch the teams play.

The third round opened with a goal by Anne, followed by another from Star. Victor made a good stop on a kick by Ashlyn, but accidentally kicked the ball out of bounds. That allowed Star to attempt a shot from the middle of the field. She turned slowly in a circle, looking at the position of the defensive players. The boys were rotating their positions as she moved, trying to keep four of the goals covered. Suddenly, she stopped, swung her right leg back as if she were going to kick the ball, but missed it. Then, bringing her leg back, she connected with the back of her heel and sent it rolling between the barrels.

"CLEVER GIRL!" Anne shouted.

"Aren't you the sneaky one?" Ethan said, impressed by her effort.

As the boys were groaning over the play, Rose quickly gathered up the ball and rolled back onto the field, right at the feet of Vallow, who picked it up, seemingly unsure what to do next.

Roland and Wart ran toward her as fast as they could, and just as they arrived, Vallow tossed the ball past the barrels with an awkward throw. When their time was up, the girls were ahead 10-7.

With the boys on offense, Wart rushed to an open goal and was rewarded with a perfectly thrown pass by Ethan. He scored. Roland scored the second goal when he simply tossed the ball over Rose's head, and it rolled between the barrels. Ryan and Ethan scored the third goal by accurate passes back and forth as they neared the goal. Ashlyn tried to stay between them to block an easy shot, but in the end, she couldn't move fast enough, and none of the other girls were able to get into position to help.

The time was ticking away, and Ethan stood in the center of the field and tried to orchestrate passes between his teammates to find a good shot. A quick scan of the field told him that most of the players were in front of him, so he yelled for Ryan to pass the ball back to him. As soon as Ryan's arm pulled back, Ethan sprinted toward an open goal. The ball touched his fingertips, and he crouched down and rolled it at the center of the goal. There was maybe fifteen feet between Ethan and the goal. The ball rolled straight to the middle. From the corner of his eye, he saw a blond blur of movement. Two feet from the goal, Star scooped the ball up and held it in her arms.

"TIME'S UP!" Breeze shouted. "THE GAME'S OVER!"

Pulling the blond tendril of hair that hung down her face behind her ear, Star gave Ethan a smile and another curtsy. The crowd watching the game cheered, and the game finished in a tie.

Ethan walked over to Star, put his arm around her, and gave her a hug. "When did you get so fast?"

"I've always been that fast. You've just never seen me run before."

He spent the next hour trying to explain the game of Borkin to the townspeople, who had never witnessed such a thing. There was question after question, and Ethan patiently answered them as best as he could. Where did you learn this game? Is it being played in the rest of NHHMM? Do you have a paper that lists the official rules? He couldn't answer the first question, and he didn't know the answers to the last two questions, either. They left the barrels and the ball at the field, as several of the locals wanted to try out the game. It was a good afternoon, much-needed escapism, and for a brief time, the worries and dangers of life were put on hold, allowing them to relax. But that calm in the midst of a storm was fleeting, and it wouldn't last for long.

Maze, the cat, was about to pounce. She sat on a shelf and silently watched the mouse move around the barn floor looking for something to eat. Only the very tip of her tail would twitch occasionally, but the rest of her was as still as the statues in the New Marchant Museum. The mouse moved closer to Maze's part of the barn, and her body began to flex. A few feet more, and she would make her jump. The rodent paused, quickly looked around the barn floor and froze in place.

The hum started quietly, and bright light filled the barn. As the humming grew louder, the mouse scurried behind some tools, and Maze's ears pulled back, and she let out an audible hiss.

In the hayloft, Ethan woke up with a start and squinted through his nearly closed eyelids at the light. When the humming stopped and the light vanished, he saw four large crates in the middle of the barn floor. Climbing down the ladder, he rubbed the sleep from his eyes and took a closer look at the crates. Three looked to be medium-sized squares, but the fourth was skinny and flat. Maybe five feet in length. Locating a metal pry bar, Ethan forced the metal into the edge of the flat crate and began to work the nails loose when Ashlyn entered the room.

"I thought I heard a humming sound. That would be the supplies that Mr. Vanderschmidt promised."

The top of the crate popped up, and Ethan pushed it off to the side. He whistled. "Wow! This is amazing."

Inside the crate were four crystal rifles and four pistols. Ethan reached down to pick one up. "Eh..." Ashlyn reprimanded. "Is it loaded?"

"I don't know."

Quickly aware that both Ethan and Star needed some training with the weapons, Ashlyn replied, "Just leave them where they are. I'll have Roland or your dad give you some basics on handling weapons. But the first rule is always to assume that a gun is loaded and ready to fire. You don't want to shoot me or anyone else by accident."

Her words bothered Ethan. They made him feel like a child. He understood her logic and concern, but it didn't change how those words of caution made him feel. "Can I open the others?"

"Of course," she answered.

The first crate held ammunition, and Ashlyn estimated there were five hundred rounds packed safely inside. The second crate held an assortment of breathers and shooting masks. The third contained five compasses, a variety of identical metal bracelets, and some round metal pendants that were the size of a strawberry and as thick as a slice of bread.

"May I?" Ethan asked as he reached down for a pendant.

"Go ahead, but be careful. I don't know what it does." In the rectangular box rested a sealed envelope addressed to Archibald

Bingham. "Let me give this to Pops and let him know the supplies have arrived." Ashlyn then left the barn, and Ethan heard her call out, "RO! RO!"

Examining the pendant, Ethan turned it over. There was nothing but metal and five small screws that he guessed held the front and back together. On the edge, however, were two small buttons positioned at a 90-degree angle from the top on either side. Nothing happened when he pushed either button independently, but when he pressed both at the same time, a bright light came from the front side of the pendant. Walking over to the darkest part of the barn, he saw that the pendant illuminated the area and made it easy to see everything. He pressed the two buttons again, and the light disappeared. Ethan put the pendant chain over his neck and let it hang in the center of his chest. *I wonder what else this genius has invented.*

Voices came from outside the barn, and he looked up to see Ashlyn, Star, and Pops entering from the large door opening. Pops had his head down, reading the letter addressed to him.

"I never took you to be the kind to wear jewelry," Star teased when she saw the pendant around Ethan's neck.

"Watch, and be amazed," he said, as he pressed the two buttons on the side. "LIGHT!"

"Outstanding," Pops said, looking up from the letter. "Jonathan has sent one of these for all of us. He said the bracelets will allow us to find each other on the watches. In a group of blue dots, the wearer will show up as green on the watch fob."

"Did he send more watches?" Ashlyn asked.

"No. He's working on it, but for now, they will only be of value to Ethan, or if you are wearing the shooting mask. Evidently it works with them as well."

Ashlyn walked over to Star and spoke to her in a low voice that neither Ethan nor Pops could hear. Star nodded her head vigorously. Reaching down, Ashlyn took one of the new rifles, two boxes of ammunition, and one of the shooting masks. "See you boys later. Star and I are going to do some shooting." Before anyone could object or comment, the two left the barn and headed up to the meadow.

"It's not as heavy as it looks," Star said, as she held the rifle up to her shoulder. Ashlyn first brought her up to speed on the shooting mask, making sure she could work the buttons quickly and efficiently.

"True, but it will get heavier the longer you hold it. If possible, always use a tree, a building, or something similar when shooting more than a couple of shots at a time. Fatigue and breathing are your enemies. If either of them gets the better of you, your chances of making an exceptional shot quickly fade."

"Breathing?"

"Yes. Your heart will beat faster when you're about to shoot at something other than a target. Your breathing will become rapid, and that will cause the barrel of the gun to move with every breath you take."

"But I won't be able to shoot for very long if I can't breathe, will I?"

"You just need to learn to control it. What I'm about to tell you will sound cruel, and you may think ill of me when I say it, but you have to find the right state of mind. It's hard to explain until you're faced with it, but if you have to shoot someone to save the ones you love, you can't look at them as a person. They must be a target, just like that dead tree on the other side of the meadow. They don't have a family, a husband, a wife, parents, or children. The person you aim this weapon at must be a direct threat to someone that you love, or you should never have the gun in your hands."

"I... don't know if I can do that," Star replied, uncertainty in her voice.

"You can," Ashlyn answered softly, "and you will if you are ever faced with that situation. Trust me, I know from experience. If it's your mother, your father, your brother, or your sisters, you won't have an issue with it. My husband tells me that you nearly killed him with a pitchfork."

Star laughed. "I think he's exaggerating a bit based on what I remember."

"Perhaps." Ashlyn smiled. "But I think you would have done anything to protect Ethan, even if it meant killing my husband."

Star smiled but did not reply.

"Think about the rifle this way. It's nothing more than a long-distance pitchfork, and you can stop the threat before it ever gets too close."

"Well," Star said, "I still don't know if I can use this, but I know I need to learn, so what's next?"

"The best part is that you already have a two-step advantage over everyone else. The sound of a black powder gun is loud, and most people flinch in anticipation of the sound. And if the expected sound doesn't get you, the recoil of the bullet as it leaves the gun will hit your shoulder with a kick. Again, anticipating that can also cause your shot to miss the target. But these guns are silent, and there is little to no recoil. You don't have to anticipate either the sound or the kick. All you have to do is focus on the shot."

"Mrs. Flynn, can I try at the tree? The explanations are great, but I need to try this out if I'm going to learn anything more."

"I understand. I'm like you. I need to learn by doing something rather than just hearing about it. When I propped up that dead tree on the other side of the meadow, I placed it where there was a large knot just about in the middle. Did you see it?"

"Yes, ma'am," Star said as she adjusted the mask. "I'm looking at it now."

"Good. Do you want to rest the rifle on the tree branch next to you, or would you prefer to lay it on the ground and use your elbow to shoot like I showed you earlier?"

"The ground," Star said, as she lay on her stomach and propped the gun up with her left elbow.

"Ok, that looks good. Now, focus on the target. There is a tiny crystal on the end of the gun, and when the gun is over the target, what happens?"

"The mask shows a red dot."

"Perfect. Now take a deep breath, relax..."

WHOOSH!

Before Ashlyn could finish her sentence, the bullet left the gun, ripped through the air, and tore into the dead tree on the other side of the meadow. The wood wobbled side to side before falling over on the ground. "How did I do?" Star asked.

"Let's find out." Ashlyn took the rifle from Star and helped her up with the other hand. They walked across the meadow in silence until they were fifteen feet away from the deadwood. "It's ok if your shot was off, it was your first time. You hit the tree, and that's all that matters. You'll get better with each shot if you practice and think about what you're doing."

With her foot, Ashlyn rolled the six-inch tree over until she could see the knot. Half an inch below the knot and to the left was the hole left by Star's first shot.

Laughing out loud, Ashlyn leaned over and kissed Star on the top of her head. "Young lady, that is perhaps the most amazing shot I've ever seen."

"Maybe, but I missed the knot I was aiming at."

"That's it," Roland said, with satisfaction in his voice. "The last tunnel to the barn is finished." Covered in dirt and sweat, Ethan offered his hand to Roland as he reached the top of the wooden ladder leading down into the ground.

"I'm glad this job is over," Ethan said, helping Roland into the barn.

"Yeah. I've never been fond of dirty work and cramped spaces."

"So, what's next?" Ethan asked, sitting down on a wooden bench.

"Nothing," Roland said. "We've done everything that we set out to do. We've made this place as secure as possible, and we've a plan in place for escape if needed. Now comes the hard part."

"What's the hard part?"

"Waiting for what we do next."

Ethan didn't like that answer, especially in light of how his last request was received. They didn't want him and Star to leave the group, and they seemed intent on waiting for trouble to happen. He didn't like waiting, especially for things he couldn't control. So much of his life now seemed like it was dependent upon someone else. What does the Resistance do next? What do his father and mother do next? What does the chancellor do next? NHHMM was never meant to be a monarchy. When his grandfather was chancellor, he assumed power with an election. Ryan O'Connor wasn't viewed as a successor to the throne, but more of the best person to lead the Resistance. Ethan was beginning to wonder. Yes, his father was a convenient figurehead, but he didn't seem to want to lead the Resistance. The Council did most of the work. Perhaps it was because Ryan and Anne had been in hiding for so long, or maybe it was because they knew Ryan didn't want the job.

"Can I ask an awkward question?" Ethan finally asked.

"Sure, but we aren't going to have that conversation again, are we?"

"No," Ethan quickly replied, blushing. "Why does everyone assume my father will lead NHHMM?"

Roland wiped the sweat from his face with a rag from his pocket and nodded as if he'd been expecting the question. "Your father is a great man. He is strong, charismatic, and has good looks. I'm sorry, but unfortunately, we are a shallow people. We somehow believe that because someone is strong, famous, and attractive, they will be a great leader. Your father is the perfect rallying point for the Resistance. At some point, sometime soon, we will not be a group that operates in the shadows but a group that asks for the support of the people to oppose Chancellor Brighton. None of the people on the Council can serve as a rallying point. Jack has the looks and the charm, but we both know my son lives in a place where there is very little black and white, and most everything is gray. Charlotte Mayberry is brilliant, eloquent, and beautiful. Still, her financial background will always cause the less fortunate in NHHMM to doubt her compassion for them."

"You could do it," Ethan interjected.

"I'm the last person you would want for the job. I loathe politics, and for the most part...politicians."

"But does Dad want to do this?"

"I've known your father all his life, and I can tell you he is an honorable man who will do what NHHMM needs."

"Sorry, but you didn't answer my question," Ethan replied, cautiously.

Roland thought for a moment and then shook his head. "No. I don't think he wants the role."

"I'm confused. You always taught me that if someone doesn't want to do something, they will never do the job well. How can Dad be the right person for the job if he doesn't want it?"

"He is the right person to be the figurehead, but if we are successful, I believe he'll only stay on in an interim role until the next leader can be elected. He hasn't said any of this, but I believe it to be true."

Ethan wasn't comfortable with how the conversation was progressing, so he changed the topic. "So, we're going to wait here until someone tells us otherwise or until something changes. I get that. I don't like it, but I understand that is the decision. How long do you think we will be here...waiting?"

"Not long," Roland replied. "Not long at all."

"But why? What makes you say that?"

"Instinct. Something I can't teach you. It's what you know to be true on the inside, even if you don't have the facts to back it up." Roland sat down opposite Ethan and gave him a serious look. "You tell me. Push everything else aside, your feelings, your emotions, your wants and desires, and tell me what you think. Do you think we will have to wait for a long time?"

"No," Ethan said, with hardly a thought. "I'm actually surprised that we are still here."

"And why is that?"

"Because this is one of the first places I would have looked."

"I know," Roland agreed. "And what does your instinct tell you we should be doing?"

"We should be in a place that isn't predictable. We should leave before we have to, and spend less time in preparation that involves waiting and more time in action."

Roland grinned as he nodded and held out his hands. "Welcome to the bureaucracy of life. The Council wanted you to have time to heal and grow stronger, and your parents wanted the same thing. Your parents have been here for two years, undiscovered in their new life, and they believe this is the safest place for us to be."

Ethan frowned and twisted his mouth. "I'm healed. I'm stronger. We need to leave. If the group won't let Star and I leave, can't we get to someplace safer for everyone else? Surely we could go to the Vanderschmidt research facility. We could even go back to Arcborne. It's sealed off and we now have portal access."

Pops nodded his head. "I'll talk to your parents," he said. "But if they think it's best to stay, the Council will agree with them. And we will stay."

CHAPTER 14

The Beginning of the End

The summer days in Tearmann proved to be tolerable for Ethan. While the weather was warm, it wasn't unbearable. The nights were cool, and almost every day there was a short rain that would roll in and cool off the mid-afternoon heat. The evenings were his favorite part of the day. The day's work was done, dinner was over, the kitchen was cleaned, and everyone had time to relax. Roland and Ryan would talk for hours about their friends on the Council from the reports that Roland would get every few days, and Anne would often help Vallow with Star's brother and sister. Ashlyn and Victor were the ones who didn't have a real place to fit in. Ashlyn was more comfortable plotting ideas and strategies with the men; the maternal instincts didn't burn intensely in her, and Victor...Victor could be happy just about anywhere because he had a way of being able to ignore everything around him and let his mind go wherever it needed to.

The interaction of everyone else gave Ethan and Star more time to talk, and he enjoyed that, as he was able to learn things about her that he never had time to learn at Arcborne. She had a twin sister who died at birth, and somewhere up in the meadow was a marker that bore the name Brett. She didn't have one favorite color, but two. Star loved the soft blue of the flowers that grew only up in the higher altitude around Tearmann. And to Ethan's surprise, her other favorite color was black. She said it was mysterious and made her feel rebellious when she wore it. When he heard that, Ethan laughed and told her she had no problem being rebellious, regardless of the color she was wearing.

For every new thing he learned, every little thing that made him say Ah-ha, there were ten more things that made him think, I knew that, yet there was no way he could possibly have known any of it. Just the same, most of the time, what he learned about Star was more of a confirmation of what he felt like he already knew.

The bench-swing hanging from the tree limb was their favorite place to talk. They could sway back and forth and listen to the tree leaves rustle, and the rope groan with each movement.

"Has anyone told you about the night we had a visitor?" Star asked one night as they sat on the swing

Ethan shook his head. "No."

"The night before you woke up after the shooting, I don't think anyone believed you were going to last the night. My father finally figured out how to slow down the bleeding, but you had lost so, so much blood... There was a loud crack of lightning, but there was no rain that night, and no clouds. A woman named Muriel knocked on the door and demanded to see you. Roland and Ashlyn were trying to be protective of you, but she said that if she didn't get to you in time, you would surely die. She asked about what type of blood you had because you desperately needed a blood donor. While the adults were debating who should give you blood, I told her that I should be the one.

She didn't argue and told me to lie down next to you. She connected a tube between you and me, and the blood going from me to you turned a blue deeper than a sapphire."

"What? Blue?" Ethan questioned.

"Yes. Blue. When I asked her about it, she said it was very rare, and it was called 'Kai'lain'. It seemed like she was telling me things that were supposed to be secret. It was so...strange."

"Did your parents know her?"

"No."

"Has anyone seen her before?"

"No."

"And she just appeared?"

"Yes. I was wondering if she was using the same type of technology that we use to jump from place to place."

"That would make sense," Ethan mused. If we've figured out how to move between places and worlds, and the Yehud can do it, there are probably other worlds that can do the same thing."

"And she told me to tell you something. She said something along the lines of 'that no matter when or where you are, the choice is always the same. You either become what they want you to be or become what you were born to be'."

"What does that mean?"

"I have no idea," Star mused.

They sat in silence for a few minutes, both content to be doing nothing but sitting on a bench swing.

"You know," Star finally said with a shiver when the night air became brisk and the breeze began to whisper of fall, "your parents are talking about having another child."

"Yeah?" Ethan said as he thought about her words.

"Yes. Your mom is worried that it will be hard for you."

"Why would that be hard for me?"

"Because you never grew up with your parents, you've only just gotten to know them, so how will that make you feel having a brother or sister that gets the relationship that you didn't have?"

"Honestly, it doesn't bother me at all. I mean, they are my parents, and I love them, but I have a stronger relationship with Pops than I will ever have with them. And why should they miss out on the things they missed out on with me?"

Star shivered. "I should have worn a jacket." Ethan lifted his arm, rested it on the back of the bench swing, and around Star's shoulder. "My mother and your father tell her it won't be a problem. Roland says the same thing, but it's really got her worried."

"Do you want some tea?" Ethan asked out of nowhere. "Your mother usually has the kettle on."

"You are so odd," Star said, looking over at him and smiling. "I'm talking about your mother, and in the middle of it, you want tea?"

"Yeah, tea. Do you want honey?"

"Just a little, if you are determined to go."

"Trust me, I'll be back in just a few minutes, I promise." Getting up from the swing, Ethan went inside, and Star pulled her feet up onto the bench seat and hugged her legs to keep warm.

True to his word, in about seven minutes, he was walking back outside carrying two cups. Handing one to Star, he sat down next to her and put his free arm around her shoulders. "Ok. I took care of it."

"Took care of what?"

"Mom. Your mother and Ashlyn were inside talking, and as I was leaving with the tea, I told Mom that it was ok with me if they had another child. That I was perfectly great with it."

Star nearly spat out the tea she was sipping. "You didn't?"

"Yes, I did. You said she was worrying about it, and I told her that it was ok."

"What happened?"

"My mom was shocked, speechless, your mom looked embarrassed, and Ashlyn just started laughing."

"Oh, I wish I could have seen their faces. So that's what the 'Would you like some tea?' was all about?"

Ethan grinned. "Well, not completely. I really did think you might like some tea. But it made sense to take care of the other during the same trip."

Ethan couldn't see Star's eyes as they were slowly swinging back and forth, but if he could, he would have seen them sparkle in the moonlight.

Jochem Pardue watched the man enter through the doors of the lobby and guessed him to be an undertaker. Extraordinarily tall and thin, with skin the color of a white porcelain plate, and hair that was smooth and oily, the man looked around the lobby and, after spying Pardue, walked awkwardly toward the doorman. Reaching into his coat pocket, the man pulled out his identification and gave it to Pardue.

"Ministry of Intelligence," the doorman said, looking over the paper.

"Precisely," the man said, giving Pardue a forced smile that looked more like the grin of a hungry wolf. "My name is Eugene Hogge. I wonder if you might help me with something?"

"I'll do my best," Pardue said, with caution.

"I have a key, and on the key is the number 531. Does your building have an apartment with that number?"

"Yes."

"Would I be correct in assuming that this key," he said, holding it up for Pardue to see, "would be to a mailbox somewhere in the lobby?"

"Could be," the old man answered.

"And where would I find this mailbox?"

"Just past the corner on the left."

"Thank you." With an awkward gait, Hogge walked across the lobby and into the hallway, where the wall of resident mailboxes was located. Running his finger across the boxes until he found 531, he then stopped, inserted the key in the lock, and gave it a turn. The box was empty, but the name COLTRANE was written in ink on a small placard above the mailbox door. Returning to Pardue, who sat on a metal stool near the door, the man smiled again. "Thank you for your assistance. Would you be so kind as to provide me with the resident's first name?"

"Not allowed to do that. I can't disclose personal information to anyone without a written document authorizing me to do so," Pardue said, crossing his arms.

Hogge smiled again, and then he spoke in a soft voice. "Perhaps you forgot what my identification papers said. It's normal for a man of your mature years, and it can happen to any of us, I suppose. You read or hear something, and the next thing you know, it's gone from your memory as if it were never there."

"There's nothing wrong with my memory," Pardue replied. "Your name is Eugene Hogge, like the swine, but spelled a little differently, and you are with the Ministry of Intelligence. Did I get that right?"

"And you know that I can get you the written request that you require, but then that would come at a great inconvenience to me. You don't really want to do that, do you? After all, right now this is simply business. You don't want to make this personal, do you?"

"Are you finished?" Pardue said, straightening his back and clenching his chin. "Because I don't care if this is personal or business. You get nothing from me without a request in writing. You can leave now, and I'll have that key, as it's the property of the building owners." He held out his hand.

"You," Hogge said, as he quickly grabbed Pardue's hand and twisted it backwards, "will get the key when I'm ready to give it back to you and not before."

The twisting of Pardue's hand sent him to his knees, and he groaned as he felt the bones about to break. Still, he remained silent and made no pleas for Hogge to stop.

"Very well," Hogge said, releasing Pardue's hand. "I'll be back with your paper."

When Hogge had left the building, Jochem Pardue hurried over to the desk in the lobby. Taking a pen and a piece of paper, he wrote five words, folded the paper, and rushed up the stairs until he reached the fifth floor. Moving down the hallway, he stopped when he arrived at apartment 531. He then knocked on the door and hoped that Ginger Coltrane would answer so that he could warn her. But he knew she kept odd hours, so he slipped the folded paper under the door.

Sometime

after Jochem Pardue's shift was over, Ginger finally came home and meandered up the stairs until she arrived at her apartment. Unlocking the door, she stepped inside, immediately saw the folded note, and opened it.

DON'T COME BACK. NOT SAFE.

Recognizing it to be Pardue's handwriting, she quickly moved over to a table with an oil lamp resting upon it. She lifted the metal lamp and peeled back the green felt that covered the opening in the base. Inside the base was her remaining money in a lace bag. Taking the bag, she made one last look around the apartment. Content that there was nothing else she needed, Ginger stepped into the hallway and closed her apartment door.

With only the lace bag and Jochem Pardue's warning, Ginger left the building and walked to Charlotte Mayberry's place. It was three o'clock in the morning, and there was virtually no one on the streets. She was alone, she had just received a warning letter to leave, and if anyone was watching the streets of New Marchant, she would be the one they would see.

Her heart began to race, and she increased her pace. When Charlotte's residence was finally in sight, it was all she could do not to run to the front door and instead forced herself to slow down to a more casual walk. If anyone was watching, she wanted them to assume she was walking to a destination, not running to sanctuary.

She couldn't see any light from the residence, but she climbed the steps to the front door and knocked. Then she waited. She knocked again and waited for a second time. The lights never came on, and the door never opened. Her knuckles started to strike the door for a third time, but then she pulled her hand back.

Taking a deep breath, Ginger took the steps down to the street and began walking to The Black Mule.

"Please. Please," Vanderschmidt said in the loudest voice he could muster. "There are a great many things to discuss today. So please, may I have your attention?"

Slowly, the other conversations finally stopped, and when it was quiet, Vanderschmidt began.

"First, I'm sorry to say that, as Jack and Charlotte are not here today, and we will not have their input on the first topic. I've already briefed Roland, Ashlyn, and Ryan by telegram, and they have given me their votes. It's not ideal, but this is something we need to decide... preferably today. Otis Walton has made an offer to the Council, and I am bringing it to you. He doesn't need our approval, as he is free to come and go as he pleases, but he would like our blessing."

"Our blessing to do what?" Professor Wimberly asked.

"He wants to talk to the chancellor. He wants to tell him what we have discovered in the hope that we can find a way to work with the chancellor to stop the invasion that now appears imminent."

"That is foolishness," Gordon shot back. "He's going to expose us all. Under torture, Walton could completely undermine everything we're doing. We can't trust the chancellor. Surely you aren't really considering this?"

"In light of everything we've learned, how can we not consider it? Can we fight two enemies at one time? We plot, plan, and work to overcome one enemy. How are we supposed to defeat two at the same time?"

"What is he proposing?" Merten Ashwillow asked.

"Otis doesn't know exactly where we are. We transport him by buggy to New Marchant, and he will be blindfolded the whole way. When he gets to the city, he makes contact with the chancellor, no one else. He tells the chancellor only about the invaders and a vague description of how they seem to arrive out of nowhere. After he informs the chancellor of what is happening, he offers to broker a treaty between the government and the Resistance."

"It can't hurt," Chamberlain said.

"Think about what you are saying," Gordon exploded. "Walton has seen our airship. He's been on it. He's seen our weapons close up. Stop and think about what he already knows. Do you want his knowledge in the hands of the chancellor, or even worse, an invader?"

"I know Otis Walton," Vanderschmidt argued. "He will not betray us. He will die before he gives the chancellor anything."

"I agree with Captain Gordon," Professor Wimberly said sternly. "This makes no sense. We are putting too much trust in someone who has only been with us for a short time. You may trust him to do the right thing, but I don't trust him that much. Not yet."

"Have you spoken with those in Tearmann?" Captain Gordon asked.

"I have," Vanderschmidt replied. "And their votes were not unanimous. When we vote on this, their individual votes will be added to the tally."

They argued and debated for the next hour, and when they were finished, the Council put it to the vote. Carstairs, Chamberlain, Ashwillow, and Vanderschmidt all voted yes, with the explanation that they had very little choice but to try and find an ally in the home of an enemy. Ryan O'Connor voted yes as well, and Roland and Ashlyn voted no, along with Captain Gordon and Professor Wimberly. The final vote was 5-4, and at the end of the day, they were divided more on strategy than on a ballot. The division was deep, wide, and forced them to act as individuals rather than the unanimous decision of the larger group. And when the meeting broke up in the early afternoon, the members of the Council left the research facility and went their separate ways.

They assigned a man named Nick Turley to act as Walton's bodyguard and driver. Before the night was over, Turley drove Dr. Walton back to New Marchant and had him situated in a hotel near the Chancellery. Tomorrow, Walton would present himself and demand an audience with Chancellor Brighton, presenting an offer that would either save their world or plunge it into chaos none of them had ever experienced.

CHAPTER 15

The Discovery

At nine o'clock in the morning, Otis Walton entered the massive lobby of the Chancellery. Everything about it was intimidating. Every stone of every intricately carved column was designed to intimidate anyone who made it past the ornate doors. He spied a desk beneath a sign that read Information Desk.

"How may I help you?" asked a perky young woman.

"I'm here to see Chancellor Brighton," Otis answered.

"And when is your appointment?"

"Alas, I do not have an appointment, but it is imperative that I meet with him."

"That's a problem for you, because the chancellor never sees anyone without an appointment."

"Then I need you to get this message to him immediately," Otis responded and placed the envelope in front of her.

"But I can't..."

"Please," Otis interrupted. "He must see this. Our world is about to be invaded, and the chancellor has no idea."

The woman had no idea how to respond. She had heard every strange excuse one could imagine for why someone needed to see the chancellor. But nothing she had heard before ever mentioned an invasion. "Sam," she called out to one of her associates. A young man approached and stood next to her. "I need you to watch my

191

desk for a few minutes. I've got to deliver a request for a meeting with Chancellor Brighton."

The woman walked across the lobby and through a guarded door that opened up into a mechanical lift. When she arrived on the top floor, she was greeted by an army major, who asked her intention.

"I have a request to meet with Chancellor Brighton, and this person is someone important. He says we are about to be invaded, and he wants me to give Chancellor Brighton this envelope." Without opening the letter, the major carried it and set it before the chancellor.

"What is this?" Brighton asked.

"A man in the lobby says we are about to be invaded and wants you to read this."

"Just a moment." Brighton took the envelope and removed the letter inside. He scanned the page and then looked up at the major. "I know this man. Bring him up."

Otis Walton was accompanied by the major from the lobby of the Chancellery, and into the lift that would take him up to see Chancellor Brighton. Having experienced a similar mechanism in the Vanderschmidt research building, this was just another ride to another part of the building. When the lift stopped, he was greeted by an officer, who took him to the chancellor.

"Otis, my friend," Brighton said, shaking his hand, "it's so good to know you are still with us. Please, have a seat."

"Thank you, Chancellor," Otis said while sitting. "But why wouldn't I still be here with you?"

"We didn't know what happened to you. You were in Arcborne, but after the evacuation, we couldn't get any word about where you were. You weren't on the list of those who got out before the explosion."

"Obviously, I was able to get out," Walton added.

"But how? I mean, no disrespect, but you aren't exactly in the prime of your life. And the climb out must have been both exhausting and brutal."

"I had help. There were members of the Resistance in Arcborne. They helped me get out."

"And why would the Resistance help you?"

"Probably because I'm an old man who needed help," Walton replied.

"Your note said something about an invasion? Now, Otis, who would be invading us?"

"They are called the Yehud. They are from another world, and they want two things. They want to steal our natural resources, and they want to steal our children. They currently have people placed inside your administration who are paving the way for this invasion."

Brighton tried hard to hold back the shock he was feeling, but Walton could see it. This news shook the chancellor.

"And do you have proof of this?"

"The Resistance sank a ship that had just arrived." Reaching into his jacket, he removed a well-folded cloth and then held it up for Brighton to see. "It says, YEHUD SUBDUES ALL."

"And how do you know this?"

"Chancellor Brighton, can we stop this cat and mouse game? At some point, you are going to have to trust what I know, or we really don't need to have this meeting."

"I agree. So, let's say for the moment that I believe everything you are saying about the invasion...this Yehud. Is that why you're here? Just to give me information?"

"No. I'm also here to make a proposal."

"Then let's hear it. What is your proposal?"

"You and the Resistance are currently expelling energy against one another. I suggest we focus our energy on defeating the invader. If their goal is to subdue us, then what do we gain by fighting against each other?"

"I see your point," Brighton said with a nod. "But by the very definition of the word, your side has to be resisting against someone, or something, and it appears that I am the someone. I'm not fighting with the Resistance. They are fighting with me."

"First," Walton replied, "it is not my side. I don't have a side. I simply see that this conflict is not good for our world. And second, I want to paint a realistic picture, and you will be angry with it. Regardless, the picture I paint is true." He paused for a moment, then added, "Right now, you aren't winning. Despite your best efforts, the Resistance gnaws at you, and you've proven that you can't shake them loose. How are you going to contend with a new enemy when you can't subdue the one you currently have?"

"You make a fair point, Otis, but why don't you give me the specifics of the proposal?"

"Make an open declaration that you welcome anyone who cares enough about our world to defend it. Give them some political concessions. Make them an ally instead of an enemy. Let the Resistance fight the war they are best at fighting. You can let your military manage the army-to-army battles. Let your new allies fight the battle they are better equipped to fight."

"Surely you see the danger in that, Otis. And when we defeat these supposed invaders, do you think the Resistance will still be my ally? No, they will resume their efforts to unseat me."

"Flip it around and look at it the other way. What assurances does the Resistance have that after the Yehud is defeated, you will not declare them to be your enemy? There is no easy victory here. There is no option that is void of risk. For anyone... Including you."

"Otis, you are providing a persuasive argument. What I need from you is more evidence. Something more concrete than a flag that could have been made in a tailor's shop in New Marchant."

Otis was churning inside. He wanted to talk about the notebook and the similarities in the language of the two worlds. He wanted to discuss the man Charlotte had captured and the existence of Ryan O'Connor. But he couldn't talk about any of those things. To give him one piece would eventually lead to other questions that would reveal more than anyone wanted the chancellor to know.

"I'm staying at The Hotel Dumond, just down the street. I don't have anything else to give you at the moment, but if something changes, can I come and see you again?"

"Of course," Brighton said. "And should something change on my end, rest assured that I will reach out to you. Thank you so much for being brave enough to come and speak with me."

When Otis Walton was well beyond hearing anything Brighton could say, the chancellor let out a scream of rage. He picked up a small metal ornament from his desk and wanted to hurl it against something, but everywhere he looked, there was something of value. Finally, in frustration, he put down the ornament and pounded his fists on the desk.

Her hands trembled when she read the message. Irena Krueger studied it for a second time, and a smile came over her face. Disgraced by her failure on the train from Arcborne and the escape of Shy Shepherd, Krueger was relegated to little more than a missing persons' hunt. She had only one assignment: find Ethan Scott and Star Chastain. She turned New Marchant upside down, and it was clear they were not in the capital city. Oppolsby delivered the same result. Her life had become little more than one plodding search after another in the many small towns and hamlets of NHHMM.

And then the telegram arrived. One single piece of paper, the one she held, could change the future of her career. She looked over at the map on her office wall. Fortunately, there hadn't been another error by her team. The village wasn't even in the next zone for searches. It was a tip that was driven by nothing more than greed. Tell the ministry something unusual that might aid their search, and there would be gold.

She opened a file and quickly scanned it, and there, at the bottom of the first page, was the one word she was looking for: Tearmann. Quickly gathering up an armful of paper, she left her office, made her way through the hallways, and up the stairs until she came to Udi's office.

"I need to see her," she demanded of the stern man sitting behind a desk outside Udi's office.

"She's in a meeting," he replied with an uninterested air.

"I don't recognize you," Krueger said.

"I'm new. Today is my first day."

"Then you need to know that if I say I need to talk to her, it's urgent that I do."

"She's in a meeting," he replied again.

"Is she with the chancellor?"

"Director Udi said nothing about making her scheduled appointments your business."

Krueger took a moment to think and then opened the door and burst into Santa Udi's office.

"You can't go in there..." she heard from behind her.

Santa Udi looked up from her desk and stopped her conversation with a director from the code-breaking department. "You've interrupted a meeting," she snarled. "I trust you can see that."

"We need to talk."

"Make an appointment," Udi replied.

"This can't wait." I've found them, she mouthed, so the director wouldn't overhear.

Udi turned her attention back to the man sitting across from her. "You may leave now. We will cover this topic later."

"But," the man argued, "I had to wait two weeks to get this meeting."

"And you may have to wait three weeks more to get another, but leave...now."

The door closed behind him, and Santa Udi motioned for Krueger to sit in the chair across from her.

"May I?" Krueger said, motioning to a larger conference table.

Udi nodded, and Irena Krueger began to spread out her papers on the table. "Tearmann," Krueger said, as she pointed to a map. "They are in Tearmann."

"And how do you know?" Udi asked, looking at the map.

"We got a tip," she answered, and showed her the telegram. "A local was visiting Gray Hawk, just below the foothills, and was talking about an odd new game they were playing up in Tearmann. He called it Borkin. One of our informants heard the conversation and passed it on to our people, for gold, of course. The name was familiar to me, but I couldn't place it. I had one of our people ask some questions of the known former residents of Arcborne, and their reply was that Borkin was a game created by the former headmaster Otis Walton, and was played by the students."

"There were over 4,000 people in Arcborne," Udi commented. "It could be any of them that carried the game out beyond the mountains. It means nothing."

"But there was only one resident of Arcborne who was from Tearmann. The girl, Star Chastain."

"And if the girl is there...then the boy will be there as well."

"Exactly. That was my thought, too."

"But why wasn't Tearmann searched before now?"

Krueger's heart sank. "It was on the list, but you wanted a systematic search performed, and it wasn't due to be visited for another two months."

Santa Udi ignored the excuse. "And how old is this information?"

"We received the tip three days ago, so...maybe two weeks?"

"How many troops do we have nearby?"

"Soldiers, or ministry agents?" Krueger answered.

"Our people, agents."

"We have twenty within a day's travel. There is a military installation within half a day's travel from Gray Hawk that has two hundred soldiers."

Santa Udi thought it over as she looked at the map. "I want all twenty of our people to rendezvous here." She tapped the map. "I want another thirty soldiers from the base to join them. They camp outside of Gray Hawk until I get there. No one, absolutely no one, leaves the camp and goes into Gray Hawk. I will personally shoot them if they do."

"I can take care of this, Minister Udi. Let me be the one to bring them in."

Udi laughed. "You will stay here, do as you are told, and nothing more."

Krueger hid her disappointment and replied, "Yes, Minister. But what do I tell them? What do I tell their supervisors?"

"You," Udi seethed, "will tell them I ordered them to be there. They don't deserve any other explanation, and you will give them none. And Krueger...do not mention this to anyone, destroy the telegram, and any notes referencing Tearmann."

Irena Krueger started to question the minister, but then thought better of it. "Yes, ma'am."

When Krueger gathered up her papers and left the office, the man was waiting for her. "Next time," he said, "when I tell you she is in a meeting, you will wait until she is finished."

"Or what?" Kruger replied. "Do you think I'm the least bit interested in the fact that I made you look as inept as you are stupid? You aren't an officer, I've never seen you before, so why don't you tell me your name so that I can have you fired for insubordination?"

"You may call me Mr. Lattimer," he said, standing up from his chair. "All you need to know is that I have the minister's ear, and that she values my counsel far more than she values yours."

Something about his look sent a shiver up Kruger's spine. Still, she kept up the façade of power. "We shall see, Mr. Lattimer, we shall see."

Santa Udi began to pace back and forth in her office in front of the large window that opened out to the city below. It would be risky. If anything went wrong, she would be exposed and have to answer questions. She needed to be able to tie up loose ends, and there were at least fifty of them. She thought for a moment, stopped her pacing, and then said aloud, "No...fifty-one."

Walking to the door, she pushed it open and looked at her assistant. "Find Hogge. I want him in my office in five minutes."

Closing the door behind her, Udi sat in the chair behind her desk, crossed her legs, and waited. Eugene Hogge entered her office three minutes later and closed the door behind him. Tall, slender, with white hair and hollow eyes, Hogge wore the same black suit and white shirt as everyone else in the Ministry of Intelligence.

"This is a surprise," he mused. "We don't normally meet during working hours."

"We need to adapt the plan."

"Of course. Life rarely plays out like we plan it."

"Can you trust your people?"

"I wouldn't have placed them where they are if I couldn't trust them."

"I need a simple, yes or no," Udi commanded.

"Yes."

"Everything depends upon what you have to do next. Everything. There can be no mistakes. None."

Hogge shrugged and put the tips of his fingers together. "Sounds like every other assignment that comes my way."

"I'm going to lead an assault team in two days," Udi said quietly. "There can't be any survivors."

"How many people are you sending?"

"Fifty."

"Troops or agents?" Hogge queried.

"Both."

"And how many people are you hunting?"

"Not sure. At least two. Probably no more than ten."

"Then why do you need my people? Fifty sounds like a respectable number to address the problem."

"You don't understand. Apart from me and you, there can't be any survivors on either side."

Hogge raised an eyebrow and gave Santa Udi a surprised look. "Cleaning house, are we?"

"In a manner of speaking. I need someone to blame. If I send only soldiers, then suspicions could come back to me. If I send only agents, then we will be accused of being heavy-handed with the local population."

"So, who is going to be blamed?"

"The Resistance. They opposed the troops. The targets die, and then our people die. It needs to be an ambush in retaliation for our attack on the kids."

"Kids?" Hogge asked with a raised eyebrow.

"Yes. The kids and the family. We've finally found the last two from Arcborne."

"Wickedly clever," Hogge said, giving her a thin smile.

"And there is one more loose end inside the building that needs to be resolved."

"Just give me a name."

Udi took a pen from her desk and scribbled a name on a piece of paper. "I need to know now if you have a problem with this," she said, handing him the paper. "There can't be any internal moral struggles. When the mission is over, the troops and agents carrying out the mission must die. All of them. No exceptions."

"You know where my loyalties lie, and you know the price of my loyalty."

"I haven't forgotten," Santa Udi said, with a nod of her head. "New Marchant will be yours."

"It will be done," Hogge smiled. "And I have some good news."

"What?"

"I found the woman. Yvette Dupuee. The one who was asking about you."

"And?"

"Her real name is Coltrane. She has an apartment in the same building as our friends."

Santa froze, and a chill shot up her spine. "That can't be a coincidence."

"Not likely," Hogge mused. "I checked the records in the office after the doorman refused to be cooperative, and she moved in shortly after our friends arrived."

"Who is she working for?"

"I don't know...yet. She's obviously not on our side, and we would know if she were with the Ministry of Intelligence. She could be reporting directly to the chancellor, but that would mean he already knows we're here."

"That would change everything."

CHAPTER 16

The Painted Lady

Paint and a creative hand can hide a myriad of faults or disguise unimaginable strength. In the case of The Painted Lady, the latter was true. On the outside, to the casual observer, The Painted Lady was a ship that was well past its prime and into a later stage of life that was not kind. She was a conundrum. She looked slow, but she was the fastest ship in the water. The visible guns looked dated and ill-maintained, giving the impression that she was only dangerous to the poor fool stupid enough to light the fuse. But, in reality, everything about her was lethal. She was, in fact, the younger sister of The Darkest Night. If there were one hundred people who knew of the capabilities of The Darkest Night, there were twenty who knew about what The Painted Lady could actually do.

The ship was a living experiment between Jonathan Vanderschmidt Junior, Jules, and Jack Flynn. It was the evolution of what Jack needed and what Julian created. Military strategists in the Ministry of Defense examined scenarios of aggression and defense. Meanwhile, the duo of Jules and Jack imagined the unimaginable, and it all started with one question...What if?

If the fusion of crystals could make the barrel of a gun lighter than the grip it rested upon, and stronger than the steel it replaced, what if it were used to make the hull of a ship? The Painted Lady was the result of the idea. A small-scale model proved that it would float, but would it be strong enough to withstand a traditional cannon shot? Working night and day for six months at a secret base in the northern pole, Nordterre, they crafted the forms for the hull and created the fused crystal pieces that made up the foundation of the ship. It was launched into the water and towed to a place out of sight from accidental onlookers or curious workers.

A ship equipped with traditional military cannon came alongside and fired a direct broadside into the crystal hull. It rocked back from the impact of the broadside, but the hull remained intact. After each round, a team of engineers led by Jules examined the hull for cracks and damage. There wasn't even a scratch on the hull. It was as if the ship had spit out a pebble against a mountain of stone. While the builders completed the boat, a different team was focused on how to disguise a nearly transparent ship made of crystal. After a few weeks, the team was able to create a new paint that would adhere to the crystal surface while still being resistant to water. All that was left was to apply the paint to create the illusion of a ship that could barely stay afloat.

The technical issues were easy to resolve; the most challenging part of the project was finding a ship's captain who loved research as much as being at sea. As far as Jack and Jules were concerned, they hoped The Painted Lady would never be used as an active weapon, but more as proof of the marriage of need and science. It wasn't a common mindset for a ship's captain, and that's what made it so difficult. A captain wanted to be at sea, embarking every day on a new challenge or a new adventure. If that was hard, finding a captain willing to commit to a life of secrecy and an unwavering commitment to the Resistance made the task virtually impossible.

A year before Ethan arrived at NHHMM, Jack Flynn found the perfect captain seated at the bar of The Lying Fisherman, drinking ale along with a shot of whiskey. She was a surly-looking, short woman with gray hair and an uncomfortable look about her. Jack watched her for a few minutes, taking in her every movement and action. She came into the bar demanding to speak with the owner. Thrasher York passed on the message, and Jack studied her, seeing what he could learn before they spoke. Her back was ramrod straight as she sat on the barstool. She wore the trousers and boots of a sailor, but not the uniform jacket or the white scarf that all officers wore. The woman shifted in her seat and her right foot tapped on the floor nervously.

She tugged on the shoulder of the casual jacket she wore, clearly unhappy with the fit. Jack watched as she stared into the mirror behind the bar, carefully studying everyone behind her. Ex-military. Or maybe she is still. Maybe she is a military plant sent to gather information. But clearly, she has come up through the military system. And she looks angry. Jack waited until Thrasher looked his way and then motioned for him to send her over.

The woman paid for her drinks, and with her eyes followed Thrasher's pointed finger toward the man sitting at a table in the shadows. She thanked Thrasher and walked with a quick step toward Jack. "You are in charge?" she asked curtly.

"That would depend on what we're talking about. I'm not in charge of the weather. I'm not in charge of the government, and I'm not in charge of the military, but you would already know that. I am, however, in charge of having rude, demanding patrons thrown out of my establishment."

"May I sit?" she asked, ignoring his comments.

Jack nodded.

Taking a seat opposite him, she quickly began. "My name is Valerie Ortega, and I want a job."

"Jack Flynn," he replied, offering his hand.

"I don't have any openings behind the bar, and you are a little small for a career as a bouncer."

"I want a job on a ship. I'm not interested in working at your pub, but I can assure you that I can physically toss anyone out of this bar if I had a mind to."

Jack laughed out loud. "Fair enough. Let's take the military out of consideration, because that's clearly where you came from. I know all of the merchants in the city, but I'm not exactly on good terms with any of them. Not as many as there used to be once the tunnels were cut. It's now faster to move cargo by land than by sea."

"That's not the kind of job I want," Ortega said flatly. "I want another kind of position. On a ship that operates outside the scope of the law."

He scratched his chin and sat back in his chair. "So, tell me, Ms. Ortega, what qualifies you as a pirate? That is what we're talking about, isn't it?

"I graduated from the NHHMM Naval Academy. I served on the military ship The Lightning as first officer, and I taught strategy and tactics at the Academy after that."

Shaking his head, Jack looked up and stared at her with a stern stare. "I don't buy it. You have a textbook career with the Navy, and now you sit in front of me wanting to be a pirate, the exact opposite of the life path you've been living? You aren't telling me the whole story."

"It's personal," Ortega said, her eyes expressionless.

"No. You come here wanting me to introduce you to people who operate on the wrong side of the law, and you say it's personal? You can leave now." Jack waved his hand.

They sat for several awkward seconds, Ortega refusing to move and Jack refusing to talk.

"How old do you think I am?" she finally asked.

Jack smiled. "No idea. My father taught me never to guess a woman's age or her weight."

"I'm fifty-eight. I've followed the rules, I've played the game, and I've excelled at every task I've been given. I've destroyed every enemy I've faced in war games. And when the captain of The Lightning retires, do they give me the commission? No. They give it to a forty-year-old woman whom I taught at the academy." Till now, she had sounded forceful but spoke just above a whisper. As her emotions ramped up, so did the volume of her voice. "If they won't let me serve because of my age, then I want to use what I know to beat them in the only way I can."

"Did they tell you that? Did they tell you they didn't choose you because of your age?" Jack questioned.

"Of course not!" Ortega fumed. "It's illegal to discriminate against someone because of their age."

"But still you believe that they did."

"I know they did."

"So, then you must agree that laws mean little to the people who hold power?"

"You and I both know that's true."

"Did you ever break the law in your career? Did you ever decide to ignore a regulation or a rule because you didn't believe it was the right thing for a particular situation?"

Ortega shifted in her seat uncomfortably, and with a twinkle in her eyes, she replied, "I've bent a few rules."

"The people you want to work with take pride in breaking them. They wear their natural rebellion like the stripes and ribbons you wore on your uniform."

"I know things," she replied curtly.

"So do I," Jack said, as he picked up his pipe from the table and reached into his pocket for his tobacco pouch. "Everyone here in the room knows something that you don't know. Why is your knowledge more valuable than what they know?"

"That's a fair question," Ortega said, resting back in her chair. "Do your people know what the next two generations of NHHMM warships will look like? I do. Do they know the speed of the ships, the size of the crews, or the changes in ammunition and number of cannon? I do."

"So you are willing to pitch away everything that you've done and believed just because you didn't get a job?"

Ortega shook her head before she responded. "I don't like what NHHMM has become since Chancellor Brighton took over. I thought the best way I could force change was as captain of The Lightning. That's not an option anymore."

Jack pressed the greenish brown tobacco into the bowl of the pipe, lit a match, and held it up to the bowl. "That, Ms. Ortega, is not the same thing. You said you wanted me to introduce you to pirates. Pirates operate on profit, nothing more. There is no politics in pirating. What you describe is rebellion. Do you want a job pirating or do you want a job in the Resistance?"

"Which pays better?" she asked with a grin.

"Pirating, but the Resistance helps you sleep a little better at night."

"I want both," Ortega quickly replied.

"The Lightning, who got the job?" Jack asked, changing the subject after a long draw on his pipe.

"Elise Fougera," Ortega said bitterly.

"Really?" Jack was genuinely curious. "I hadn't heard Elise got The Lightning."

"You know her?" Ortega asked with a raised eyebrow.

"We've met," Jack replied evasively. "I would love to say that she got the job because of her relationship with the admiral, but she is ruthless, smart, and she does know a good bit about sailing."

"Well, she obviously isn't that good or she would have caught you by now," Ortega quipped.

"I couldn't comment on that."

"I would have caught you."

"Doubtful," Flynn mused, "as I'm not a pirate."

"I would never have confused you with a pirate." Ortega smiled slightly. "I would have taken you for more of a smuggler."

Jack grinned. "I'll drink to that." He raised his glass, then called out, "Thrasher," motioning for another round to be brought over.

She was tough, tenacious, and by all accounts, brilliant. And best of all, she knew how to run a ship.

The day before he departed for Retribution, Jack was forced to spend the day travelling for meetings that couldn't be postponed. A buggy took him to the coast, a dinghy carried him to The Darkest Night, and the ship carried him three hours away from the main shipping lanes. It wasn't a trip Jack had really planned on making. But when he found an envelope wedged between the door and frame of his residence the day before, the trip became essential. He pulled on the envelope and studied the front. Jack Flynn was written in his father's handwriting, and in the upper left-hand corner were the initials JBVJR. The letter was in the code that he and his father used, and it took a little time for him to translate. When he absorbed the words and their meaning, he sent both messengers and telegrams and hoped they would arrive in time.

He asked Thrasher York to accompany him, along with two of his crew, on another short trip further away from The Darkest Night.

"How does she look?" Jack asked.

"They gave her the right name, that's for sure," York replied, laughing. "When was the last time you saw her?"

"Just after I got back, when I could navigate without the crutch."

"She has changed. I'm telling you, that boat is one ugly bitch."

"I'll tell Captain Ortega that you said her baby is ugly."

York groaned and shook his head. "And I thought we were friends."

Jack grinned. "We are. It's just my little way of paying Captain Gordon back for letting Scarlett and Miner take target practice on my approach to The Darkest Night."

"That was what...six months ago? And I'm not Gordon, why take it out on me?"

"It could have been two years ago. Doesn't matter. I have a very long memory, and I want to keep Gordon on his toes."

"Well, you won't have to wait long to get us in trouble. Here she comes now."

Jack looked over his shoulder and then carefully shifted in the dinghy. Coming up from behind him was The Painted Lady. Everything about her looked as if she could barely float in the water, and Jack listened intently. The only sound he could hear was the hull cutting through the surface of the ocean. She was silent.

"Evening, boys," Captain Ortega said, looking down at them from above. "Are you lost? Do you need help?"

"My friend here," Jack said, pointing to Thrasher, "says his captain reckons a ship so old and ugly, couldn't be used for anything other than moving refuse or livestock. In fact, he said that he smelled your approach long before he could actually see the 'ugly bitch'. And that's a quote."

"Spoken like a man who has never been downwind of his own ship and crew," came Ortega's retort.

"Do you wish to come aboard?"

"Yes, ma'am," Jack replied. Then, turning his head to Thrasher, he spoke with a deadly serious expression. "You understand the orders I've left for Captain Gordon?"

"Perfectly," Thrasher answered.

"No matter what happens, no matter what orders you receive, he can't deviate from what we spoke about."

"No deviation at all. I understand. Are you sure you don't want us to stay and bring you back?"

"No, Captain Ortega will get me back safe and sound," Jack answered.

Thrasher positioned the dinghy alongside The Painted Lady, and Jack grabbed the rope ladder and climbed up the side of the ship. When he got to the top, he grabbed Captain Ortega's waiting hand and pulled himself up on deck.

"Well...?" Ortega said, waiting expectantly for Jack to comment.

"She really is an ugly bitch, and I mean that in the most genuine and positive way. I mean, I know how she is built and what she can do. Still, you have truly turned her into something that no one would believe was capable of being even remotely seaworthy."

Ortega laughed. "And she is more lethal than she is ugly. My crew has been dying to show you what she can do."

"Yes, but we need to talk. It's important."

"I gathered that from the word you sent ahead, but you really need to experience this. You've only seen her during construction. Now you get to see how special she really is."

"Ok, we'll talk afterward. Show me what this girl can do."

"This way," Ortega said, walking quickly to the bridge. "And you might want to lean back against the rail there."

"Nah," Jack said, shaking his head. "This isn't my first time on one of my ships."

"Have it your way," Ortega smirked, then gave the order for the sails to be lowered. Two members of her crew managed that in seconds. "Liu," she barked.

A small man in his forties quickly moved on deck and into position behind the ship's wheel. "Mister Liu is my helmsman, and he can make this ship go anywhere it needs to go. Mister Liu," Ortega said as she shifted both her weight and her feet, "what is our status?"

"The crew is below deck, the drive is active, and all I need is your order."

Ortega looked over at the water around her. There was little to no wind, and the ocean was calm. A smile came across her lips, and she leaned forward. "Full speed, Mister Liu."

"Aye, Captain. Full speed."

The Painted Lady lurched forward with such force that it threw Jack backward and down to the deck. He quickly got back up to his feet and leaned into the wind as the ship continued to accelerate. "I warned you," Captain Ortega said as she looked over to him.

Even though Jack knew the ship was supposed to be fast, he hadn't experienced it firsthand. The Vanderschmidts connected a specialized crystal generator to power an electric motor, which was connected to a shaft that was attached to a propeller with a large blade. That then provided the thrust to move the ship forward or backward.

Finding the correct configuration for the propulsion system wasn't an easy task. Several of the drive shafts were broken until they could match the right size and metal to the components. The motor was so powerful that it could snap the drive in half when accelerating from a complete stop. Yes, Captain Ortega enjoyed seeing Jack take a fall on the bridge, but more than anything, she was excited to know that they had indeed finally found the right mix of metal and design.

"How fast can this thing go?" Jack yelled over the roar of the wind as they moved faster and faster.

"We don't yet know for sure," Ortega replied. "Our speed is as much a factor of the condition of the water as it is the motor that propels us. We've yet to find water smooth enough to see how fast she will really go. Do you notice anything else?"

"Silence?"

"Exactly. The only thing you can hear below decks is the hum of the engine. Above deck, all you can hear is the water as we move through it. I'm going to ask Mr. Liu to make a hard turn to port. You might want to hold on to something this time."

Jack grabbed the rail with both hands as Ortega ordered Mister Liu to drop to half-speed and begin a hard turn to port. The Painted Lady began to slow and make a turn shaped like a 'U' rather than a long sweeping arc. To his amazement, the ship seemed to run flat on the water without listing to one side.

"In the tests we ran, we found that she was most vulnerable to a broadside attack, not because of the damage, but because of the force of the blast. She is so light that she was susceptible to being capsized by the force of a broadside blast. So, we added fins on the hull about thirty degrees out on either side of the keel to add stability. That solved the problem of a broadside blast, but also made her run smoothly on a tight turn." Looking over to the helmsman, Ortega ordered him to bring the ship to a complete stop.

"How many crew are on board?" Jack asked.

"Today, only eight. If we were going into a fight, we would have close to forty."

"Do you want to see the gunnery deck?"

"No," Jack answered. "I'm sure you wouldn't take her out if you didn't know you could defend yourself. It's more important that we cover the things I came for. Can we go to your quarters and talk?"

"Of course," Ortega answered, disappointed that she couldn't show off her ship's firepower.

Jack followed her to the captain's quarters, went inside, and closed the door behind him. "Have a seat," she said, pointing to the chairs around a wooden table. Around the walls were an assortment of charts and maps, and on the far side of the room was Ortega's personal living space. Everything was clean and in its proper place. But Jack noticed there was nothing personal around the room to show that it belonged to Valerie Ortega. No photos, nothing artistic, and nothing that would tell anyone anything about the occupant.

"Do you remember when you told me that if I gave you a choice of being a pirate or a rebel, that you would choose both?"

"Yes."

"Is that what you still want?"

"Nothing has changed," Ortega answered.

"Well, you are about to get exactly what you want."

Jack told her about the invaders. He walked her through what happened, the design and firepower of the ships, and the limitations that Drake Gordon had provided. The hardest part of the conversation was telling her about the crystals and how they could open a hole in space and time. Grasping the idea that an enemy could appear out of thin air right beside her was challenging. It took her almost an hour of answering questions before Jack saw it click in her mind, and when it did, her whole expression changed. She sat a little straighter, and her eyes went from unsure amazement to cold and calculating.

"When will they be here?" she asked.

"I have no idea. Tomorrow? Never? They already have spies spread out around NHHMM. We have intercepted some of their plans and are using them to construct an alphabet, an understanding of their language, so that we can now spy upon them. We simply don't know."

"And what do you want from me?"

"When they come, I need you to make life miserable for them. You must not get into a battle with multiple ships. There is too much risk. However, you can accelerate faster, so there is no way they can catch up to our ship. If they come, when they come, I want you to make them bleed a slow death. I want you to use The Painted Lady to destroy their ships and supplies faster than they can rebuild them.

Hit them hard, and then run away. And then circle back and hit them again."

"Those are basic tactics," Ortega said with a puzzled look. "I would have done that anyway."

"But here is the twist: I'm going to be away for a few months, maybe longer, working on a project, and it will be almost impossible for you to reach me, and I you. It is critical that no matter what the Council or any other Resistance leader says, you do not back off from this approach."

"Having a division in the ranks of the Council?"

"No, but I know at least one person who influences the Council who will want to try to make the chancellor our ally against the invaders. The chancellor will want us to share our weapons. That cannot happen, no matter who gives the order. We cannot give over our strength to appease those who desire peace and goodwill."

"So, you want me to be..."

"A pirate and rebel, which is exactly what you wanted."

"And what if the Council and the chancellor align? What am I supposed to do then? Am I supposed to fire on our own ships and our own people?"

Jack paused for a moment before he answered. "Where I'm going, I'll be faced with the same thing. I will have to make the same decision. And, Captain, if you can't make the same decision, and if you're unwilling to do what is necessary...then I've hired the wrong woman."

"You don't need to worry," Captain Ortega said with a steely look. "I don't care what flag the enemy flies, or what uniform they wear. I will do what's needed, and you have my word on that."

"Good. That's all I need to hear."

"When are you leaving?" she asked.

"First thing tomorrow morning. I'm actually missing a critical meeting of the Resistance, because this is probably more important than anything they are discussing there."

CHAPTER 17

The Danger of Love

Jack saw the two buggies approaching and waved them over to his location at the train station platform. He motioned for them to stop when they were in position and then looked them over to make sure their cargo was still intact. The first buggy had a wooden bed behind the driver, with two crates and his personal trunk. The second buggy carried two more crates.

Putting his thumb and forefinger to his mouth, he whistled at a group of porters standing around and waiting for work. Two young men came to him, pulling L-shaped trolleys.

"Which train?" the first one asked.

"The eight-thirty," Jack replied.

"There's no eight-thirty train. There's one at eight-ten, and one at eight-forty. Which one do you want?"

"Take them over to the ticket agent, and we'll sort it out there. But boys, please be careful with them. They break."

Walking over to the ticket agent's desk, Jack reached into his pocket and retrieved a folded paper. He handed it to the agent and introduced himself. "I'm Wilhem Klein. I have a reservation on the eight-thirty train."

"Ah," the agent said, looking up over his glasses, before glancing towards the porters. "Boys, take him to the Red Special." He then motioned to the crates. "Are all those things yours?"

"Yes."

"The trunk can go, but the crates will have to stay. Not enough room in the passenger car."

"But I was asked to bring these crates. It's my job."

"What's in them?"

"Spirits. I'm the new manager at..."

The agent held out his hand. "I don't need to know, and I don't want to know. You see the guards off to the left where the porters are going?"

"I do," Jack replied.

"If you are telling the truth, then you'll have something to bribe them with, because nothing gets on the train without their approval." The agent stamped Jack's paper and gave it back to him.

Jack took the paper and smiled. The beauty of being a smuggler was that he knew how transportation worked. You knew who could be bribed, and the kind of bribe you needed to have. So far, Jack's plan was working perfectly, and now he just had to hope he had the right type of guards. It took him less than two minutes to find out.

The Red Special wasn't a locomotive, but three train cars parked on a spur with nothing else around. The first of the three appeared to be a passenger car, and the other two were for cargo. Each car was painted black with a red diamond at its center.

"Did the agent tell you the crates are not allowed?" a tall officer with a thick neck asked.

"He did mention that," Jack said, "but I'm hoping we can find some kind of compromise."

"What's in the crates?" the officer enquired.

"Can I show you?" Jack asked.

"Sure, why not?" The officer motioned to two uniformed soldiers. "Open 'em up."

With quick, practiced movements, the soldiers used a bar and popped open each of the crates.

"You know that some of this is illegal stuff?"

"The Glow? Of course, I know. But all of this is for the officers at the base I'm headed to. I got a list of what I needed to bring a few days ago. I'm going to be running the tavern there, and I wanted to make sure I brought them what they wanted."

"Well," the officer said, as he took a bottle of Reaper's Glow from one of the crates, "you got the good stuff. Which one is this?"

"That one is peach, but I've also got apple, spice, and melon."

"The spice is my favorite, but then I've never tried the melon," the officer mused. "What are these other labels. The small ones."

"Those are the names of the officers and administrators who requested them."

"But you really aren't supposed to be taking extra cargo."

"I understand," Jack said, taking the bottle of peach Glow from him and placing it back into the crate. "And while I really want to keep the officers happy," Jack continued, as he looked over the contents of one of the crates and selected a different bottle, "I couldn't, in good conscience, bring them a damaged bottle. Could I?" Using his thumbnail, he scratched the label of the bottle of Reaper's Glow Spice. "Can I leave this here with you?" he asked, pulling off the small label he had made up and attached the day before.

The officer looked around and then placed the bottle behind the steps that led up to the passenger car.

"Anyone important tried a bottle of the melon?" one of the soldiers asked. "Maybe it's damaged as well."

Jack looked over to the officer and raised an eyebrow. The officer smiled. "And what do we have here?" Jack said aloud as he looked for a bottle of the melon Glow. "Another damaged bottle!" he exclaimed, as he ran his thumbnail across the label.

"I trust you will use the utmost care in loading my crates into the cargo cars," Jack said as he gave the second bottle to the officer. "And that the rest of my cargo will arrive at my destination, undamaged..."

"You have my word," the officer said.

"Should I board now?"

"Yes, sir, take any available seat."

Jack walked confidently to the passenger car, sure that the crates would undergo no further examination and that the false bottom hiding the two masks would never be discovered.

Shy climbed the steps into the passenger car and saw that there were already three other people on the train, including a man at the end of the car who was slouched in his chair with his feet crossed and resting on a small table that was bolted to the floor. His hat was pulled down over his eyes, and Shy recognized Jack without seeing his face.

She sat down next to a man and a woman, introduced herself, and made small talk while she waited for more passengers to arrive. It didn't seem wise to sit next to Jack immediately. Continuing to play her part, she met everyone who boarded and did her best to remember their names. Her clothes were simple: a blue buttoned blouse and a beige dress that covered her ankles. It took her twice as long as usual when she got out of bed, because she had to work so much harder to look so bland.

By 8.25, there were fourteen passengers on the train, and Shy had introduced herself to everyone. At 8.30, a young blond woman with her hair pulled over to one shoulder stepped into the passenger car, accompanied by two men carrying metal trays. On each tray was a pitcher and seven small glasses, about the size of a whiskey-shot glass.

"May I have your attention, please?" Everyone looked at her except Jack, who continued to sleep. "MAY I HAVE EVERYONE'S ATTENTION PLEASE!"

Jack stirred, resituated his hat, and looked up at the young woman. "Sorry. Just napping."

"You are all about to depart to a destination that is top secret. You are not allowed to know the location of this facility or how to get to it. Inside each pitcher is a sedative, a sleeping tonic, if you will. It is completely harmless to you, but it will put you into a deep sleep. You will awake in your assigned housing a few hours after we arrive. You will each take a glass from the tray, we will pour the tonic into the glass, and you will drink every drop. When you have swallowed the tonic, you will open your mouth and stick out your tongue. When we are satisfied that you have swallowed the tonic, the train to your destination will depart, and not a moment before."

A young woman raised her hand, and the blond nodded to her.

"I really don't think I want to do this after all. I'm going to leave if that's alright."

"Your ability to change your mind stopped the moment you boarded this train. If you don't do this voluntarily, we will open your mouth for you and pour the tonic in. Do you understand?"

The young woman started to cry.

215

The blond nodded to the men on either side, and they began to walk down each side of the passenger car. When they got to Shy, knowing she had no other choice, she threw back the tonic like a shot of whiskey and prepared for a sleep she didn't want.

Jack was the last to be offered a glass. "You know, I was already asleep. You woke me up just so you could give me something to make me sleep. How idiotic is that!" Taking the tonic, Jack put the glass back on the tray, propped his feet back on the table, and put his hat back over his eyes. "Wake me up when we get there."

He had a splitting headache. It felt like his eyes were about to explode from their sockets. It took him about thirty seconds to realize this was worse than any hangover he had ever experienced. Jack found himself in bed, and swinging his legs over the side of the mattress, he sat up and tried to compose himself. He smelled beer, and he heard loud, rowdy voices. I must be near the tavern.

Standing up, he steadied himself by putting his hand on the wall, and he cursed. He saw the door, opened it, and saw a flight of stairs heading down. Wonderful. I'm above the bar, and I have a staircase to manage.

With cautious steps, he went down the stairs and squinted as the light got brighter. At the bottom of the stairs, he stopped and looked around the room. It was a good layout as taverns go. The bar was long, and there was plenty of room before the tables. He figured they could easily handle guests two-deep at the bar. He smelled food and saw patrons eating at their tables. The biggest problem he noticed, however, was the staff. There wasn't nearly enough.

"Want to give me some help?" a voice called out from behind the bar. A woman who looked to be in her mid-thirties was staring at him. "Now? Now would be good."

Jack pulled his hair back and tied it with a leather strap, then stepped behind the bar. "What's your name?" he asked.

"Savvy."

"Ok, Savvy. I'm Will. Let's get this party started."

"Will, the party's been going on for four hours. It's ten o'clock."

"Well, that's not good."

"I'll keep the tabs, if you can make the pours. Beer's on tap, the cheap stuff is behind you on the shelves, and the good stuff is directly in front of the cheap stuff beneath the counter. Wine is in the middle behind you. The open bottles are right in front of you."

For the next two hours, Jack didn't do anything but meet customers and make drinks. Every now and then, Savvy would look at him to see if he was keeping up, and he was.

Just past midnight, a fight broke out between two soldiers of low rank. "Savvy," he called out. "Have we got anyone to take care of that?"

"Yeah," she said with a sly grin. "He just got here this afternoon."

"Of course, he did," Jack mumbled as he walked around the bar towards the fight.

"Gentlemen, you will take this outside. NOW!" The men were clearly drunk, and the largest of the two decided to throw a punch in Jack's direction. Brushing it aside, Jack grabbed the man's wrist, twisted it behind his back, and pushed him out of the only open door he could find. The second soldier found someone else to hit and was sitting on top of the customer, throwing punch after punch to the man's face. Jack pulled the soldier up, slapped the man on both ears at the same time, and then knocked him out with one fist to his face.

Leaving the man where he was, Jack grabbed the back of a wooden chair and dragged it over to the bar. He then stood on the chair, jumped up onto the bar, and yelled as loud as he could, "YOU WILL ALL PAY VERY CLOSE ATTENTION TO WHAT I AM ABOUT TO SAY!"

The tavern was so loud that only the people nearest to him could hear. Savvy stepped over to the center area behind the bar and grabbed the rope on a large bell that hung from the wall. She started ringing the bell and didn't stop until everyone in the tavern was quiet.

"Thank you," Jack said in a normal voice. "Obviously, I'm new here. I don't know you. I don't know your rank. I don't know your occupation. I don't know your reputation, and to be completely honest. I... Do... Not... Care. Did everyone just hear what I said? I don't care who you are or who you think you are. There are rules that you must follow to be in this place. Rules. Now, who wants to know what the rules are?"

Jack's question was greeted with silence.

"Well," Savvy finally said. "I want to know the rules."

"Rule Number 1," Jack said, holding up his forefinger. "You

never fight in my tavern. Ever. I don't care what you do outside of this building, but if you throw just one punch or shove just one person, you will be banned from here for a month. Do the same stupid thing again, and you will never get back inside this building. You get one chance. You will not get two.

"Rule Number 2," he said, holding up his middle finger also. "You never, ever touch my staff...unless they invite you to do so, away from this property. Touch them, grab them, slap them, pinch them... It doesn't matter. You are banned, and I will personally throw you out the door and probably break whichever hand did the touching."

"Are you going to try that with me?" an officer asked from the back of the room. Whispers started all around the tavern.

"Absolutely," Jack said without hesitation, as he jumped down from the bar and walked toward the officer. "There are no exceptions. No matter your rank, no matter your title, and no matter your gender," he added, noticing the voice belonged to a woman. "Touch one of my staff and you are done." As soon as the words left his mouth, a chill ran up his spine.

The officer was Elise Fougera, captain of The Lightning, and she knew him as Jack Flynn.

"I'll drink to that," Elise said in a loud voice. "And you are buying the next round, because I just saved you from a month of bar fights," she added in a whisper.

"DO YOU UNDERSTAND THE RULES?" Jack said, turning from Elise. A few voices murmured agreement, so he addressed them again. "I'M BUYING THE NEXT ROUND IF YOU UNDERSTAND THE RULES. DO YOU UNDERSTAND THE RULES?"

The customers responded with both cheers and applause, rushing to the bar.

"So, Jack, can I call you that?"

"My name is Wilhelm, Captain. But my friends call me Will."

"Once you get settled in, Will, we should sit down and catch up."

"Absolutely. But if you will excuse me, I need to help out the staff. Some idiot just said he would buy the next round."

The tavern shut down at two o'clock, and when the clean-up was finished, Jack sat down with his staff. It included five wait staff, one cook and her assistant, and three others who cleaned the tables and kept inventory coming in and trash going out."

"You hungry?" the cook asked Jack.

"Very," Jack replied, realizing it had been eighteen hours since he had eaten.

"What do you want?"

"Just surprise me."

Fifteen minutes later, the cook brought him some grilled venison, a slice of bread, and something with a baked crust on top. "Vegetables," she said, pointing to the baked crust.

Jack called out and motioned for everyone to join him as he sat on top of the bar. "Pull up a chair." The staff grabbed chairs and sat around him. "I haven't been formally introduced to any of you. My name is Will Klein, and I'm the new manager if you hadn't figured that out already. Please introduce yourself so that I can start remembering your names."

The cook's name was Bridget, and her assistant was Toby. The five servers were Andi, Shawn, Pat, Jen, and Darby. He had already met the bartender, Savvy, and the two who kept the spirits flowing were Truss and Mags. Magpie, her given name, but she promised to hurt anyone who called her anything but Mags.

"I've run a few pubs in my time," Jack continued, "so I have a little idea about what I should be doing. And the first thing I noticed is that we are understaffed. There's too much work and not enough people. Are we allowed to recruit other staff here, or are people just stuck doing what they are told to do?"

"You can recruit from the inside, but it's hard to get additional help by train," Savvy answered.

"Fair enough. The first thing I'm asking you to do is to get some additional people. I'm not looking to hire your best friend or your friend who doesn't like to work. I want to hire people who will make your lives a little easier."

"Did you mean what you said earlier?"

"Which part?" Jack answered.

"The rules. Did you really mean what you said about the rules?"

"Yes, both parts. I will not allow you to be in the middle of a fight, and no one is allowed to touch any of you when you are here."

"Then we will have no problem finding good help. The money is better here than most places," Savvy commented, "but up until now, none of us have been safe."

"We're going to fix that part. You have my word."

They spoke for another fifteen minutes, and Jack tried to eat his food between questions and other topics the staff brought up.

"Are we open for lunch?" Jack asked.

"No," Mags replied. "We don't open until four in the afternoon."

"Ok." Jack nodded. "Do what you usually do for the next few weeks, and I'll observe. Once I get a feel for what's going on, we'll make changes as needed. If you know of someone who wants to work here, have them show up at three o'clock. We'll talk then."

When his staff was gone, Jack stepped outside the tavern and decided to explore the new city that he called home. He noticed the first difference less than fifteen steps from the tavern door. The security presence was dramatically increased with armed soldiers in every direction, and he wondered if they would stop him as he passed. They didn't. Evidently, if you made it into Retribution, you were supposed to be here. If they weren't monitoring the people, then what were they guarding? There wasn't any logical pattern to how they were positioned. They could be in front of any building, regardless of size, or standing by a tree with no buildings around. I need a map.

He decided to try an experiment to see how focused the guards really were. Approaching one of them stood in front of a three-story building, Jack spoke. "Sorry to bother you, sir, but I just came in on the train today and I have a question."

"Of course, Mr. Klein. How can I help you?"

"How do you know me?" Jack asked with a genuine look of concern.

"There were fourteen new arrivals today, sir, and only one of them threatened everyone who lives in this place. Including the most beautiful officer we have in our military."

"Beautiful? Really? It must have been darker than I thought, or I'm just worn out from my travels, because it's pretty rare that I miss a beautiful woman." It was all a role he was playing, of course. He knew precisely who Elise Fougera was, and he had always thought of her not as beautiful, but as stunning.

The guard smiled. "We all know exactly who you are, and I'm afraid that some of my friends are going to end up with broken hands."

"Well, then, just make sure that you aren't one of them. What's your name?"

"Private Ramas."

"It's good to meet you, Private Ramas," Jack said, offering his hand. Ramas shook it, then stepped back into position.

"A pleasure to meet you as well."

"Do you know of anywhere I can find a map of this place?"

"Not at this hour, but there are several places that sell them. I believe the shop behind you carries them, as well."

"And where can I find food?"

"There's the military dining hall, but that's only for soldiers. We have a lot of restaurants in town, but it just depends on what you like."

"Thank you, Ramas," Jack said with a wave. "Come and see us sometime."

"Good night, sir."

As he walked away from Private Ramas, Jack realized that he needed to check the tavern's storeroom to see if the crates he brought had been stored inside. It wouldn't do for someone to mess about with them and discover the false bottoms. Yes, that would get him into trouble, but that was probably nothing compared to the trouble an ex-lover could cause.

CHAPTER 18

The Unexpected Visitors

Ethan finished his morning training routine and left the barn with his muscles quivering. His legs felt like jelly, and his arms felt as if they couldn't lift or move one more thing. Walking to the back of the barn, he cupped his hands and dipped them in the cool, fresh water. Mrs. Chastain was always considerate, leaving the bucket of water she drew up on the top of the well wall so that he didn't have to do it. He splashed the water on his face and neck, and then reached in a second time, this time with a cup, to get some water to drink. It tasted good, and he wanted more, but he had learned to pace himself. Walking between the barn and the Chastain house, he noticed the barn pitchfork that had been left outside by the entrance, and he made a mental note to put it back in the barn when he'd cooled off. Sitting down on the bench swing under the large oak tree, he rested his arm on the back rail and began to swing back and forth.

"How did it go?" It was Star, standing behind him.

He turned to look at her, and out of the corner of his eye, he saw something moving toward his face. Instinctively, his hand came up, and he grabbed an apple she tossed his way.

"How did you know I would catch that?" he said, a grin spreading across his face.

"I didn't," she said, grinning back. "I'm just glad you did catch it."

"Thanks." He took a bite. "The training was good," he said, after he swallowed. "I think I need to change up the routine, though. The run is getting boring."

"It sounds like you and I are both restless. Ashlyn said there's no more target practice until we get more ammunition. So just like we planned, we've wrapped up the rifle and ammunition in a tarp and put it in the hollow oak on the edge of the meadow, just up the hill."

"No one would find it there." Ethan nodded and thought about the word Star used. Restless. Was that it? Was he restless?

"Maybe, I'm restless. I don't really know. I just feel like we're all waiting for something." He took another bite of the apple. "It seems like all we're doing is preparing and waiting."

"But it's not such a bad place to wait," Star replied.

He smiled again. "No, it isn't, but I can't help feeling that we haven't gone through everything we have, just to sit and wait."

"We won't have to wait much longer."

"Pops said the same thing. Why do you say that?"

"Just a feeling. It's kind of like the end of a school term. You know that the year is almost over, but you aren't exactly sure what will happen next."

"Yeah." Ethan nodded. "That's it. I don't know what is going to happen next, and I feel completely out of touch with what's happening in the rest of NHHMM. I think Pops knows more than he tells me. If my parents are supposed to lead a rebellion, they really can't do it all from up here, if they want to. Sooner or later, something's going to explode, and then it will all begin."

"I miss half rounds," Star sighed, changing the subject.

"Yes. I agree. Maybe we can recruit Anton or Gustav into the Resistance."

"Which would be your choice?"

"That's a good question. I would never admit it to Anton, but I believe Gustav's were better."

"I hope I get to meet some of the people you told me about," she said after a moment.

"Like who?"

"Jack. Charlotte. The pirate...Captain..."

"Gordon," Ethan finished.

"Yes, Captain Gordan. Mr. Vanderschmidt."

"You will. They're at the heart of the Resistance. So I have no doubt you will meet them."

"And I want to see Mr. Vanderschmidt's factory. It sounds like there are all kinds of exciting things there."

"Yeah, it's like Arcborne, but real. And from what I hear, his family is just as creative as he is."

"Can you imagine the pranks that he and his family play on each other?"

Ethan laughed. "That's kind of scary. The thought of them using their inventions to prank one another."

"Well, as long as they don't use poison ivy or dye, it can't be too bad."

They spent the next half hour talking about Arcborne, the feud between the students, and the crazy pranks they came up with. Ethan didn't miss Arcborne. He missed the seemingly endless things to learn and explore, but he didn't miss feeling like a prisoner or an experiment.

He couldn't put his finger on it, but something in him had changed. A year ago, he was a fourteen-year-old boy who avoided trouble rather than embracing it. A year ago, he had no one to care about but Pops. A year ago, the closest he ever came to adventure was playing a game of Conquest. Now, he had parents, he had Star, and now he had friends who were willing to sacrifice for him.

But now, he also had responsibility and was beginning to understand that evil exists, and that when you run from evil, it will ultimately catch you and consume you. A part of him wanted to be a kid again. A kid who could read whenever he wanted, study anything his mind could comprehend, and live a quiet existence. The other part of him, however, was growing stronger and stronger every day. He was tired of feeling hunted and tired of waiting for somebody else to decide what was going to happen. Maybe there would again be a time when he could relax and let the world go by. A time when there were no enemies, no hunters, and a time where sleep could be deep, and nightmares few. But he didn't see that happening anytime in the near future.

He reached over and took Star's hand. She slid her fingers between his. "Mom should have breakfast ready," she said after a moment.

"In a minute," Ethan said. He whistled, and Quinn came running from behind the barn. He tossed the half-eaten apple to her, and Quinn promptly dropped down to the ground and began to eat it.

"Huh," Star said, surprised. "She likes apples?"

"And carrots," Ethan said.

"Carrots?"

"Yeah, this dog seems to like things other than meat. I don't think there is anything that Quinn won't eat."

"Well," Star said, standing up from the swing and pulling Ethan up with her, "my mother's made a good breakfast, so come on, it's time we had something to eat."

Quinn finished off the apple and then sniffed at the ground to see if there was more. Inside, Vallow Chastain had prepared her usual breakfast of sausages, flat cakes, eggs, and the pastry of the day. Today it was a blueberry tart. It would be the last breakfast she ever made in their home.

It was just after two o'clock, and Wart Pinsley was less than a quarter mile down the trail from Tearmann to Gray Hawk. A cloud of dust caught his eye from further down the hill, and he slowed down his horse to a stop and looked carefully. Just before the trail made a hairpin turn, he could see men. Lots of men. Soldiers, in fact. Most were on foot, but four, maybe five, were on horses.

He quickly jumped down from his two-wheeled cart and unhitched his dapple-gray horse. Leaving the cart in the middle of the trail, Wart climbed onto his horse's back and turned back to Tearmann. He pressed his heels down hard and forced the horse up the hill at a pace she wasn't accustomed to. When he reached Tearmann, he pulled hard to the right on the reins and rode fast to the edge of town.

"VICTOR!" he called out as he arrived at the Chastain home. "VICTOR!"

Vallow Chastain opened the door and stepped outside, wiping her hands on her apron. "What is it, Wart?"

"Soldiers. Coming up the hill. Lots of soldiers."

"How far away?" she asked.

"Five, maybe ten minutes."

"Oh my." Running to the barn, she grabbed the rope attached to the bell clapper and began to swing it back and forth. The bell rang out, loud and strong, echoing across the valley.

Anne O'Connor burst out of her home, saw the frantic look on Vallow's face, and knew what was happening. Ashlyn followed her out, carrying a long crystal rifle and a bag slung across her shoulder. Her steps were calculated, and her face showed a look of resolute defiance.

"Wart," Ashlyn asked, "how many?"

"Thirty, maybe forty. I don't know. A lot."

"You need to get out of here," she said. "You don't need to be mixed up in this."

Roland and Ethan emerged from the barn covered in dirt from the tunnels. "Let's take our positions," Roland said calmly. "Vallow, can you get everyone inside the barn?"

"Victor is in town, the children are in the house. I don't know where Star is."

"I'll get Mr. Chastain," Wart said, lunging the horse in the direction of town with a kick.

"Where is Dad?" Ethan asked.

"He was working at the school," Anne replied. "He can hear the bell from here. I'm sure he's on his way."

"Ms. Chastain, where is Star?" Ethan said, turning to her.

"I don't know," she replied quietly.

"I'll find her," Ethan replied, and he sprinted off to the lavender fields that she often enjoyed.

"Get the children in the barn," Ashlyn repeated. "As soon as Victor is here, we start moving them out."

Vallow rushed back into her house and quickly emerged again, pulling her two youngest children by the hand and leading them into the barn. Anne followed them in, and Ashlyn strolled to a tree in front of the barn and rested the rifle against the tree trunk. From the bag, she removed her mask and placed it over her right eye, then she toggled the button until the magnification was where she wanted it. "Ok," she said, reaching for the rifle. "No sign of the troops, but Wart seems to be coming back. He's got Victor."

Roland stepped back into the barn and then emerged with a pistol stuck in the waist of his pants, and his cane without the covering sleeve. "Any sign of the others?"

"Not yet," Ashlyn replied, keeping her eyes on the road into town.

Ethan sprinted back up from the lavender fields and shook his head. "She's not there. I'll check the meadow." He turned to run up the hill toward the meadow when he saw a squad of ten men emerging from the trees. "POPS!" he called out.

Roland's head snapped to the left, and he started in a sprint toward the tree line. He didn't need to tell Ashlyn anything. She kept her eye on the road going into town.

Wart arrived back in front of the barn, and Victor slid off the horse and onto the ground. "Get into the barn," Ashlyn ordered. "You know what to do. Two by two."

Victor didn't reply but rushed into the barn, and within seconds, a low hum and a bright light followed the seventh chime of the clock. "Get out of here, Wart. You've got to go, now."

Wart nodded and pushed the horse across the road and into Farmer Cleo's lavender fields.

The sound of gunfire came from the tree line. In one hand, Roland held a pistol, and he shot back as he ran, and in the other was the steel blade from his cane. Two of the soldiers fell, and then Roland was in the middle of them. Ethan watched in awe as the blade flashed, and soldier after soldier fell to the ground. An officer then stepped from behind a tree and pointed a pistol at Roland's back.

"NO!" Ethan screamed.

As the soldier steadied his aim, Ryan O'Connor emerged from the trees in a full sprint, drove his shoulder into the officer's back, and flattened him against a tree trunk with a sickening crunch. Taking a knife from his boot, he charged at one of the last three men while Roland fought with the other two. Within a minute, the battle was over, and the barn had glowed and hummed a second time.

The second group of men got into position too early, and now they would only have to defend one area of attack instead of two. "You and Anne need to go," Roland said. "Ash and I can hold off the rest. We will be right behind you."

"But..." Ryan started to argue.

Roland interrupted him. "No, we all agreed. You are the most important one. Don't argue with me. We don't have time."

"Let's go," Ryan said, putting his hand on Ethan's shoulder.

"Here they come," Ashlyn said, as she squeezed the trigger and dropped the first man that appeared in the street. Roland reloaded his pistol while Ryan and Ethan entered the barn.

"Ok, you and your mother go next," Ryan said as they neared Anne and the clock sitting in the middle of the barn floor.

"No," Ethan replied. "That's not the plan. You and Mom go first. The rest of us will follow. You two are the priority."

"But you aren't going to leave until you find Star," Ryan argued.

"Then I'd better find her quickly."

"Promise me, you will follow," Anne demanded.

"Go, Mom. I'll be right behind you."

Ryan reset the hands of the clock to the top of the hour, and it began to chime. Ethan took three steps backward and watched as his parents disappeared into the light. When they were gone, he rushed to the small box beside the barn door, retrieved a pistol, and crawled down into the tunnel that led to the Chastain house.

The soldiers were smart. They spread out using the trees and town buildings as cover. Ashlyn was patient. She waited until one of the soldiers was careless and showed too much of himself, and then she would fire. Three more soldiers dropped, and then a small group of five began to rush toward them. She sighted the lead soldier, took a deep breath, and... Something behind and above her whipped past her head, and before her eyes, the soldier's chest turned crimson, and he dropped to the ground.

She sighted the next target, and the same thing happened. And then she smiled, just a little. Star. Gunfire started as the soldiers got closer and came into range. All around her, shots began to whiz through the air, methodically, shot after shot, she dropped everyone she aimed at.

The back door of the Chastain house was kicked in, and three soldiers entered with their weapons drawn. One watched that door while the other two crept to the front door to get a better shot at Roland and Ashlyn.

Ethan's mouth went dry as he watched the people he knew he was about to kill. He remembered Pop's words when he taught him how to shoot a few days earlier. "Firing at a target isn't the same thing as shooting at a person. The person moves. The person breathes. The person has a beating heart. Your deliberate actions will stop that heart.

Always make sure you are ready to make that decision before you ever point the barrel at anyone."

Standing in the shadow of the hallway, he saw the two men walk to the front and heard the whispers of the third man. His hands were shaking as he raised the weapon, his heart pounding. He felt sick. Ethan didn't question what he was going to do; he was just empty inside because he had to do it.

The man by the back door was staring intently outside. He was the first to go. Ethan's gun made no sound. The man simply fell forward out of the back door and onto the ground. Without hesitation, Ethan then turned and shot the man closest to him. He then fired at the third man, but missed, and the man fired his own gun while turning to face Ethan. The shot was wide, but Ethan's fourth shot landed in the center of the man's chest.

For a moment, the street sounded like explosions from every angle, and then little by little, gunfire became more sporadic. Glancing out the back door to make sure it was clear, Ethan ran around the back of the barn and approached the corner where Roland and Ashlyn were standing.

"Everyone ok?" he asked.

"Yeah," Roland said. "The bulk of them are gone. There may be a few left, but they aren't going to rush the building. Now is a good time to leave."

"I agree," Ashlyn said.

The three stepped quickly inside the barn, and Roland closed the doors behind them. "You and Ashlyn go first," he said

"Ok," Ethan agreed, kneeling beside the clock.

Ashlyn turned the hands of the clock until it started to chime, and Ethan looked over to her, placing his hand on it. She gave him a curious look, which he didn't understand as the hum started.

Two. There were voices outside the barn door.

Three. A man screamed, and there was shouting, while inside, a bright white light filled the barn.

Four. Ethan looked at Ashlyn and said in a quiet voice, "Not this time."

Five. In a blur of movement, Ethan stood up, grabbed Pops by the collar, and swept his legs out from under him. Pops fell backward to the ground, landing on top of Ashlyn and the clock.

Six. "I'm not leaving Star," Ethan said, flinging himself away from the clock.

Seven. The humming stopped, the light vanished, and Ethan was alone in the barn. Standing up, he brushed off the straw from his pants. The barn door opened, a gun fired, and the clock in the middle of the barn floor exploded.

"So, they left without you?" Santa Udi said, standing in the doorway.

"Who left without me?" Ethan asked. Her gun was pointed directly at him, and he knew from experience that she didn't miss. His pistol was still in his waistband, and he didn't think he could reach it before she shot him.

"Still trying to play the clever game," she said. "Slowly, very slowly, take the gun from your waist and toss it over here."

Reaching down, he removed the gun by the end of the handle and deliberately tossed it behind him. Udi scowled.

"You really are as arrogant as they say. But it doesn't make any difference. I don't know how I failed to kill you the last time, but I promise you, this time I will succeed."

"I doubt that. I don't think the chancellor wants me dead, and I think you will deliver me to him exactly as you have been ordered."

Udi laughed. "You don't understand," she said. "I don't care what the chancellor wants. I don't really work for him. He thinks I do, but he's mistaken."

"Then what do you have to gain by killing me?"

"Everything. You see, the chancellor wants you so that you can beat the machine, and he can get what's inside. I, we, don't want you to do that. We don't want the vault opened. We don't want the chancellor to have what's inside."

"Do you know what's inside?" Ethan asked, trying to buy time.

"Not really. We suspect it's the key to how you open and close the doors between worlds, but we already know how to do that. We just don't want the chancellor to know."

"But why?"

"Because if he knows, it only makes him more powerful, and our task more difficult."

"Task? What task?"

"We are going to take over your world, Ethan Scott, just as we have done to countless others. We want the chancellor to be weak, and unfortunately for you...We don't need you to be alive."

Santa Udi raised her pistol and focused her aim on Ethan's chest. But then her eyes grew wide and her body shifted, as her gun arm began to waver. Her fingers loosened their grip, and the pistol fell to the barn floor. Across her chest, four spots of crimson appeared and then quickly spread across her white blouse. She tried to swallow, and blood began to seep from the corner of her mouth. Her knees wobbled before her body fell forward, face-first into the straw. In her back was a pitchfork, and behind her, standing in the doorway, was Star.

The room was in chaos. The Chastains wanted to know where their daughter was. Anne and Ryan wanted to know where Ethan was. Ashlyn tried to explain, while Roland was demanding that someone explain to him why he couldn't go back. Everything on the local apparatus was set correctly; Roland had a watch containing the crystals to open the portal, but nothing happened. He couldn't go back.

A young woman stood in the doorway to the arrival room in the Vanderschmidt research facility. She had no idea what to do, and panic showed across her face. "Is Vanderschmidt here?" Roland roared.

"No...sir," she stammered.

"Then who is in charge?"

"Mister Clyde."

"Get him in here, NOW!"

Moments later, Jonathan Vanderschmidt's grandson came running into the room.

"How long until it's dark outside?"

"Two, maybe three hours."

"Get it ready to go the moment we have darkness. If you need a crew, find one."

"Does anyone remember if Ethan and Star were wearing the bracelets we got in the supply crates?"

Figuring out what her husband was doing, Ashlyn smiled and nodded her head. "Brilliant!" she said aloud.

"Yes," Vallow answered. "I saw Star wearing hers this morning."

"And Ethan, did anyone notice if Ethan was wearing his?"

No one answered.

"Then let's hope Star and Ethan are still together." Looking over at Clyde Vanderschmidt, Roland spoke clearly. "My wife and I will be going with you. If we are lucky, we will have two others returning with us. How long is the roll-up ladder we used in Arcborne?"

"Ten feet," Clyde replied.

"Make sure you bring a rope," Roland ordered. Then he turned and left the room to start the preparations.

Star stood in the opening of the barn and looked down at Santa Udi. Her face was pale, and her hands were shaking and making fists until she released them, hoping the shaking would stop. It didn't. She tried to control her breathing, but she wasn't having much luck. Her blue eyes finally looked up at Ethan. "I was out of ammunition. I didn't have a choice. She was going to kill you."

Rushing over to her, Ethan held her tight. "I know. Thank you."

"Came from...from the meadow. Heard the bell. I just aimed, pulled the trigger, and then looked for the next one."

"I understand," Ethan said quietly. "I do."

Her head was buried into his shoulder, and her body trembled. "Did everyone get away?"

"Yes. Everyone but us."

"You should have left," Star said.

"No. I wasn't going to leave you behind," he reassured, holding her tightly.

"Can we still join them?"

"No. Udi destroyed the clock."

"What do we do?" she asked, looking up at him.

"We've got to pack what we can. We need to hide the guns since we have no more ammunition, and we need to leave. We need to find a way to get in contact with members of the Resistance, but for now... we are on our own."

"Ok." Star pushed back from Ethan, her eyes seeming to focus again. "The rifle I used is leaning against the side of the barn. I'll gather up some food from the kitchen, and I'll see if my father took the gold he keeps hidden away."

"Good. I'll hide the guns and what's left of the clock. Then I'll check my parents' place for anything of value we can take."

"We aren't coming back, are we?" Star asked, afraid she already knew the answer.

"No. We aren't coming back. There are probably more soldiers already on their way."

"Then we need to get Quinn. She was with me in the meadow. I tied her up when the shooting started. I'll go get her."

Ethan watched her run up the hill to the meadow, then he walked back to the remains of the clock. It was hopelessly shattered, beyond repair. He picked up the pieces, left the barn, and walked over to a water well in the back. Taking the rope, he raised the bucket and positioned it on the edge of the stone circle. Then, he took off his shirt, wrapped the mechanical pieces of the clock up in the fabric, added two stones, and tied it up in a knot, before tossing it down into the well. He placed the bucket down into the well until it met the water below.

He wrapped up the rifle and pistol tightly in a tarp and slid them behind one of the support beams in the tunnel under the barn. He was on his way to his parents' house when he remembered the paper trays from Dean Vasquez's office. Taking the trays from the feed room, he returned to the tunnel and placed them on the ground. He didn't have time to cover them up. Ethan could only hope that if anyone searched the property, they would never find the tunnel.

He then went into his parents' house, shoved some clothing into a shoulder bag, pulled on a clean shirt, and then went to the place where he knew Ryan kept his money. There wasn't a lot, but it would probably be enough to get them to where they could get help. He came out of the house and saw Star and Quinn waiting for him. She had her back to the barn, and Ethan understood why. There wasn't enough time to clean anything up. No time to move the bodies. No time to cover up Santa Udi.

"Ready?" Ethan asked.

"Ready. I've got food in one bag," Star said, holding up her left hand. "And clothing in the other."

"Thoughts?" Ethan asked.

"I vote we go across Cleo's fields. Stay off the roads and try to get to Gray Hawk."

They followed the tree line on the outside border of Farmer Cleo's land until the sun began to sink below the mountains before them. Using the amulets sent by Mr. Vanderschmidt, they walked on into the night until they could walk no more. Ethan cleared off the ground as best he could to give them a smooth place to rest. A massive rock wall protected them on one side, and a fast-moving stream was just to their left. Sitting on the ground in silence, they ate some bread and fruit before lying down on the grass. It was only then that the events of the day caught up with them, and Star moved closer to Ethan, laid her head on his shoulder, and then cried herself to sleep.

"How far away are we?" Ashlyn asked, an hour into the trip.

"We are over the mountains," Clyde answered. "You said that Gray Hawk was a hundred times the size of Tearmann, so I'm going to find Gray Hawk, then turn around and look for the other. Once we find Tearmann, I'll circle the area until we find the exact location."

Even though the windows were closed in the carriage, the night air was even cooler higher up in the sky. Just before they departed, Ashlyn threw a coat in the passenger compartment, and she was happy that she did. If she had only brought gloves, too.

"When we get there, I'll use the filter to scan for the bracelets. Ash, use the one that will show body heat," Roland said

"Why don't you both use the filters for body heat?" Clyde asked.

"Because the bracelets will show up even if there is no body heat."

"Oh," Clyde said, understanding his meaning. And a bracelet on a body that's cold would give them a different answer. Not one that they wanted, but an answer, nonetheless.

Fifteen minutes later, they were circling Gray Hawk and heading back to where they thought Tearmann would be located. "That's it," Roland said, pointing down to the right. "Just starboard, there. The houses should be just to the right."

"Got it. I'll start a wide circle. We can stay up here as long as you need."

"Uh, Roland," Ashlyn said as she looked toward the ground. "You need to change filters."

Clicking the button on the side of his mask, he switched the filters. "So that would be the reinforcements cleaning the house. How many do you see?"

"Twenty. Maybe twenty-five." Ashlyn watched as the officers on the ground checked the dead bodies and looked for the living. "And they are spread out all over the area."

"Yeah, they're looking for someone."

"Did you see any bracelets?"

"Not yet," Roland answered, switching the filter back.

Clyde looked over his shoulder at Roland. "I'm not trying to rush you, but if there are twenty people down there looking for something, there's a good chance that one of them will see us when we pass in front of the moon."

"And how long do we have before that happens?" Ashlyn asked.

"Maybe...fifteen seconds?"

"Then turn NOW!" Roland growled. Clyde sent the airship into a hard bank to port and went in the other direction.

"Now what?"

"Take us back. There are no bracelets down there around the house or the barn, so they're either still alive out there or...their bodies have been removed."

"But shouldn't we keep looking?" Ashlyn argued.

"No. We can't have the airship discovered by the chancellor's people, and even if we found them, we couldn't rescue them without exposing the airship."

"Then why did we come?" Clyde asked.

"Because I wanted to make sure they weren't already dead. I owe that to their parents. I want them to have at least some hope."

If the soldiers weren't searching the area, and the airship hadn't changed direction, they would have flown right over two bracelets still attached to living bodies.

CHAPTER 19

The Invasion Begins

Chancellor Brighton sat in a leather chair positioned before an enormous floor-to-ceiling glass wall, overlooking the heart of New Marchant. To his left was a small round table, where his glass of whiskey rested. On the other side of the table was an identical chair where his guest would soon sit. The sky before him was giving way to night, and the tall buildings cast dark shadows on the city below. The harbor garrison was in clear view, and beyond were two dozen ships resting on the dark water. One of the ships caught his eye as, from the main mast, a bright red flag, bigger than a sail, fluttered in the breeze.

One more meeting and it would be time for dinner. It was a rare evening for the chancellor. There were no events to host, no people to entertain, and no last-minute crisis to consume the rest of the day. It would be dinner with Esmerelda, his wife. He doubted she would actually make the dinner, after all, there were other people to do that. She would oversee the meal, the pairing of wine to food, the appetizer, and the dessert that would follow, but none of it would be created by her hands. Esmerelda, actually working in the kitchen? Those days were long passed.

One of the housekeepers, one Brighton hadn't seen before, worked on a bookcase with a duster made of feathers. He was average by any standard. His age, height, weight, and style made him look like just another man wearing a uniform. The man had no scars, no tattoos, and his hair was an unmemorable brown.

He stood in front of a bookshelf about twenty feet away from the chancellor's desk. He paid no attention to Brighton, seemingly content to simply do the job he was paid to do. There were some cleaning supplies on an ornate wheeled cart, and occasionally the man took a rag to remove something he noticed on a shelf before he went back to his dusting. None of the books on the shelf were the same size, but a set of eight smaller ones had been pushed back further from the others, looking distinctly different.

The housekeeper pulled these smaller books, one by one, dusted them, and placed them on his cart. When he was finished, he took an ornate stone box from the bottom shelf on his cart and put it in the open section of the bookcase, then pushed it against the back wall. Then, making sure to keep the books in order, he replaced them on the bookshelf, determined to keep them in a nice row that aligned with the rest of the books.

"Sir?" the uniformed soldier announced as he approached, "Your next appointment is here."

"Of course," the chancellor answered, sipping on his whiskey. "Send her in."

Footsteps approached, but Chancellor Brighton continued to look out over the city. It was only when he noticed the tall, slender man in the reflection of the window that he finally spoke. Turning his head, he looked at Eugene Hogge and raised an eyebrow. "I was expecting Minister Udi. Has she been delayed?"

"She's dead," Hogge replied, showing no emotion. "So it would be accurate to say she has been delayed."

"And why am I just now hearing about this?"

"I was notified by telegram less than ten minutes ago. The people in her office said she was scheduled to meet with you, so I came in her place."

"What happened?"

"She was killed by the Resistance, along with thirty of our soldiers and twenty of her officers."

Brighton stood up and walked over to the bar to pour himself another whiskey. "Have a seat and tell me the story." He poured a second glass for Hogge and turned back to the chairs. Hogge sat down, and he passed him a glass. "Here, drink up."

"Thank you," Hogge replied, "but I don't drink."

"My father taught me never to trust a man who won't share a drink with you."

Hogge took the glass and placed it on the table. "No doubt your father was a wise man." He sat back in his chair and crossed his legs.

"Is this about the Scott boy?"

"Yes, but how did you know?"

"I'm the chancellor, it's my job to know when my Minister of Intelligence utilizes troops without first consulting with me. Hogge, I know the things that you know and the things you have yet to discover." Brighton's tone was both confident and condescending, and his tone was intentional. He wasn't sure if Eugene Hogge had an agenda or if he was simply being a messenger bearing the bad news. Either way, he needed to reinforce to Hogge who was still in control. "Did we catch him?"

"No. It was an ambush. As best we can tell..."

"You are speculating?"

"Yes, Chancellor. There were no survivors. All we could do was to examine the scene and draw conclusions based upon the facts."

The veins in Brighton's neck began to budge. "We lost fifty people..."

"Fifty-one," Hogge corrected.

"We lost fifty-one people at the hands of the Resistance, and we have no survivors?"

"That is correct."

"And there is no sign of the boy?"

"As best as we can tell, the Resistance carried away their wounded and dead further up into the mountains and took the Scott boy and the girl with them."

"What were they doing there?"

"Tearmann is the Chastine girl's home. We think her family and a few others left with them."

"Who were the others?"

"A couple who taught in the area's school, and another couple who were visiting. The man who was visiting fits the description of the man who escaped from Hardscrabble."

Brighton gritted his teeth and twirled the glass around between his forefinger and thumb. "I want names. I want a complete background on everyone who could have been involved. My Ministry of Intelligence doesn't seem to be able to find these people, so get me the information, and I will do it myself. I want everything. EVERYTHING!"

"You can rest assured that I'm doing everything I can to find them."

"And that is supposed to buoy my confidence?"

"I'm not trying to buoy your confidence. To be completely honest, I'm having this conversation with you out of simple courtesy because you and I are going to be working together."

"Brash. Impertinent. You think I am going to give you Udi's job simply because you gave me this update?"

Hogge ignored Brighton's question. Reaching into his jacket pocket, he removed a watch and checked the time.

"I asked you a question," the chancellor bellowed. "Quit looking at your watch and answer me!"

"We have five minutes before it starts, so I suggest you listen very carefully. We need to discuss your transition to a new role."

Brighton's face took on a perplexed look. What he heard didn't register, but for once in his professional life, he had no witty retort or smooth comment. "What are you talking about?"

"We've been planning this for over two years. We had to recruit the right people and slowly and quietly put our resources in place. Yes, Minister Udi died today, but it would have happened anyway. The Resistance simply did the work for me."

"Who are we?" Brighton demanded.

"We are the Yehud. We are from another world, much like this one, but still different. And we have decided to make this world, NHHMM, a part of our empire. It's really not that complex. We are going to seize power from you, just as you took it from Chancellor O'Connor and the people of NHHMM."

"GUARDS!" Brighton called out. "GUARDS!"

Within seconds, an officer and five of Brighton's personal guards burst into the room.

"Arrest this man. I want him in irons, and I want him in Hardscrabble. NOW!"

"Chancellor," Hogge said, as the guards lifted him up and jerked his hands behind his back. "I am unarmed, and I am no physical threat to you. I suggest that your men check me for weapons, and that you have them wait outside. What is about to happen, what I am about to show you, will be best managed if you are the only one who hears my words. If you don't believe what I've said to be true, then you will no doubt place me in Hardscrabble to rot. But you alone need to hear this message."

Brighton paused and motioned for the guards to check Hogge for weapons. Curious, Brighton nodded his head. "Lieutenant, take your men and wait outside."

"Yes, sir," the officer answered and ordered his men from the office.

Hogge rechecked his watch. "We have sixty seconds. We do not wish to spill blood. We do not wish to cause injury to your cities or your people. We want this to be as painless as possible, but make no mistake, we want your world, and we will have it. Cooperate with us. You will have a role to play, and you live a life that is both comfortable and with some degree of power. The power will be ceremonial, but it is better than the alternative. Now...watch."

"Watch what?" Brighton demanded.

Hogge pointed to the harbor. A few seconds passed, and Brighton was about to summon the guards again when the sky lit up. Beyond the harbor, a dozen warships appeared. Brighton's jaw dropped. The ship nearest the one with the red flag fired first. The rest followed seconds after. Cannons thundered, and the sound echoed off the buildings. The windows in the chancellor's office rattled, and he took a half-step back. Smoke filled the harbor, and when it finally cleared, the warships were gone, and the only thing left were splinters floating on the water.

"The boat with the red flag was one of ours. The men on the ship were our own. None of your people have been killed, and we have not fired on either your garrison or the other ships in the harbor."

"What do you want?" Brighton said, still looking at the harbor.

"I've already told you. We want your world. I'm going to tell you what you are going to do next. You have no options and very little time to make your decisions."

"Or...?"

"Or we come back and take what we want."

"I'm listening," the chancellor said in a cautious voice.

Chancellor Brighton missed dinner. He missed dessert. His conversation with Eugene Hogge lasted for another thirty minutes before the visitor left, leaving the chancellor alone to contemplate the ultimatum. Everything the Yehud demanded was possible, and while most of it was unpleasant, some of the demands actually worked to his advantage.

Before he called the necessary meetings of his government leaders and his top military aides, he summoned General Mobius T. Lloyd to his office. Mobius arrived to find the chancellor seated behind his desk with his left hand on a glass of whiskey and his right hand resting in his lap.

"Mobius," Chancellor Brighton said as the officer entered the office. "Please forgive me if I don't get up. Join me. Sit down."

"Chancellor," the general replied. In his fifties, with close-cropped gray hair and a square jaw, Mobius T. Lloyd was the textbook military officer. Medals were draped across his chest, and every crease in his clothing was precise and clean. "I trust you have called me here to discuss what happened in the harbor. I must confess that I have next to nothing in terms of information, and I..."

Brighton held up his hand to stop him. "I know everything there is to know. For the moment, I need you to listen and answer my questions."

"Yes, sir."

"How many people know about Retribution?"

"Not counting the people working or living there?"

"Yes. How many people outside the place know of it?"

"One hundred and twelve."

"That's fairly exact, isn't it?"

"Yes, sir. There are only one hundred and twelve people in the government who have authorization to know of, or be involved with, Retribution, and I was responsible for approving every one of them. Some are military officials, some are in the Transportation Ministry, some work in accounting, and some simply move papers from one place to another. But outside of the people in Retribution, there are only one hundred and twelve who know about it."

"Good." He paused before he started the next sentence, knowing that depending on the general's response, Brighton would have a trusted ally, or he would shoot the general with the pistol resting on his lap under the desk. "I need you to pick five trustworthy and expendable people, and I need you to purge any document regarding Retribution, and anything that references Retribution. It would be better if the five you chose were part of the one hundred and twelve you just mentioned."

"Chancellor, I don't understand. What do you mean by 'trustworthy' and 'expendable'?"

"I mean that once you have purged the information, you need to purge the people." Brighton moved his finger to the trigger of the pistol and tightened his grip.

"Why? What is this about?"

"We are about to be invaded by an enemy that we are unprepared to face. Within three days, I must inform the people of NHHMM that they will be an unwilling part of an invading empire, and that this transition will be peaceful. If I don't, they will destroy our cities, our people, and our lifestyle to get what they want."

"But, sir, can't we at least devise a plan to defend NHHMM? You have generals and admirals for that. Surely…"

"Mobius, we don't have time. What we can't do is allow these invaders to get their hands on what's in Retribution. What we have working there could allow us to fight, but we need time to learn our enemy and launch an attack. We simply can't lose that place or the people in it. Retribution reports to you, and that's why I'm ordering you and your family to leave once your other task is completed. Take your family to Retribution. It is the safest place for you to be."

The general's face showed his internal turmoil. He was already thinking about the people who would die. Some were friends, others loyal comrades, but fortunately, no one who couldn't be replaced. "May I make a suggestion?"

"Of course," Brighton answered. "I trust and value your input."

"We have a logistical problem. There are eleven members of our military who coordinate the transport and people into Retribution. Removing them could cripple the whole project, but I believe there is a solution."

"I understand your concern. What are you suggesting?"

"Move them and whatever family they may have into Retribution. We give them both an incentive and a threat."

"Threat?" Brighton asked.

"Yes. By moving them in, we make them a target should any of the logistics team consider betraying the project to the invaders."

"Brilliant!" Brighton exclaimed. "Absolutely brilliant. Do you have any other concerns?"

"None that can prevent the fulfillment of your request. I can do it. It will be done."

"Thank you, Mobius," Brighton said, releasing his grip on the pistol. "I know this is hard, but it is the right thing to do."

"I do have a question. Why didn't Minister Udi know about any of this invasion? She is the Minister of Intelligence."

"She did know, because she was behind it. And her assistant is working for them as well. I simply can't trust anyone other than you."

The general sat a little straighter in his chair, and it was clear that the chancellor's flattery was making an impact.

Roland and Ashly barely spoke on the way back to the Vanderschmidt factory. Neither knew how to tell Ethan and Star's parents that the only good news they had was that they didn't see any sign of the bracelets. They didn't know for certain if they were dead or alive. They could have been captured and already removed from the area. They could be in hiding, or...Their bodies could have already been removed.

While the airship made no noise except for the spinning of the propellers, the commotion of the actual landing and securing of the craft drew a crowd. The four people they least wanted to talk to were present and waiting. As the cabin door opened, Ashlyn exited first, followed by Roland and finally Clyde. When Clyde closed the door behind him, Vallow Chastain burst into tears and buried her head on her husband's shoulder.

"Nothing?" Ryan asked.

"Nothing," Roland replied. "No sign of them, or their bracelets."

"So, they could still be alive," Anne asked with a trembling voice.

"Yes," Ashlyn said, trying her best to sound optimistic. "They could have made it out of the area, and it's possible they could be in the tunnels under the barn."

"We just don't know," Roland added.

As the group made its way into the factory, Ryan motioned for Roland to wait until everyone else was in the building.

"Why did you come back if you didn't see them?" Ryan asked when everyone else was inside. "You still had a few hours before you had to turn back."

"The area surrounding the barn in every direction was crawling with reinforcements searching for survivors, and we had another problem," Roland said, pointing up at the sky. "Full moon. We couldn't chance someone seeing the airship from the ground."

"You don't have anything?" Ryan said in frustration."

"Yes, Ryan, I do have something. I have confirmation that they weren't dead around the barn. We saw no sign of the bracelets they were wearing, so I'm pretty confident they weren't dead on the ground. They could have been captured. They could have escaped, or they could be in hiding."

"I just can't believe you didn't try harder."

Roland clenched his jaw and paused before responding. "Ryan, do you want to know what I think?"

"Yes."

"I think that Ethan and Star are still alive, and if anyone can find a way to survive, they can. I also think that I'm a little tired of being lectured by you, and I'm sure that Clyde can take you out to search for them every night if that's what you want."

Roland turned and walked into the factory, leaving Ryan standing in the darkness.

CHAPTER 20

The Third Enemy

Otis Walton gripped the frame of the seat and could hardly breathe. The night was as black as he had ever seen, and he was counting on a driver wearing a mask to navigate the journey from New Marchant to the remote Vanderschmidt facility. The note he clutched had been delivered to his hotel room just after midnight by a man in uniform. Walton skimmed the words, saw the signature and seal, and immediately knocked on the door of the man who served as his bodyguard and his driver. Nick Turley answered the door with tousled hair and the wide-eyed look that comes from being awakened from a deep sleep.

They left the hotel thirty minutes later, and Walton's personal terror began. With every turn of the wheel, the buggy pitched right and then left, leaving Walton to hold on or be thrown to the side of the road. The filters in the mask allowed Turley to navigate the journey, but Otis Walton was effectively blind. The full moon was blocked by low clouds and gave his eyes shadows, but little more. And his greeting at the Vanderschmidt facility was just as hostile as the journey. Ryan, Roland, Ashlyn, Merten Ashwillow, and Jonathan Vanderschmidt Senior were the only members of the Council present to hear what Otis Walton had to say.

"This letter," he said, holding it up for the rest to see, "was delivered to me just after midnight. It is signed by his hand, and his seal is attached."

"Well, what does it say?" Vanderschmidt groused.

"I'll read it aloud...

Dear Mr. Walton,

Tonight, I was visited by a member of the invaders that you referenced. Surprisingly, I found him to be a member of my own intelligence ministry. You may already know that an attack took place at the New Marchant harbor, but what you don't know is that it happened right before my eyes. I saw the ships appear from nowhere and destroy a vessel they said was one of their own. I now realize that what you said in our previous meeting was correct. We do not have the power to fight these people as a divided nation. Our only chance is to work together.

Their representative informed me that an invasion would occur within three days. He told me that we could either give power to them peacefully or that they would take it by force. I must address the people of NHHMM and explain what happened in the harbor, and I only have four options. I can blame the attack on pirates. I can blame the attack on the Resistance, or I can tell them the truth while our world is already fighting against itself. The only other option is for us to work together to defeat a common enemy.

For the latter to be a reality, you and whoever represents the alliance need to meet with me before the deadline issued by the invaders. We no longer have time for games. We need a strategy and a plan developed by individuals capable of making informed decisions. I will expect both you and your representative to be in my office the day after tomorrow to work out our differences.

Matthew Brighton
Chancellor

"He's seen them. He now has validation that what we warned him about is true," Walton added.

"Can we prove what the chancellor says happened, really happened?" Ashlyn asked.

"Mr. Turley says he heard the cannon just before dusk," the old man said.

"And you didn't?" Roland commented with a disbelieving look.

"No, but my hearing isn't what it once was," Walton added. "But while he was at dinner, Mr. Turley both saw the smoke and smelled the gunpowder."

"Proving or disproving the chancellor will require little effort. But assuming he is telling the truth," Vanderschmidt argued, "what do we do?"

"We need to send someone to meet with him," Merten Ashwillow answered.

"I disagree," Roland argued. "We simply can't trust the man."

"We don't really have a choice," Ashwillow said with a shrug. "Do you have a better solution?"

Roland started to reply, but Ryan O'Connor cut him off. "I'll go. It should be me."

"No. No." Roland shook his head with agitation. "He's already had your father killed. And you would walk right into his hands. No."

"If he is sincere... If... Who else would he believe could speak for the Resistance? Who? There isn't anyone else. If we do nothing, how can we expect to lead the people forward? We will be cowards who did nothing when our world needed us most."

"But if he is lying," Vanderschmidt argued with his soft voice, "we will have given him our future."

"Jonathan," Ryan answered, "we all know that I'm not the future. While the Council has been working and plotting, I've been hiding in the mountains teaching school. My name will give credibility to what we discuss. He knows me. I grew up with him. He will recognize my face, and I stand the best chance of working out some kind of arrangement. I know the government, I know the military, I know the people, and I know the Resistance."

"And what if he holds you hostage?"Ashlyn added. "What if he demands that the Council surrender to save you? Or, even worse, what if he demands Ethan in exchange for your safety? You aren't thinking this through. Too much can go wrong."

"All I offer is a name. I know that. I am the most expendable person here. You all know that it's true. However, I ask each of you to consider this from a different perspective. If the chancellor is telling the truth, then we have a greater chance of influencing the future of our world. Roland," he said, turning to his mentor, "don't fight me on this. In your heart, you know it is the right decision."

"Let's vote on it," Roland shot back, hoping to circumvent Ryan's decision.

"No," Ryan replied, shaking his head. "This doesn't require a vote. I'm making the decision that needs to be made. You can't stop me from leaving, and I don't think you want to try."

No one else in the room spoke after that, and after several minutes of silence, Ryan turned and walked toward the door. "Where are you going?" Roland asked.

"I need to tell Anne," he said as he walked down the hall.

"Well," Ashlyn commented under her breath, "that's not going to be a fun conversation."

"No, I don't suppose it will," Roland whispered. "We need to pack our things."

"Are we going with him?"

"No, he won't agree to that. We're going to find Ethan and Star. We've got to find them before anyone else does."

Even though the days were still warm, the nights in the foothills below Tearmann were cold enough to be uncomfortable without a coat or a blanket, and Ethan found himself wishing he had brought his silver waistcoat. It was still blood-stained, but it would keep him warm. He knew better than to start a fire for warmth. For all he knew, the chancellor's people could be anywhere, and the smell of wood smoke could lead them right to his location. Looking back over his shoulder, he saw Star start to stir. Quinn was lying next to her as if she understood that her body heat was what Star needed to stay warm. Using the pendant Mr. Vanderschmidt supplied, Ethan was able to study the map while Star slept. What he wanted was a city large enough that they wouldn't stand out like strangers. They needed a place where they could be lost in the crowd, and the map confirmed that Mason Point was the best place and the closest.

Situated where three tributaries made up the Bethune River that emptied into the ocean several hundred miles away, Mason Point was the ninth largest city in NHHMM. Because of the river, there was a constant flow of strangers in and out of the area, and the only people who would notice them were the ones intent on looking for them. That gave them the chance to literally hide in plain sight.

If they stayed off the main roads and didn't venture from the tree line, he guessed the trip would take just under two days. They had enough food to last that long, and there were plenty of streams and small lakes along the way, so they should be good with the water they would need. The challenge was to avoid being seen.

"Morning," Star said from behind him. "How long have you been up?"

"A while," he replied, avoiding the direct answer. The reality was that he hadn't slept all night. "You had nightmares."

"I did," Star replied, as she got up and then sat down next to Ethan. "And I'm guessing I will for some time. Please wake me up if I start to get loud. It's ok."

Ethan smiled. "You were fine. I've found that in real life, we never speak or cry out as clearly or loudly as we do in our dreams. Hungry?"

"Yes, I'm famished." Reaching into the food bag, she pulled out a small loaf of bread and tore off a piece. The outside was crispy, but the inside was still soft. She offered the bread to Ethan.

"Thanks." He began to chew, and Quinn walked over and sat in front of Star, giving her a look that said...Hey, where's mine?

"Beggar," Star laughed as she tore off a piece for Quinn. "Do you think they're looking for us?"

"I have no idea, but I've been thinking about that. The way that Santa Udi shot at the clock tells me she'd put together at least some of the pieces as to how we escaped from the chancellor. But does anyone else know?" He shrugged. "Sooner or later, someone from the government will start identifying the bodies that were left back there. I'm not sure if that's happened yet. When they don't find any of us among the dead, they will either assume that we disappeared to another place, or that we're on foot, running as far away as we can."

"I heard what she said before...Before I killed her. Do you believe her?"

"About her not working for the chancellor and being a part of the upcoming invasion? Yeah. But she's dead, so I don't know who we need to avoid more: the chancellor or Santa Udi's people."

"Is there anyone we can contact for help?"

"Everyone went to Mr. Vanderschmidt's facility, but I don't know exactly how to get there or how to contact them. Our best bet is to send a telegram to Professor Wimberly. We would have to word it carefully, but we could probably make contact with her before the others. The next option would be Vanderschmidt's shop in New Marchant, or O'Connor's, the clothing store."

Star finished her bread, put the rest of the loaf back in the bag, and shook her finger at Quinn, who was still begging for more. "That's it. You will have to wait until later.

"Thank you," Ethan said after the dog wandered off looking for something else to eat.

"You are very welcome," Star said softly.

"I'm afraid that last one is going to give you nightmares."

"Probably, but I think they'll all give me nightmares. I wouldn't change anything that I did. I just hope killing people doesn't ever become so easy that it doesn't bother me. Does that make sense?"

"It makes perfect sense."

From behind them, further up the mountain, they heard shouts. The voices were neither excited nor hurried. They were systematic and sounded like someone was announcing a completed action, like in school when the teacher would call out a name to check attendance and the student would reply, Present.

"We need to go. They're working their way out from your home to see if they can find tracks of anyone. Let's stay in the trees and off the main paths. We've got to stay ahead of them."

And then, from up the hill, they heard dogs barking. "Run," Ethan said. "Run!"

The buggy ride to New Marchant was one long conversation between Ryan O'Connor and Otis Walton. Since the driver was one of Mr. Vanderschmidt's employees, they were able to discuss the upcoming meeting with Chancellor Brighton freely.

"He's going to want to take over the Vanderschmidt research building. He'll want our weapons and all our technology," Ryan argued.

"Every partnership requires some sacrifice. Every merger requires some compromise," Walton mused.

"We can't give that to him."

"We must give him something."

"Yes, I know that, but we can't give him our weapons until there's no other choice. I have no doubt that if the invader is defeated, he'll use whatever we give him against us."

"Then what will you give him?

"I'll give him my name," Ryan replied, as the buggy pulled up to the main entrance of the Chancellery. After getting out, the two men climbed the steps and made their way to the information desk.

"We have a meeting with the chancellor," Walton said.

"Name?" the young woman asked.

"Otis Walton, and my guest."

"His name?"

Ryan paused before answering. Until this moment, he had been a ghost in the eyes of the chancellor. He didn't know if Ryan was alive, dead, or in exile. Once he announced himself, there would be no more doubt. "I will give my name only to the chancellor. If that is not acceptable, we will leave."

The woman looked over to an officer in uniform standing beside the desk. He nodded his head slightly. "Very well," she said, then gave them each a badge with a large N on it and a date. "Please keep this with you at all times and return it to me when you depart. Major Birchfield will be your guide from here."

"If you will follow me," the major stated flatly. They followed him down a long corridor until they reached a set of sliding metal doors. Opening the door, the major gestured for them to enter. With the door closed, the machine moved upward until it reached the top floor of the building. "Please place your arms out," the officer ordered. A junior officer then searched the men for any kind of weapon or knife.

As the searches took place, the major walked down the hallway and called out in a loud voice, "Mister Otis Walton and his guest."

"Send them in," the chancellor replied from the balcony overlooking the rotunda.

Brighton turned as the men entered the office area. "Mr. Walton, I'm so glad that you came. And..." He paused when he saw Ryan. "And, Ryan. It has been a long time. You've hardly changed since I saw you last. I wasn't really sure if you were dead or just hiding somewhere. I heard rumors, of course, but I could never track you down."

"Matthew," Ryan acknowledged, refusing to address him with the title Brighton stole from his father.

"I'm certain this is an awkward moment for you," Brighton said. "After all, the last time you were here, your father occupied this office.

Fortunately, we are not here to discuss the past today, but to discuss the future. I take it you have been able to verify what happened a few days ago in the harbor?"

"Yes," Otis replied. "Our sources confirmed your description of the events."

"Do you have a plan?" Ryan interrupted.

"Several," Brighton said, smiling. "Please, take a seat and I will lay it out for you."

When the men were seated, Brighton sat down in the chair behind his desk. "I've already given the order to move our best soldiers and weapons to a secure location. When the Yehud come, they will immediately take over our military and confiscate our best weapons. Once we know their strength and tactics, we will launch a series of non-military strikes to weaken their supply chain and their resolve. Once we feel the odds are in our favor, we will launch a global counterattack and drive them out. I've tasked the scientific institute with determining how they travel between our world and then developing a method to block their movement. When everything is in place, we will force them out of our world."

"And you want what from us?" Ryan asked.

"I want you to sign a document as the head of the Resistance, saying that you support all my efforts and dealings with the Yehud. And when the time is right, I want your people to do what they do best. I want you to nibble at them every day and weaken them. That's how we will win."

"And what do we get in return?"

"You get to live. You see, if I agree to make a bloodless transition, and you don't support it, the Yehud will put their focus on you. They will extend all their efforts to crush the only part of our world that stands against them. They will have all our intelligence files, and they will not care about our politics. They will round everyone up who opposes them, and you will all die. In my plan, most of us get to live, and we can fight them when we are ready to fight them."

"And you want nothing else?" Ryan questioned.

"No. Nothing."

"I'd like to see the letter," Ryan said, without emotion.

"Of course." Brighton opened a drawer in his desk and removed a letter written on his own letterhead. At the bottom was his signature and seal as a witness to the signing. "If there is anything you see that is contradictory to what I've already said, I am happy to revise this so that it is acceptable to you."

Ryan carefully read the letter and then passed it over to Walton. When the old man was finished, he put the letter on the chancellor's desk and pushed it toward him.

"I need a pen," Ryan said, ready to get the meeting over with. Thus far, he had been able to keep his emotions in check. But seeing Brighton sit in the chair where his father had sat, and using letterhead that once bore his father's name, was wearing his self-control thin.

Brighton took a pen from his desk and dipped it into the inkwell. Without a word, he then handed the pen to Ryan. With a flourish, Ryan signed his name and gave both the pen and the signed document back to Brighton.

"Excellent," Brighton said with a smile. "This was a wise decision that will serve us all well." On his desk was a small brass bell that he picked up and rang. "I've taken the liberty of having dinner prepared for you. Think of it as a last supper before the war for our world takes place."

"No," Ryan said. "We didn't come here for a meal, and I really don't have the appetite to share one with you."

"Honesty," Brighton said. "I appreciate honesty. It is so rare these days. But...I really must insist."

"You are in no position to insist on anything," Ryan snapped, and he turned to leave.

Walton grabbed Ryan's arm with his right hand and spoke up quickly. "Of course, we will stay. Perhaps over a meal, we can mend some of the bridges that have been burned."

Ryan shot Walton an angry stare and then looked at the chancellor. "I will give you dinner, but I will not give you forgiveness."

"Excellent," Brighton said, nodding his head. "I wasn't asking for forgiveness, so let's have dinner."

The conversation was decidedly awkward. And while Walton willingly engaged with Brighton, Ryan hardly said a word. When the main course was finished and they were waiting for dessert, the chancellor finally asked a question that only Ryan could answer. "And how are your wife and son?"

Ryan looked the chancellor dead in the eyes and replied, "We lost my son right after you had my father killed, and my wife just wants to live a quiet, peaceful life."

"I'm sorry to hear about your son. But I'm surprised you haven't had another by now. I mean, you are both well within the child-bearing years."

Ryan's jaw clenched, and his hands curled into fists. Walton quickly interjected. "Chancellor Brighton, we thank you for your hospitality, but it is time we were on our way."

"Thank you for coming. Tonight, we have taken a great step forward in protecting our world and our people. Before you go, however, there is someone who wants to meet you." He motioned to the soldier guarding the door, who nodded and pushed the door open wide. In walked Eugene Hogge, and he moved across the room like a man with purpose, a tall, thin specter of death coming to claim yet another life.

"Mr. Hogge, allow me to introduce Mr. Otis Walton and Mr. Ryan O'Connor. Ryan is the son of the former chancellor and the leader of the Resistance. Mr. Hogge is the representative of the Yehud, and he has something for you."

Reaching into the folds of his jacket, Hogge produced a pistol, pointed it at Walton's chest, and pulled the trigger. Before Ryan O'Connor could move, the gun fired a second time, and Ethan's father was dead.

"Really?" Brighton said as he shook his head. "You had to kill them here...in my office?"

"Remember, Chancellor, it is only your office as long as I want it to be." With that, Hogge left the room, leaving the chancellor alone with two dead guests.

All in all, it was a good evening for him. His dinner was exceptional, he had a letter from the Resistance giving him their full support, and the last O'Connor who could rally the people against him was dead.

"Will someone come in here and clean up this mess?" he called out to anyone who could hear.

Before anyone could respond, a low hum began to permeate the room, and twenty feet away from the dining table, a bursting bright light caused Brighton to shield his eyes. He blinked and stared in disbelief at a woman who now stood before him. Wearing a black dress, a black hat, and a black veil that covered her face, she leaned slightly to the left, resting her weight on a slender black cane. Black lace gloves covered her hands, and Brighton noticed the last two gloved fingers were tucked into the palm and sewn in place.

"That is a pity," she said, as she looked at Brighton and the dead men at the table. "That's the real problem with time," she mused. "It's quite unpredictable."

The same guard who had announced Eugene Hogge rounded the corner and started to draw his pistol. "WAIT!" Brighton ordered, intrigued by the woman before him. He studied her. She could have been in her late sixties...maybe a little older. Her voice sounded younger, though, with a playful quality to it.

"Thank you," she said, then looked at the dead men slouched over the dining table. "Clearly, enough people have died tonight, and we don't want your guard to be yet another casualty of an unnecessary war."

"If I'm not mistaken," Brighton said with a smile that curled on the edge of his lips, "my guard is the one with the gun, and you were not invited to be here. And the funeral attire," he added, motioning with his hand, "did you come from a funeral, or is this look for them?"

"I now prefer black; it hides the flaws of life. There was a time when my dress was pompous and overdone, much like yours, but I outgrew that." The woman sighed. "May I?" she asked, as she walked with a stiff hobble over to Ryan.

Chancellor Brighton shrugged and gestured to the man.

The woman grabbed Ryan's dark hair and lifted his head up from the plate it was resting on. "I was trying to help you avoid all this, and not without serious risk to myself, but what you have started here may well be your undoing."

"Then take it up with Hogge. You just missed him," Brighton said. "I'm assuming you work with him."

"Bless your heart," she cooed. "There is so much that you don't understand. I don't work for or with the Yehud. Think of me more as their competition. Think of me more as an interested party that wants to offer you a better deal."

Brighton looked at the woman, at the two dead men at his table, and then over to the guard. "Leave us," he said, with a dismissive gesture of his hand.

When the guard was gone, Brighton stood up, walked across the room, and pushed the button that opened the secret door leading to the conference room. "What shall we talk about?" he asked, as he gestured for her to enter.

With a noticeable limp, the woman walked into the conference room, her fist gripped so tightly on the handle of the cane that her knuckles under the lace gloves looked like a piece of knotty wood. She gave Brighton a gentle nod of her head as she passed him. "So much to talk about...so, so much to talk about, and so little time. Well, that's not entirely accurate, but let's talk anyway."

To Be Continued

ACKNOWLEDGEMENTS

Special thanks to Eugene, who creates covers that compel the human eye to study the small details.

www.ingramcontent.com/pod-product-compliance
Lightning Source LLC
Chambersburg PA
CBHW070500030726
47503CB00004B/1120